HOTEL EUROPA

OTHER WORKS BY DUMITRU TSEPENEAG IN ENGLISH TRANSLATION

Vain Art of the Fugue
Pigeon Post
The Necessary Marriage

HOTEL EUROPA   Dumitru TSEPENEAG

TRANSLATED BY PATRICK CAMILLER

DALKEY ARCHIVE PRESS
CHAMPAIGN AND LONDON

Originally published in Romanian as *Hotel Europa* by Editura Albatros, 1996
Copyright © 1996 by Dumitru Tsepeneag
Translation copyright © 2010 by Patrick Camiller
First edition, 2010

Library of Congress Cataloging-in-Publication Data

Tepeneag, Dumitru, 1937-
[Hôtel Europa. English]
Hotel Europa / Dumitru Tsepeneag ; translated by Patrick Camiller. -- 1st ed.
  p. cm.
Originally published in Romanian as Hotel Europa in 1996.
ISBN 978-1-56478-570-1 (pbk. : alk. paper)
1. Romanians--France--Fiction. I. Camiller, Patrick. II. Title.
PC840.3.E67H6713 2010
859'.334--dc22
                    2010025173

Partially funded by the University of Illinois at Urbana-Champaign and by a grant from
the Illinois Arts Council, a state agency

Partially funded by the Translation and Publication Support Program of the Romanian
Cultural Institute

www.dalkeyarchive.com

Cover: design and composition by Danielle Dutton, illustration by Nicholas Motte
Printed on permanent/durable acid-free paper and bound in the United States of America

HOTEL EUROPA

I unstick my knee from her thigh, let out a faint groan as I turn over thinking of the word sciatica. Then my hand knocks against the wood of the bedside table—an agreeable sensation. I ought to be getting up.

It's pitch-dark in the room, winter outside. I can only just make out the tree branches at the window: threatening or protective, I'm not sure which. A huge skeleton preserved in the cold. Nocturnal refrigerator. The words don't bode at all well for the book I'm planning to write.

I make the necessary effort, though. My left arm leans on the table, the right acts as a spring; one leg swings over the edge of the bed, immediately followed by the other. I find myself perched on the corner, hands on knees and a little dopey. I take deep breaths, turn my head to look at the woman still asleep there. She is snoring softly.

I stand up, go to the bathroom, and switch on the light. I experience it as an assault. Raise my arm to parry the blow. Then I see myself in the mirror.

We always think about ourselves in clichés: the same words keep seeping into our consciousness, forming a kind of schematic, coded monologue that at least has the merit of preserving some mental continuity. On the other hand, what's the point of repeating over and over again something that can no longer be called an observation, still less an appraisal of a particular state of affairs, because it's no longer linked to reality directly through a process of perception, but only vaguely through one of recognition—not an image but an idea, and in the end an *idée fixe*? I don't take the trouble to verify it: I've grown old!

Is this a leitmotif of mine, or the mirror's?

It's no longer a question of angst; it's become something mechanical by dint of repetition, like the flicking of a switch. It's not a thought but a label stuck to the mirror, an intertitle in a silent movie. Or a subtitle in a sound movie in a different language: I see an image with the word underneath; I no longer try to fight it, as I would have done a few years ago, nor to study it more attentively, to inspect it for plausible arguments against this "accusation," to plead that at least there are extenuating circumstances. I no longer defend myself in any way. I shrug my shoulders—and the accusation becomes a verdict, a final sentence.

Without thinking I grab the toothbrush and toothpaste. I always squeeze out too much. I turn on the tap, but I'm too lazy to use the glass in which I've already replaced the tube of paste. Besides, her toothbrush is also in it—the sleeping woman's. She is still asleep, still snoring gently. What I should do is remove the toothbrush and put it on the edge of the sink along with the tube of paste, then rinse out the glass. Too complicated. So I cup my hands and bend over to drink the icy water. Why don't I let the hot tap run a little so that I get the right temperature? What's my hurry?

I scrub my teeth, with a vertical movement of the brush, as it's written in the book—I mean the book of life. Here's one argument against the verdict that I've grown old: even if I don't still have my full set—a couple of bridges and a host of fillings—I haven't yet reached the stage of false teeth.

"But your grandmother died with all her teeth, and she was seventy-plus."

A prosecutor's voice that seems to come out of the shower nozzle, if not straight from the tap a few steps away. It's high-pitched and malicious. Like hers when she gets hysterical.

I spit out the paste, which has filled my mouth and trickled into my throat. I continue to brush my teeth and gums, opening my lips as wide as possible and pressing my tongue out of harm's way against the roof of my mouth, as if in preparation for an exercise in how to pronounce the English "th" sound. You are supposed to keep brushing for three minutes—at least three. I see myself grinning in the mirror with that pinkish-white foam that creeps onto my nose then drops over my chin and pajama collar: a grotesque sight, a clown's act repeated every morning. It's a comical moment and I need only trace a little inward smile to poke gentle fun at myself. I can't manage it. Especially in the morning . . . the inevitable internal monologue is so serious as to be ridiculous.

"I'm getting old and I wish it wasn't true . . ." The refrain from a popular song echoes in my head, sung out of tune at a party by my father and his friends. One of them was a priest: he at least sang well, or that's what my mother said, but the others drowned him out with their bleating, prevented him from showing off his talent. (The same song, somewhat modified, was performed by the young people I met in Bucharest. One was called Mihai, another Ion. I can't remember the rest of the names; I should make an effort, but I'm not capable of it now. And what does it matter! Ion and Mihai promised they would write to me.)

I rinse my mouth and move on to the next task: shaving. As if I couldn't go just as I am! If I've already made up my mind, what's the point of dragging it out? But have I really made up my mind?

I straighten my back and feel a sharp pain. Is it sciatica, or maybe arthritis of the hips? I should see a doctor. Only it's come at a bad time. Either I leave or I stay put and try to write as and when I can. And if I'm going to leave, I should do it before she wakes up—without explanations. I mean, without any more explanations. Marianne knows very well that I need a change of scenery from time to time. A change of air, and climate.

I can't stand the winter. I detest it.

I reach out for the shaving cream: an aerosol spray, the most harmful for the environment. How many times have I sworn to buy it in a tube, and how many times have I forgotten! We live inconsiderately, toward ourselves and others. We drift along from one day to the next, carelessly and in a constant hurry—as if we were just on a trip, just passing through.

"Speak for yourself. Why do you misuse the plural like that?"

She's right. Why do I feel representative? Why do I think I speak for anyone but myself? Is it just because I sometimes take a pencil in my hand and scribble on sheets of paper, or tap with my fingers on a keyboard?

I lather myself with care, although my beard doesn't grow fast and isn't at all rough. It's a teenager's beard, an aged adolescent's . . . I'm playing for time. In fact I'm waiting for the woman in the next room to wake up, to put the coffee on, to toast some slices of bread that we can both spread with butter and cherry jam or marmalade. Little by little, though not without bluster and not without indignant protests against the conjugal yoke, I convince myself that there's no point in leaving today either.

"Can't you see it's raining?"

"So what if it's raining? I have an umbrella. The metro's just around the corner, and then it's only ten minutes to the station."

"Have you forgotten that you wanted to see a doctor?"

"I'll do that later . . ."

"And when's that likely to be?"

She has so many commonsense arguments—how the hell can you resist? I cut myself on the cheek out of irritation. Blood trickles out beneath the white foam. I bend over and wash my face. It's quite a deep cut, so I think of using some gauze. I look in the little cupboard. One cheek remains unshaven, the other marked with a piece of gauze. I look like a cartoon. How can I leave in this state?

Well, maybe I'll take a bath instead! I turn on both taps, at the risk of waking her up, and before I step into the tub I promise myself that tomorrow morning I won't shilly-shally around anymore, I won't waste any time in front of the mirror like an ageing coquette. I'll also do without the shave and the bath—even the brushing of my teeth. In any case I've already bought the ticket, and my suitcase is packed and hidden in the storage room next to the kitchen. I only have to get dressed and take off.

How nice it is to set out, a light suitcase in your hand, never so much as glancing back! In the morning. Whistling idly and looking with pity or scorn at all the people rushing to work, their backs bent as they hurry along staring at the ground.

Maybe I'll call her from the station, so she doesn't start imagining God knows what. What exactly? That I was kidnapped during the night? Murdered, hacked into pieces and dumped in the Seine? She knows very well that I need to get away from time to time, to go into the big wide world, even if I eventually return without a line written.

"If all you're going to end up with is a blank sheet of paper, you might as well stay at home."

Of course she's being sarcastic; it's easy for her. She no longer even bothers to show she's jealous.

I take off my pajamas, get into the bath and stretch out. I close my eyes. A sensation of well-being comes over me: the backache dissolves in the warm water.

It was warm, unnaturally warm, especially when you think that Christmas was approaching. He walked quickly, sometimes breaking into a run, bumped into a passerby here and there, came to a halt, started up again. He was panting and sweating. The tails of his raincoat swelled like a ship's sails in the wind or like clothes put out to dry on a line (your choice!); they impeded him, slowed him down. He was going to meet Ion, behind the Hotel Intercontinental in Bucharest, opposite the Hungarian airline office. He was late. He had spent the morning trying to get through to Ana, who was staying with her parents in Timişoara. The line was constantly busy, and the one time it did ring there was no answer. Maybe he'd dialed a wrong number.

When he reached Piaţa Rosetti, he looked at his watch. He was already a quarter of an hour late. It's not so terrible, he said to himself, Ion will wait. He'll be pleased to have something to complain about.

"You're always late," Ion said. "I've never known anyone so unpunctual."

Then he would pass from lack of punctuality to lack of seriousness, the second character trait implying and encompassing the first. Or else, if he didn't have the patience to dig up more general aspersions, or if he was simply unable to continue because his interlocutor protested at having this stupid widening of the issue forced upon him, he would jump straight to the specifics of their national character—and then, then there was no stopping him. It was Ion's passion to list all the characteristics of Romanian identity, naturally beginning with the defects . . .

"But don't we have any positive qualities?" Mihai asked, perhaps less than serious.

"Yes, we do," the other replied. "But we're in a situation where we can't take advantage of them. They're like the dark side of the moon."

"As bad as that?"

"Let me explain. Negative and positive are always found together—I mean they are two sides, two possibilities for any given element."

"Hum!"

"We are doomed by circumstances to remain in the negative, like an undeveloped photograph."

"Wait a minute, you're beginning to wander," Mihai said. "You can use better similes than that to demonstrate your point. Why not a coin, let's say one leu, or even twenty-five bani? Or better still a dollar bill."

"Come on, wiseass, don't get all pretentious if you already know what I mean."

"I'm not being pretentious. I'm helping to perfect your theory—which I've heard dozens of times before, remember. Logically speaking, the idea is very interesting, Gestaltist. Saussure already made use of it, though for different, more scientific purposes."

Mihai was almost running now, yet was managing to keep up the dialogue with his friend. It's easier like that, when you imagine it in your head, than it is in reality. And it's even easier when you're in the bath—even if the water's getting cold and you have to sit up and turn on the hot tap. At first that's also cold and you'd turn it off again if you didn't have faith in the written word, in the letters imprinted on the tap—*CHAUD*. You wait. And of course you let some of the tepid water drain away.

Now it feels good again.

Mihai no longer had any reason to run. He could already see the Hotel Intercontinental. There were more people than usual on the sidewalk. The traffic seemed to be blocked on University Square: neither cars nor buses were moving. A truck covered with tarpaulin had come to a standstill, surrounded by an excited crowd. A police car was honking like crazy to clear a way through.

Something's happened! Maybe a flying saucer landed . . .

Mihai slowed down and put both hands in his raincoat pocket. He stopped. Someone's banging on the door, louder and louder. Marianne has woken up and is furious that it's locked. She'll shout:

"Are you planning to spend much longer in there?"

Yes, I guessed right—except that she adds my name, so I'm sure she's talking to me, not anyone else who might be in here. But she doesn't shout. It's not the voice she uses when she's in full flow. She still sounds a bit sleepy. I don't answer. So there! Let her think

I've drowned. Or electrocuted myself by dropping the hair dryer in the water.

"I've told you again and again not to dry your hair in the bath!"

I don't answer. I try to imagine what might be going on in Mihai's head. Why has he stopped? Is he afraid? If he took a few more steps he'd be in front of the National Theater.

"What are you doing in there?"

He's obviously unsure whether to go any further. Maybe it's not a question of fear; maybe, on the contrary, he's thinking of joining the others in the square. And Ion? Is he there too, attracted by the crowd, or is he waiting at the place we arranged on the phone? That's why he's undecided, doesn't know what to do, feels like lighting a cigarette but can't find his matches. He doesn't have the nerve to ask any of the sullen passersby for a light. He takes another step and then comes to a halt. One pedestrian seems to have a cigarette in the corner of his mouth. Then he vanishes, swallowed up by the human torrent. No, he can't stay there rooted to the spot; he has to make a decision.

"Open up! Do you hear me?"

I have no choice, I have to answer her. Mihai looks at the people flocking into the square from every direction. Ion, a man of his word, might still be waiting where we agreed . . . He can't just leave him there . . . I pat the water with the palm of my hand; it doesn't seem so hot any more.

"I'm taking a bath."

Of course she could have worked that out for herself. It's not really pertinent information, not what interests her. She wants to know why I locked the door.

"Open the door! I need to brush my teeth."

I can't keep it up any longer; she'll get too mad at me. So I raise myself out of the water and stretch to unbolt the door. She comes in without even glancing at me. I stand there uncertain, a Neptune dripping suds and water. She goes to the sink and turns the taps on, hard. Grabs her toothbrush with one hand, the tube of paste with the other. I admire the way her hips shake in time with her brush strokes. Vibrating all over, she tries to tell me something, an idea that develops in her as more and more of the toothpaste turns into froth. An idea or maybe an urgent message. I don't understand a word, but I do see that the mirror is becoming dotted with little white specks. I lie down again in the bath and remember that I can't leave Mihai rooted to the spot in the middle of the sidewalk, jostled on all sides by the people heading for the square. Probably he's already reached the meeting place and noticed that Ion isn't waiting there, that he's left—or never arrived.

"—want a bath too!"

The last few words were audible—and peremptory. No point in protesting, in saying that I wasn't finished, hadn't even had time to soap myself properly; nor in shamelessly divulging that because of her I had botched an important scene, one of many from the famous December of 1989, which would have helped me to work out other scenes that had unfolded on the same square a few months later. So, I have to get a move on. If Ion wasn't in front of the travel agency, Ion who always keeps his word, it wasn't at all out of the question that something serious had happened to him. Maybe he's been arrested, for example, picked up from the student hostel that very morning. Two thugs in gray raincoats went up to the third floor, knocked on the door, banged on it with their palms and fists, and getting no answer pushed the handle down and went into his room. Ion was in the communal washroom taking a shower. When he came back he surprised them leafing through his books. That was one hypothesis, the most serious. But there were others to be taken into consideration; even before Marianne started hammering at the bathroom door like a woman possessed, I had thought of having Ion meet Petrişor that same morning, the Petrişor who had news fresh from Timişoara and knew of a demonstration due to take place in Bucharest itself.

"Where? Who's organizing it?"

Ion knew there were all kinds of rumors about the events in Timişoara, but as he was not very trusting by nature he told himself that the general alarmism and excitement of those days did not yet justify speaking of what might, pompously, be called a "revolution." "A heap of mashed potato doesn't just explode all of a sudden!" he liked to repeat to anyone who would listen. Which doesn't mean he wouldn't have gone to University Square, at least to have a look. That was why he'd arranged to meet Mihai at the travel agency behind the Hotel Intercontinental. It was an excellent observation point.

The agency was closed. Ion was nervously pacing the sidewalk; Mihai was late as usual. In the square, larger and larger groups of people made it difficult, soon impossible, for traffic to pass through. And here comes Valeriu, sprung from God knows where, who gives Ion a hug. He's just left Petrişor, on his way into the square. Ion is easily persuaded to go along too, not to wait around any longer. Maybe Mihai is already there, in one of the groups discussing Timişoara and the tens of thousands killed.

Even the Paris papers, and especially French television, were quite alarmist: they quoted figures that now seem off the wall, but at the time, in the heat of the moment, we'd all lost our critical faculties. Logical thinking only served to make the horrors more plausible. The climax came when the TV news showed pictures of the bodies dug up in Timişoara: the abnormally pale infant on its mother's sallow belly, the corpses, all sewn up with wire, or so it seemed to me . . . Really harrowing.

It's true that Marianne, more Cartesian than the general run of French journalists, was skeptical from the beginning:

"Well, I can hardly believe that . . ."

But one reason she could hardly believe it was that I was the one who communicated the news to her, before her favorite Channel One reporter commented on the situation and broadcast a series of new images, each more appalling than the last.

"You Romanians, honestly, when you—"

She didn't finish the sentence because the telephone rang and anyway she might have been unsure what she wanted to say. I didn't reopen the discussion but slipped out into the street. Only that evening, when we saw the pictures on television, did her heart finally go out to a people who couldn't really be considered guilty just because I happen to be what I am—that is, riddled with defects . . .

"But don't I have any positive qualities?" I asked.

"Sure you do," she said. "But as you get older they're less and less noticeable."

In bed, reading by the light of the night-table lamp: as bourgeois a couple as you're likely to see, in a bedroom deserving the same epithet. I think that's the impression we'd give if we were ever filmed. But we aren't: no one's staring at us; no one is paying us the least bit of attention. Does that mean we're invisible? Marianne sticks her left foot out from under the duvet, wriggles her toes mechanically, unconsciously. Her conscious mind is absorbed in a Marguerite Duras novel, it doesn't matter which, let's say *Le Camion*. Nowadays women read much more than men. I mean literature, novels. That may be why there are more and more female novelists, and not only in England, where it was already quite striking in the nineteenth century. They set the tone, they listen to the music. I read the paper. Now I come across a news report that I can't refrain from reading aloud:

"'Nicolae and Elena Ceauşescu were executed in Târgovişte but were buried in Bucharest . . .'"

"I know," Marianne yawns. "They announced it on television. I even saw the trial. Horrible!"

"Just listen for a second! '. . . but buried in Bucharest, it was revealed on Friday in an interview with . . .'"

"I must have missed that."

"Then you missed the man with the beard. Do you remember? You said you liked the look of him back in December. Anyway, they mention him here, and his white beard especially."

"They're making a Santa Claus out of him."

"I'm just telling you what's here."

"But you skipped his name."

"Yes."

"Why?"

"'. . . who took part in the trial of the two dictators.'"

"Two?"

"Yes. Husband and wife. A couple."

"Together until the very end," Marianne adds, not at all ironically. Admiringly, in fact—almost enviously.

I look at her but say nothing. I rustle the paper, a little annoyed.

"Listen!"

"What do you think I'm doing?" she asks, jabbing me with her foot, or rather her knee, her left thigh.

"The place where they've been buried will be kept secret, he said: '. . . because we're afraid the public would desecrate the grave.'"

"The public, poor things! They sure have to carry a lot on their shoulders."

"Don't you believe Romanians hated Ceausescu?"

"Sure I do. Why shouldn't I? I believe everything you tell me . . ."

"It's not just me. The papers, the television . . ."

"Okay, whatever you say. Now come on, read what they write about Rostropovich."

"The violinist?"

"The cellist."

"What do you want me to read?"

"Read what's written right here."

"There's nothing especially interesting."

"Just read!"

" 'The cellist Mstislav Rostropovich has recovered his USSR citizenship by way of a special decree of the Presidium of the Supreme Soviet published yesterday . . .' "

"A decree?"

"Yes."

"I thought they could only take it away from you by decree."

"Well, if they can take it away by decree, they can also give it back by decree. That's clear enough. Look what else they say: 'The musician went into exile from the USSR in 1974, and he was stripped of his citizenship in 1978.' "

"But it doesn't say anything about a decree."

"What?"

"It doesn't say they stripped him of his citizenship by decree."

"How else would they have done it?"

"No idea."

"Anyway, they did it by a special decree."

"Like the Légion d'Honneur," Marianne titters, resting her thigh against mine. Then she stretches out some more.

"Rostropovich's wife, the singer Galina Vishnevskaya, has also regained her citizenship, by the same decree."

Marianne sprawls all over me now, not bothering about the paper, which falls crumpled off the end of the bed.

They only arrested Ion in the evening, after he reappeared at the hostel.

He had spent nearly the whole day looking for Mihai in University Square and the streets around it. Once he'd even hurried all the way down the boulevard to Piața Romană, where he heard there would be another demonstration, but the few groups that attempted to gather there in the hope of attracting other citizens on their way home from work were immediately dispersed.

When Ion returned to University Square, the crowd was considerably denser. It was even necessary to send in a few APCs, and at the sight of these green armored vehicles everyone scattered like partridges or made a run for the subway. A few particularly courageous ones began to throw stones they'd found on a nearby building site. Some even hit their targets. Probably out of fear, an APC let loose two or three bursts of gunfire. A few soldiers remained on the street. A little later the traffic started flowing again. Ion lay sprawled on the sidewalk, exhausted like the others by all the running.

My eyes are closing on me, the lids itch, I don't feel like pretending to read the paper anymore. Marianne is fast asleep beside me.

Another huge crowd formed toward nightfall: they were mostly young people, who shouted something or other about the people killed in Timișoara. The armored cars returned too. I switch off the lamp and turn onto my side. I hear volleys of gunfire, the shouts of paramedics, the rumble of police vehicles. When Ion saw that the APCs were back, he ran off in the direction of Colțea Hospital. Someone behind pushed him over. He picked himself up and sprinted as far as Strada Lipscani. He was with a number of others now, including Petrișor.

It's easy to imagine a snatch of dialogue, interspersed with their panting for breath:

"Have you seen Mihai?"

"No," Petrișor said, putting his hand over the tear at the knee of his pants. He was bleeding.

"There were too few of us," Ion said. "So they started shooting."

"And what about Timișoara? Didn't they shoot there too? There were plenty of people there . . . the way people talk, it sounds as if the whole city was on the streets."

"I don't know what to tell you."

"The workers must be got to come here. All of them—here in the center."

"But would they want to?"

"Of course. Don't you think they've had it up to here with what's been going on?"

"But how can we get everyone together? Do you have some kind of plan?"

"No, I'm not sure. The only chance would be if the Midget called some big meeting in connection with Timişoara. He's a big one for giving speeches. So, with any luck he'll mobilize them himself."

"You think he's that stupid?"

"Well, isn't he?"

"Come on, stop all this shit."

"Listen!"

"To what?"

"The bells are ringing."

A group of people had taken refuge in the church next to the hospital, and some had managed to get into the belfry. Mihai was with them. (Historically speaking, the above exchange is inaccurate: it couldn't have taken place either before or after December 21. Thus, a very Romanian piece of dialogue . . .)

Ion was a skeptic at heart—it was a hard habit to break, and his friends tended to hold it against him. He's a real albatross! they would say. All he wants is to run away to the West. As if he were the only one!

A third-year student in French, he had become friendly with Georges, from Lebanon, who claimed that his father was rolling in it and had promised to invite Ion to his house in Beirut. Georges had perfect manners and was indeed generous with everyone, not only pretty girls. But Ion wondered how it was possible to be rich in a country ravaged by years of bloody civil war. Well, here was proof that it was possible! Georges showed him a photo of a luxurious villa, half-destroyed though it was by artillery shells. It was his parents' home.

"We'll fix it up to look like before," he said.

Some of the people fleeing University Square headed for the subway. Night was falling, and it had turned bitterly cold. Ion walked huddled up, but as quickly as he could. Petrişor, who lived in the same hostel, could hardly keep up with him. Underground, then, an apparition: a woman, perhaps—but when Ion looked more closely he saw a goat's mouth. The thing was swaying its hips and bleating softly.

"Keep away! Can't you see it's a crazy old woman?"

But Ion was fascinated and stopped. He let himself be led down a side passage. Maybe it was an arcade. He saw a leather-goods shop, its shutters not yet drawn.

"Do you want to buy a suitcase?"

Further along, the brightly lit window of another shop. An eagle, or rather a hawk, a stuffed harrier; no space to spread its wings. The apparition took two steps back, still wiggling itself left and right. She was wearing black mittens with only one finger each. Petrişor stopped at the entrance to the side passage. He'd walked through a puddle and the water had soaked his shoes.

"What are you doing? Are you crazy?"

There wasn't just one puddle but dozens. They were everywhere, getting deeper and deeper. The water was up to Ion's ankles and kept rising as he advanced. The woman was walking backward, bleating from time to time. There was more and more water, and with it more and more of the greenish light that came from the recessed lamps along the floor and in the shopwindows, all switched on, and from garlands of variously colored Christmas lights. There was also a parrot, or anyway some brightly colored exotic bird. The water had reached Ion's knees. The woman had vanished. He heard Petrişor call after him, but the voice sounded a long way off. Then all the lights suddenly went out, and for a few moments Ion was aware only of the rippling water, now waist-high, which slowed and muffled his movements. It felt warm and pleasant. Then, after that brief sensation of wellbeing, he heard two bodies fall into the water with a loud splash—unless it was actually the sound that divers make when they break back through to the surface. Someone had grabbed him by the neck and arms. There was no point in shouting out—in this country no one hears you when you scream . . . He awoke in a dark cellar and immediately went down on all fours, because that made it easier to squeeze through the mass of bodies he saw sprawled everywhere. No, they weren't corpses—anyway, some of them were moving. Shining between them were what looked like the scales of some fish. Before long, he heard Petrişor's voice:

"This time we're really fucked!"

"We've been fucked for a long time already," Ion replied at once, with a kind of joviality.

Petrişor said no more: he was afraid of waking the others. Ion crept alongside a wall, which, though damp and foul-smelling, gave out a little warmth. A hot water pipe, he assumed. He touched the wall with the palm of his hand. It was smooth, almost velvety. And soft: like skin, like the ass of a woman asleep beneath a duvet. He couldn't control himself. He sank his hand into the fleshy matter and heard a shout. Marianne, rudely awoken, is hitting me on the hand:

"*Vieux cochon*! *Salaud*!"

I fall asleep again. I see the truck with the khaki canvas, spot it from a distance. Yet I'm approaching it, moving forward like an automaton. My mouth is dry. Petrişor catches me by the arm, pulls me, tries to hold me back.

"Don't go, Ion. They're here to arrest us."

My arm has gone numb. The corpses, the sleeping bodies, began to speak all at once, and their words lit up the room: a captain was banging his fist on a wooden table, which echoed like a hollow cask. He was seated behind a huge barrel, perched on a tennis umpire's chair. Propped up against the barrel was Petrişor, in only his underpants, holding a goat that struggled and bleated.

"I think I'm going crazy," Petrişor shouted.

"And are you sorry?"

The captain was grinning from ear to ear. Or no, he was brushing his teeth, and then he spat a greenish fluid straight into the barrel.

There's someone in the barrel.

Fear now. Dripping with sweat.

I jump out of bed and hurry to the bathroom. Flick the light switch. See the mirror appear above the sink, my face trapped inside it. My captive vacuous face, its tousled hair and bulging eyes. I move closer to it, to myself. This early-morning double ought to startle me, to bewilder me. But that's not how it is. Maybe because I've come from a long way away. I don't feel the least surprise.

The idea came to me just now in fact . . . From the table where I'm seated, I can see a mirror through the half-open door into the next room. If I lean to my right, I can make out an ear and part of a cheek. If I wanted to see my nose, my other cheek, or my whole face, I'd risk toppling over, along with the chair. Even now, the chair is balancing unsteadily on two of its legs. It's true that I could just move the table . . .

Apparently it's good for the mind to look in the mirror, to see yourself as you are. In my case that means an exiled writer, getting old fast. With a bit of a bulge, although I've lost nearly ten kilos. I suck in my cheeks, round my lips, raise my eyebrows. That's worse! Anyway, the bags under my eyes, the two lines descending from my nose to the corners of my mouth, the wrinkles that are beginning to form on my brow: I can't escape all that, whatever faces I pull. I'd have to resort to cosmetic surgery—and in the end, well, why not? There's nothing to be embarrassed about. It's become quite trendy, even if the idea is more readily accepted in the case of the so-called weaker sex. A woman who struggles to preserve her looks, at least in part, declaring war on old age and those wrinkles in the mirror . . . no one thinks of her as some old bag preening herself while the country goes to wrack and ruin. Besides, what can an old woman do—the country's a mess, no one lifts a finger, and the young just want to get out while the getting's good. No, surgery is considered an entirely legitimate defense, even a right, for women . . . but this doesn't apply so easily to men. How unjust. Nothing but an unreasoning prejudice. Men are supposed to bear old age stoically, to stoop with a smile on their lips, to let themselves wither with a brave face. They're not allowed the same little tricks, either when they're young or when they're old.

"Enough with your absurd theories. You're making a laughing-stock of yourself."

"What do you mean? I'm taking a widespread prejudice and subjecting it to rational discussion. I want to hear arguments, not simple exclamations or interjections. And, by the way, your attitude is precisely the sort of thing that fuels inequality between the sexes—directly or indirectly. Shall I explain?"

"No, thanks."

"So you refuse to discuss it. You're afraid that I might somehow convince you."

"Cut it out: you're ridiculous. Besides, can you really see me going to a surgeon to make my skin smoother?"

"That's your business. And you do have your creams, after all—all those little jars."

"Do you want some too? Be my guest."

I have to admit that the discussion is pointless. Besides, for me, what the mirror serves to verify is not beauty or youth but identity. I need to check whether I'm still more or less the same, to confirm that I haven't changed at all . . . or only a little. Inside myself, I mean. But how can I see inside myself? There ain't no mirror for that.

"So get down to work! Write!"

That's it, that's what I should be doing. Instead I waste time, rant about one thing or another. I'm not capable of leaving, of isolating myself, of concentrating on just one thing. I write in fits and starts, as and when it comes to me: bits and pieces, notebook entries, not even a whole scene followed through to the end, only discrete actions outside of any context, tangled fragments. And many days not even that. I make do with dreaming of something that I've promised myself I'll write when I have the necessary peace and leisure time, a place where I can happily stay put, or rather bolt myself down, pen in hand, in front of a ream of blank paper that I can blacken as quickly as possible, covering one sheet after another with little signs illegible to everyone else, and vigorous deletions too, ticks and arrows referring to margins that soon fill up with even smaller letters, an ungenerous, tortured handwriting interspersed here and there with absurd, delirious drawings that nevertheless help me to survive the moments of blockage when my mind empties like a vase with a hole in the bottom and I no longer see anything but what happens to be visible through the window: grass and flowers, trees, the neighbors' house, more trees in blossom, I imagine it's spring, a wagtail is moving with difficulty through the long thick grass.

I take off my pajamas and remember that I still have to shave, and then take a bath. To lie in the hot liquid and forget aches and pains or sciatica, to stop thinking of my body, of myself, to escape this carapace of flabby flesh. I tighten what's left of my biceps, my pectorals. The effort swells my cheeks more than my muscles, and the face in the mirror seems so comical that I burst out laughing. I laugh to myself, in the mirror. Then I feel better.

We both spread butter on slices of toast. Marianne adds some cherry jam, but I don't like that. Maybe I'll put some orange marmalade on the last piece. It's slightly bitter.

I didn't answer her immediately. I chewed on my bread, sipped my cup of coffee, and buttered another slice. Of course I want to go, but not right now. I feel like writing the novel that I've been thinking about ever since that trip I made in the truck. I hadn't been able to stop myself from going, even at the height of the "events." The truck, chartered by *Médecins sans frontières*, was carrying food and medicine. We crossed the Danube into Romania at Giurgiu, having driven through southern France, northern Italy, Yugoslavia, and Bulgaria. We avoided the route via Timişoara because we were afraid of the "terrorists"; we were simply terrified of them. By the time we reached Bucharest, there no longer seemed to be any danger. It was a few days after the Ceausescus were executed.

Marianne was not about to give up. She repeated her question.

". . . to write the novel first," I replied with my mouth full. Then I took a teaspoonful of marmalade and, instead of spreading it on what was left of the toast, put it straight into my mouth.

"A novel!"

"What's so surprising about that?"

Marianne got up to toast some more bread. She said over her shoulder:

"Do you mean like the ones you've written up to now?"

Keeping a dignified silence, I put my teaspoon down again; the orange peel tasted even more bitter on its own. I heard the bread pop up in the toaster when it was done. Marianne interpreted my silence as a sign of weakness, of insecurity. It gave her the confidence to press on. She sat down at the table and looked straight into my ear:

"The things you write are anything but novels."

"So what are they then?"

She hadn't expected this riposte, which shot out like an arrow from a bow. I looked up at her ready for a fight. She spread another slice of bread with butter and jam, while starting to move her cheeks and lips. But she held back from uttering the sounds: she preferred to bite into her bread. I took the opportunity to give a little speech about the so-called traditional novel, which is not so old, in fact, and which really only developed in the nineteenth century. In the eighteenth century, novelists hadn't yet taken refuge in the heaven of omniscience . . .

"In what?"

"The author hadn't become Almighty and All-Knowing yet, nor had he made himself invisible. It hadn't occurred to him that he could try and mimic that other creator—you know, the one with the capital letter."

"With the what?"

"To mimic God. The author was a modest presence in the pages of his book, often even addressing the reader as straightforwardly as in ordinary conversation. And readers, for their part, had a tolerant and sophisticated relationship to the author, feeling that they'd been invited into a fictional world and that it was in everyone's interest to respect its conventional character. They didn't confuse that world with reality . . . whatever that might be."

"Eh?"

"They didn't imagine they were looking out of a window onto the street, or from the street into the houses of people like themselves. They didn't identify in that way. They became involved, maybe passionately involved, but still kept a distance from the characters. And they didn't dare venture the opinion—on the basis of their own experience—that the subject or plot was 'true to life.' They accepted the novel as a novel, without complaint, just as the author constructed it."

"You could say they were still following some of the rules of classicism that had survived from the seventeenth century."

"If you like—but that's not so important. The key thing is that they accepted the author's visible presence in the text."

Here the telephone interrupted us. Marianne got to her feet and went into the living room to pick it up. The speed with which she did this showed me that she was glad to end the conversation. It wasn't the first time that breakfast had been the occasion for a theoretical dispute.

But, to be honest, this narrator must admit that he can never control himself in such situations. After making a few points fairly calmly, he raises his tone of voice almost against his will and begins to hold forth; he waves his arms without noticing that he has a knife in one hand and a slice of bread in the other, while the female character, that is to say Marianne, pulls back, almost frightened, drops her ironical repartee, and looks for the first pretext to retreat from the field of battle, where the narrator, upset that he has again failed to persuade her, is still roaring so loudly that the neighbors can probably hear him.

If you're unable to persuade your own wife—or lover—what hopes can you entertain in relation to other men's wives and lovers? Because women are the real readership for a novel. Men have other things to worry about. Some read the newspapers. Others not even that.

I was in the cab of the truck, squashed between the driver and Doctor Gachet. Until then I had managed to keep our conversation centered on the events, or anyway not to let it stray outside the realm of politics, whether French or international. It was our second day on the road and we were somewhere in Serbia, past Belgrade and heading for the Bulgarian frontier. It was drizzling, and we knew the fine drops of water might turn into snow at any moment. The doctor was rather bored. He asked me the question point-blank, so that I had no way of dodging it or of drawing him onto another subject before it was out. He knew I was a writer, since I had presented myself as one to *Médecins sans frontières* and it was on that basis that they'd agreed to let me go along as an interpreter. It's true that I could have lied and said I was a bank clerk or a Radio Free Europe journalist, but the fact was that the friend who recommended me had already told them I was an exiled writer and all that. As far as my friend was concerned—I can understand it perfectly—being a writer was no big deal. That's how Doctor Gachet saw it too.

"So, what kind of things do you write?" he asked. He was much younger than I, good-looking, successful with women. At the Yugoslav—or rather Croat—hotel where we put up for the night, he seduced our waitress before you could say presto. She had worked in Paris and could get by in French quite well. I saw him disappear with her down a hallway.

"Kind of novels."

"But what kind of novels?" he insisted. "About exile, about emigration." The tone was no longer questioning: he thought it evident that an émigré should write about emigration.

"Not really . . . not yet . . ." I stuttered vaguely in reply.

We were driving through a village, where a big sheepdog was lazing dreamily in the middle of the road. The driver swerved to avoid it and we ended up in a ditch. We climbed down. The other trucks in the convoy naturally stopped as well. We struggled for nearly an hour to get ours back on the road. A few local farmers came to help us. We were muddy right up to our waists.

I had been let off the hook. But at dinner that evening the doctor brought the conversation round to literature again. He spoke enthusiastically about Solzhenitsyn, and I nodded away as I wolfed down my food.

"A truly great writer," the doctor sighed.

I stuffed myself with a huge lump of steak that I was barely able to chew. I moved my jaws furiously, in such a way that my head and whole body might have seemed to be enthusiastically agreeing with this statement. But Dr. Gachet had some doubts—or perhaps he simply wanted to prolong the conversation, because there he was once more, staring at my right ear with a broad smile on his face.

"Excellent, don't you think?"

He clearly wasn't referring to the steak, which was actually rather shriveled and as tough as a cowboy's boots. I struggled to get the bolus down: it must have been the size of an apple, though a little softer, so that in the end it did pass from the gullet into the esophagus, helped on its way by a draught of white wine, and then another.

"You eat too fast," the doctor remarked. He politely avoided saying "like a pig," which is surely what my scarlet perspiring face must have suggested to him.

I latched on to the new topic and informed him that, some years before, I had developed an ulcer from eating too fast and too greedily. He asked me a few questions, and I answered them with a wealth of detail. I even told him about how I had broken an arm and a leg once when jumping, or rather falling, from the second floor of a building.

"Did you fall or did you jump?"

"I jumped—but I saw there was a sofa waiting . . ."

"A sofa?"

"Yes, a kind of round sofa, I'm not quite sure what to call it."

"But what was it doing in the street?"

"It wasn't in the street."

"But . . . Where exactly did you jump from, then?"

"From the top of the staircase that led to the ground-floor reception room at the Writers' Union."

Happy to have escaped from Solzhenitsyn, I supplied more and more biographical details of interest to the doctor, although they were far from being as spectacular as those narrated by the great Russian writer. I was never in prison, never in a cancer ward. Nothing I could do about that! I wasn't going to start inventing things, wasn't going to come up with some bullshit just so a French doctor would think more highly of me. I did try, though, to inject a lot of humor into my stories. And self-irony. Two or three times he even deigned to laugh, and then I joined in too, really cracked up. The driver laughed along with us, but he kept his cool and used a napkin to quickly wipe up the sauce trickling from my chin onto my shirt collar. And then we ordered another bottle of wine, again white.

The female character is back from the telephone, while the other character, who's also the narrator, gives her a questioning look, and when she pours herself a cup of coffee without replying I wait a few more seconds and then open up the quotation marks, start with a capital letter, compose my sentence, with a comma before the final vocative and a question mark at the end—the whole works.

"Who were you talking to for so long, my dear?"

She sips her coffee and remains silent. Then she informs me that, thanks to one of her best friends—whom the author knows too, though he won't mention her name because he isn't sure whether she will play any role in the narrative, and anyway he still has plenty of time to make up his mind—that, thanks to this friend X (whose name she repeats), she could get an appointment for me soon with the doctor.

"With the doctor?" And I light a cigarette, as if this proves I'm in the best of health. In fact I say as much, after taking a few quick puffs.

"If you're in the best of health, why do you keep moaning about your back all day?"

"Really, do I keep moaning?"

"Yes, you do. And in your sleep you even start groaning. When you wake up in the morning, you totter around like an old man. Then you go into the bathroom and gape at yourself in the mirror for minutes on end."

"I have to shave, don't I?"

"And you turn on the taps, as if you couldn't care less whether I want to go on sleeping. You get in the bath and lie there for ages in hot water, saying that it helps with the pain. So, I'd say you were in bad shape. There's no point pretending now that you're healthy because you want to run away somewhere, supposedly to write a novel. As if those things you scribble were novels anyway!"

"You can call them whatever you like."

"They're certainly impossible to read. I'm surprised you can still get them published."

It might be noted that at this point the narrator, or rather the author, anyway the guy sitting at the table in front of sheets of paper darkened with his tiny handwriting, stretches his legs and coughs or sighs, leans back like so many times before on the hind legs of his now rickety chair, regains a more or less upright position, picks up his pen, leafs through the pages and reads a sentence here or there with an air of disgust, and then, instead of writing more, begins to cross lines out with a furious energy of which his few presumed readers would never have thought him capable. One particularly violent motion leaves a page torn in two. Perhaps it's where the author, or to be more precise the narrator, is trying to answer the questions put to him, on the subject of literature, by Dr. Gachet.

"You'd do better to write about that winter journey to Bucharest," Marianne says, comfortably installed on the terrace in a white wickerwork armchair that she's padded with red and blue cushions. She has a novel by Marguerite Duras on her lap, and on top of that is a Siamese cat, which yawns out of sheer boredom at what it hears.

I lower my just-opened newspaper and peer at her over my glasses. Of course I chuckle:

"I could call it *Journey to the East.*"

Marianne shrugs, a little annoyed, but she controls herself. I think that, for whatever reason, she really was trying to help, that afternoon. She's sweet as pie as she goes on:

"The title doesn't matter. You could call it *The Winter Journey.*"

"Why not *The Truck*?" I suggest, still on guard. I glance at the cat, who's surprised that I'm showing him any attention; he mutters something or other, but in such a mewling tone I think even Marianne doesn't understand it.

"You passed through so many interesting places," she persists calmly. "First of all there was Milan, Venice . . ."

"We didn't stop in either of those places. It wasn't a honeymoon trip, you know."

"Then Trieste, the city of Joyce's friend, Svevo."

"Joyce who had Beckett as his secretary, who was himself the friend of Pinget, who died alone like a dog."

"Then Zagreb . . ."

"We went around it on the highway . . ."

". . . and Belgrade. Yugoslavs are very passionate . . ."

"The blood rushes to their heads pretty quickly, it's true."

"Prague, Budapest—no, of course not, you crossed straight into Bulgaria . . . Now *there's* a mysterious country, with its rose perfume and its solemn male voices . . ."

"They have thick necks."

"That's not necessarily a defect. What's wrong with thick necks?" she asks with a laugh.

I concede that she has a point. I should have known not to quote Eminescu to a Frenchwoman. National poets should remain on national territory.

"And all the adventures you must have had during those three days. There must be a lot to tell . . ."

"What adventures?"

Marianne loses patience. She pushes the cat away and raises her tone by nearly an octave.

"How should I know? Make some up. Aren't you supposed to be a novelist?"

". . . novelist!" the Siamese repeats like a parrot.

I fold the newspaper and place it on my knees. Supporting myself as well as I can against the back of the chair, I cough to clear my throat. The cat jumps back onto his mistress's lap and pricks up his ears.

"'The day after his own adventure with the waitress, Doctor Gachet realized that his wallet was missing. He no longer had any money or even his ID. And we were already at the Bulgarian frontier. I don't know if they were being friendly or incompetent, but the Serbian border guards just waved us through; we were leaving their patch, so what did they care? The Bulgarians, on the other hand, were delighted to hear that a Frenchman had been robbed in Yugoslavia. 'The Serbs are all a bunch of thieves,' a Bulgarian policeman told us in French. I didn't contradict him, or point out that the waitress had been a Croat. Actually I wasn't sure of that: she could have been ethnically Croatian, Serbian, Macedonian, Bosnian, Montenegrin or possibly even Romanian. There are a lot of Romanians in Yugoslavia. You also find Hungarians, Czechs, Slovaks, Slovenians, Turks, Bulgarians, Albanians . . . My list seemed to confuse Dr. Gachet, but for some reason it made the driver laugh. He probably found it funny that there were so many nationalities in Europe. Anyway, the Bulgarian customs people were happy with the automobile documents and our instructions endorsed by the French ministry of foreign affairs. But what about later? How would we manage if Doctor Gachet wasn't able to show any ID? He didn't look too worried, but he did eventually go to his embassy in Sofia. And, after a couple of hours that the rest of us spent drinking beer with some Bulgarians who were very interested in the Romanian events, he returned with an official slip of paper that would get him to Bucharest.'"

"Not the most thrilling of tales."

"We were pretty wasted by the time we got back in the truck. Even Roger was more than a little tipsy."

"Weren't you ever stopped by the police?"

"Who was going to stop us? We had a French tricolor on the windscreen."

"Ah, right."

"But listen to this. It was getting dark by the time we reached the Danube region. Dr. Gachet reopened our literary discussion by talking about Zinoviev, whom I hadn't even read. All I could say was: 'Yes, yes, a very interesting writer.' 'A philosopher!' he shouted back. 'A philosopher of anticommunism.' I didn't contradict him. 'Have you read how he describes *Homo sovieticus*?' the doctor went on. As a matter of fact I hadn't. Through the window I caught sight of a bunch of scrawny dogs, with ash-gray fur. They were running to the right of the truck—which was probably why the driver hadn't spotted them. 'They look just like wolves,' I said absentmindedly. Roger laughed: Ha, ha, ha! Then two of the nasty creatures suddenly crossed into the road. The driver didn't have time to avoid them: he hit them head on. 'Maybe they really were wolves,' Dr. Gachet mused. Roger lowered his window until we could hear their characteristically mournful baying. There was a whole pack of them. They were still running by the side of the road, their tongues curving down out of their mouths."

"No kidding, were they really wolves?" Marianne asked suspiciously.

"Who knows? All I can say is that their howls made our hair stand on end."

"But how could they howl and run at the same time?"

"Don't ask me. Maybe it was a division of labor: some ran while the others howled. Roger accelerated and they gradually faded out of sight, although for a time we could still hear them in the distance."

"They were howling from hunger . . ."

"No idea. Anyway, after a few more kilometers, the engine began to cough and sputter and snarl—we soon ground to a halt. 'Why you motherfucker!' Roger bellowed, and he smashed his fist twice into the steering wheel."

"That's not possible."

"What do you mean not possible? The engine had broken down. Roger switched off the ignition and scratched his thick red neck. The other trucks in the convoy also stopped. 'I'll have to see what's up,' he said, but it was obvious that he didn't feel much like getting out. 'Come on, the wolves are way back behind us,' Dr. Gachet said, trying to encourage him, 'and it'll be dark soon.' 'Let's make a fire at least,' Roger suggested, and he opened the cab door. The doctor bravely climbed down with him."

"And what about you?"

"Me? I was shivering from the cold. It had begun to snow again, a real blizzard. Besides, someone had to stay in the cab, in case Roger needed a pedal or a button to be pushed."

"But you don't even know how to drive."

"No, but I do know how to push. It's no big deal to press on a pedal or a button. Anyway, Gachet and the other members of the expedition began to build a fire with planks that had been keeping some boxes in place inside a truck. But they couldn't get the fire going because of all the wind. 'There are some binoculars in my briefcase,' the doctor shouted up to me. 'Would you get them out?' I found the binoculars and handed them down. He assumed the role of lookout, scanning a landscape that looked almost empty to the naked eye. A hawk was circling overhead—or maybe it was an eagle. The drivers had their heads beneath the hood, where the engine was rattling and from time to time coughing or choking. I pressed now on the accelerator, now on the button that operated the wipers to clear the snow from the windshield. I also switched on the headlights. Then I saw the wolves. It was probably a different pack, which had run up from the Danube ahead of us. Dr. Gachet was keeping watch in the opposite direction, convinced that the danger, if any, would come from there. I hesitated for a few moments, spellbound by the animals' sudden appearance in the blizzard, right in the middle of the road. "The wolves!" I screamed, and I banged furiously on the horn. Roger climbed back in right away, without bothering to close the hood, while the other drivers hurried off to their own trucks. Dr. Gachet didn't lose his sangfroid; once inside he continued to survey the landscape through his binoculars, giving the impression that he actually enjoyed the situation in which we found ourselves. As for the wolves, they didn't approach the truck but gathered by the roadside as if to fight over some piece of meat. 'They've found a dead body to tear apart,' the doctor muttered. At that moment one of the trucks behind us revved up and drove directly into the pack. The wolves yapped like little whipped dogs."

"Maybe they were just dogs after all."

"Maybe. What's for sure is that the wolves, or wild dogs, ran yelping from the truck. Dr. Gachet could see through his binoculars that the mangled corpse they'd congregated around was that of a human male: one leg had been ripped from its joint, an arm had been eaten all the way up to the elbow, one eye hung down over a cheek, and the face, missing its nose, was swollen from a string of bites. Although it was getting dark and the blizzard was still raging, huge blue eagles were flying round and round in the sky above us. The carrion would be theirs: they just had to wait for us to leave. A driver more daring than the others, the one who had chased the wolves away, got down from his truck and took what turned out to be a German passport from the dead man's body. You see, not even a German passport could save him."

"What on earth was he doing in Bulgaria?"

"He was a journalist who had tried to get through to Bucharest in the first days of the uprising, when the airport was still closed."

"And didn't the wolves come back?"

"What wolves? They were stray dogs that had ganged up and were roaming the countryside in search of food."

"So, what did you do in the end? Did you get the engine working?"

"Yes, there wasn't much wrong with it, although it's true that I wasn't helping when I stepped on the brake instead of the accelerator. We crossed the bridge at Giurgiu that same evening, rested for a few hours under blankets in the truck's cab, left for Bucharest at dawn, and arrived around midday."

"Sounds like you've touched your story up quite a bit," Marianne said, finally satisfied with my storytelling abilities. "Now let me read Duras for a while."

I didn't say another word. So she didn't get to hear about my brush with the Romanian security guy at the frontier, who wanted (or pretended that he wanted) to arrest me. He made us unload all the boxes from the truck, on the pretext that he was looking for weapons. Nor did I tell her about the journey from Giurgiu to Bucharest: friendly groups of peasants waved at us with triumphant, happy gestures, as if we were "the Americans" who had finally come to free them; snow on the highway prevented us from making faster progress, then we ran into huge puddles and concentrations of mud on the outskirts of Bucharest; we kept getting lost in the streets of the capital, which I no longer recognized.

"Everything's changed!" I exclaimed to the others. Dr. Gachet understood what I was feeling and tried to console me by pointing out that it had been the same when he went to Brazzaville with a colleague who was returning for the first time in ten years; the African had been so emotional that he burst into tears.

"How long is it since you were last in Budapest?" the doctor asked me. I didn't bother to correct him: what was the point? Did I care what went on in his head? I was tired, weary of a journey I should never have undertaken in the first place.

It was no longer snowing. The sun had come out. We stopped in a street somewhere and asked a passerby to explain how to get to the center of town. He was a young guy and seemed nice enough. Although I called out to him in Romanian, he insisted on speaking French, and, once he had climbed onto the side of the truck, directed his instructions to Gachet rather than me. But we couldn't hear him very well, so it occurred to the doctor to jump down and let our guide sit in his place.

"I'll ride in another truck," Dr. Gachet said.

The young man was more than delighted to climb into the French truck and wanted to know exactly where we came from in France. "Really? From Paris itself?" he repeated several times. He also wanted to know whether the Americans would be sending aid. He spoke briskly and kept switching between Romanian and French. Roger was beginning to lose patience.

"What's your name?" I asked him in Romanian.

"Mihai."

"Right, Mihai, please tell us how to get to the center of town: to University Square, for example."

But Mihai felt like talking some more. He said he was an English student, but a friend of his was studying French and dreamed of traveling to Paris. This friend was called Ion Valea, he said. When I tried to interrupt him, he quickly added:

"He was picked up by the Securitate before Christmas and came within an inch of being shot. He was one of the last to be arrested."

"So, how about University Square?"

I was getting tired of all the talk.

"There were more victims in University Square than anywhere else. They opened fire on us there. Then the workers came from the rally: it was our big lucky break!"

"Let's go," I said. "To University Square." And I signaled to Roger to pull out.

Happy to stay in the truck, Mihai proved to be a pretty good guide from then on. But he felt he had a duty to tell us how the revolution had unfolded: for example, how it had been when the 'terrorists' opened fire from the rooftops. No one could see them, and in the street they looked no different from the rest of the population—in civilian clothes. It was just that their eyes were glazed-over, as Maria, a friend of his, had once put it. Still, they were the most extraordinary marksmen—the very best, they'd been given special training. And they had imported rifles, with telescopic sights and infrared scopes. They even climbed onto the palace roof.

"Which palace?"

"The royal palace—well, you know, it's been turned into an art museum. They didn't quit until they were sure that their boss, the Midget, was well and truly dead."

"Did they hate him that much?" I pretended not to understand.

"No, sir. The terrorists were Ceausescu's men, the most loyal of his security forces. His praetorian guard."

"And where are they now?"

"I don't know. They gave themselves up. Some of them were drugged to their eyeballs."

We passed through University Square, where candles were alight and loaves of bread had been placed as an offering on the edge of the sidewalk. The bread was the touch that Roger liked most. Then we finally arrived at the embassy. Mihai wouldn't get out until we'd promised to phone him in the next few days.

"I want to introduce you to my friends," he said.

Moved by the pride in his voice, I shook his hand warmly and watched him walk off. He turned around and raised his arm, with two fingers in a victory salute. Dr. Gachet took me by the shoulder and muttered something about these young people who have the honor of saving Europe. Then, with the gestures of a host welcoming a guest into his home, he made way for me to walk first through the little black iron gate.

"This is a wonderful novel!" Marianne exclaims as she stops reading and puts her book on her knees. She looks up at the man. A little while ago he was sitting on his chair with his eyes open, but now he's walking up the flight of steps into the French embassy in Bucharest.

I kept my promise. I called Mihai and went to the address he'd given me, somewhere on Calea Moșilor, in a filthy run-down block with peeling walls like all the others. I'd bought two bottles of whisky at the Hotel Intercontinental. Mihai was waiting for me downstairs, in front of the elevator. He took the bottles, as thrilled as though I had handed him a champion's cup or trophy. We went up to his studio apartment, where a number of boys and two girls were crammed together in a cloud of cigarette smoke. Mihai showed them the bottles, raising them above his head in a triumphant gesture, then introduced me to everyone. The girls were called Maria and Ana. Ion was there too—tall, thin, with a long neck and a prominent Adam's apple, a real apple of an Adam's apple. And Petrișor. I didn't remember all the names. They were drinking plum brandy, țuică, but when they saw the whisky they hurriedly emptied their glasses.

"Rinse your glasses out first," Mihai ordered, "so the whisky doesn't smell of țuică."

I didn't carry my patriotism as far as to pretend that I preferred plum brandy to whisky. But, to be different, I chose the middle way of asking if they had a little vodka. Mihai smiled and said no.

"Then I'll have a whisky," I said, sitting down on the sofa between the two girls. To be precise, one of them—Maria—was perched on Ion's knees. Mihai brought another chair from the kitchen.

"I can also make some tea," he offered.

"It's only half-past four," Maria joked. She was stroking Ion's neck and playing with his Adam's apple. She was rather plumper than Ana, and had a fairer complexion—much fairer, in fact, because Ana was really quite dark.

They asked me how the journey by truck had been. I told them we were robbed by a Hungarian woman in Zagreb, who had been a waitress in Munich and looked like Marlene Dietrich. I also explained that Dr. Gachet, the leader of our expedition, had been most susceptible to her charms; she had been seated at a nearby table, with a cigarette holder more than half a foot long, sticking out from between her thick, red, rounded lips.

"And you're sure you didn't want her for yourself?" Ana asked on my left.

For some reason that made everyone laugh. They asked for more of the Scotch concoction, but I greatly abridged the rest of that little story . . .

"At the Bulgarian frontier Gachet suddenly announced that he couldn't find his wallet or his watch. Even his passport was missing."

"Maybe she was a spy," Petrișor said.

"Why a spy?" Ion dissented. "Just a thief."

"But why steal the passport?"

"Wouldn't you have been tempted?"

"What for?"

"How do you mean, 'what for'?"

"You think it's easy to tinker around with a French passport?"

Finally Ana broke in and asked coaxingly, "Won't you tell us some more of your adventures?" She glued her leg to mine and emptied her glass.

It was better to move on to all the other things I remembered than to dwell any more on the business of the passport. I swallowed another mouthful of whisky. Jesus, was it strong!

"On our way through Venice we witnessed a crime of passion."

"Oh, please, tell us all about it."

"An American woman shot a casual lover of hers, a young gondolier who couldn't have been more than twenty. We were leaning on the parapet of a bridge and admiring a façade. It was a little cross-canal, with no one in sight. Then we saw the gondola. The woman took a Browning from her handbag and pointed it at the man's chest. Until then he had been laughing as he pulled on the oar—probably a mocking laughter, you know, heedless of her reproaches. But then she screamed: 'I'll kill you! I'll kill you!' The voice was rough, thick, too deep for a woman's. '*Che fai, che fai*?' the young gondolier murmured, as if refusing to believe the statement of intent. Three shots rang out, and I saw the boy sink to his knees. I think the last bullet penetrated his skull—from less than a yard away, just imagine. The force with which the killer grabbed the body and hurled it into the water cemented my suspicions: the American was in fact a transvestite."

"A what?" Maria asked.

"A guy dressed up like at the carnival," Ion answered wisely.

"So it wasn't a woman at all?" Ana asked, slipping a hand beneath my sweater.

"Let me finish . . . I was so taken aback, so terrified, that I let out a yell. The American looked up and saw me. I realized that I had to vanish from his field of vision post haste, so I made a dive like a rugby player. I lay flat on the ground as two bullets whistled over my head."

"The bullets whistled here too," Petrişor said, or maybe it was the boy sitting next to him on the arm of the chair.

"Yes, but it wasn't Americans who were firing them," Mihai said.

And they began to kid around. Ana ran her fingernails up and down my spine.

"More like Libyans."

"Lidobyans . . ."

"Come off it: they were Oltenians."

"Yes, from our own good old Oltenia. Not so far from here."

"From *your* good old Oltenia. And the Midget's."

"The Midget was no Oltenian," Petrişor protested.

"What was he, then?"

"A Tatar."

"Petrişor's from Oltenia, from Craiova in fact," Ana whispered in my ear. I could feel one of her breasts on my shoulder, her nails on my spine, and her half-bare thigh against my knees. A real challenge to the law of the impenetrability of matter!

After a third glass of whisky, and with one of the bottles already empty, Ion began to talk to me in French. He spoke it quite well but in a very precious way, using imperfect subjunctives and all kinds of grammatical touches that sounded pretty pedantic. He wanted to know where I lived in Paris, what I did with myself there, and how it was that Mitterrand was still in power after so many years.

"But didn't Ceausescu last nearly twenty-five years?" Mihai chipped in, having pulled his chair closer to us and put Ana's legs on his lap to stop her from sprawling all over me. It was quite crowded!

"We shouldn't compare things that are incomparable!" I said severely, and began to cough. Ana tried to get her hand inside my pants, but I stood up and went to the kitchen for a glass of water. Mihai came after me: he took a clean glass from the cupboard, filled it from the tap and handed it to me. The room was a complete mess, and filthy as well. A cockroach was running around the sink, another on the cupboard. God knows what there was underneath. Mihai waited for me to finish drinking and then said:

"I know why you got up. You're a serious guy, someone who can be relied on."

I looked at him as if I hadn't immediately understood.

I put the glass in the sink. I hear Marianne shout from the living room, asking if I plan on ever making that cup of tea we talked about. The water is already bubbling away. I snatch the kettle from the stove. Huh, I must have let it boil too long. *Tant pis!* I take a tray and cover it with cups, spoons, teapot, sugar, artificial sweetener (for me), and the everlasting cherry jam.

I didn't respond to Mihai—except to say that I had to leave for an important engagement. I said good-bye to everyone from the door. Ana gave me a languorous look, but I didn't have the courage to make the slightest movement of my eyes or head in return. Only now am I winking, in the living-room mirror. I see myself carrying the tray like a stylized waiter—an ageing one, though, it must be said . . . Yes, dear readers, here I am, a bilingual waiter at your service! Only the bow tie is missing. I haven't put it on because I can't stand that feeling of tightness at my throat. There's no danger, absolutely none at all, that I'll ever commit suicide by strangulation. Maybe some other way, who knows, but not by strangulation!

Mihai saw me down to the street door, which meowed like our Siamese cat. I noticed then that Mihai had blue eyes. He asked me if he could walk a little way with me. Why not? I had nothing against it.

"Did you come over by car?"

"By car? I can't even drive."

That was the last thing I should have admitted to him. His lips broke into the same smile he'd had when I asked for a vodka, only this time it lasted longer and seemed more disdainful. I tried to correct the bad impression I'd made, but I only succeeded in making myself look worse.

"Have you forgotten that we came in that truck?"

"Via Venice, no?"

There was something unpleasantly aggressive in the way he said it. They learned to be like that when they were little kids, with the red Pioneer scarf round their neck. Anyway, I kept trying to find a defense.

"I joined the convoy in Trieste."

I expected him to mention Joyce, given that he was studying English. This would then change the topic of conversation. But Mihai had completely different things on his mind: he looked at me very attentively, as if he were trying to decipher a rebus.

"I flew to Venice first," I added with a touch of panic. Today's readers, especially younger ones, won't accept anything that sounds implausible. I ought to remember that, to pay more attention to little details that, while seeming trivial at first sight, are in the end not exactly decisive, but . . .

"And from Venice to Trieste by train, I suppose."

He spoke softly, but his look was piercing and watchful. Was he laying a trap? What if there was no train service between Venice and Trieste? But how would he know something like that?

I said yes, by train.

"My God, you're going to take forever," Marianne calls out from the sofa. She's wearing her lilac-colored silk robe, with a few of the buttons undone, so that a white thigh gleams out appealingly like fresh cream.

"I'd have liked to tell you how the revolution happened." Mihai had given up pestering me with questions. "But I can see it doesn't interest you."

"What are you talking about? Of course it does—enormously! Why do you think I've come all the way here? Three days in a truck and all kinds of danger, or anyway unpleasant incidents. Lousy hotels, junk restaurants, aggressive, officious border police. It wasn't exactly a picnic."

To tell the truth, I probably had him all wrong: he was neither suspicious of me nor jealous over the girl. He simply wanted to chat and felt disappointed, even angry, that I was leaving so soon. He would have liked to get me to stay a little longer.

"I haven't much time," I say as I pour the tea into the cups.

"What do you mean?" Marianne asks, quickly covering her thigh with the robe.

Mihai lowered his eyes. I feel sorry about it now: I was too rushed, or anyway too offhand—and impolite right from the beginning. Instead of getting them to tell me about the revolution, those intense few days when people put their lives at risk, I started to spin all kinds of yarns about things I'd never experienced. It's true they'd been egging me on with their rather naïve curiosity, but was that any excuse (to whom?) for reeling out that string of pulp adventures? Unforgivable! To make up for it, I suggested to Mihai that we meet at the bar of the Hotel Intercontinental in a couple of days' time. He cheered up.

"You're a serious type after all," he said, looking straight into my eyes.

"Why are you looking at me like that?" Marianne seems annoyed. I'll have to give her my full attention until sometime this evening, stop thinking about the novel, put it right out of my mind. Otherwise I'll be in for the same trouble as a few days ago, when she called me an impotent exile and said I was much too full of myself.

"At least if you were more modest!" she had said as she went into the bathroom and slammed the door.

I skim the papers that Marianne has put aside for me. She does keep her word when she promises something.

I discover that the defense ministry revealed as early as January 3 that there had been a plot. "Militaru: The Council of the National Salvation Front Has Existed for Six Months."

So what? The question isn't whether there was a plot against Ceausescu. Good for them if they managed to organize themselves, maybe with the help of the Securitate! But, in that case, it isn't clear where the famous terrorists came from. Or where they disappeared to.

"Well, maybe they just let them all go."

"That wouldn't matter one way or the other. The question is whether there were any terrorists or not."

"Some people were certainly shot at."

"That's it. Who?"

"You, me, the people!"

"Oh yeah. Come off it!"

The French press concentrated only on the trial of the presidential couple. One psychoanalyst-journalist (or vice versa) wrote, under the title "Romanian Hypnosis": "There is no resemblance between the man on the balcony and the stubborn amnesiac peasant [in the courtroom] who looks at his watch and signals for his wife to keep quiet. What happened to the promised secrets, to the revelations we were expecting to hear? It was pointless shouting that the film footage had been stolen from us. The truth is that the Ruler only exists on the horizon of our imagination. Cut open his pot belly and you will find nothing inside. He is his own tomb."

Marianne isn't home. I have no one to share my comments with. So I just have to read and be quiet.

FNAC, the booksellers, are sending five tons of books to Romania. I ask myself what kind, and who'll end up with them.

Euphoria is giving way to suspicion.

Careful! Something's rotten here. The revolution isn't what we thought it was. The revolution is being controlled.

The article refers to Militaru's declaration. I ask myself whether the Front has an interest in denying that there was a plot—I mean, that the revolution was a plot. But what about the dead? There can't be a revolution without dead people: it would be like the proverbial omelet without broken eggs. But dead people without a revolution?

The *Libération* journalist goes on:

"Who can rationally believe that this dictatorship, protected for years and years by an inextricable web of security forces, could have collapsed unless elements within those forces, even leading elements, had colluded with opponents working to bring down the regime? Of course, this is not to deny the importance of the popular revolt, without which nothing would have been possible . . . But, in short, if there was a revolution on Christmas Eve, it was because some revolted and others plotted."

I glance at the review of a book translated from Italian: *Democracy as Violence*, by Luciano Canfora. Originally the term "democracy" denoted a political break rather than a communal assembly, for which the Greeks had the word *isonomia*. According to Canfora, by asserting the rule of the *demos* over the citizen elite, radical democracy made intolerance a form of political struggle. Among the Greeks, in the fifth century BC, democracy was anti-individualist . . .

The Front is keeping to the story that there was a revolution. Brucan said as much at a press conference. Of course they need a popular, revolutionary legitimacy.

My eyes are beginning to close.

László Rajk: ". . . that the Romanian-Hungarian frontier should no longer be any more than a line on the map . . ."

The wallpaper in the bedroom has fine blue and white lines, with a motif of silver flowers. In the wardrobe, a collection of poor-quality shoes liberally spread with polish, some showing advanced signs of wear. The cheap shirts had probably been bought at Prisunic for a hundred and fifty francs apiece. Around twenty suits on hangers refute Pacepa's claim that Ceausescu's fear of germs led him to wear a new, disinfected set of clothes every day.

In his office, a complete dearth of reading material.

The beds, all of the four-poster variety, are draped in a gaudy violet, mauve, or emerald-green satin.

As for the Romanian Communist Party and its four million members, no one says a word. A little patience is in order . . .

Students were the first on the barricades, hoping to bring down the dictator, and they are again the first to challenge the new regime. At rallies held yesterday in Bucharest, they openly disputed its representative character.

"The Soviet Union tacitly agreed to the overthrow of Ceausescu several weeks before he fell," Silviu Brucan stated yesterday on British television.

I prefer to turn the page and read more about Home Sweet Home.

Elena Ceausescu's bathroom is the most extraordinary room in the whole house. Rare earthenware tiles, wallpaper with gilded arabesques, a rose-colored bathtub and washstand, with huge gold taps in the form of swans. A stack of towels in acrylic. (If they'd tried to use all that as a set on *Dallas*, people would have accused the TV people of going too far.)

Copies of *Paris-Match* and *Jours de France* at the foot of their bed. A photo album documenting the birth of a lamb!

The ewe of popular legend . . .

My eyes open again with several blinks.

People in the village of X claim to have seen a flying saucer on their football field. Night was falling. No match was being played that day, and the stands were empty. The eyewitnesses who later reported the machine to the police saw it from quite a distance, then. All their accounts are quite similar and resemble others from various parts of the world, including those from the former communist countries of Eastern Europe.

The tree branches at the window are naturally darker than the black night, especially as the night begins to fade, to grow paler, as night nears its end. This time my mind is made up! I'm on my way . . .

I hoist myself up and remain seated for a moment on the edge of the bed. I switch on the bedside lamp and turn to look at Marianne, who is sleeping with her mouth half open. She isn't snoring—whistling, rather, like a samovar when the pressure is building up. I switch off the light.

Then I go to the bathroom and turn on the light there. The mirror greets me with a treacherous welcome. Servile and hypocritical! I try to avoid it by looking away and busying myself with the taps. I wash my face and brush my teeth, but don't bother shaving this time; it would be too difficult without looking in the mirror. I return to the bedroom and grope around for my clothes. I feel the cat's head, then its body stretched out on my shorts. Its fur is so soft, irritatingly velvety. I give it a push, and when it meows I tweak its ears. Marianne is breathing gently and whistling.

I find the suitcase exactly where I hid it a few days ago. I put on my padded coat, step into the hallway and close the door behind me. My back suddenly begins to ache as I walk down the staircase. *Tant pis!* Nothing's going to stop me this time. Outside the dawn is slowly breaking. I head for the metro.

At the street corner, a midget is trying to climb up a rope. What's holding it in place? Preferring not to look, I cross over to the other sidewalk. My suitcase isn't heavy, and I try to convince myself that I am cheerful and carefree. I whistle an aria, but I get it so wrong that even I can't tell where it comes from. I can't resist the temptation to turn my head for a moment: the midget has wriggled up nearly three meters, so that his head is now level with a few second-floor windows. He is wearing a wide-brimmed hat. I quicken my pace. A car speeds past, and I have just enough time to glimpse a woman inside, dressed in white, like a bride. Also wearing a veil. Beside her, in a cage, a bird that looks just like an eagle. Yes, it must really have been an eagle. A bad omen, I say to myself, and I switch my suitcase to the other hand.

I walk down the steps into the metro. Two young people run by, then another chases after them. I think I can see a knife in his hand. I flatten myself against the wall, hesitate for a few moments, then start again in the same direction—even though I feel a lump in my throat and a shooting pain in my lower back. I have to get to the Gare Montparnasse, and from there catch a train to Brittany. A friend has offered to put me up there in his summerhouse, which he only uses one month a year, sometimes even less. I'll have one room on the second floor, with a bathroom next to it. The window looks out onto some wooded hills; the village, behind the house, serves as a kind of last outpost before the mysterious country beyond. Perceval passed that way one still morning—a morning that will never be repeated.

I had forgotten the wild kids. When I reach the platform, I see all three of them chatting like the best of friends. I look at my watch: there's plenty of time. Is Marianne awake by now? There's a public telephone on the platform, and I think that maybe I should call and let her know I'm on my way to Brittany. Yes, at the very least I ought to tell her where I'll be. But she's probably still asleep, whistling and gently breathing. What's the point of waking her? I'll phone from the station.

When the metro arrives, the boys don't even think of getting on but start racing to the other end of the platform. A policeman, brutally professional, pushes a ragged gypsy out of the car that stops in front of me. The gypsy winks at me and smiles, not looking at all perturbed . It's not out of the question that he's been hoping this moment would come. Now that the police have picked him up, he won't have to worry about tomorrow.

"Nonsense!" Marianne would have said at once. "Do you think that freedom counts for nothing, that it's just an empty word?"

"Yes," I reply provocatively in my imagined dialogue—just to see what she'll say, what arguments she'll use against me. Both of us enjoy arguing, contradicting each other. "Freedom isn't much use when you're hungry."

She takes a sip of coffee, as if to buy herself time to come up with a crushing response. Unable to find one, she makes do with asking me some (let's say, pointed) questions.

"Is that how you spoke to the young people you met in Bucharest? Would you have the courage, or the effrontery, to tell *them* something like that?"

She thinks she has shut me up. In fact, when I met Mihai at the bar of the Hotel Intercontinental, I tried to explain to him that the important thing is not being free but *struggling* to be free. The road to freedom is more valuable than freedom itself, especially if it's the kind that gets handed down by previous generations and becomes yours without a fight. Freedom like that . . .

"How come?" Mihai asked.

"Because all you can ever inherit are formal liberties, enacted by legislation and limited by the liberties of others. In a supposedly normal . . ."—I should have said *normative*—". . . democratic society, people *know* they are free but don't *feel* it. When you struggle for freedom, in a totalitarian society, the little freedoms you manage to snatch, like in a battle, are more euphoric, if you see what I mean. They're more intoxicating than the same freedoms when they become legal rights. In a struggle it's as if you can feel freedom—in and of itself."

"You feel fear, then the pride of overcoming it," Mihai said, almost in a whisper.

"Exactly. That's what real freedom feels like."

"Like when I pulled for dear life on the bells in the Colţea church tower. During the revolution . . ." Mihai added wistfully.

The time had come for him to talk, and for me to keep quiet. I encouraged him to continue, to speak of those giddy days of intense emotion.

He moved the whisky bottle a little further away. It was meant to represent the Hotel Intercontinental, where we happened to be sitting at the time. He had arranged a meeting outside with Ion, at a point just behind the bottle. A lot of people were gathered nearby in University Square: Ion was probably somewhere among them, lost in the crowd; anyway he hadn't shown up at the agreed meeting place. Then Mihai too had moved toward the square. The traffic was at a standstill on Bulevardul Magheru. He moved a glass to show me where the University was.

"I know it very well, believe me," I mumbled. "I was a student too, a long time ago."

Mihai drank some more whisky to gather strength, then indicated Bulevardul Magheru between his glass and the bottle.

"The first barricade went up about here," and Mihai marked it with the saltshaker. How? "Easy. They just blocked the boulevard with a bunch of taxis and cars, which they pushed there from in front of the Intercontinental, Strada Biserica Enei, wherever." He completed the barricade with the pepper shaker, a cigarette packet, and a lighter. It was impassable.

"And what were the police doing about it?"

Mihai shrugged—didn't know what the police had been doing about it. No sign of the army either; the APCs only arrived later. Mihai's fingers advanced along the tablecloth, the nails chewed right down.

"Did they start shooting?"

He nodded. "At one point they did, but everyone ran for it." Mihai was laughing as he said this, but at the time he had been afraid, his legs like jelly. When he reached Colțea Hospital—he didn't know how he made it—the gate swung open, or perhaps it had never been locked; everyone raced toward the little church. He took my glass—there was still a drop of whisky in it—and used it to locate the church at the edge of the table. He had no idea how he got into the belfry. The ropes were hanging motionless, and the bells seemed not to have been rung for years. He grabbed the end of one rope and pulled on it, but not hard enough; the clapper barely grazed the bronze frame of the bell. The first sound was so faint you could have mistaken it for the strumming of a guitar. Then another bell ringer came along, and another, and another.

"But how many bells were there in that belfry?"

He didn't answer. I grabbed the church and emptied it, while he did the same with the university. He clicked his tongue and said:

"I won't forget it as long as I live."

I envied him. Now he has memories that will last him the rest of his life. He'll have things to tell his children, then his grandchildren. I refilled his glass. Around midday the workers who had been at the rally appeared on the scene. Slogans began to spread over the walls of the University: *Down with the cobbler! Down with the president who can't read or write! Murderers! Freedom!*

I brought the conversation back to theoretical matters, my voice sounding more and more like a teacher's.

"We shouldn't confuse liberty with the right to do this or that. Freedom of expression, for example, is a right, laid down by the law, but also restricted by the law."

"Restricted?" Mihai had a puzzled look. "Can't people say what they like in France?"

"Of course they can. But, if you mention a person by name, you have to be able to prove what you say. Otherwise you risk being accused of libel."

"Ah yes, I see what you mean."

"Anyway, that's not the freedom I'm talking about. Formal liberties are actually rights. You enjoy them, and in theory they are guaranteed. They're meant to protect you—not just you but everyone. And that's how things are. You feel defended . . . But that's not pure freedom. It's not freedom but security."

"Security?"

"Protection, defense, safeguarding. Do you understand? Whereas freedom should be a kind of intoxication, almost a mystical state."

I gulped down my whisky. Mihai seemed to accept the theory, well sprinkled as it was with alcohol. He too emptied his glass and stared at me. I kept quiet, waiting to hear what he would say. He came straight to the point.

"You're an anarchist."

It wasn't a question but a statement—no other way of describing it. I see the sign for "Montparnasse" and just manage to leap out of the metro with my luggage in time. I was lucky. I step onto the moving walkway and wipe my forehead with a tissue. I see the young threesome from before on the walkway in the opposite direction, and they recognize me and make faces. Is that also covered by freedom of expression? Probably—although the law doesn't mention it specifically, and it might be considered a breach of public order. Those young hooligans are taking a risk—which according to my theory enhances their sense of freedom. But what about me? I stick my tongue out at them, grimace like an escaped chimpanzee, and am so astonished by their expressions that it is I, not they, who break into laughter. I wave to them: so long, guys! And I proudly puff out my rib cage.

The first telephone at the station is in use: there's a girl holding the receiver to her ear but crying rather than speaking. I can't bear to watch her, so I walk away. Eventually I find an empty booth, but it only works with cards and I don't have one on me. I go to the station restaurant.

"The telephone is for customers only," I am told.

"Look, I'm in a real hurry. My train's in ten minutes."

"Why don't you order a glass of mineral water?" the waiter suggests.

I do what he says. Marianne takes a long time to answer: she must be in the bathroom. What's she up to in there? Then I hear her voice, sounding like an announcer on an airport PA.

"I'm at the station. My train leaves in ten minutes."

"Where to?" she asks calmly.

"Brittany."

"Is your ticket stamped already?"

"Not yet. I'm in the station restaurant. I'll do it in a minute."

"Don't stamp it. Come back home."

"What for? I'm going there to work—to write my novel, or at least get it under way. It'll be easier afterward. I'll be able to continue it in Paris."

"Drop the novel. Is that really your priority, in the state you're in?"

"What state's that?"

"You're sick. Come back here. Your test results have arrived."

"When?"

"This morning. Your cholesterol has almost doubled. I phoned Gachet. He said you should go see him this afternoon."

"Gachet said that?"

"Yes, this very afternoon."

She's managed to outmaneuver me. I stand there in a daze, still holding the receiver. Realizing that she's won, she doesn't press the point. She hangs up.

I sit at a table, order a calvados, wipe my neck and forehead again. I'm soaked in sweat. But what if she was lying? I brush the stupid idea away with the back of my hand. I know she doesn't lie. I finish my glass and ask for another . . . Mihai looked at me suspiciously; when I didn't respond, he probably thought he had offended me. So he assured me that that hadn't been his intention. In the end, an anarchist isn't the same as a communist. Communists are Marxists. He talked a lot, making frequent gestures. I watched him as though he were on the screen of an ancient television, with lines and dots all around him like a swarm of flies or mosquitoes. I couldn't hear him properly either. We had both really been hitting the bottle, and it was just at that moment that Ion showed up. Showed up in the nick of time, as it were . . . He was wearing a suit and a multicolored silk tie. He had a book in his hand and casually placed it on the table with the title facing up: *The Lover*, by Marguerite Duras. I asked him to take a seat.

Marianne is right: it's just too risky, especially since I'd be alone in Brittany and completely cut off. I should definitely see a doctor first, to get a prescription and some advice about treatment . . . But why Gachet?

"I met that French doctor you came with," Ion said. "He told me you're a writer."

"Is that what he said?"

"Yes."

"Well, I think he must have gotten confused."

Ion didn't dare ask what my real profession was after that. I'd have answered that I worked for Radio Free Europe and had come to do some research for a show. That would have shut him up. As it was, I kept him under restraint by taking the initiative myself:

"Was it Dr. Gachet who gave you this book?"

I was mumbling a little. At the other end of the room, a peasant in a fluffy shepherd's hat was being shown the door by a couple of waiters. No one seemed the least bit flustered.

"Oh no, that was someone else. Dr. Gachet told me I really must read Solzhenitsyn and Zinoviev, the apostles of anti-communism. That's what he called them."

"Are you a communist?" I asked.

"Me? God forbid! All they could do was sign me up for their youth organization. It was compulsory."

"So what do you need Solzhenitsyn or Zinoviev for? They wrote their books for the likes of Gachet, who were Maoists or Trotskyists fifteen years ago."

Ion looked at me in disbelief. Maybe he was sorry he had spilled the beans by telling me he'd been in the Communist Youth. Mihai, a little quicker on his feet, had understood what I was getting at. He poured out what was left of the whisky and generously handed his glass to Ion. Then he began to curse the Western intellectuals who had pretended for so long not to notice what was happening in Eastern Europe. They just sat there and waited to see if the great experiment would work, if the guinea pig would hold out. You certainly couldn't say they weren't interested—after all, it was their theory in the first place.

"And Lenin's," Ion added.

"But, since they weren't the ones in charge, they could complain from time to time and claim that their principles weren't being properly applied . . ."

But that wasn't exactly my point. I would have qualified the attack on Western intellectuals in a couple of ways—the first being that they are by no means all of a piece, and never have been. Secondly, as intellectuals go, they are neither more nor less hypocritical and conformist than their Eastern counterparts. Maybe we should just steer clear of generalizations entirely. Yes, that's more or less what I would have said, but given my state I preferred to keep quiet and nod.

"Anyway they believed in it—or some of them did," Ion muttered.

"In communism?"

"I don't know. In communism, in socialism, or in capitalism. But they believed in something. Whereas we . . ."

I order another calvados and a *croque-monsieur*. I look at my watch: the train for Brittany left two minutes ago. What can I do now except go and see Dr. Gachet—and listen to him ramble on about *Homo sovieticus*? Then he'll give me a prescription and I'll be able to go off and write my novel.

I turned to Mihai, who'd given me a wink. Or at least I thought he had. He probably wasn't really in the mood for one of Ion's famous speeches about the Romanians' national characteristics, about their sheep-like fatalism and other qualities, each more dubious than the last. He tried to change the subject:

"You know, Ana asked about you."

I didn't know what to say. I raised my glass, then changed my mind and put it back on the table. My head was aching.

"'How is the gentleman from Paris?'" Mihai continued, making his voice squeaky.

"I wouldn't mind going to Paris myself," Ion sighed.

I called the waiter and settled the bill. Holding out my hand to the two students, I told them I wasn't feeling at all well and absolutely had to lie down. And I left.

It's cold outside, and my suitcase is heavier now that I'm on my way back. From behind I look like a man limping along with a stoop; from the front I look lost in my thoughts. Where am I heading, blindly, like this? I ought to turn around and go into the metro. It would only take ten minutes to get back to my local station, and from there it's a short walk home. Very handy, I have to admit. I think about all this as I keep shuffling in the same direction.

A young boy with a satchel on his back walks toward me kicking a tin can along the ground. He doesn't try to avoid me, nor do I have time to move out of the way. He gives the can another kick, so that it comes rolling to my feet. Then he stops too, a yard or so from me. He looks up. His eyes are cold and severe.

"You'll end up like Jean-Pierre Papin if you keep being late for school."

My "dumb footballer" joke falls flat. The kid stares silently into my eyes, waiting for me to step aside and let him pass. Children are generally lacking in humor. Some stay like that all their life, right into old age. Humor! But just look at them: they manage perfectly well without it, even better than people who think they have to be funny morning, noon, and night, that their purpose in life is to make others laugh. Do people like that ever laugh themselves? Or do they just expect it of others? Some people laugh with a forced titter, others until they're blue in the face. They say that humor is the politeness of despair. Maybe it's true—although I don't see why it should be more polite to giggle than to frown. Or just to remain serious. Dignified. Not to mention that that kind of politeness borders on cowardice . . . as does any politeness carried to the point of servility.

My nimble movement to avoid the boy's tin can was executed with the suitcase in one hand and my left arm raised above my head, as if I were dancing a hora in the Romanian countryside. Here we go—hippety-hop, hippety-hay! This doesn't amuse him either; no doubt I just look ridiculous in his eyes. He would think it much more natural if I pushed him roughly aside or swore at him, or at least acted in a threatening manner. Instead I skip and dance around him. A real weirdo! With a final sidelong glance, he sends the can another few yards and is on his way.

I put the suitcase down and turn to watch him go. His movements are rigid, almost robotic. The can doesn't travel far, so each time he takes another few steps and kicks it again. No passion, no sense of pleasure; not a game, not sport. What is it, then? Maybe a great sadness, a despair that cannot express itself, a gesture of rage: he really doesn't feel like going to school. Childhood is pretty sad on winter mornings.

Because we can't see into other people's minds and are never even sure what's in our own, all we have left is to concoct what they are doing and thinking—to transform everyone, including ourselves, into characters in a play.

Now there's a profound idea! I take the suitcase by the handle and start off again. I no longer see anything around me. My thoughts are elsewhere—my body too . . . When I bumped into Roger, I was trying to cross the boulevard before the lights changed. He seemed far away too. I took him by the arm. The traffic lights turned yellow, then green, a bluish-green.

"Too late!" I shouted.

He turned his bereted head, with its thick Bulgarian neck. He looked pleased to see me. We shook hands for a long time and asked each other how we were doing—a stereotyped exchange of pointless questions that lasts longer in French than any other language. I guess he wanted to chat, or even to reminisce about the Balkan trip we had taken together, as he put it. He suggested having a coffee somewhere.

"Or maybe you're in a hurry . . . Where are you off to with that suitcase?"

I'm not quite sure what I should or shouldn't tell him. I mention a railway station, my appointment with Mihai and Ion at the bar of the Hotel Intercontinental.

"I got here yesterday with a different convoy," he says. "I'm here for three days this time."

Then he fills me in about the French interest in Romanians. "Especially Romanian women!" He laughs with a kind of whinny and adds, "It's wild: they all seem to have French on their lips."

I said nothing, thinking that sometimes every word just makes the ambiguity of a situation worse. I'm no longer even sure which tense I should be using, here. It's best if I just let him talk. He gives me a whole song and dance about a woman he knew who'd been a terrorist's mistress. He saw it with his own eyes: the rifle with telescopic sights—a German model. She'd hidden it behind the headboard, but because the bed shook like in an earthquake . . . And he roared with laughter.

"What's this, a rifle?" Roger asked, climbing out of bed. The woman couldn't stop him. She covered her breasts with both hands, like she'd seen them do in the movies, and perched there on her knees while the French truck driver turned the weapon this way and that. He didn't report her to the authorities. What the fuck did he care?

"That's all in the past now anyway."

Roger looked at me to see if I agreed with the easy absolution he'd given to the tyrant's henchmen. I kept quiet. I simply pointed out that, being a foreigner, he probably didn't know that it's almost impossible to find a café open at this hour in the morning. Even the bars are closed—especially in the city center.

We parted with a friendly handshake. I didn't have the nerve to ask whether he was on his way to the terrorist's girlfriend again; or warn him that it could still be a dangerous thing to do; or tell him that he should keep his eyes and ears open, even though the terrorist had almost certainly been caught and sentenced by now. But, then, how come his rifle had been left behind? Or rather, how had he had the time to go and conceal it behind the headboard? Did that mean he had managed to blend into the crowd, to escape without leaving any trace? Full of mysteries, this country! One headline covering the front page of a paper read: "Where Are Our Terrorists?" I didn't read the article inside, but I remembered the title. Roger's lucky not to know any Romanian, I thought, and I started walking again as if I had a goal in mind. I couldn't help going wherever I was going . . . It wasn't that cold any more. Perhaps that's why I was in a better mood: that, plus Roger. I liked him, even though he was a bit of a shady character. The truth was that I envied his travels by truck all over Europe; not everyone can handle that kind of nomadic lifestyle. I was walking quite fast now, without hesitation. But I had no clear destination, just wandering wherever chance would take me. I did vaguely think that I would probably end up at home, where I would dump my suitcase, change my clothes, and then head out to the doctor's. Again, the thought of Gachet was enough to make me break into a sweat . . .

When I found myself at the apartment block, I hesitated for a few moments before going in. I started to climb the stairs and felt the pain in my back. My mouth was dry and I was itching to go into the kitchen and pour myself a glass of water. A cat crept along by the wall. It had blue eyes, but since it wasn't the Siamese there was no point in asking it whether anyone was home. On the second floor, a man wearing a wide-brimmed hat was waiting in front of the elevator.

"I think it's out of order," I said, as if to justify climbing the stairs with my suitcase, instead of waiting as patiently as he.

He ignored me. He had a coil of rope around one arm, and was holding out the other to press the call button outside the elevator. I managed to squeeze past him. Without my having noticed it, the stairs were now taking me down. What do I need the elevator for if I can get to the third floor by going down? Maybe I'm in the metro again and the moving walkway is out of order. It's always breaking down!

The descent lasted a long time. I was already below sea level, as I could tell from the fact that the deep-sea diver was resurfacing with a girl in his arms, quite a pretty young miss, even if her body did end in a fishtail. I've seen girls like that before . . .

"The elevator's out of order," I said.

Of course the diver couldn't speak because of his helmet. Maybe he didn't hear me. But the girl gave me a smile: she looked pretty happy, snuggled up in those thick rubbery arms. The rumble of the metro could be heard—unless it was something else, I'm not really sure, the sound could easily have come from a ship about to raise anchor, or even from the elevator if it had somehow been repaired meanwhile. I was fed up with descending. I turned and began to go up again. The diver and the girl were no longer to be seen. Perhaps they'd gone off down a side corridor, or should I say a gallery?

I was a little lost, a little uneasy, but I didn't panic. I'll get somewhere in the end. The key thing is to keep cool. It was getting dark: the more I went up, the darker it became. I stopped in front of an apartment door; I could just make out the name printed on a visiting card: Ana Pînzaru. I felt like laughing. All these detours, all these ups and downs, and nothing to show for them. What am I going to do now? It's not a hypocritical question, please believe me. I'm so tired of this story, so bored with it all. And I also risk running into Mihai or Ion or other characters I don't have the faintest idea what to do with yet. But I can hardly beat a retreat now that I'm in front of her door and only have to lift my hand to ring the bell . . .

I rang and waited, but the door didn't open. Maybe she's not in. Frankly, I was a little annoyed to have made such a long journey for nothing. Then, with the tenacity of a postman, I rang a second time—long and hard. From there on the landing I could hear the bell ring inside. Why hasn't she heard it? I glued my ear to the door: the sound of bare feet on parquet. She opened the door bleary-eyed, wearing a short see-through nightdress. I apologized for bothering her at such an early hour.

"I missed my train. And, as I was in the area . . ."

"It's okay. Do come in."

I went into the vestibule and put my suitcase next to a motorcyclist's helmet—or could it have been a deep-sea diver's?

"Take your coat off," Ana said. "They give us plenty of heating nowadays." She crossed her arms. I looked at her large wide feet and painted toenails. I took off my coat and, feeling a little nervous, went through into the little, modestly furnished living room.

"I'll make you some coffee," she suggested. "You know, Maria's still asleep. She got back late last night."

I sat down in a frayed armchair, its springs in bad shape. I felt a shooting pain in my back. Walking that much is no joke! I smiled in embarrassment, but Ana had gone to the kitchen and my smile beamed into empty space. A book lay on the table beside the armchair. No, it wasn't Madame Duras's *The Lover* but *Lady Chatterley's Lover*. I picked it up and began to leaf through the pages, but I soon put it down again. Ana was already back, carrying the coffee on a tray. She had donned a robe and brushed her hair, keeping the loop at the back. She had also put on some pink slippers with pompoms. She put the tray on the *Lover*, then noticed the book and rescued it to show me. I lowered my eyes and began to tie a shoelace that had come undone. When I looked up, Ana was holding out the sugar bowl and giving me an encouraging smile.

"No, thanks. I'm on a diet."

"What's wrong with you?" she asked.

"What's *not* wrong with me, my dear Miss Pînzaru! Some test results arrived this morning. My cholesterol has shot up, and urea is running wild in my bloodstream."

"Urea too?"

"Why are you surprised? As you get older . . ."

"I'm not surprised, but you don't look all that bad. Maybe the lab sent the wrong results . . . I work in a hospital, so I know stuff like that happens. There's nothing easier than to get the jars mixed up."

She was laughing. She pulled up a stool and sat at my feet.

"You're too kind. But you know, I also have sciatica." I bent forward and felt my back with both hands. She made the same movement, doubtless out of sympathy, so that our heads collided with each other—or, to be more precise, my chin rubbed against her forehead. But then I pulled sharply back as she inched forward with her face, her mouth, her nose—what was it all for? Where would it end up? The tails of her robe had spread open and her skimpy nightdress seemed to have climbed even higher—or perhaps she no longer had it on. I was propped against the back of the chair.

"And I have arthritis here, in the neck region. I've been wearing a brace the last few months." I held my neck tightly to show her, although, since she worked in a hospital, she must have known more about it than I did. Ana was laughing by now.

"You're probably like that German officer—what was his name?"

"There were a number of them."

"The one with a monocle who was bald or had his head shaved. I can't remember. As stiff as they come, he was."

I ran my hand through my hair. It had been getting thinner recently, but nevertheless . . .

"I have to see Doctor Gachet this afternoon. Believe me, I'm not looking forward to that."

"I believe you," she said, resting her elbows on my knees. One of her eyes was green, the other blue. I reached out to take my cup of coffee.

"Excuse me," I said.

I was afraid I might drop it on her. She took a pack of Marlboros from her robe pocket and offered me one.

"No, thanks, I gave up a year ago. I was starting to get asthma." Then, to steer the conversation away from my myriad ailments, I whispered:

"The elevator was out of order. I met a deep-sea diver on the stairs."

"Ah, you mean Valentin. He's off looking for that slut again."

She was obviously a little upset about something, but since I couldn't take back mentioning the diver, I asked her to tell me more:

"Is he a professional deep-sea diver? Or does he wear that getup for fun?"

"Diver? Like hell he is! He's a mining engineer."

I couldn't make much sense of it. If I had asked which mine he worked at and Ana had answered Lupeni or Petroşani, I still wouldn't have understood what a deep-sea diver was doing in the cellar . . . or those galleries. Who knows where they lead—maybe to the metro, or maybe somewhere else, God knows . . . My eyelids were growing heavy and I seemed to be seeing her through a mist. My chin was drooping onto my chest, my arms and legs felt shaky;

in vain did Ana massage my calves and then my thighs . . . I could hardly feel her fingers.

"You're tired," she murmured. "Why don't you come and lie down?"

I went into the bedroom, where Ana ordered me to undress. Maria was asleep in bed. I stripped to my briefs and undershirt. The barrel of a rifle was sticking out from under the bed frame.

"Get in. There's room for all three of us."

I crawled in on all fours beside Maria, who moved an arm and muttered without really waking up:

"Who's this?"

"It's the gentleman from Paris," Ana said. "Go to sleep!"

I twisted onto my back, taking care not to wake her up, and let out a sigh of relief. No matter what, it's always better in bed! Ana took off her dressing gown and stretched out next to me. I didn't move and kept my arms glued to my side so as to occupy as little space as possible. Ana turned over with her back towards me. I touched her buttocks inadvertently: they were hot. So were Maria's. It was warm and soft there. I could feel the urea and the cholesterol rising in my blood.

When I awoke I saw the tree branches at the window, still without leaves but familiar and protective. Marianne is in the bathroom.

In the novel my plan is to fall in love with both of them: Maria and Ana. Marianne thinks that's quite ridiculous.

"Fall in love with both? How old-fashioned! And unlikely too, at your age. They're not even twin sisters."

"Ana's a sister, at the hospital. Or anyway a nurse."

"Good luck to her. Listen . . ."

"Are you jealous?"

"I'm fed up with your awful sense of humor: it's absurd and stupid at the same time. Are you all like that out there?"

"Jokers?"

"Phonies. And look where it's gotten you."

"You mean, in the shit?"

"You said it, not me. But that's not what I'm talking about. Look, do you want to discuss this seriously or not?"

"I do."

"Okay. Well, it's ridiculous to think of yourself as falling in love with both. You seem to have forgotten that Ana and Mihai are lovers, and that the other one, whatshername, Maria, is Ion's sweetheart. Anyway, that's how you introduced them to me."

"I don't know—I'm not so sure any more. Maybe they just had a fling."

"And then there's Valentin, the mining engineer."

"He's just Ana's cousin. He doesn't count."

"How can you be so sure?"

"He doesn't even live in Bucharest. He goes there now and again for some underwater fishing."

"In Bucharest?"

"Yes, at Snagov—a few miles from the city, where there's a big lake. It's not the only one, either. Underwater fishing is his only passion in life."

"A strange passion for a miner to have. Besides, why doesn't he just go to the sea?"

"The Black Sea is too polluted. It's almost a dead sea."

The Siamese joins in the discussion and, surprise, surprise, says he agrees with me.

"You shut up!" Marianne snaps at him.

"You always start shouting when he doesn't take your side!" I say, eyeing the cat with satisfaction. He puts on an offended look and heads out of the kitchen, but then stops in the doorway to mew a parting shot:

"There sure is a lot of chatter in this novel of yours."

"It's his novel, not mine," Marianne clarifies.

"What novel?" I ask. "I haven't even started to write it. I need some peace and concentration for that. I need to get away to the country somewhere."

"You can go after you've been to see Dr. Gachet," Marianne says. She takes a bite from the slice of bread and butter that she has spread thickly with cherry jam. Realizing that, no matter what, I'll have the last word when I start writing, she changes the subject in order to remain on the offensive. It's an eminently feminine tactic, which I've never really known how to counter.

"You should really go back to Romania. And not only to Bucharest."

"Really? Again?"

"Yes, really. A writer needs to keep abreast of things, especially when they keep changing so quickly there."

I don't dare tell her that my mind is there all the time. My body too, in a way.

"I have correspondents," I reply self-importantly. "Just yesterday I got a letter from Mihai."

"What did he say?"

"Things are changing with dizzying speed, you're right about that. People are already challenging the government. There's one demonstration after another. The students have been occupying University Square for days, right in the center of the city. The traffic's blocked on Bulevardul Magheru. In the evening there are open-air meetings, anticommunist speeches, group singing, and all kinds of slogans: for example, better an anarchist than a communist—no, what am I saying?—better a hooligan . . . I forgot to say that the head of the provisional government described the demonstrators as a bunch of hooligans. What's his name?"

"Iliescu."

"Yes. Well, it seems that he used to be secretary of the Communist Party."

"I thought the other one was secretary . . ."

"No, he was *general* secretary."

"Ah!"

"I tell you, it's not easy to get your head round it all. In Timişoara they issued a kind of proclamation signed by I-don't-know-how-many millions of citizens."

"That many?"

"Yes, I don't know the exact figure. And one of the demands in it is that people who got their job through the party should no longer be allowed to hold positions of responsibility in the country. It's clear that that's mainly directed against . . . What's his name again?"

"Who?"

"The former secretary."

"Iliescu."

"Right. He's the direct target."

"But the party had I-don't-know-how-many millions of members. On television they said four million. Apparently a lot of jobs were never offered to you under the old regime if you didn't join. What are they going to do with all those people?"

"Don't ask me. They could all be booted out."

"And who would replace them? You can't have a purge like that overnight."

"How would I know? It's better if I read you a bit from the letter. I've got it here in my pocket. Listen: 'Yesterday evening there were nearly ten thousand people in the square—and not only young people, believe me. We shouted and sang ourselves hoarse. Then the speeches began, from the balcony of the geology department overlooking the square. One of the speakers shouted his lungs out and ended up asking everyone who hadn't been a party member to kneel on the ground.'"

"Hang on. Does it say everyone who had been or hadn't been?"

"I'll translate it again word for word: everyone who *hadn't* been a party member."

"*What* did he ask them to do?" the Siamese asked in surprise, having meanwhile returned to the kitchen.

"To kneel on the ground. That's clear enough."

"What was the point of that?" Marianne asks in turn.

"I don't know. So they could be told apart from those who had been members. Let me go on."

"Sorry."

I fairly melt with pleasure when the Siamese acts polite. I offer him a sugar cube dipped in coffee.

"Don't give him sugar, or he'll get fat again!" Marianne protests.

"So: '. . . everyone who hadn't been a party member to kneel on the ground. Of course we all knelt down—or nearly all. A little way off, there was a guy of around fifty wearing a raincoat that had obviously been bought abroad, and next to him another, even older man. Well, both of them remained standing. I couldn't help going up to them and shouting: "On your knees, you communists!" They ignored me. I think they were afraid, but they didn't budge an inch.'"

"I'm sorry to interrupt, but I simply don't get it. We agreed just now that most of the active population had been party members—which means that none of them were in the square; they must have stayed at home watching television. Most of them didn't support the demonstrations. Is that right?"

"I'm not sure it's so simple. Some party members may have been there and knelt on the ground along with everyone else. Didn't members and non-members alike clap their hands just a few months earlier? When the dictator appeared on the balcony . . ."

"Nevertheless, what an idea to make them kneel down! You claim they wanted to tell them apart from the others . . . but if, as you say, all the members and non-members there knelt down together, apart from the two old men, it would have been a pointless exercise."

"Maybe differentiation wasn't the real point."

"What was it then?"

"I don't know. Stop pestering me with your questions. I wasn't there, was I?"

"What else does he write in the letter?"

"He says that several dozen people began a hunger strike, right there in the square."

"What for?"

"To support the Timişoara Proclamation."

"Had they been in the Party too?"

The Siamese was getting bored with the conversation. He said: "Pretty weird, these Romanians!" and sauntered off. Marianne laughed, and so did I, though in a forced kind of way. It's true that the Siamese can be funny once in a while.

"All nations are like that," I said, becoming serious.

"Not quite like that," Marianne corrected me.

I was a little angry now.

"Tomorrow, or the day after, I can see you joining Le Pen."

Marianne laughed even louder.

"Well, if we suddenly find everyone from that square here in Paris . . ."

"Ha, that's a good one! Why should they come here? You can see they're fighting to change things where they are. Do you think it's easy after forty years of dictatorship?"

"Okay, okay, I was just teasing you."

"No doubt they'll come to Paris, as tourists, sooner or later. I hope you'll accept that."

"What do you think I am? The police department?"

"I meant, in principle . . ."

"In principle I'll accept whatever you like," she said, to patch things up—although she knows that what irritates me more than anything else is that falsely conciliatory tone she adopts to end a discussion, so that she can always have the last word.

I say no more, I leave her in peace. After all, I'll write whatever the hell I like in the novel. And I won't write anything I don't want to write—will I?

I go for my appointment with Dr. Gachet, who welcomes me with open arms.

"Long time no see!" he says effusively. His face seems somehow different—yes, of course, he's shaved off his mustache.

"It really suits you like that," I say. "Reminds me of a famous painting."

"A painting?" Dr. Gachet confesses that he doesn't know much about art. He neither understands it nor has a feeling for it. He seems embarrassed to admit this, but he can't pretend, can't brag and claim to be a connoisseur, when in fact . . .

"But what does it matter?" I say.

He asks me how the novel is coming along. When did I ever talk to him about a novel? Then I remember that, a month or so after I returned from Bucharest, Marianne invited him to dinner and he came over with a woman called Smaranda, who had been in France at the time of the events and asked for political asylum. In fact, she'd left Romania in the early autumn with a delegation from the health ministry, to take part in some international conference in Austria. She was a doctor, and had been the head of a department at the ministry back home. She had traveled from Vienna to Germany and spent a couple of months with some people she knew in Frankfurt, but not knowing a word of German she had come to Paris in December. One thing led to another, and we'd ended up discussing the Romanian people. It was probably then that either Marianne or myself had said that I was writing a novel connected to the situation in Romania—more realist than my previous novels. At that moment the Siamese had crawled out from under the table and mewed ironically. The Romanian people . . .

"We're an ancient people," Smaranda said, "older than the English, for example. And the Romanians wouldn't have found their way to communism if the West hadn't allowed the Russians to occupy Eastern Europe. We're a traditionalist people, who had nothing at all in common with the social-political theories of Western modernity."

Dr. Gachet was feasting his eyes on her.

"So why did Romanians join the Communist Party *en masse*?" Marianne asked. For some time she had considered herself a great specialist in Romanian questions.

"For that very reason," Smaranda replied without hesitation. "To undermine it, to destroy it from within, to leave nothing but a shell, an empty form."

"Bravo, bravo!" Dr. Gachet couldn't restrain himself and began to applaud like a man possessed. I didn't dare applaud, nor contradict her. I looked at Marianne, who was biting her lips, and told myself she'd just have to cope!

"Presumably you were in the Party yourself," Marianne murmured.

"Of course! From my first year at university."

"But why did you stay here, then? I mean, why didn't you go back to Romania? Forgive me for being so blunt. Why did you ask for political asylum, right at the last minute—how shall I put it, as soon as the revolution started off?"

Smaranda didn't reply at once. Gachet looked a little uneasy, but he didn't want to get himself in trouble by speaking in her place. He'd been in the truck during the revolution, en route for Romania. He hadn't even met her yet. They got to know each other only after he came back to Paris. Anyway, the doctor now seemed head over heels in love. Marianne was smiling.

"Do you think that what happened there was really a revolution?" Smaranda asked, turning the question around.

"What else would you call it?"

"It was a plot hatched by the Securitate, on orders from Gorbachev. Precisely to save communism, which had been heading for disaster under Ceausescu."

"So, Ceausescu was a victim?"

"Exactly. The victim of a plot. If you'd seen the video of the trial, you wouldn't be in any doubt."

"But can you be so sure?"

"Yes, I can."

"Did you know this last December already, at the time of the Timişoara revolt and the uprising in Bucharest?"

It was a real interrogation. Smaranda was red as a beetroot, while Marianne's tone kept growing sharper. The Siamese jumped onto her lap, and I was afraid that, rude and spoiled as he was, he would try to butt in on the conversation. Gachet could no longer bear the tension, which was mounting with each riposte. He stood up, asked for a glass of water, and maneuvered the conversation in such a way as to halt the escalation of hostilities. Marianne and Smaranda then started chatting about something else and got on like a house on fire. Dr. Gachet seemed fairly content again by the time they left. Afterward, Marianne asked me:

"Don't you think that girl worked for the Securitate? Or maybe the KGB? They're not mutually exclusive. Wolton shows in his book that . . ."

"How should I know, dear?"

"Definitely for the Securitate," the Siamese decided.

Then all three of us went to bed.

Now Dr. Gachet is frowning and muttering as he pores over my test results.

"Is it serious?" I ask, nervous. The main thing I'm afraid of is that he won't let me go to Brittany: I'd got it into my head that I wouldn't be able to write the novel otherwise. Here in Paris I mostly took notes, jotting down everything that occurred to me, or simply copied whole passages from newspaper articles about Romania.

"It's no joke at all," Gachet replies, with that wonderfully French gift for euphemism . . . maybe it comes from the language itself—anyway, what does it matter?

He asks me to strip to the waist, so I take off my jacket, shirt, and vest. When I raise my left arm I feel a shooting pain just below my neck, but I don't tell the doctor about it, so as not to complicate things.

"You should lose some more weight," Gachet warns.

"But I've already lost ten kilos or more," I say, looking at the bulge over the waist of my trousers.

"Lose another ten."

Easy for him to say: he's young and slim, not like me, who somehow or other acquired all this fat during the long years of exile, when all hope deserted me. Maybe that's how it happened—losing hope invites obesity. And now, if I have to lose even more weight, I might as well join the hunger strike in University Square; then at least I'd be of some use . . . anyway, more than by writing a novel. Yes, that's what I should do. When you're on a hunger strike you can lie down all the time; no one forces you to kneel because you weren't a communist. I can see myself there in a nice sleeping bag, maybe by the architecture department, with a beard and a mustache. But Ana still recognizes me: that's the gentleman from Paris, she says to Maria, who leans over to get a proper look at me. And the others appear too. "Where do you say he's from?"— "Paris."—"So what's he doing here? He's too old to be starving himself."—"He doesn't look like he's doing too well, either." They laugh, crouch down, and snap their fingers at me, but perhaps they also admire me for my courage, for having come all the way from Paris to starve myself on a filthy Bucharest sidewalk that no one ever dreams of cleaning. "They'll let us rot here, without sending anyone out to talk things over with us."—"Why isn't the television here?" Maria shouts, moving her ass in time with a dance of her own invention. There's also a guy with a guitar, and others who clap their hands to the music. It feels good, a fun place to be.

I tell Gachet of my idea and he laughs:

"Unfortunately, from a medical point of view, it's not at all advisable in your present state. Your heart couldn't take it."

"So what *is* advisable in my present state?"

"To spend some time in the country, following a proper diet and going for short walks, out in nature. Choose somewhere mild, not too cold or damp like it is in Paris, but also not too hot like the summers are in the south. Avoid eating too much of anything, stay away from alcohol, cut out animal fats, and even lean meat, as much as possible—and eat more fish and vegetables. Don't do anything strenuous, don't let yourself get excited—a calm, simple life. And, of course, make sure to take the medicine I'll prescribe for you in a moment. You can get dressed. I see you're getting goose pimples."

"What about writing? Can I do that?" I ask as I grapple with the sleeves of my shirt.

"Yes, but only an hour or two a day, and only about pleasant things—if possible, with a lot of humor, ironic detachment. You have to avoid any emotion. Do you understand?"

When I tell Marianne about all the advice and prohibitions, she looks at me triumphantly.

"You see! And you wanted to write a novel about the revolution . . ."

Even if I'm no longer allowed to work myself up, I can't let her get away with that kind of inanity. I have to contradict her. I can't help it.

"Who wants to write about the revolution? Where did you get that idea from? Anyway, are you sure it was a revolution?"

"Don't you start that. Are you letting that Securitate woman influence you?"

"I'm not letting anyone influence me. But yes, I'm beginning to ask some questions. Maybe the revolution is only just beginning . . ."

"On University Square?"

"Why not?"

Marianne shrugs. With her back turned to me, she starts preparing dinner in the space between the oven and the dishwasher. This doesn't stop her from giving a little speech, one I don't need to listen to because I already know it by heart.

"You don't know yourself what you want. You've decided to write a novel, but you haven't a clue what it'll be about or who the characters will be. You haven't even written a general outline so you know where you're going. You stumble along from page to page, choosing one direction and then another. You don't manage to put together the simplest action, to say anything remotely interesting or significant so that the reader will feel like persevering. I know you inside out! Once again you won't be capable of writing a proper novel. You may try to convince yourself that you're working on a realist novel, but you don't even know what reality is. Everything's mixed up in your mind, you live with your head in the clouds. For you, reality is just a meaningless jumble—not to mention that you've been eaten away by nihilism like a leper. Since you don't believe in anything, the results on paper can only be confusion and ambiguity."

I've heard it all before and I know what will come next. So I inch my way out of the kitchen on tiptoe.

Mihai's letter. I should quote at least a few fragments—apart from the one I read out to Marianne, of course.

In connection with that earlier fragment, by the way, I ought to include a newspaper clipping here, from an article signed by an émigré writer. It rambles a bit, I know, but there are a few interesting touches. For example:

> I was at University Square in late April 1990, with Cornel Regman and his wife. We were impressed by the excitement in the crowd, by the songs and the anticommunist slogans. At one point a student appeared on the balcony and shouted:
>
> "Kneel down, those of you who aren't communists!"
>
> Everyone knelt down, or in Mrs. Regman's case crouched down. Only two of us, Regman and myself, remained on our feet.

"I can't kneel, because I wouldn't be able to get up again. I have rusty joints," the literary critic explained to me, a little embarrassed. I smiled at him, thrust out my chest and went on standing. Deep inside I said to myself with pride: See, even at my age I can still take a stand!

Those who had knelt down looked at me with disapproval, some even with hatred.

"You commie!" one of the heroes of the square said, grinding his teeth.

I gave him a look that was more serene than defiant.

Was I afraid?

I was feeling too happy, too proud of myself, to be afraid. They could have beaten or tortured me, but I still don't think I would have testified that I had never been a Party member, or even joined the Pioneers. Nor would I have told them that I was So-and-so, whom our "departed leader" stripped of his citizenship by decree in 1975, after I had turned everyone against me by doing my own thing and refusing to bow to the "general interest." Nor would I even have mentioned that the present government has still not rescinded the decree.

At one point in the letter Mihai refers to Ana, who, having finished work at the hospital, takes a shower, makes herself up, and returns to University Square to attend to the hunger strikers. Some of them haven't eaten for two weeks. All they drink is tea with sugar. Ana takes their blood pressure with a device she has probably purloined from the hospital.

Then, one day, a harrowing scene: Ana was kneeling beside a striker who seemed about to expire; "he could barely speak, but the few words he was able to get out were enough to express his firm resolve to continue the struggle to the end." Everyone around "looked at her with admiration and respect." This lean, lanky guy suddenly showed up then, but Ana was "concentrating on the hunger hero" and didn't notice him. The beanpole elbowed his way through, shouting that he was her cousin. People let him approach Ana, and without further ado he grabbed her by the arm "as if it were a wing," dragging her to her feet.

"Valentin!" Ana shouted. "Have you lost your mind?"

"Under the indignant eyes of the crowd," Valentin pulled like a lunatic on Ana's arm, and as she didn't have the presence of mind to drop her sphygmomanometer, the hunger striker "found himself being dragged out of the little tent that had been put up to shield him from the sun." Mihai rushed over to help the damsel in distress, but the "cousin" was stronger than he. Luckily some others stepped in too. In the end Valentin—who, according to Mihai, "had the typical mug of a Securitate agent"—was forced out of the way, narrowly escaping a beating at the hands of two "dark-skinned heavies," one armed with a bicycle chain, the other with a winch. Oddly enough, the two gypsies calmed down as soon as the students in charge of keeping order appeared on the scene.

"No violence! No violence!" they said—whereupon both the gypsies and Valentin made themselves scarce.

"Is he really your cousin?" Mihai asked Ana when they were back on the sidewalk outside the Hungarian Airlines office.

She didn't deny it, although she was visibly ashamed.

"And what kind of guy is he?" Mihai continued. "What does he do for a living?"

"He's a mining engineer."

Mihai didn't write any more about what had happened, but passed on to less interesting matters. They had probably left together and gone to eat and drink something at a café-bar; they weren't on hunger strike themselves, after all. It's not out of the question that they came across the mining engineer again, either in the street or seated at the back of the bar; he'd have spotted them and staggered over. If that had been the case, anything was possible: maybe they yelled and came to blows, or else made up and went on drinking together until midnight. Thus do facts lose their significance for the reader.

But another variant is also worthy of consideration: namely, that the mining engineer really was a Securitate agent, and that Ana was either in the dark about it or had no interest in revealing the fact. That doesn't necessarily mean there was any complicity between them. Why complicate things?

Yes, but if that's how it was, if the engineer wasn't an engineer but a secret policeman, or else both (which is actually the most likely scenario), and if the nurse was not au fait with his double job, then, well, the cousin (that is, the Securitate agent) wouldn't have been the least bit interested in making a scene in the bar, any more than he would have wanted to earlier at University Square—and then, after what had happened in the Square, he certainly wouldn't have wanted to expose himself even further by tailing Ana and Mihai. So, where does that leave us? There's only one hypothesis that can explain his behavior. I mention it only because of my professional scruples, since it's my duty as a novelist to keep looking for anything that might shed light on the plot. (Such conscientiousness is, I admit, rather at odds with my promise not to complicate matters further.) Anyway, the only rational hypothesis is that the cousin had fallen in love with his cousin. Pretty banal. And then, why would he be jealous of a hunger striker, of a "hunger hero," as Mihai put it—especially one who wasn't exactly young, who had served time in the 1950s under Gheorghiu-Dej and looked rather the worse for wear . . . ? There must be more to it: for example, that the cousin wasn't in fact Ana's cousin (or only a cousin thrice removed). He *passed* for Ana's cousin, but in fact he was her husband, her lawfully wedded spouse. That would certainly be the spicier option, but then what was forcing him to act the part of her cousin? Why did he need to do it? For whose benefit? The only logical explanation I can think of is that they were both working for the Securitate. In fact, if you're interested, that's actually how they met in the first place. And now they were on an assignment . . .

But what kind of assignment?

Making one conjecture after another, the novelist risks turning into an amateur detective, painting his characters in the gaudiest colors imaginable. And the reader, who already has to endure the assaults of life's dismal routine, probably won't take kindly to finding them in the book he or she has chosen to read, but will simply put it down, or else ostentatiously fling it into the garbage—especially if all the unsettling revelations are communicated in a single sentence or paragraph, without nuances, without the subtle gradations that create an air of suspense . . .

"Only the reader's curiosity can save the novelist in the end," Marianne said to me a little while ago, and I nodded in agreement. Faced with such a profound truth, I was even more helpless than a hunger striker. After all, a hunger striker can still hope to defend himself by arousing people's pity—or anyway some people's. Some of the spectators, in person or on TV, will end up identifying with this or that hollow-cheeked protester, with his glassy, sunken eyes—so much so that they'll start to feel hungry themselves, and dash to the nearest café or sausage stall (it's easier for TV viewers, since their fridge is in the next room). But wait, that's not the point I was trying to make: I think I've lost the thread, which was something about the danger of boring the reader with my tall stories. So, let's go back to the café-bar where Mihai, Ana, and Valentin are washing down sausages and roasted peppers with muscat wine, laughing and whispering like real partners in crime. It's natural that they're so excited. The next day, their assignment will take what you might call a colorful—or even "novelistic," for God's sake—turn. I take the other letter, Ion's, from my pocket and wave it for a few seconds under Marianne's nose, waiting to see her bubble with curiosity.

"I've received a letter that explains everything," I say triumphantly, proud that my novelist's intuition has again borne fruit. But Marianne keeps her poise and doesn't allow any curiosity to show.

"Who from?" she asks, grudgingly.

"Ion," I reply, continuing to wave the letter like a fan.

"You're getting tiresome."

She gets up and walks out of the kitchen. The Siamese looks at me a little contemptuously.

"That's what you deserve for going on like that."

He's right. I pulled too hard on the rope, and it snapped. Of course it's no great tragedy: all I need do is give up the direct dialogue (the dialogue with Marianne) and give a sober summary of Ion's letter, without any cheap stylistic effects. Or I could simply reproduce it word for word, maybe adding a sentence of my own here and there. I'll preserve his style, however rhetorical and melo-dramatic it seems to me . . .

"Yes, read it to me, won't you?" the cat mews.

Dear Mr. XXXX,

As I write the lines you hold before you, the tears have not yet dried on my cheeks. I've been crying all day, like a child! At first it was partly because of the pain. Then, as the physical pain faded, I cried out of bitter disappoint-ment. All is lost! For us, the battle is over!

Oh, the villains, the foul, vile wretches! How patiently they waited for the elections, and then, emerging victori-ous, stepped forward to do what they'd been preparing all along! Everything was planned in the minutest detail. First they sent in the police to clear the hunger strikers—as if they cared a fig whether they starved to death or not. It was just a pretext to get at us, and to put us to the test. We didn't give in, of course. Most of the strikers stood firm. It was clear from our parleys with the police that they'd been given orders to provoke us. We refused to leave, and so they drew their rubber truncheons.

We retreated at the first assault. But then we came back in force, with stones, bottles of gasoline, and various con-coctions—Molotov cocktails or whatever they're called. I was in the crowd of young people who launched the counterattack. "It's like at the Battle of Plevna!" Mihai shouted, at the head of what was mainly a group of gyp-sies. And so what? Who was looking at the color of their skin? "So what if they're gypsies?" I said to Maria, who stuck as close as she could to me, even though she was screaming and crying with fright. Just as long as we don't become racists like in South Africa!

But they weren't just gypsies: they were probably gypsy-provocateurs, brought in to spread mayhem! Mihai was the only one who really believed that the police had pulled back to spare us. In fact, they *wanted* us to set fire to the interior ministry and smash things as we went along. At one point we found ourselves in front of the television studios. Mihai was right at the front, shouting his head off and throwing anything he could lay his hands on. He was one of the first to break into the building. How courageous he was! Then I lost sight of him: he seemed to vanish into thin air. I'm afraid something may have happened to him, because I didn't see him the next day either, when the miners arrived and all hell broke loose.

The miners' picks were more effective than police truncheons or water cannons. It was pandemonium! I saw with my own eyes how they pummeled a geology student I know: Constantinescu—Vasile Constantinescu, I think; his friends call him Sile for short. They hit him till he was flat on the ground, with blood pouring from him like from a slit pig. Others came (miners too?) and swung him into a truck like a sack of beans, on top of other bodies lying there. I was watching from a hiding place in an arcade, hardly daring to stick my nose out. I'd already been hit on the back with a cudgel and punched several times near the throat. I'd only just managed to get away from them.

Maria and Ana disappeared at the same time as Mihai. Anyway, there is no hope now of our holding out: the miners were too strong and had the support of Securitate types. I'd bet my life on it.

I stopped writing to watch the news, and there was Iliescu thanking the miners and that despicable bearded bandit. If I cry now, it's out of fury! People say it was the bandit who shipped those miners in. Those monsters will stop at nothing to hang onto power, they don't even bother to hide it, and yet the masses, still in a stupor from the years of the Midget, went out and voted for them anyway! The people applauded the miners: yes—ruffians, airheads, and dimwits, that's the people for you! (Excuse my language.) Penguins of the cobbler Ceausescu! A frightened mass, willing to do anything just to survive—that was the Romanian people during the communist period! We all complained that we were living in a totalitarian state, with a monstrous police apparatus watching our every movement. But what movement? Was there ever any movement? And weren't the police and Securitate Romanians too? Weren't they recruited from the ranks of the people? And now, aren't the miners also the people? And the tongue-waggers and costermongers who cheered them on after voting as they did . . . and the gypsies too, some of whom, as I said, were probably put on the payroll by the new regime to lead us astray: aren't they Romanians too? Don't they also live in this sad country, where people are so fond of jeering at others?

Forgive me my rage! All I can do is rant and rave: but what else is left? During those December days, I began to hope that our "mioritism"—if that word, with its pastoral overtones, is not a vacuous invention of intellectuals steeped in cultural theory and desperately seeking something more than a purely individualist identity . . . if, that is, it expresses a national or ethnic reality—well, I hoped that it might finally have some beneficial effects after being forced into an accommodation with Russian-style communism for so many years. Yes, I thought that the heap of mashed potato had finally exploded, in the end. And some people really did sacrifice themselves in December! When we faced APCs on the streets and shouted that death would liberate us, it was no longer a question of mioritic passivity; the sheep were no longer lining up passively for the slaughter but advancing toward their butchers with chests (so to speak) bared. If mioritism means overriding the will to live or even facing death with indifference, like the Dacians of old who joyfully fell in battle, then why should we not sacrifice ourselves for a whole nation pining for freedom? That's what I said to myself: that's what I thought most people were thinking. But I was wrong. In December, of course, the majority of people stayed at home in carpet slippers watching television. And, when they finally went out, it was to rejoice, not to sacrifice themselves!

The Romanian people didn't change during the years of dictatorship. Or, if they did, it was for the worse: communism just accentuated their defects.

I cannot and will not remain in this country. I'll go out into the big wide world. Now that's much easier than before. At least we've got that: passports!

Once again please excuse me for this overlong and whinging letter. I shall allow myself to hope that we'll meet again before long: not in Romania, but somewhere, somewhere in Europe.

Respectfully yours,

Ion Valea

"We'll wake up and find him on the doorstep," the Siamese mewed, with disgusting egotism.

But I say nothing. I don't feel like commenting.

I go to the bathroom, automatically look at myself in the mirror, feel my puffy cheeks, study the rising slope of my forehead that accentuates the constant hair loss. "That's life," I say, shrugging my shoulders. I notice an odd taste in my mouth and decide to brush my teeth. I take the toothpaste and only squeeze a little onto the brush, because if there's too much foam it ends up on my ears. I turn the tap. I'm too lazy to use the glass, which holds the tube of toothpaste, so I shape my hands into a bowl and lean over to sip some water; it's lukewarm, then positively hot. I chose the wrong tap, so now I turn the one marked FROID and get a pleasant temperature. That's civilization for you: all you need do is turn a tap, press a button or lift a lever. I brush my teeth well. Although I don't have my full set of teeth anymore, I haven't needed any false ones yet, and the ones I still have will keep me going for a few more years. I rinse my mouth and think that maybe it would be a good idea to shave before leaving.

This time my mind is made up. There's no point putting it off any longer. I must start writing the novel, writing it seriously, from beginning to end.

I've been to the pharmacy and bought the medicine prescribed by Dr. Gachet. My suitcase has been ready for a long time; the keys to my friend's house are in my pocket. I look in the mirror again and smile: how pleasant it is to be leaving; to go out in the morning with a light suitcase in your hand, whistling, without a care in the world, not once turning your head, not once looking around with pity or contempt as you pass all those care-bowed people hurrying off to work.

I should put in a sentence or two somewhere to indicate that Ion was one of the first in line at the passport office; he got up at five in the morning, but when he reached Strada Iorga he noticed that a few dozen people were there already, mostly the same age as himself. Women could have an abortion now whenever they wanted, and everyone could leave the country for wherever they wanted. So that's freedom, in the full sense of the word. It was February, a little over three months before the *euphoric and tragic* (author's emphasis) events in University Square.

Anyway, everything needs to be looked at again, tidied up and rewritten. The few notes and scenes that already exist in draft will have to be reworked and fitted into a coherent whole. It wouldn't hurt to draw up an outline. I cobbled one together in Paris, but I forgot it in my rush to get away, along with various other papers, clippings, and notes that I'd kept in the margins of other texts. All I brought in the end was my yellow folder.

Now I'll have to call Marianne and ask her to put everything in a big envelope and mail it to me: the red folder marked ROMANIA, and the blue one marked EUROPE.

What if she refuses? What if she says: "Why couldn't you be more careful and pack everything you needed?"

"I was in a rush."

"Yes, you rushed out like a thief, without even saying good-bye. Well, now good luck to you!"

Everything has to be rewritten, including these last few sentences (how can I know what Marianne will say to me over the phone!). In any case, I'll delete nearly all (why not all?) the passages where I talk about myself. It's ridiculous to keep pointing myself out: here I am, the author! This text didn't write itself! I'm the one pulling the strings behind the scenes! It's not as if I look in the mirror the whole time I'm writing . . . Actually, there *is* a mirror to my right, in the next room, and just now I looked up at it and saw myself in the act of writing. I quickly turned my head back again, because otherwise the pen would wander off. It's unnatural to spend more time talking about myself than about the (other) characters—even if I can claim that this helped me to find my characters and my subject . . . I mean, even if it was by writing about myself that I also managed to write about the others.

But now it's time to remove myself from all the scenes where I was in search of my characters. Or at least I need to scale myself down, so that I only appear now and again, and even then only discreetly—between the lines, as it were. I turn my head to look at the mirror again and for a moment I don't see myself in it—or, to be more precise, I see only my stubborn hand continuing to move across this sheet of paper. A hand and an arm, with no head.

I take off my glasses and light a cigarette.

Okay, let's say I manage to do it: to write myself out of the text. But what about Marianne? If I get rid of myself, she disappears too (plus the tomcat). On the other hand, if I leave her in the first part (as a less and less important secondary character), can I really eliminate her from the rest? Having used her from the beginning, discussed my characters with her, made her listen to all kinds of bullshit . . . even if she blew up sometimes, slamming the door in my face, abandoning me (fortunately the Siamese is a good conversationalist!), can I really dump her now . . . just like that, in cold blood?

Besides, how would I get rid of her? Divorce?

I couldn't do it. I can't stand being cruel to anyone, especially not to my characters. Who was it who said that, when a character in a novel commits suicide, it might as well be first-degree murder? To divorce her in a situation like this, in order to write her out . . . it would be tantamount to . . . Well, what if she killed herself out of despair? Or simply out of spite? She's capable of it. Anyway, why should I divorce her? Why give up a woman I'm fond of? A woman who is, in the end, a pretty decent person? Because she sometimes teases and makes fun of me? Because she doesn't like what I write? Because she voted for Mitterrand last time and we don't always see eye to eye, politically? What real grounds for divorce could I cite in a court of law? And anyway, what would I do afterward? The only possibility would be to leave for Romania and fall in love with Ana or Maria, or both, never to return.

I have to think all these things through before I make a decision. In the end, the legendary Master Manole did not personally remove the scaffolding and sacrifice his loved one—it was done for him, by force. In the end, of course, at the last minute!

I reread Ion's letter and am tempted to tone it down, especially toward the end. But I eventually decide to leave it as it is: they're his opinions, not mine. So, now what? How should I go on from here?

Of course I could wait for another letter from Ion, who, having written once, will probably write again. I could also reply (but to where?) and urge him to tell me more about his trials and tribulations, or even send him some money from time to time, both as a reward and as an enticement to provide me more material in future. But how can I be sure that things will turn out in a way that suits me? I'm not even sure that he'll emigrate, leave behind his family (about whom I know nothing), his friends, and his sweetheart. Maria vanished without trace after the miners appeared: she may be sick or injured, in the hospital. It would make sense for Ion to try and find her. I can't be sure about anything. All I have to go on is a letter that arrived a few days ago, which I keep rereading in the hope that it'll shed some light on what happened in University Square—and, above all, on the Romanian students' state of mind. They've had so many illusions shattered—how many is too many?—since the beginning of the year, and now, in their disappointment, they're getting violent instead of calmly weighing up the situation. Maybe in time they'll be capable of that . . .

There's something else, too. If I want to write a real novel (a realist novel), I shouldn't even mention Ion's letter. First of all, who'll believe that I didn't just cook it up myself? The epistolary novel is an old genre—it's had its day. It's not so easy to pull the wool over modern readers' eyes. Maybe Dr. Gachet would believe me, since he knew both Ion and Mihai. Maybe Roger too remembers them. Nobody else. Marianne's testimony wouldn't count for much, since no matter how gullible you are, she's still going to look like my accomplice. (In fact, Marianne hasn't actually read the letter: I just waved it playfully under her nose at breakfast. And—I know her—she's capable of just shrugging her shoulders if anyone asks her about it.)

It's not a simple decision. I have to give it more thought—and give Ion more time to make up his mind, to travel at least as far from Bucharest as Timişoara. He has a friend there who could put him up, give him advice. Ion's looked for Mihai everywhere since he went missing: he even contacted his parents, whom he'd never met before (the father was a former officer, but in which branch of the military?). But Ion's been thinking of leaving the country with an old friend of his, Tiberius, who studied with him in Bucharest before he realized that it made more sense to switch to a college in his native Timişoara.

"You people down south are a bit too gypsified," Tiberius had said to him once.

Ion was not a true-born Bucharester—his father had moved there in the sixties from somewhere in Transylvania—and so he hadn't really risen to the bait, especially as Tiberius's comment was entirely tongue in cheek.

If Ion decides to leave and stops in Timişoara, he'll need some time after that to make it to Budapest . . . although he could also go by way of Belgrade on his journey to the West—or to "Europe," as he put it in the letter. Belgrade, Zagreb, Trieste, Venice, Milan, then across into France, which is probably his final goal. But that would mean bypassing Germany, and there's been nothing to suggest that he's a Germanophobe; he might well want to pass through it, at least out of curiosity. What the other route has going for it—through Yugoslavia and Italy—is that I've already made it sound really interesting . . . I filled the heads of those guys I met in Bucharest with all sorts of stories about my truck ride to Romania, all sorts of adventures I concocted to make myself look big. I never even told Marianne the banal, monotonous truth about that trip: I invented other fairy tales for her, and I confess I was afraid she might repeat some of them (for example, the whopper about the wolves in Bulgaria that ate a German journalist) when Dr. Gachet came over for dinner with Smaranda. At the time, I thought Marianne had probably assumed there was no point in mentioning incidents that the doctor had witnessed himself . . . so in the end I got off scot-free. On reflection, however, I can see that I was never really in any danger: not because Marianne blindly believed everything I said, but because, in fact, she didn't believe a word I said. I probably noted down the conversation we had when I returned from Romania . . . and, although I can't find the page in question, I remember very well what Marianne said at the end of my report:

"I think you're exaggerating."

And she went back to reading Duras again—a novelist I have nothing against, believe me, any more than I do against Solzhenitsyn. I sometimes even make use of them and their reputations to express my own often dark and tangled ideas . . . I have to do what I can!

I get up to close the door, so that I won't keep seeing myself in the mirror. I pause for a few moments at the other window, from which I can see the forest. Perhaps I should move the desk here.

No sooner said than done: I drag it over with everything still on it. From here the mirror isn't visible at all, even with the door open. I don't like keeping it closed; the radiator doesn't work in this room and the only heat comes through there. But I'm not sure I'm doing the right thing. Instead of the mirror I now see the forest. The landscape fascinates me in winter too, when it seems more mysterious than ever, and I'm afraid that I'll waste time gawking out at it instead of concentrating on a text that only takes shape with such difficulty beneath my hand, beneath my pen. When all is said and done, these little strokes that make up my writing depend on nothing other than myself. As to the forest, nature, the world's hieroglyphs, who knows what's behind them, what hand draws and arranges them, subjecting them to a new metamorphosis every day . . . It's anyone's guess who pulls the strings behind the scenes!

Nothing obliged Ion to leave as soon as he had a passport. And, indeed, he got one in February but was still in Bucharest in June. On the morning of the picks and bludgeons, some of those bruisers from the bowels of the earth probably spotted him as he ran from entranceway to entranceway hiding from their paroxysm of blind rage. Now he's at Petrișor's, together with a group of other students, not all from the same year or even the same school at the University. Some he only met for the first time in December, but under the kind of exceptional circumstances that bond people together far more tightly than months or years of shared drudgery. There was Toma, for example, whom he'd first met in the cellars of the Securitate on that never-to-be-forgotten night . . . and, as for Petrișor himself, it had all shaken him far worse than it had the other students—even worse than Ion. What terror he had lived through, that night . . . he'd thought it would drive him out of his mind. Toma nodded, and Petrişor said he couldn't believe the miners were half as scary as that night had been.

"You only say that because you didn't see what they looked like. You didn't get to admire them at work," Ion interrupted, his fingers, hands, and arms all emphasizing his point.

"What do you mean he didn't see them?" Toma asked in surprise.

"He wasn't in Bucharest," Ion said. "How could he have seen them?"

"I was at my folks' place, in Craiova," Petrişor confirmed.

"But didn't they pass through there?" Valeriu asked loudly.

"Who?"

"The miners."

"No way. They took a direct route: Tîrgu Jiu—Piteşti—Bucharest. No one stopped them, and there were no detours," Petrişor sighed.

"Could anyone have stopped them? Eh?"

"Sure. It would have been easy." Petrişor was getting worked up.

"How?"

"All anyone had to do was cut the electricity on the railroad."

Everyone nodded in agreement. Only Toma refused to give in so easily:

"That would have meant disrupting the whole railroad network."

"So? Nothing could have been worse than what happened," Ion said, sitting on the floor beside Toma.

"Some came by truck, though," Valeriu noted.

"They made fools of us in front of the world," Petrişor groaned.

"In front of *Europe!*" Sonia stressed, and Ion looked over at her with interest. He'd noticed her on his way in: she had been sitting by the window, with an ultra-long cigarette-holder, looking out into the yard of the apartment block. She'd probably come with Valeriu. Toma had shown up later, but since Ion was sitting next to him now, within easy reach, as it were, why shouldn't he ask a few things about Sonia, *sotto voce*? But Toma didn't know much.

"She's a student at the School of Fine Arts," he said.

"Is she going out with Valeriu?"

"No idea. I've only ever seen her in a group. Ask Petrişor, he'll know more. But what's up with you and Maria? Have you split up?" Ion lit a cigarette.

"Maria's vanished."

"What do you mean?"

"Vanished, that's all I know. I've looked everywhere for her: at school, at her aunt's place . . . the one who took her in and brought her up when her parents were killed . . ."

"Both parents?"

"Yes, in a car accident. Maria was only four or five at the time. She'd stayed at home that day, and the same aunt, her mother's second cousin and still a spinster, was looking after her. The aunt got married later, to a Hungarian from Satu Mare, after her old father died; her mother had already died of cancer."

"Is any of this relevant?" Toma muttered, a little dizzy from the flood of details.

"Yes, because one day the Hungarian ran away. He crossed the border and headed for Budapest."

"Plenty of Romanians made a break for it too, didn't they?" Toma interjected.

"Romanians too. Yes, of course they did."

Out of politeness, or maybe real curiosity, Toma diligently kept up his end of the conversation:

"But weren't the parents also Hungarian?"

"Which parents?"

"Maria's."

"No idea. I don't think so. Maybe her mother was. Anyway, the aunt has an accent."

"A Hungarian accent?"

"Hungarian or Czech. I can't tell."

"Well, so what happened to the Hungarian? When did he run away to Budapest?"

"When the going got rough. A year ago, no, two years ago—in the summer. As for Maria, they arrested her."

"No kidding."

"That's what she told me. They only held her for a few days, then let her go."

"Why did they arrest her?"

"They were all under investigation. It seems the Hungarian was running a spy ring."

"What kind of spy ring?"

"I don't know. Maybe he wasn't, really. The Securitate was obsessed with spies. They saw them everywhere."

"What are you two chattering about?" Petrişor asked, coming over with a bottle of wine to fill their long empty glasses.

"It seems Maria's disappeared," Toma replied.

"What do you mean, disappeared? Have you been to see Ana?"

"I've been to Ana's and everywhere else. Ana's shacked up with a guy called Valentin these days. I went to her place one morning.

But maybe it was too early, because she opened the door in her nightdress looking like she'd just woken up. She didn't even ask me in. At the far end of the room I thought I could see a great hunk of a man, dressed like a deep-sea diver."

"Like what?"

"Well, I can't be sure. Ana was in a see-through nightdress. 'Where's Maria?' I asked. 'Not here,' she said, moving to close the door on me. That was when I thought I saw the diver."

"Maybe it was a biker," Petrişor suggested.

"What he had on his head wasn't a motorcycle helmet."

"Or maybe a fireman?"

"Not a fireman's hat either. But I couldn't positively swear it was a diver."

"Anyway, it's not important," Toma said. "I mean, it has no bearing on Maria—unless you think she's been drowned."

"Who by?"

"The miners?"

"Quit fooling around!" Petrişor snapped, and Ion looked at him gratefully, as though he had just then saved Maria from drowning and was carrying her—dripping—out of the water in her nightdress.

The conversation had taken an absurd turn. But who was to blame for getting Ion to mention the diver in the first place? Hah, hah! We know who it was! Petrişor looked straight into Ion's eyes, smiling beneath his mustache.

"Ana sure likes to fool around," Valeriu said.

"She's never struck me as the clowning type."

"No, not that kind of fooling around . . . you know what I mean. She likes to play the vamp—to flirt, to get her claws into . . ."

"Yeah, I suppose so."

"Do you remember what she did to that poor writer from Paris? She climbed all over him like ivy."

"He was so embarrassed that he didn't know what to do or say. The sweat was pouring off him."

"He couldn't string one proper sentence together."

"In the end he just got up and went."

"I know, I know," Ion said. "I was there, I was sitting next to him. With Maria . . ."

A stumpy, greasy-looking guy—Ion didn't even know his name—walked over then and broke into the conversation:

"I've heard she's in Paris."

"Who, Maria?" Ion asked—with such panic in his voice that everyone burst out laughing.

"Not Maria. Ana."

"I heard that too," Petrişor said.

"What's she doing there?"

"Seeing the sights: the Louvre, the Eiffel Tower . . . She's entitled, isn't she?"

"Sure she is. I'll just get some more wine," Petrişor added, walking off.

"And what about Mihai? I haven't seen him lately either," Valeriu said.

"I have," Sonia told him. "I saw him in the street, with a brunette who was carrying a suitcase. They may have been going to the station."

"Ana's a brunette too."

"Oh? I've never had the honor," Sonia said, a little annoyed.

"She's never met her," Valeriu confirmed.

"So how can she say she saw her in the street?" Toma yelped.

"I didn't. It wasn't her."

"Who wasn't?"

"Aw, come on, we're going round in circles."

"It's the booze talking. We should really go . . ."

". . . to Paris."

". . . home."

"I certainly wouldn't mind leaving for Paris."

"Why stop at Paris?"

"You're turning green with envy."

"I'm . . ."

"I'd also like to see Budapest."

"So who's stopping you?"

"Have you got your passport yet?"

". . . or Prague . . ."

"Well, get going then."

"Prague is a wonderful city!"

"Sure, it's the center . . ."

"The center of what?"

"Of Europe."

"Bullshit."

"Yes sir, the center of Europe!"

"Europe's a big place."

"As big as a cow. It goes all the way to the Urals."

". . . all the way to the heavens."

"Maybe Siberia's Europe too?"

"And what about Turkey?"

"Yeah, why Greece and not Turkey?"

"That's how the cookie crumbles!"

"Or Bulgaria in that case!"

"Don't make me laugh!"

"And Romania!"

"Now you're making me cry."

"After the business with the miners . . ."

"Yeah, that's the end of that. Bye, bye, Europe!"

"The miners . . ."

"What have they got to do with it?"

"What do you mean? You call that democracy?"

"I was talking about geography, not democracy."

"You can starve to death if your geography isn't right."

"And with democracy you soon find yourself out of a job."

"Like in France . . ."

"So what, don't we have unemployment here?"

"Sure we do."

"But we still don't have democracy."

"What democracy could we possibly have? Don't make me laugh!"

"You laugh till you cry."

"You cry from laughter."

"Romanians together—from the Nistru to the Tisa . . ."

"And on to the Seine and the Rhone!"

"Or laugh from crying . . ."

"That's better. At least that way you end up laughing."

"He who laughs last, laughs . . ."

". . . till the sheep come home."

"A flock of sheep . . ."

". . . making us all weep . . ."

". . . as we leap and we leap."

"Humor and transhumance . . . that's the genius of the Romanian people. We're all a bunch of comic nomads," Ion declared, raising his glass solemnly to his mouth and then gulping it all straight down.

Everyone wants to get away, everyone wants to beat it for the West. Since the "setback" on University Square, their vague desires have turned into definite plans, a program for the future. To these young people, emigration seems like their only chance for salvation. After the springtime euphoria, and especially after the elections, large numbers of them have made up their mind.

A survey published in *Cotidianul*, admittedly an opposition paper, suggested that ten out of thirty young people interviewed in the street would like to leave Romania forever, while another eight were at least planning trips to the West, "to see what things are like over there." Most disturbing was the fact that many acting on this desire to go abroad were leaving common sense behind in the process.

For example, the French press reported that eight young Romanians were discovered in a shipping crate already sealed for departure—they were hoping to reach Canada. By the time they were found out, they had already been in there for ten days and were starving and frozen. They were lucky that the French, who must have suspected something, carried out a last-minute check—in their cautiously thorough way. A few days later, according to *France Presse*, five more young Romanians were discovered in exactly the same situation, trying to stow away on a ship bound for Canada.

Even more interesting, and more depressing, was a report in the daily *România Liberă*: "There has been fighting in the streets in front of the Argentinean embassy in Bucharest, at 11, Strada Drobeta. By the beginning of this month, 25,000 Romanian citizens had already completed forms to emigrate to Argentina—Patagonia, to be precise, an entirely rural area reserved for immigrants.

"The waiting goes on day and night outside the embassy building, where people camp out for four or five days at a time, desperately shoving and clambering over one another to get into the office and start filling out their applications, as if this were their last chance in this life. Yet most of them know nothing about Argentina, and the Argentinean ambassador has recently appeared on television to declare that his country will in no way assume responsibility for this influx of Romanians: immigrants will receive no state support, and will have to work hard from the moment they arrive. Some of the people lining up at the embassy have come from the provinces: there is one unemployed father of four; and a crane operator who has to bring up five children on 14,500 lei a month. (As of the first of May, the price of one trip on Bucharest public transport will be a hundred lei, and we estimate that it will cost 8000 lei a month to heat a three-room apartment next winter.)

"Most of those applying to leave the country have no special skills. The largest group of professionals represented here are engineers . . .

"Street vendors have appeared with juice, sandwiches, snacks, and instant coffee; others are working impromptu currency-exchange booths, and still others offer to provide valid application forms—or more often invalid photocopies—for between 500 and 2000 lei each. Impromptu Spanish translators offer—for a price—to translate the resumes of anyone lucky enough to have made it inside and obtained an application. A rumor has started that people with families will be given preference, and so idyllic adventures take shape on the spot. In reality—as a foreign ministry spokesman went on to say, and as the Romanian embassy in Buenos Aires has been informed—the Argentinean authorities prefer individuals who can bear the costs of traveling to Argentina and settling there, especially those between eighteen and twenty-five years of age who intend to engage in agriculture and livestock farming.

"The Bucharest bureau chief of the World Health Organization stated in an interview that what shocked him most about the Romanians' behavior was 'their desire to go anywhere, just to get away.'"

A few other quotations from the press:

"Seven thousand five hundred illegal Romanian immigrants have been deported from Germany since the beginning of the year." (*Libération*, Berlin correspondent)

"Barcelona police have uncovered a ring of child-beggars. They picked up six adults and eleven minors for questioning, all of Romanian nationality. The child beggars were netting around $8,700 a week for the heads of the organization, which is made up of the Cârpaci and Constantin families. The children have been placed in a shelter for minors. The adults were all carrying false papers for political refugees, issued in Madrid." (*France Presse*)

"Two individuals, both aged about twenty, have been found dead in an English port, hidden in a truck that had been driven from Romania. The police assume that they were refugees who had concealed themselves and died of asphyxiation." (*AFP*)

To a survey question that asked whether she would make love to an extraterrestrial, young Juna, a nineteen-year-old "freelancer," replied without hesitation: "Absolutely! I bet those guys are so civilized they couldn't possibly have things like AIDS, syphilis, or other venereal diseases. But I'd be even happier if they took me with them!" (*Express Magazin*—a Bucharest weekly)

He took a newspaper out of his pocket, unfolded it (with a lot of crinkling), sat down, and crossed his legs. He leaned over on one elbow without bothering too much about the man sitting next to him, and began to read.

The headlines.

The beginning of an article.

The train slowed down, as if it was about to enter a station, then picked up speed again. It was early July, therefore after the elections and after the "day of the miners," which had been a major theme for several weeks. Of course, Ion would only have been reading an opposition paper such as *România Liberă*—or a vaguely literary weekly like *Contrapunct*, considered the youth paper (in Bucharest), where Stoiciu published his interminable report on University Square. If I had just one issue of it from that period, I could glean a few lines from it to use as my starting point for some new chapter . . . or hone in on one of the people mentioned in the letter from the editor, if only in passing. I could then present this person in such a way that Ion would identify with him: how about that, we have the same name, and he's studying literature or French (or it might be English).

"What year are you in?"

"Third."

"So? Tell us what happened. Leave your shirt for now, tuck it back inside your pants. You'll be showing your bruises on television."

"You don't think they'd stick their noses in here, do you?"

"Well, anyway, a photographer might. Let's hear what it was like. Tell me."

Or maybe I could at least find a passage to work with from Stoiciu's book. I'll ask Marianne to send it to me with the folders.

I take another narrative fragment from my travel diary. The scene is set on the Vienna-Munich express. Two girls drinking red wine and giggling as if no one else is around. The wine drips and stains their snow-white jumpers. They're getting tipsy. Here an oneiric digression about the old man in the compartment, who turns from a slightly disapproving spectator to an actor in a rape scene. But it is the girls who pounce on him, not the other way round. The scene is more suggested than described. The lead-up mentions that the old man (who's actually not so old) is a journalist (therefore a writer). His identity?

That's no good. Let me tell it again. Like an old wives' tale. Begin at the beginning. Ion goes into the Gara de Nord in Bucharest. The station is swarming with people, as if it's been turned into a bazaar. A description of the Turkish-style stalls (stores!) and of the ragged kids wandering around with glassy eyes. Ion pushes his way through the crowd, which is itself a terrifying character, though one painted so often that there's no point in my dwelling on it. I'd do better to explain why there are so many newspaper stands in Bucharest. Ion buys *România Liberă* and, let's say, *Contrapunct*, although I might be accused of a certain lack of realism there, a lack of documentary evidence. An irritated reader might take me to task:

"Go on, find me a single copy of *Contrapunct* or *Contemporanul/Idea Europeană* at the Gara de Nord, and I'll chew it up and swallow it."

"Actually, I did see *Contemporanul/Idea Europeană* there once. There was just one copy, at the corner of the stand. The vendor was amazed when I paid for it—so amazed that he forgot to give me my change."

"Yeah, yeah, tell me another one!"

"Fine, I won't insist."

So I give up the newspapers, and Ion does too. He was carrying a suitcase—which is normal enough. But he also had a bunch of flowers, of roses—which is no more normal than *Contemporanul/Idea Europeană* at the Gara de Nord. Ion held them as though they were a chicken on its way to the chopping block. He was walking fast, almost running.

The departure signal had already been given. After placing his foot on the first step, he looked over his shoulder as if he'd heard someone call out to him. But no one had called out. Then he climbed the other steps into the car, and with no further hesitation moved along the corridor clutching the flowers and his suitcase in one hand. He opened the door to a compartment where two other men were seated; they looked like peasants at first, dressed as they were in thick homespun clothes. One seemed to have had his head shaved, but he was getting on in years and couldn't still have been in the army. Prison, more likely. The two mumbled something in reply to Ion's greeting. They weren't in the mood for conversation, each one dozing in his corner. Ion returned to the corridor and pulled the window down. The train was moving off. He wanted to jettison the flowers, but changed his mind, turned back into the compartment, put his suitcase in the luggage net and laid the flowers on top. The old man's trunk was next to it, large as a coffin, painted green. Didn't the other guy have any luggage at all?

It was only then that he noticed the woman seated at the window. She smiled at him, her face glowing as if a lightbulb had come on behind her blue eyes. A strapping young man who had been sprawled out opposite her pulled his long legs together as if to make some space. But Ion didn't need to be near the window. The train had picked up speed.

The man who'd seemed not to have any luggage had a wicker basket stashed under his seat. It's safer there: you never know what might happen on a trip; you nod off and when you wake up your stuff's vanished into thin air. Who can you complain to then? Who can you blame? Besides, the old man opposite looks as if he's just been released from prison—although it's hard to believe he'd start stealing again so soon. No, the one with the flowers looks more suspicious . . . The man bent down to feel the basket, then pulled it out and began to check the contents, starting with a huge block of foul-smelling cheese, which he'd wrapped in a red handkerchief. The woman by the window pinched her nose with two fingers and opened her mouth to breathe; it was as round as a fish's, or a siren's. She also lifted her feet onto her seat, folding them tightly underneath her so that all you could see were her knees; this allowed the man opposite to stretch his long legs as much as he liked. The peasant put the cheese back in its rag, then reached inside the basket up to his elbows as he carefully replaced it at the bottom. His large calloused hands reappeared with a transistor radio. He should switch it on, Ion thought. But, after looking ruefully at the rectangular box that he did not dare hold by the handle—what if it broke!—the man put it back in its place, rummaged around again at the bottom of the basket, and came up with a chunk of bread into which he sank his teeth with great application. He chewed slowly and rhythmically, with jaws covered by several days' growth of dark prickly beard. When he had finished the bread, he pushed the basket back as far as possible under the seat, then sat thoughtfully with his palms on his knees.

The woman by the window was now smiling at the man opposite her. Her legs had gone to sleep, so she executed the maneuver necessary to swing them out from under her. Her skirt was pulled high up her thighs. Ion heard the man say a few words in Italian, or maybe Spanish. The woman nodded and abruptly stood up, giving the Italian only just enough time to withdraw his legs. Then she turned her back on him and fumbled around in the luggage net. Ion too raised his eyes and saw a bronze-colored cage next to the suitcases. He hadn't noticed it before. It was empty. The woman pulled it toward her and turned to show it to the Italian, who laughed softly, grinning from ear to ear. His nose was hooked like an eagle's beak, and his chin stuck out quite prominently.

"It's no laughing matter," the owner of the cage informed everyone.

She was right. Behind her, at the window, a respectably sized fish was swimming in the same direction as the train.

The door opened, and a sergeant came in with two ordinary soldiers.

"How many places are there?" he growled, or maybe it was one of the privates. Ion coughed and the woman shrugged her shoulders, showing them her empty cage.

"Only one," the sergeant said, impressed by the cage. The Italian got to his feet. Everyone was tense and felt put out by the sudden entry of the sun-faded uniforms. Only the old man was unaffected, motionless in his corner, fast asleep—or pretending to be.

The sergeant too seemed a little awkward, shifting his weight from one foot to the other. But there was still a trace of the smile with which he had first appeared—hard to say whether it was expressing embarrassment or disdain.

"Hey, quit that pushing!"

He was talking to his men, in a gruff tone of voice, trying to mask his surprise, his sense of being caught unawares. Now he was irritated by the empty cage, which the woman kept holding out to him absurdly. What does she want? What's she up to? Maybe she's just making fun of me?

"There's not much room," she said. And she turned round and put the cage back in the net.

In the end the sergeant gave the order to retreat. The privates were happy to get away. As he went out the sergeant cast a glance at the old man, who had one eye open: dark and shiny.

The woman sat down and looked blankly out the window. The others did the same. No one gave another thought to the sergeant, who had disappeared down the corridor. If he'd stayed in the compartment longer, he would have seen the eagle swoop down to the window and cover it with outspread wings. It was getting dark. The peasant with the basket had dozed off. The woman and the Italian were whispering and holding hands. The old jailbird was looking at them with gentle mockery. It should be noted that the Italian was very elegantly dressed. His bony hands completely blotted out the woman's, but in return her knees and thighs were growing more and more visible: so white and fleshy that they lit up the compartment.

The conductor opened the door and switched on the light. The peasant woke with a start and began to mutter incoherently. The old man hurried to show his travel permit, but the railwayman took no notice. He clipped the peasant's ticket, then mechanically took Ion's and stood there absently holding it in his hands. His eyes were riveted to the woman's thighs.

"Your ticket, please," he mumbled, still looking at her.

The Italian with the little mustache gave a forced smile. He had released the woman's hands and was rummaging through his pockets.

"Is the train running late?" the woman asked.

The conductor replied obsequiously with a long, contorted sentence, full of parentheses, far exceeding the Italian's powers of comprehension in the Romanian language, so that he was left with one hand in his inside jacket pocket searching in vain for their ticket, while his companion rested again on her knees with her mouth wide open. The Italian asked something in his own language, but the woman didn't answer, and so the conductor felt encouraged to make his sentences even longer, adding more and more detail, explaining that it can happen from time to time that the train stops in open country because some hooligan has pulled the emergency handle . . .

"Hooligan? University Square . . ." said the Italian, delighted that he finally understood something. "Me too hooligan!"

The conductor paid him no mind and continued to explain that we live in troubled times, when we're at the mercy of any bum who, as soon as he feels like stopping the train, jumps up and pulls the alarm handle, just like that!

"What would anyone do that for?" Ion interrupted, and the Italian, who kept mumbling the word "hooligan" from time to time, smiled in his direction.

"What for?" the conductor echoed, surprised at Ion's surprise. "To jump off and run home, that's what for. When they get near their village, even if they can't see it because a hill or forest's in the way, they start tugging on the cord. Sometimes they're only minors—in the head, anyway."

"Miners? Are the miners coming?" the Italian asked, panic-stricken, leaping up again on his beanpole legs.

Everyone laughed. Or not everyone: the old jailbird's eyes were shut, and the other peasant was rummaging around in his basket with one hand, as though scratching something on the back, maybe a chick or whatever he had there. The conductor laughed the loudest. When he quieted down, he began to talk about the train's engineer, whose brother was a miner.

"A *minor* miner?" Ion asked provocatively.

The Italian gasped—he was on edge, but he didn't dare say another word.

"Ha, ha, ha!" the conductor whinnied, now leaning toward the woman, although the question had come from Ion. "It wouldn't surprise me." And then he held forth some more about the engineer, a man he obviously couldn't stomach. The Italian looked exhausted. The old man opened his eyes and again held out his travel permit. The conductor stopped short, and suddenly seemed apprehensive.

"It's nothing serious," he assured the woman, handing her ticket back unclipped. Then he spoke one more sentence from the doorway, shot a final glance at the white thighs, and crept softly, softly out of the compartment.

The old jailbird was soon back in the land of nod. Maybe he's dreaming, Ion said to himself—but what do we care? He looked at the woman, who only had eyes for the Italian. The man with the basket started rummaging again and, after a while, produced something else wrapped in several pieces of rag. For a moment Ion thought it was a child—or at least the thought crossed his mind. But he immediately dismissed it as absurd. How could it be a child? You don't keep a child in a basket under your seat. In fact it was a tortoise. The man looked at it for a long time, then put it back in its filthy rags. Two cheery girls came into the compartment wearing white jumpers that looked like they were covered in morello cherry stains. Or maybe it was wine? Or blood?

"Excuse us!"

They had the wrong compartment, so they left as quickly as they had come in. Best to forget them!

The Italian lit a cigarette, blowing the smoke in rings and playfully pointing them out to the woman, but she didn't seem too thrilled. Only when the man said something and pointed to the alarm handle did she finally deign to smile. He rose to his feet and stretched up to the alarm; no, the woman said, *ti prego*.

"What on earth are you doing?" Ion growled.

The Italian sat down: he was only joking. He smiled at all the others. The old man was still asleep, dreaming that he was being handed his ID, watch, and travel permit. He saw a bluish light shine down on him, and he heard a ringing in his ears. He doubled over, more from fear than pain; looked as if he'd suddenly been taken ill. Ion jumped up, but the old man was already flat out on the floor of the compartment. One of his arms came to rest on the knees of the startled peasant, who stood up—or tried to stand up—and in doing so knocked his shoulder against Ion's head as he was bending over to pick up the old man. The peasant uttered a curse and flailed out at random. His blow struck Ion right on the chin, causing him to swing around sharply. The peasant struck a second time. Ion was quite sturdy, however, and although he hadn't expected such violence from the peasant—or perhaps for that very reason—he responded by kneeing him in the stomach. The peasant, his leg immobilized by the weight of the old jailbird, lost his balance and fell, which made it easier for Ion to give him a punch in the ear that caused him to cry out. The woman screamed, while the Italian, trembling, was unsure whether to intervene. He was afraid of another misunderstanding that would make him look ridiculous, like the one a short while before.

The peasant summoned what was left of his strength, pulled his leg out from under the old man's body, and threw himself on Ion, who was still a little off-balance from the punch he'd just landed, jabbing him in the throat. Ion collapsed over the body, while the woman, now really terrified, gave another shout, pounced on the alarm handle and hung from it in desperation.

"The miners . . ." the Italian mumbled.

As the train came to a halt with a long loud whistle and a screeching of brakes, the woman was thrown in among the three entangled bodies. Recovering a little from the blow to his throat,

Ion tried hard to get to his feet. Then the woman, no longer knowing what she was doing, grabbed the man with the basket by the hair; he struggled to free himself, but since his arms were trapped he lashed out with his feet—or rather, his knees—at the man beneath him. On the floor, below all three, the old man was completely crushed.

The compartment door opened and the sergeant reappeared. What was he to make of it all? The woman was screaming at the top of her lungs, her hands sunk into the hair of the man she'd fallen on, while the others went on gasping and groaning. The Italian managed to calm the woman by saying something to her in Italian: she finally agreed to relax her grip on the peasant's hair, making him less inclined to hit her with the palm of his hand as soon as he was free. Ion picked himself up groggily. Only the old man didn't move.

"Go get some water!" the sergeant shouted, and the conductor's frame appeared at his shoulder. Pushed onto his seat, the peasant looked around furious and bewildered, trying hard to make sense of it all. The sergeant took the Italian by the arm and said a few words in his ear. The foreigner answered in his own language, pointing a finger at the peasant.

"What's going on here?" the conductor asked calmly, with a hint of sarcasm in his voice. The Italian replied excitedly, accompanying his words with gestures that he tried to make as eloquent as possible. Then they all turned their eyes to the old man's body, which still lay on the floor and showed no signs of life.

"Go get some water!" the sergeant barked again at the two privates in the corridor. There was no room for them inside.

"Water!" shouted the conductor.

Then a man claiming to be a doctor appeared on the scene. The sergeant left the compartment with Ion and the peasant, and asked them some quite pointed questions. He found out that Ion was a third-year student in French. And the peasant?

The doctor was examining the old man.

"He's not dead," he said.

"Dead? *È morto?*"

"Not *morto!*" said the doctor, annoyed. "But what the hell's been going on here?"

The woman was by the window, sobbing her heart out. In the corridor, the sergeant learned that the peasant wasn't really a peasant: that is, he was no longer one, as he'd been working for some time down a mine in the Jiu Valley. Ion looked out of the window. An eagle was carrying a large fish in its claws over a hill. It didn't surprise him: nothing could surprise him any longer, he thought, taking a kind of pride in his state of mind. Not even a flying saucer. And it was certainly no flying saucer, just some poor bird that had caught a fish. Still, Ion couldn't help thinking that it might be better if he got off the train at the next station. Then he changed his mind. Why should he be afraid? He'll keep going to Timişoara as planned, to talk things over with Tiberius. Then he'll see. He had a little money and a passport. Nothing stopped him from traveling further.

Tiberius was waiting for him at the station. Their reunion was not particularly effusive: a shake of their tightly pressed right hands and a pat on their upper forearms with their left, while their lips moved to let out the sounds of a greeting.

They went to Tiberius's place. He lived alone, in what was nominally his parents' apartment: two bedrooms, living room, and kitchen. Since her husband's death, Tiberius's mother had been spending more time in the country, with a sister who taught at a nearby village school. She stayed with her son in Timişoara only in the winter. Ion would be sleeping in her room. He put his suitcase in a corner there and came out again at once. Tiberius was reading a newspaper in the living room.

On the bus from the station, Ion probably hadn't lost any time before telling Tiberius about his plans. He probably also would have put the question to him, bluntly, and Tiberius would have tried to buy time: "You should have written ahead, to give me time to think it over." Or maybe Ion only asked later, as they were entering the apartment block, or while he had been putting his suitcase in the corner, or immediately afterward, without thinking that Tiberius was busy reading the paper and might not hear him. But Tiberius did hear him and even answered:

"You should have written ahead. You've caught me off-guard. It's a pretty major decision, after all."

"I made up my mind suddenly."

"What do you mean, suddenly? Didn't you have to apply for your passport first? You had to line up and wait God knows how long . . ."

"And then I forgot about it."

"Good for you!"

"I went to get my papers in January. I was one of the first ones there, I swear. I even tried to be the very first—to show off, you know. I got up at five in the morning and was there by six, or soon after. They opened the doors at eight. Well, how many do you think were waiting there already?"

"I don't know. A hundred?"

Tiberius felt under attack from the garrulity of his old classmate and friend. He lit a cigarette and looked out the window at the top of a tree. He was only listening with one ear. Ion had taken off again:

"More than a hundred. I didn't actually count them, but I think there were more—many more, even. They were shivering with cold. Nearly all pretty young, our age or even less. Some of them may even have been minors—although I guess in that case they would have needed a parent or guardian along as well, to apply for a passport. I don't know. Anyway, there was this old lady passing by, and she stopped and lined up behind me like everyone else. Ten minutes later she finally asked me: 'What are people lining up here for?'—'For passports,' I told her. —'Passports? What would I do with one of those?'—'I couldn't say, lady,' I said, getting annoyed. 'How should I know?'—'There, you see, you don't know much of anything, do you. But you still get up at the crack of dawn and come here with your teeth chattering.' And she went on complaining like that for a few more minutes before she finally walked away. A real loony!"

A pigeon had settled in the treetop, as large and dark as a raven. Its beak was hooked, but of course it didn't look like an eagle either—it couldn't have been one. Neither eagle nor raven: it was a dark-feathered pigeon.

"Didn't she ask you where you were planning to go?"

"No."

"What would you have said if she had?"

Ion was surprised that Tiberius had suddenly become so curious, and so insistent in his curiosity.

"I don't know. I might have told her something, or then again I might not have. I was under no obligation to give an account of myself."

"No. Still, I'd like to know. Where were you planning on going when you applied for the passport?"

Tiberius wasn't even smiling—nor looking out the window as he had been until then. He was staring hard at Ion, waiting for an answer.

"I didn't ask myself that at the time. I just wanted a passport—that is, I wanted to *be able* to leave. It was an abstraction. All in my head."

"I see."

The dark pigeon spread its wings and vanished. The wind was gently shaking the treetop.

"It was only after the Square . . ."

"Huh?"

"It was only after the events in the Square that I started looking for visas."

"From the French?"

"The Germans and the French. We don't need one for Hungary or Austria."

That evening Tiberius made an omelet, then they went for a walk. Not wanting to start up again about leaving the country—going to "Europe," as Ion solemnly put it—Tiberius brought their conversation round to Maria. When he'd left Bucharest, the relationship between Ion and Maria had been in full swing. Now it seemed to have cooled down. Anyway, Ion said in a calm, if not cold, voice that he hadn't seen Maria for nearly a month.

"She's disappeared. It's like the earth swallowed her up."

"How could she have disappeared?" Tiberius seemed honestly surprised, even upset. He stopped walking and put his hand on Ion's arm. Under the street lamp, Ion's face looked pallid with fear. Probably only a trick of the light.

"I don't know what to say. It's a real mystery for me too."

Ion leaned against the lamppost and took out a handkerchief. But he wasn't too upset. He noisily blew his nose. Then Tiberius said softly:

"Have you seen her since the business with the miners?"

"Yes. We spent the evening together—and the night. At my place."

"And then?"

"Then she disappeared. She left on Sunday saying she was off to see her aunt, the one who brought her up. She was like a mother to her."

"I know who you mean."

"And since then not a word . . ."

"It's really weird."

"Sure is."

Ion began walking again, taking long steps. Tiberius could hardly keep up with him, and from time to time caught him by the arm or elbow.

"Haven't you reported it to the police?"

"Oh, yeah, the police . . ."

"And what about her aunt?"

"I've been to see her. She's ill."

"Ill?"

"Yes—though still dreaming of going to Prague."

Tiberius was out of breath. He was almost running as he continued his interrogation. Ion answered without looking at him: his strides were naturally longer than Tiberius's, even though he wasn't much taller.

"To Prague?"

"Yes. She said it's the center . . ."

"Of what?"

"The center of Europe. Her aunt is Czech, originally."

And Ion suddenly came to a halt. Tiberius also stopped and then said, almost apologetically:

"I didn't know that. So that means Maria is too . . ."

"Yes."

"So . . . couldn't she have gone to Prague?"

It was Ion's turn to be surprised, and he showed it; his voice became loud and shrill.

"Prague?"

"Yes, what's so strange about that?"

They went into a bar, where Tiberius ran into some people he knew: fellow students, friends, friends of friends. They were all drinking beer and making a racket. Space was cleared for Ion and Tiberius at one of the three tables that had been pushed together. Tiberius took care of the introductions over his glass of beer:

"Ion comes from Bucharest."

In the past, the name of the capital would, at most, have elicited a polite reaction, not untinged with derision. But now, after the December events and University Square, the city had been totally rehabilitated; it even threatened to capture first place from Timișoara in the revolutionary league rankings.

Ion couldn't handle the ugly cacophony of questions that rained down on him all at once. So he just smiled and bent his head slightly, nodding repetitively in a way he'd learned from a Chinese, or rather Taiwanese, film: the secret was to keep your shoulders perfectly still. The subtlety of this movement could only be compared to that of the bobbing heads of barnyard fowl—chickens, for example, when they're looking for worms or maggots on the ground. In lieu of any input from Ion, some questions were answered excitedly by the very person who, a moment earlier, had asked a similar or even identical one. The questions moved backward, circling first around the miners and their strongarm show, then delving further into the past. Ion had nothing to contribute on the first set—what could he say beyond the fact that it had all outraged him. Should he describe how the miners had chased him and set about him with clubs? Or show them the bruise that was still on his arm—though now so pale, so inconspicuous by comparison with the wounds or scars inflicted on others, that he probably would have made a laughingstock of himself? It was better not to open his mouth. Soon the questions thinned out and became more precise, more discerning, more theoretical. Then one, from a girl sitting next to him . . . Ion answered her almost without realizing it.

"And what was it that disappointed you so much?" she asked insistently, her eyes shining with curiosity.

"It's not a question of disappointment," Ion defended himself, trying to find the right words. "I don't know how to put it."

"You said that, even before the miners, something wasn't right . . ."

"Yes, it was already looking like a real fuck-up in the making . . ."

His words rang out, stark and vulgar, in a new—relative—silence. The rain of questions dried up; everyone was all ears. The girl kept her cool and, making her lips as thin as possible, asked dryly:

"How's that?"

"We didn't have a clear strategy," Ion replied, in almost a whisper. Quiet though it now was, he could barely be heard at the other end of their tables.

"What did he say? What did he say?"

"They didn't have a clear strategy," someone repeated.

"What didn't they have?"

"But did they have an *unclear* one?" a red-bearded guy sitting opposite Tiberius asked.

Maybe he wasn't being sarcastic. Anyway, Ion addressed his answer to the girl.

"Yes, we did. It was to force the government to take our demands into account."

"That's not a strategy!" someone yelled.

"What isn't?"

"That."

"So, what were your demands?" the girl with shining eyes asked.

"You know very well what they were. For example, Point 8 in the Proclamation."

Voices began to blare again, perhaps not as cacophonously as before, but with an intensity that seemed to express local pride mingled with anger. The radicalism of the Timișoara Proclamation was questioned even in Timișoara.

The redbeard, doubtless considering himself an astute psychologist, had another question.

"Do you really think the people in the government and the National Salvation Front will get scared and saw off the branch they're sitting on?"

"I don't know," Ion said.

"Iliescu himself was one of their targets."

"Well, yes . . ."

"The man behind the revolution."

"What's he on about?" several of the others protested.

"What a load of bullshit!"

Ion looked back at the girl, who was silently running her finger along the rim of her glass.

"We were in the dark about that," Ion said, as if apologizing.

"But what was your strategy? What did you think you had on your side?" The redbeard kept his eyes fixed on Ion.

"Our willingness to protest and the resonance this had among the masses."

"The masses . . ." Tiberius muttered. Till now he hadn't opened his mouth except to drink. He'd already finished two large beers.

"At first we didn't know. How could we have? It was the height of the revolutionary euphoria . . . We thought people wanted radical change. Only later did we see . . ."

"You saw at the elections," Tiberius chipped in, his voice gentler now.

"Maybe the masses did want radical change," the redbeard said, though not belligerently.

"How do you mean?"

"Point 8 in the Declaration wasn't a bright idea. It frightened all the Party members, or nearly all—including their families."

"But Point 8 only concerned the *nomenclatura*, you know, the ones who'd gotten their jobs through the Party . . ."

But the bearded psychologist wasn't about to give in, and he could talk till the cows came home. It wasn't the first time he'd debated the call for Party appointees to be dismissed from their jobs. It was a kind of hobbyhorse of his. He let out a horselaugh and said:

"No one was making that sort of distinction anymore. In fact, the Party rank and file were the most scared. The people! Four million members. Do you realize what that means, if you add in the wives and families—sometimes even close or not-so-close relatives? Point 8 put them all in Iliescu's hands."

"You're exaggerating," someone whispered.

"Oh no I'm not! Romanians are a naturally conservative people. They react slowly, and they're skeptical about things. They've seen a lot in their time! They don't get enthusiastic at the drop of a hat. At most they'll put on a show. They learned doublespeak in the time of the Turks—then perfected it to a fine art under the communists."

Ion nodded in agreement. But the others, headed by the girl, staunchly defended Point 8, so that the discussion went on until the waiters finally began to stack the chairs and switch off the lights.

The girl's name was Livia. She hung on Ion's arm, and all three of them went back to Tiberius's place. They drank some plum brandy, real firewater, and then Tiberius went to his room to sleep.

You spin out your dialogue scenes, you go on and on without getting anywhere, as if you were writing a pulp serial: that's what the cat would say if he read the ten pages or so that I've just finished scribbling. Lucky he stayed in Paris, with Marianne.

I get up from the table. At least the novel is advancing, for better or worse. I think I see someone riding a horse at the edge of the forest. But he disappears too quickly into the trees.

Perhaps I should call Marianne. She only sent me one of the folders—the most important, it's true, but I'd like to have the others as well. I'm getting hungry. I go to the kitchen to fry some eggs. Tiberius too, who like a good host woke up before his guests, is preparing breakfast: bacon, eggs, slices of bread. English style. A real Banat breakfast would have included smoked sausage and schnapps—anyway, not tea. Ion came in wearing only his briefs, and Tiberius sent him back to get dressed.

Livia, by now in the shower, called out that she only wanted some coffee. That's her business, of course: Tiberius never let on that he cared one way or the other about things. He fried the bacon and eggs, then put them on the table along with some cheese and bread. He was hungry. He sat down and helped himself. Ion came back and sat down too. When Livia appeared, fresh and gleaming, Tiberius prompted Ion to continue the little Sunday-morning speech he had just begun with his mouth full of bacon.

"Go on!"

"I'll make some coffee," Livia said. The two men paid little attention to her.

"When an army retreats," Ion elaborated, "you agree that it's not necessarily seen as the end of the story—in people's heads, I mean. They expect it to come back."

"Who?" Livia asked.

"The army, of course."

"No, which people expect it?"

Tiberius shrugged with irritation and twiddled his fork in the air, as if to say: what does this girl want, why is she butting in, why doesn't she let us talk in peace? Ion didn't get flustered: he took advantage of the pause to pop some egg into his mouth. Livia was watching the coffee, to make sure it didn't bubble up in the Turkish-style pot. She didn't look bad from behind. Nor from in front.

"Some of the people will have gone off with the army, carrying their baggage," Ion admitted.

"Only some . . ."

"Quite right, no reason for everyone to leave."

"But their wives and children will have followed them," Tiberius suggested.

"What wives?" Livia burst out, turning round with the pot. Her eyes shone even more brightly than the night before.

"Yes, what wives?" Ion exclaimed. "The mistresses, kept women, love children: they're the ones who count. And they will all have stayed put. The veterans likewise. Where can they go? They've spent most of their life here, they have no reason to leave. And then there are all the real locals, including the offspring from a natural inclination that we share with the birds and the bees . . . Just think about it. It had been two centuries since Traian came with his legions. That's quite a few generations."

"Ah, Traian." Livia's face lit up as things became clearer.

"And so?" Tiberius almost panted, so curious that he stopped eating. Ion was still hungry, though, and his friend had to be patient. He cut himself a thick slice of cheese, slowly placed it on some bread, and only then continued:

"That was when the waiting began—in 271 AD, to be precise, in the reign of Aurelian."

Ion went quiet again. Livia made a noise sipping the coffee and excused herself.

"A former Roman province, a community that didn't have much to show for it all now except the Latin language . . ."

". . . which they spoke any old way they wanted," Tiberius said.

"Of course. They spoke it as best they could—although they did take great pains to preserve it. People didn't speak it any better in the heart of the Empire—in Italy, in France. Actually they spoke it worse, because they weren't afraid of straying from the rules a little."

"They vulgarized without fear . . ."

"So what did the community do?" Livia asked, without expecting a reply.

"All those people had in common were the Latin language and pride at having been a province of the great empire. And, as time went by, the pride became all the greater."

"Meanwhile the barbarians were advancing, the empire was falling apart!" Livia tossed in the sentence in the hope of getting at least a smile from one of them. But the young men didn't even glance at her. Ion cut himself another slice of cheese, then added:

"Waiting makes you passive. You focus on something that necessarily transcends the present moment."

"Passive and fatalistic," Tiberius emphasized.

"Well, I'll be going now," Livia said, getting up from her chair.

"Absolutely. They lived in what they thought was a temporary situation, but it seemed to go on forever. That's why they couldn't oppose any of the constant invasions. It's true that they were also very disorganized—and scattered. They'd abandoned the towns, where grass now grew over the paving. You know that well enough: the Latin *pavimentum* gave us our word for earth, *pământ*, an etymology that Pârvan already pointed out. So, how could they have resisted? They ran off like rabbits into the forest."

"Into the mountains."

Livia—her major was physics—waited on her feet for a pause in their conversation, so that she could take her leave. But they were so carried away that they no longer noticed her. In the end she tiptoed out, looked back once from the doorway as she crossed onto the landing. She heard Ion's voice ring out:

"A state of expectation imbues you with a certain femininity. Do you understand? A woman *waits*—both culturally and physiologically."

Livia slammed the door behind her. The sound made Ion jump, and both he and Tiberius looked around . . . but neither deemed this enough to interrupt their discussion. Maybe they thought it was anyway too late. They certainly weren't going to get up and run after the girl. No way.

"Do you mean to say that the Romanians became effeminate?" Tiberius asked with a note of concern.

"I'm being serious," Ion replied, thinking nevertheless that it was kind of a shame that Livia had run off like that.

"So am I."

Ion looked at the door again and even began to rise from the table. To head him off, Tiberius quickly asked him:

"Do you know the one about Arpad the Hungarian?"

"Which one?"

"I'll tell you. The victorious Arpad is on horseback, entering Transylvania at the head of his cavalry. What a wonderful country! What a poetic landscape! Hills and dales, hills and dales—and emptiness. Not a living creature, as far as the eye can see. And Arpad rides on, at the head of his men, proud and fearless. He thinks: Maybe we should pitch our tents here. Such a beautiful country shouldn't lie in waste: it deserves to be inhabited. Why go any farther? That's what Arpad thinks. And he feels the sun beating down. It's getting hotter and hotter. Goodness, what a heat-wave! Now and again Arpad wipes the sweat from his brow with the back of his hand. At some point he spots a blue lake, on the edge of a forest. He raises his open hand in a signal to stop. He orders his men to remain where they are; he doesn't want anyone to accompany him. He needs to bathe, to refresh himself a little, but also to be alone for a while, so that he can think hard and make an important decision. For everyone! So there he is, alone on his horse, heading for the lake. No one is worried. The place is deserted, far off the beaten track. Arpad reaches the lake, gets down and tethers his horse, takes all his clothes off, goes into the water, and splashes around noisily. He's happy! He swims out into the lake for a few minutes, with powerful strokes, then returns merrily to the shore. Now he looks around as if he's just woken up: his horse and clothes are gone . . ."

"Which means that waiting erodes not only a people's courage but also their moral sense," Ion concluded. While Tiberius had been telling the story, he had wolfed down everything on the table. *Now* coffee sounded good.

"Come on! Don't you think it's a sign of courage to steal the clothes and horse of a warrior like Arpad?"

"Courage? The guy was naked as a newborn babe. And he had his head in the clouds."

"What about the others?"

"Didn't you say he left the others a long way off? They had no idea what was going on."

"Anyway, that's not how you judge a people. Courage, cowardice, I don't know what else. You should judge them like you do individuals."

"Which is how?"

"With different criteria."

"Which criteria?"

"I'd say the main one is perseverance."

"What?"

"Survival."

"Ah, you think you're being clever? That sounds a bit too simple. Survival!"

"Simple? Do you know how many peoples have disappeared throughout history? Some of them on Romanian soil: the Cumans, the Pechenegs."

"They mixed in with the rest of us."

"Mixed in and disappeared."

Ion stayed on a few more days in Timişoara, or maybe it was a few weeks. He kept hoping that he might persuade Tiberius to go with him. Every other day they had a brief chat that ended in indecision. For example:

"What's up? Why don't you come with me?"

"How can I? I don't even have a passport."

"That's no problem. I'll wait for you to get one. It doesn't take so long in the provinces."

"I don't really feel like it."

"Why's that?"

"I don't know. Why should I go wandering around like a crazy man?"

"Well, we'll see."

"I've also got to take my exams."

"You'll have time before your passport is issued. While you're doing that, maybe I'll drop in on my aunt in Cluj."

"I don't know. It doesn't really appeal to me."

And then Ion would shrug and leave the room, or even the apartment. He spent a couple of days looking for Livia. She'd vanished now too; some said she'd gone to Bucharest. Tiberius crammed away for his exams, or at least that's what he claimed. Each day he took the bus in the morning and came back in the late evening.

"Where are you going?"

"To the library."

"I'll come with you."

Tiberius didn't feel much like talking. He looked out of the bus window at the houses and the people in the street—or maybe just into space. Who knows what he was thinking? Ion kept remembering the first time he'd been in Timişoara, two years earlier, when he'd spent the holidays with Tiberius. He'd just finished his first year at college. And at the end of the summer Tiberius hadn't gone back to Bucharest.

"Didn't you have a parrot in those days?" Ion asked him.

Tiberius hesitated. He probably needed a few moments to clear his mind of the thoughts that had just been weighing him down.

"I don't anymore."

"Did it die?"

"No, it flew away. One day I left the cage door open after feeding it. It was on the terrace—a sunny spring day."

"And it never came back? A parrot escaping into an environment entirely inhospitable to its species . . . that's pretty unusual."

"Maybe an eagle got its claws on it." Tiberius didn't seem too put out by the loss of the parrot, and anyway he didn't understand Ion's sudden interest. How did he even remember the damn thing? It's true that it used to make a hell of a noise, but . . .

Before they went into the university library, Tiberius asked:

"What do you want to look at in there?"

"I'm not sure. Maybe something about UFOs."

"UFOs? Why, what's got into you?"

At that moment they bumped into Tiberius's red-bearded classmate, the one Ion had met in the bar.

They resumed their UFO conversation that evening. After some beating about the bush, Ion said that he'd actually seen an unidentified flying object—which is to say, put simply, if incorrectly: a flying saucer.

"When was that?"

"Sometime in December, a little before the . . ."

"Yes . . ."

"Yes. And then . . . I thought I saw another one when I was coming here on the train. I was staring out the window, not thinking of anything in particular. First I saw an eagle catch a fish."

"What?"

"It had been hunting a fish. It had it in its claws," Ion explained, and his former classmate Tiberius Ludoşan looked at him askance.

"You said you weren't alone in the compartment."

"That's right. I told you what happened."

"Yes . . ."

"I wasn't alone."

"And did the others see it too?"

"The saucer?"

"Whatever the hell it was you're talking about."

"How should I know?"

"Weren't you all there together, on opposite rows of seats? You'd have thought someone else might have mentioned it. Or you yourself could have asked . . ."

"Asked what?"

"For confirmation that you weren't hallucinating."

"Well, I wasn't, I can assure you."

"I'm not so sure. After getting yourself knocked around . . ."

"I was a bit groggy."

"You see?"

"My head was aching. The miner had gone into the corridor."

"Who?"

"The peasant. And the old man was asleep—huddled in the corner like a whipped dog. Believe me, my head was splitting. I also told you about what happened when I got off the train, didn't I?"

"Well, you see? Maybe . . ."

"Make what you like of it. It's all the same to me."

"Meaning?"

"Maybe being knocked around put me in the right frame of mind to see what I saw. Do you remember what Svidrigailov said?"

"Who?"

"Svidrigailov, in *Crime and Punishment*."

"Yes. But what's the connection? There's a big difference between seeing ghosts and UFOs."

"Okay, but there is a connection."

"Which is?"

"Neither flying saucers nor ghosts are part of our everyday reality. So, maybe you have to be in a special state of mind to see them. I don't know: I'm just talking . . . I don't have any idea, really."

The man at the edge of the forest is on a bike. It's the mailman. He's on his way here. He could have taken a shorter route, but he likes to ride past the forest in the morning, to feel its freshness close to him.

The letter he brings me is from Marianne. She's enclosed a newspaper clipping no bigger than a matchbox. The headline is NECROPHILIA:

"A young woman in Bucharest, who had been pronounced dead by four doctors and sent to the morgue for an autopsy, woke up in the night while she was being raped by one of the guards. The rapist fainted from the shock."

In Paris, where mortuary staff probably control their necrophiliac urges better, it's been a long time since anyone came back from the dead.

Ion opened his eyes, then closed them again. He couldn't get to sleep. He had to wake up early the next morning: he was leaving for Budapest with Gyuri Farkas and his father. They'd kindly invited him to come along in their car; a German make, though not a Mercedes . . . an Audi or a Volkswagen.

"No, it's not a Trabant," Farkas laughed, shaking his rather stiff, almost muscular, Christ-like red beard. "What's so surprising about that?"

Ion turned onto his stomach and pulled the pillow over his ears. The walls smelled of damp, like the ones in his room in Bucharest. It was a familiar smell; it didn't disturb him too much.

"If you like it, so much the better," his father said, putting an overcoat over his conductor's uniform.

It was snowing outside, and it was quite cold indoors. His father was angry not because Ion liked the smell of damp—how stupid can you get?—but because he saw Ion lying in bed like a woman in a maternity ward.

"I'm cold," Ion said. "Why should I get up?"

"I certainly used to at your age! I got up, washed and . . ."

"Is there any hot water?" Ion asked, and he yawned so widely that his father lost his temper.

"Cold water for you!" the railwayman yelled. "It'll wake you up, get your blood moving."

"You think my blood's stagnant or something?" Ion asked, closing one eye. This infuriated his father, who tried to drag the duvet off his son.

The truth is that his bad mood had suddenly tipped over into rage and turned the barnyard fowl into a ferocious eagle . . . (No, that doesn't work; it's terrible.)

Ion held the duvet with both hands and moved his legs like a swimmer. The truth is, the schoolboy thought (not too many similes, now!), all this anger is really Auntie Marioara's fault . . . Auntie Marioara who had disappeared again . . . It wasn't the first time she'd taken French leave, not by a long shot. Once she only came back after six months. Dinu Valea beat her black and blue, then took her in his arms, carried her to his bedroom, and locked the door. The next morning, Marioara was laughing and trilling all around the house, in pink slippers with pompoms that clicked like a stork's beak. (There I go again . . .)

"Are you ill?" Ion's father asked more gently now, and the by-no-means slow-witted son knew he'd won again.

Even if Marioara had really made a run for it this time, the conductor still had to clock in. Work is work, he sighed. He wouldn't be back home for two days. And maybe he'd have liked to kiss the boy on the forehead: so what if he's a big strapping lad now? Dinu Valea had to pass through a transitional phase: he couldn't switch directly from paternal shouting to paternal tenderness. But deep inside he had already mellowed. Ion had never known his mother, who had died giving birth. Dinu Valea had needed to be both mother and father, then. It was a hard life. If he thought too much about it, the tears welled up—especially when he was "in his cups," as Marioara put it.

"If you're cold it must be because you're ill. Do you have a temperature?"

Dinu put his big dry hand on Ion's forehead, and it was the boy's turn to mellow and put up with what was to follow.

"No, you don't feel warm at all," the father said, leaning over to kiss him. The boy didn't shrink away, didn't press his head against the damp wall. The father was a little disconcerted by this: he brushed the kid's forehead with his lips, then stood up again and went with dignity to the door.

"Lock up everywhere when you go out. And don't wander the streets at night."

He tried to make his voice sound severe, but it just came out as sad. Dinu left, the door banged shut behind him. Ion was surprised to see a sickle in a corner of the room. No doubt it had been forgotten there, having been brought in from the shed along with the toolbox in which his father had been looking for a hammer the previous evening. He turned over and clamped his eyelids shut, so tight that his whole face was distorted. Better to think of nothing and try to sleep—to concentrate, to persevere. But then Sandu turned up.

Sandu's parents had run away, out of the country: they'd "chosen freedom," as Radio Free Europe used to put it.

"They're in Germany now," Sandu boasted, waving a letter that said his father and mother were doing better and better. "They've even bought a car."

"What kind?" Ion enquired.

"A Mercedes," Sandu replied immediately.

"You're pulling my leg, aren't you?"

"Look, see for yourself."

But Ion had no interest in reading the letter. "I couldn't care less," he said distantly.

They went to the same school together, and they also had the same passion for athletics. Sandu joined a sports club and persuaded Ion to go along with him. Then, if the club made progress—in fact, its official name was *Progresul*—Ion would be able to ask his father to get them both into the more prestigious *Rapid* club. Unfortunately, they weren't cut out to compete in the same trials; the coach, whom everyone called Mister Fane, realized after a few weeks that Sandu, with his supple body and long muscles, could be a natural at middle-distance running or perhaps even the three-thousand-meter, whereas the bulkier Ion, with his different muscular fibre and broad swimmer's shoulders, might possibly, at best, turn out a decent sprinter—although Fane was even skeptical about that.

"You'd be better off swimming," he said. "Probably butterfly stroke." But Ion wouldn't listen. He knew how to swim, of course, but he didn't like the water, couldn't stand having his head under it, dreaded getting it in his mouth or ears.

"I prefer running . . ."

"Or maybe wrestling," the coach retorted mercilessly. "You're a strong kid. You've got powerful arms."

Ion was offended, especially as he was much quicker off the mark than Sandu and had sometimes managed to beat him in a race—and Sandu himself admired Ion's abilities. On the other hand, Sandu was shorter and leaner and had the kind of stamina that Ion would never get from any amount of training. To put him off the idea once and for all, Mister Fane organized a thousand-meter race one Saturday afternoon at the Youth Stadium. Ion was off like a shot and had a clear lead after the first two hundred meters. There were a few spectators—including some girls from the handball team who enjoyed cheering on the dark, well-built young man—and he ran like a lunatic at the front of the pack. At first he felt euphoric, and at the bend he turned round to see Sandu lagging at the back. But, as he came out of the turn, he spotted a young blonde athlete with big breasts bobbing up and down; he wondered which sport she could be practicing like that, without a bra. Then he began to think about all of Mister Fane's nonsense. Maybe I'd do better to try and join Rapid right away: get myself a proper coach rather than a sour old man who's shortsighted in every sense of the word. But what would Ion do about Sandu? He worried about him, as a true friend should. By the time he went into the next bend, weighed down by all these thoughts, he was already visibly slowing—and, again because of all the cogitation, breathing with greater and greater difficulty. Two lanky blond devils overtook him, then a third, on the side closer to the stands. I'll keep a little something in reserve for the finish, Ion told himself as he allowed two more to pass. There was another lap and a bit to go. Then he saw Sandu at his shoulder. "Go on, keep going!" Sandu encouraged him, before he raced ahead like a gazelle. It was a pleasure to see him overhaul the others so easily; he hadn't been the first out of

the bend, but was almost shoulder-to-shoulder with the only run-
ner still putting up a fight. Ion, now far back at the rear, watched
admiringly and ran slower and slower himself. This stadium must
be on a slope, he said to himself—a sudden flash of humor. Now in
last place, he could relax and watch the final struggle between the
two leaders. So as not to miss a moment of it, he had the simple and
efficient idea of leaving the track and crossing the grass diagonally.
On the home stretch Sandu looked as if he was going to lose, his
easy stride doing nothing to disguise the likelihood of this result.
Ion, gasping for breath among the handball players, cheered his
friend on at the top of his voice. Sandu turned his head for a second and, probably seeing Ion among the girls, allowed himself the
luxury of a smile. Then, with greater agility than a doe, antelope,
and kangaroo combined—in fact with an agility that was truly
extraterrestrial—Sandu pulled alongside his flagging opponent,
effortlessly overtook him, and passed the finish line with a quick
glance over his shoulder. Ion ran forward to hug and congratulate him. Sandu's breathing was almost normal—certainly more so
than that of his panting friend-turned-spectator.

Nor, in fact, did Ion excel over shorter distances.

"At least you'll reach the finish in the hundred meters," said
Mister Fane, real name Ştefan Ghişoiu, a great lover of horseracing who went to the track at Ploieşti every Sunday by train. Although he was stinting with praise and rather skeptical by nature,
he became wildly enthusiastic wherever Sandu was concerned,
whistling and cheering as if he was a thoroughbred favored to win
the Derby. Ghişoiu drew this very comparison himself, in fact,
adding a few words that no one had ever heard him say before:
"You'll go a long way, kid!"

And Mister Fane wasn't mistaken. One fine day Sandu was summoned to the Passport Office, where he was given a passport and an exit visa for Germany. He was in his last year at school at the time, with not long to go before the baccalaureate exam and the national junior championships. But what did that matter? A new and wonderful life awaited him on the other side of the Iron Curtain, in the fairytale West that seemed to beckon like a huge Christmas tree, with a Mercedes perched on top.

Ion went with him to the station. Two or three of his uncles and aunts were there too, along with the grandmother to whom his parents had entrusted him before their own departure.

"What's he going to do there?" Dinu Valea growled.

"Don't you worry about that!" Marioara replied sarcastically. "Haven't you heard? His folks have bought themselves a second Mercedes."

"Butter and Mercedes!" Dinu muttered. "That's all Germans are good for."

Ion kept his eyes on his plate, not saying a word. Sandu had promised to write and send him whatever he wanted from over there. A pair of spiked shoes! You mean sprinting shoes? Ion shook his head; there was no point now for him to keep up with athletics. A few days later he went to see Mister Fane and told him of Sandu's departure. The coach looked as if he already knew all about it—God only knows how. Maybe Sandu had said or written something before he left.

"He'll go a long way," Mister Fane repeated. "So long as he keeps at it and doesn't start fooling around. It would have been better for him if he'd gone to East Germany."

"Why wouldn't he keep at it?" Ion asked innocently.

"Well, you know what the West's like, kid!"

"Butter and Mercedes!" Ion repeated playfully.

But Mister Fane seemed not to have heard. For the first time since Ion had known him, the coach began to pour out his memories. It's true that he had reminisced about this or that in the past, but it was only now—after the departure of Sandu, (or, in full, Alexandru Economu, senior at Matei Basarab University and future athletics champion)—that his tongue was well and truly loosened. Only now did he begin to blurt out everything he knew about the cities of the West, the luxury and the women, my God, you should see the women!

Ion was all ears. All his other senses suddenly atrophied so that his hearing could swell to monstrous proportions. Mister Fane's words struck his eardrums like heavenly music barely understood, although at the same time they made him dizzy with all kinds of shameful desires. Worst of all was when the coach gloated over the miracle of a blonde, a kind of countess, who played the guitar and lived in a sumptuous apartment, with a bathroom as large as an ordinary mortal's dining-room and a pink marble swimming pool instead of a bathtub . . . and, my God, what perfumes, what knickknacks, they took your breath away, made you crawl on all fours, drove you completely round the bend . . . I swear I'm not exaggerating, I'm not making anything up.

"I can't even repeat it all like it was—I'd end up mad as a hatter. It makes me feel ashamed to think of it. Come on, let's drop it!"

Mister Fane ended his story there: he didn't give in to the youngster's pleading and, to change the subject, offered to take him to the races the next day. Ion said yes, in the hope of getting the coach's tongue to do a little more wagging.

"Did she own any racehorses?" Ion asked in the train, out of the blue.

"Who?" Fane Ghişoiu lit a cigarette, pretending not to understand.

"The lady . . ." Ion said.

The coach didn't answer and buried himself in the racing form. Then he began to tell Ion how the chances for each horse could be calculated—if there was any point and everything wasn't already rigged.

"Are you serious?" Ion asked indignantly.

"They're a bunch of crooks, both the jockeys and the trainers. They stitch everything up between them and bet on a rank outsider, so they walk off with all the dough . . . A load of bandits, I'm telling you! You haven't got a chance unless you're in on their scam," Mister Fane sighed.

Ion didn't act on Ghişoiu's tip, however. He liked the name of another horse—it was called Sandoz—and so he backed it instead of whatever animal the coach had recommended.

"You put your money on that nag? It doesn't have a hope in hell, you dimwit!" Fane Ghişoiu shook his binoculars at him. "Wait and see where it ends up."

Sandoz did look pretty pathetic, as if it could barely manage to pull its sulky along behind it . . . Yet Sandoz came in first, causing the crowd to scream and shout.

"See? The race was fixed! I told you! They'll pay out fifty to one. Pity you only bet twenty lei. You were afraid, eh?"

Ion said nothing and again followed his intuition in the next race, defying the logical choice that Ghişoiu had pompously explained to him. And again Ion won. A fistful of lei.

There were two or three more races, but Ghişoiu no longer had a cent and Ion didn't feel like continuing. Ghişoiu was too proud to ask for a loan, and refused to take it when Ion made a half-hearted offer. The young man then invited him to a bar they had passed on their way in, not far from the racetrack; it even seemed to have a garden. Some tables were indeed laid out on the barren earth, a few tufts of grass peeping through here and there. They ordered some wine and *mititei* sausages. It was May, and dust was wafting up together with the smell of garlic. But the serious customers had not yet arrived. A dark-complexioned couple were arguing like marines.

"And what the hell do you call this, woman?" the man asked, taking a wad of bills out of his pocket that were so worn it was hard to tell how much money he actually had.

"Give 'em to me, I'll count them," the woman sobbed.

"Like fuck you will! You can stick 'em up your ass!" the other Gypsy replied, looking over at the two newcomers, or maybe only at the coach. And then he made an unambiguously obscene gesture with his index finger.

The waiter brought the wine first. Mister Fane was terribly thirsty and didn't have the patience to wait for some soda to make a spritzer—which is what Ion had suggested, following his father's authoritative advice: "A spritzer's the only drink when it's hot. Anything else makes you drunk too quickly." Mister Fane gulped down one glass after another, so that their bottle was empty by the time the sausages arrived. Ion ordered another and looked at the dark young woman smiling to him from the next table.

"Who are you making eyes at, you slut?" the Gypsy man barked at her, smiling under his mustache.

The *mititei*, which were salty and garlicky and came with fries and green chilies, made Mister Fane even thirstier. Soon he'd polished off their second bottle too. Yet it was he who groaned:

"We'll miss the last train if we're not careful."

The Gypsies had left. A noisy crowd of racegoers had now invaded the bar, while somewhere beneath a plane tree two fiddlers were tuning their instruments. One of them was the man who had been at the next table. But where was his woman?

It was just then that Mister Fane got it into his head to talk a little more about Paris and the blonde countess.

"Man, she had an apartment like a palace. But I only got to her boudoir once," he said offhandedly. "She had all kinds of feathered friends living there, you know. There was even a falcon or harrier in a cage. She was dressed all in white—like a bride."

The coach was well and truly plastered by now. He started giving out such intimate details that Ion grew more and more embarrassed. Luckily, however, the coach and the countess had fallen out with each other soon after. Mister Fane wasn't so clear about this part of the story. Most likely he'd gotten blind drunk and called on the countess late at night. Or he'd already been there, drunk, and made some kind of terrible faux pas . . .

"So, anyway, she shut the door in my face. And, when I banged on it with my fists, a six-foot-something black hoodlum opened up and suggested I beat it before he found time to lose his temper."

What could Mister Fane do? He took the advice—without even waiting for the elevator. Dawn was breaking out in the street. It wasn't far to the Metro station. At the corner he saw a guy climbing a rope as nimbly as a sailor (Mister Fane actually said "as a monkey," but where would a monkey have laid hands on a rope?). Ştefan Ghişoiu, athletics coach, stopped to whistle in amazement—or maybe in admiration. Then he took a few more steps toward the Metro. He heard the sound of a car, quickly turned his head, and saw the countess's brightly lit limo. On the seat beside her was a huge, splendid golden cage, looking as if it had been prepared for a condor. What a strange woman!

Ion was tired of trying to fall asleep. He climbed out of bed and began to rummage in his suitcase for the map Roger had given him, a map of Europe, probably by way of thanking Ion for having introduced him to Ana.

The telephone rang. Marianne told me a woman from the embassy had been looking for me. She had that voice she puts on when she wants to be sarcastic.

"Do you have contacts at the embassy nowadays?"

"What are you talking about?"

"I don't know, I'm asking you."

"I haven't a clue."

"What do you mean, you haven't a clue? Don't you know what you're doing anymore?" Marianne was probably looking for her pack of cigarettes.

"I don't have contacts, as you put it, at the embassy. And, even if I did, what would be so wrong about that? Why does it bother you? They're not like they used to be in the past."

"Oh sure!"

"So, in your opinion, nothing has changed in Romania?"

"I didn't say that."

"What did you say, exactly?" I'm beginning to get pissed off, to get on my high horse.

"You said . . . ?"

"Forget what I said. Tell me what *you* said."

"Let me speak, *merde!*"

"Go ahead."

"You said they're not like they used to be."

"Who?"

"The people at the embassy, I guess."

"So?"

"What do you mean, so? Did you say it or didn't you?"

"I also said, 'Why does it bother you?'"

"And I said . . ."

"Is that why you called, to talk about the embassy?"

"You're rude, plus you're full of shit. Why don't you just give them your phone number there, so they stop pestering me? I'm not your switchboard operator."

"Did you give them the number here?"

"No, I didn't. But next time . . ."

"Okay, okay, but didn't she give you her name?"

"Yes, she did."

"Who was it?"

"Ana."

"Ana?"

"That's right."

"In that case, please don't give her the number. Absolutely not. And what did you tell her? Did she ask you where I am, what I'm doing?"

"I told her what she already knows: that you're writing a book."

"How does she know that?"

"Isn't she one of your characters? Have you started hiding from your own characters? Running away from them? Is that where you're at now? What are you afraid of, really? Are you afraid of her?"

"No, I'm not . . . But how do you know Ana was calling from the embassy?"

"She told me. This is the Romanian embassy, she said."

"So Ana's in Paris?"

"Of course she is. Why are you surprised, you hypocrite?"

"Does that mean she's working at the embassy?"

"Are you asking me?"

"Who else? You talked to her on the phone."

"I talked to her, but I didn't ask any questions."

"What else did she say?"

"Not much. At one point she spoke to someone there without putting her hand over the receiver: 'She says he's not at home,' she said. She meant you. Or rather me. I said you weren't at home, I guess it sounded like I was lying. Do you get it?"

Marianne's voice again showed signs of irritation. It was no longer as jovial as when we'd started. Jollity gone, annoyance in its place. That's the way it goes: she fell into a trap of her own making; she wanted to play games with me and ended up getting herself upset. But I'd like to find out more. I'm not sure she's telling me everything—all the things she talked about with Ana.

"Was it a man she spoke to, when she reported what you'd said?"

"Could have been."

"He wasn't called Valentin, was he?"

"How should I know, dear?"

"And did Mihai phone at all?"

"No."

"What about Maria?"

"No. Mihai didn't phone, but I think he's sent you a letter. I put it on your desk."

"Why didn't you say so? And why didn't you send it to me?"

"I was waiting for there to be more of them. It seems odd to send you only one. I thought I'd wait for the other one to write as well. What's his name?"

"Ion."

"Yes. Same as Iliescu."

"Ion means John."

"And Iliescu?"

"It comes from Ilie—Elie, Elijah, the thunderer. He passes across the sky in a chariot of clouds. Then he sends down thunder and lightning."

"A kind of Jupiter!"

"You've got it. *Jupiter tonans . . .*"

Whenever we got round to talking about Iliescu, it meant we'd exhausted all the other topics. Marianne holds President Iliescu in a kind of esteem, since he was elected by universal suffrage. Anyway, it was time to put an end to our telephone conversation. I thanked her for calling and asked her again to send me Mihai's letter, as soon as possible. Marianne was no longer irritated. Now she felt like talking some more.

"And what about me? Don't you want to see me?"

"Sure I do . . ."

I could hardly say no, for God's sake, or tell her that having her around cuts off my inspiration . . . I've been here almost three weeks and have hardly written anything new. Mostly I've transcribed or rewritten what was already down on paper. I've scribbled a few more pages, sure . . . but too little. Ion hasn't even reached Budapest yet. Not that it's his fault.

"Whatever you like . . ." I added, rather tentatively. Another time my hesitation would have been enough to annoy her all over again, but right now she felt like getting out of Paris to breathe some fresh air . . .

"How's the weather there?" Marianne asked, obsessed as usual (like all French women?) with weather reports, which she watches religiously on television.

I look out the window: the sky is bright and blue. The sun seems to be shining over the forest more than it is here. An airplane is passing overhead.

"It's raining," I said.

"Raining?"

"Yes, nonstop."

"Hmm. They said it would be nice there, in Normandy."

"It's close to Brittany here."

"That makes no difference."

An airplane passes and leaves a long white trail like a wedding dress. The weather has been good ever since I arrived: not a cloud in the sky, like in the South. Even a bit boring in the end . . .

"Hello?" Marianne shouts, intrigued by my silence.

"Hello."

"What's up? Why have you gone quiet?"

"I'm fine. What do you want me to say?"

"Tell me whether to come or not. The cat's missing you too."

"Look, let's leave it for a little while longer. I'll call you when the weather improves. Is that okay? And do send me Mihai's letter."

Marianne agrees to postpone her visit. We say good-bye and hang up. At that very moment I remember that I didn't say anything to her about the folder. She only sent me the red one, and now I urgently need the blue one marked EUROPE. I look out the window again. The whitish trail left by the airplane can still be seen above the forest.

I go downstairs to the hall, where a huge map of Europe hangs on the wall. I move the little rectangle on which I've written Ion Valea to somewhere between Timişoara and Budapest, in the vicinity of Kecskemet. I stick Ana in Paris, along with Valentin. They're both working at the embassy . . . I don't know for sure that Valentin's there too, but I'll take the risk: I don't like not knowing where he is. As for Mihai, I leave him in Bucharest—where Roger's been too the last few days. He parked his truck in a little street near the block where Ana used to live. He's looking for her desperately all over the city, wandering the bars like a lunatic and complaining about the Romanian wine he has to drink.

"Of course the wine is bad," Mister Fane said, when Roger met him just now in a bar on Bulevardul 1 Mai. "It's bad if you compare it with French wine, but not so bad if you don't. Wine is like a woman: she can't bear comparison. Anyway, it's stupid to start comparing instead of, well, drinking." (Variant: Wine is like Romania: it can't bear comparison, etc.) "Do you understand?"

Roger nodded that he did. He liked the old coach's philosophizing. So he ordered another bottle and began to talk about Ana.

On the other hand, I don't know what to do about Maria. I twist her marker between my fingers and scratch the tip of my nose with it. Shall I stick it in Bucharest too? Again, Ana's the only one who might know something about her. Maybe I should take the plunge and call the embassy. I make another rectangle for Sandu, although I'm not too sure where to put it. He spent some time with his parents, in Tübingen. Ion got a few letters from him—shorter and shorter, though, and not very informative. He was learning German. He met a waitress, a Swiss girl. After a while Ion got a postcard from Berne, then another one from Frankfurt. Sandu had made friends there with someone called Georg Wilhelm Friedrich Gogel. Good luck to him! His latest news, a little before the revolution, had come from Jena. He was working in a laboratory and hoped to join an athletics club. He didn't have his hopes up, but he'd taken part in a couple of cross-country races, one in Nuremberg, the other in Bamberg, and had done reasonably well. He didn't say which place he'd finished in. His parents were living in Heidelberg, and he hoped to move there soon and study at the university. Why don't you go to Berlin? Ion wrote. Now that the Wall's come down, no one's stopping you. Yes, that makes sense. I take a thumbtack and stick the cardboard square in the center of Berlin, where the wall used to be.

"He was extraordinarily talented," Mister Fane sighed. Roger had ordered a third bottle of Târnave and said with a bit of a slur:

"It's a pity he didn't come to France."

I go back upstairs and sit at the desk. I push the typewriter to one side and pick up my pen.

After he left Fane Ghişoiu, Roger walked aimlessly around the streets, even though it was hot and he had all that white

Romanian plonk inside him. He found himself somewhere on Calea Victoriei. He'd figured he'd just go into one of the hotels, the Bucureşti or the Athénée Palace, where they might actually have something halfway decent to drink—perhaps even a French wine. Now someone was shouting to him from the opposite sidewalk. It was Mihai, together with a girl and Petrişor. The girl was called Sonia. After just a few seconds, Roger naturally asked about Ana.

Mihai was pretty tongue-tied, so Sonia took over: "I've heard she's in Paris."

"You don't even know her," Petrişor added, to set the record straight.

But Sonia wanted to be nice to Roger at all costs and ignored Petrişor's remark; anyway, he had spoken in Romanian, which was all Greek to Roger. The girl put her little hand on his hairy, rather sweaty arm and repeated:

"She's in Paris, with Valentin."

"Who's Valentin?" The truck driver was getting worried. He remembered the gun barrel sticking out from under the bed.

Mihai was mumbling something, trying to change the subject. But Roger wanted to know more and more. He took Sonia aside, his hands on her shoulders, while the other two men just stood there looking stupid. Unfortunately, Sonia couldn't tell him anything more. She didn't even know Ana.

"She's a brunette." Roger tried to jog her memory.

"I can't picture her. Anyway she could have dyed her hair before she left."

"She could have dyed it any color under the sun, I'd still recognize her. But are you sure she's in Paris?"

It seemed less and less unlikely to Roger—natural even—that Ana was in Paris. He could see her on the streets, or perhaps rather in a nightclub. And then . . . He forgot about Sonia, who, resting on his big strong arm, told him in minute detail how she'd heard of Ana's departure to the City of Light.

"I was at Ion's place," she specified. "There were a lot of us. In fact, Petrişor was there as well, but he's playing dumb now for some reason . . ."

I stop writing. I need to get a new sheet of paper but I'm feeling lazy—no, not lazy, just sick of it all. Another plane appears over the forest: it looks different from the first, more rounded, hard to describe . . .

I see him pedaling on the edge of the forest, happily breathing the fresh morning air. The mailman brings me a batch of newspapers from Marianne. Recent copies of *Libération*, which I immediately start to leaf through.

The American senator Robert Dole (from Kansas) has expressed the view that the granting of most favored nation status to Romania should depend on how it behaves in the field of human rights. Dole, head of the Republican minority in the Senate, arrived in Bucharest on Friday, together with six other congressmen. In order for that status to be granted, he said, his colleagues will have to be convinced that "Romania has an exemplary human rights record."

The delegation of senators met President Iliescu and representatives of the opposition parties. For his part, Petre Roman stated that he would be happy to go to the United States and to have a frank discussion with anyone interested in what was happening in Romania.

Most of the paper is, of course, devoted to the conflict in the Gulf, especially since Baghdad turned all foreign citizens on Iraqi soil into hostages. But this doesn't mean that journalists have lost all interest in Eastern Europe. Here, for example, is a quote from an article entitled *The Rabbi of the Great Departure*:

"'I'd have shaken hands with Hitler if it would have led to the saving of Jewish lives.'

"Moses Rosen will go down in history as the man who orchestrated the largest exodus of Jews from Eastern Europe (not including the USSR) to Israel. Thanks to his Zionist tenacity, 380,000 Romanian Jews—ninety-seven percent of the total—have managed to leave the country since the Second World War. Moses Rosen considers that he has fulfilled his mission to save his people. Many still hold the price of this policy against him, however: intense collaboration with a regime for which he became a kind of itinerant ambassador . . .

"By allowing the Jews to leave, the regime in Bucharest would obtain most favored nation status from the United States, and the international Jewish community would praise the 'humanitarian' merits of Ceausescu. The Jews became a bargaining chip. Israel paid between five and seven thousand dollars, sometimes much more, for each exit visa, in accordance with the demands of the Romanian authorities. Ceausescu accumulated a personal fortune of sixty million dollars through this 'traffic' alone.

"In 1968, Rosen sang the praises of Ceausescu, and 'in my own name and that of the Jewish community in Romania' expressed 'the gratitude and boundless affection we have for him.'

These encomiums did not go unrewarded. In a country where religious practices were violently repressed, Rosen managed to expand the activity of Jewish organizations. Although the number of Jews in Romania continually declined, so that more than half the Jewish population is now over sixty-five, there are eighty synagogues and sixty-eight Jewish community centers in the country. Several Talmudic schools teach Hebrew, approximately five thousand elderly Jewish people enjoy special medical treatment, and four thousand Jewish individuals eat meals in kosher restaurants.

"These benefits for Jews led to an exacerbation of the latent anti-Semitism among Romanians. But Rosen justified himself as follows: 'We must preserve the traditions for those who remain, and prepare the young people who leave for Israel so that they can emigrate as true Orthodox Jews, unlike the Jews from the USSR, who seek only to escape from communism and to become American citizens. I have been accused of making a pact with the devil, but I have never repudiated the state of Israel.

"Ten years from now it is possible that not a single Jew will be left in Romania. Moses Rosen will perhaps have been the last great rabbi of an exodus community. And he has done his duty to the end."

(It can't have hurt that he was named Moses. Probably made him particularly tenacious in his fight to return the local Jews to Israel.)

And some encouraging news items:

After the miners' leaders recognized, at a meeting in Braşov, that they had been manipulated in June, Miron Cosma and Marian Munteanu shook hands in a gesture of reconciliation.

In Sofia, reformers and neoconservatives fought for control over the Socialist Party (formerly the Communist Party) at a special congress. The economic chaos is more and more beneficial to the opposition.

A verdict has been announced in the trial of Nicu Ceausescu: The youngest son of the former Romanian dictator was sentenced to twenty-five years in jail by the Military Tribunal of Bucharest. The charge, which was initially "genocide" and "violation of the laws concerning the possession of firearms," was changed to "incitement to extremely serious crimes." On August 23rd, the Bucharest Regional Court provisionally released Nicu Ceausescu "on medical grounds" . . . and since then he has been hospitalized with cirrhosis of the liver somewhere on the outskirts of Bucharest.

Yesterday, at the temporary presidential offices in West Beirut, head of state Elias Hraoui solemnly declared the founding of the Second Lebanese Republic and promulgated the most important constitutional amendments since the country's independence. The President also announced the formation of a government that will reform all the political parties, dissolve the militias, and put an end to the war.

Iraq has freed its hostages and called for a "holy war."

At Vultureşti, 150 kilometers from Bucharest, children with AIDS are dying like flies, in the most appalling conditions.

The first bases to be abandoned during the Soviet troop withdrawal scheduled for completion in June have brought to light an ecological disaster: For nearly forty years, the soldiers buried huge empty gasoline canisters on the precincts of the base. Neither watertight nor rustproof, these have begun to leak. The result is a microtide of black liquid that threatens groundwater layers in the region.

The Soviets are leaving, and an American environmental protection company, Martech, is arriving in their place.

That silvery point on a background of blue sky has appeared again. It seems to be growing larger and larger.

Ion might accuse me of speaking more about myself in this novel than him, despite the fact that he's the main character. Of course, it would be easy for me to reply that he doesn't decide who the main character is . . . But that, I admit, would be unworthy of an author who hates appearing to his readers as a god or a father in relation to his characters—especially since Ion (or anyone else) would have every right to ask me, with a show of innocence:

"Fair enough, but who does decide? And when?"

That would leave me stumped. So, I need to go about it differently. Maybe I should give Ion a little lecture about the function of the narrator, that mysterious intermediary between myself and him, between him and the reader, that voice which fills (or whose task it is to fill) the acoustic space of the novel, and without which you might think that nothing could exist. No, he's not the author. The author is like the Holy Spirit: full of ideas but invisible, inaudible. He pulls all the strings, it's true, but whose strings? I mean, he needs characters, even if they are miserable puppets . . . And all those creatures, who aren't human beings—that's why they're called characters!—need a voice in order to exist, in order to express themselves. That's what the narrator is: a voice! A voice that seeps through all the interstices of an unstable, evanescent construction built out of words and meanings. As in a dream, the narrator's voice cannot be located; it gives you the feeling that it can burst out anywhere—unreal and ubiquitous. Of course, from time to time we seem to hear the voice of the characters. But that's an illusion. In reality it's still just the narrator: he dubs in all the parts, not only their speech but also their thoughts. Concealed somewhere among the props, he's the one who thinks aloud.

Thus, if Ion could see me at this moment, he would realize that I'm as silent as the grave: I don't even move my lips. And I can assure him that I'm no ventriloquist. (No, this ventriloquism metaphor complicates things. Forget I ever mentioned it. I said nothing!) I cover my mouth with my hand. So, if Ion looked at me with, as they say, eagle eyes, he would probably begin to understand what the narrator is all about. And he would be able to explain it to me! Yes, he would explain that it's no good balancing centaur-like on the chair's hind legs and wriggling to catch sight of myself in the mirror, no good craning my neck, pursing my lips, and torturing myself, I still won't manage to see my reflection from where I am here by the window. No, it's best if I stop going on endlessly about the narrator, because I still don't know how to explain it properly. How can I explain it if I don't really understand it myself? Perhaps there should be no mention of a narrator at all.

And aren't there more than one? Eh? And then, what are readers? Aren't they also narrators of a kind, since we don't all read the same text—even if it's in the same book? Well, okay, I don't want to insist. I think it would be easier to tell Ion—who must already be in Budapest, surprised that the suburbs have the same slowly crumbling prefabricated apartment blocks as in Bucharest—to tell Ion that I tend to write more about myself simply because I know myself better than I know him or the other characters. How *could* I know them? Did they exist before I put their names to paper? Before I tuned in to the voice of our intermediary, who speaks like an evangelist employed as switchboard operator, and who now and then lets out a high-pitched squeak . . . ?

Mihai told me about Ion that first time. But who could have told me about Ion passing through the town of Kecskemet? It takes a real superhuman effort to follow him on his European tour. I've never been to Kecskemet—where Dr. Farkas left his car at the parking lot by the theater and invited the young men to a café. He had to take a short break before he took the wheel again. His son Gyuri still didn't have his driver's license. Nor did Ion.

"Have you ever been to Budapest before?" Dr. Farkas asked Ion, and I have no idea what the student from Bucharest replied.

For my own part, I've only been to Budapest once, which, despite its Stalinist suburbs, is a splendid city, a real European capital. I was there a few years ago, for the official "rehabilitation" of Nagy Imre. I've forgotten the name of the hotel where I stayed. I remember it was on Lenin Utca, the main thoroughfare whose name has doubtless been changed by now. The elevator boy was a Romanian or Hungarian from Transylvania, so we could speak the same language. He told me that Budapest was full of Romanians. Many had crossed into Hungary intending to get to Austria, and from there to Germany, France, or Italy—anywhere, just to be in the famous West, now metonymically baptized "Europe," as if the countries that didn't belong to the European Community weren't Europe at all but Asia, as if Prague and Budapest weren't right at the heart of Europe. If, like De Gaulle, we reckon that Europe actually stretches from the Atlantic to the Urals, then even poor old Bucharest is closer to the center than to the edge—the eastern edge, I mean.

"But isn't Russia also in Europe?" Ion asked, if only to please his benefactors.

"Not really . . ." Dr. Farkas answered, with a sudden note of sadness in his voice. His son began to laugh.

So, they were somewhere in Europe, where, as everyone knows, everything you could possibly want will just drop right into your lap. All you have to do is lean forward and pick it up. Yes, it's all easy as pie. The only problem is, at some point, you might get a little sick of pie. You might want something else for a change.

"I'd like a croissant," Gyuri said. He knew a café in Budapest where . . .

"In Budapest or Vienna?" Ion asked, with enough skepticism in his voice to irritate Farkas Jr.

"I said Budapest."

Ion raised his arms as if to say that he had nothing against the idea, that in any case he had no desire to argue or indeed to suggest that he thought the Viennese more civilized or better fed than the inhabitants of Budapest. In fact, he was an admirer of the Hungarians, as Farkas Senior and Farkas Junior very well knew. During the dictatorship he'd even thought of running away to Budapest.

The Hungarians treated Romanian emigrants quite well. This was hardly surprising, since they hated Ceausescu so much: above all for the way he treated the Hungarians and Saxons in Transylvania. In the Stalinist period there had been an "autonomous Hungarian region" there. Maybe things were more or less okay for the Hungarians under Stalinism, but in any case they got quite a bit worse when Ceausescu figured out how useful nationalism could be—and nationalism was an excellent diversion on the other side of the River Tisza too. So, although Hungarian guards were supposed to be just as vigilant as their Romanian counterparts, they usually turned a blind eye to runaways of any ethnic group. Besides, how could they have told them apart? Through a pair of binoculars, a Romanian and a Hungarian sneaking across the border look as alike as brothers. That's one of the advantages of extreme situations: they allow us to imagine that we belong to the same species. Afterward, we forget. No doubt membership in a single species doesn't provide us a sufficient sense of identity; it's only good for borderline cases. When life gets easier, your criteria become more selective—until, after a few successive selections, you wake up in a concentration camp or a gulag. But even that kind of selection isn't discriminating enough . . . it's too dependent on other people. You could take the initiative and carve more and more groups out of your society without waiting for anyone's help . . . except that not even the narrowest circle (the family, for example) can ensure total solidarity.

"You're right," said Farkas *père*. "Man is a wolf . . ."

". . . a lone wolf," Ion specified.

But Farkas *fils* thought differently. In his view, there was a cure for everything. Of course, he said, the dissolution of the unity between animal and nature, bringing the advent of consciousness (which can only ever be unhappy) and the subject-object opposition, have made man a solitary being, have alienated him, split him in two. They have atomized the human species.

"But that's only the first stage of man's development," the young man continued, now almost shouting.

"And what comes next, if I may ask?" his father enquired.

Ion smiled sardonically. He'd heard this kind of Hegelianism before—in the Marxism classes at school. The car overtook a tractor that was pulling a piece of agricultural equipment—let's say a harrow. It looked like an instrument of torture from one of Kafka's short stories.

"Next comes the contractual stage—the stage of society based on contract rather than conflict."

"The multilaterally developed socialist society!" Ion exclaimed, and Dr. Farkas shook with laughter at the steering wheel. This didn't fluster his son, although the idealist did scratch his red beard and pause for a moment to recharge his batteries. We shall use this pause to contemplate the countryside around them, through Ion's somewhat melancholy eyes. Only now did he realize that he had left his native land behind and had no idea when he would see it again. The Hungarian Puszta is certainly not a pastoral or "mioritic" landscape, and suddenly unfamiliar surroundings usually provoke a sense of nostalgia, accompanied with a slight heartache or a little lump in the throat. —But isn't the Walachian plain of Bărăgan similar to the Puszta? Transylvania is a real mioritic space . . . —Have you seen Burgundy, or Bourgogne, as it's called in French? *That's* a mioritic space all right: hills and dales, hills and dales, as far as the eye can see; acres of vineyards; and the high-speed train cutting through like a butcher's knife . . .

Gyuri returned to the charge, addressing himself to Ion.

"The way you mix things up is typical of people acting in bad faith. What I'm saying has nothing to do with socialism—not even theoretical socialism."

"Well, I'm sorry," Ion said in a conciliatory, newly sincere tone. His mind seemed to be elsewhere, though he still made a polite effort to follow the discussion. Besides, he was looking at the countryside, not at his traveling companions.

Farkas Jr. went on to explain about the relational or relativist morality that can be established through a kind of negotiation, you might even call it haggling. It doesn't rule out some pretty violent gestures, although these are subsequently defused and taken on board by society as a whole. Gyuri appeared to know what he was talking about. From time to time he used the phrase *consumer society*, which to his mind was less a model or ideal—though Ion wasn't concentrating and missed these finer points—than a kind of stage in a process of transformation.

"A process?"

"Yes, a fairly slow evolution, certainly not without conflicts or latent contradictions."

Ion closed his eyes. Farkas *père* yawned with boredom. Budapest was getting closer.

He wandered the streets, window-shopping. He stopped in front of a leather store: it had good but terribly expensive suitcases of every kind. He didn't really need a suitcase: his own was still okay, although Maria had made a hole in one corner with a knife—no, it had been a sickle. He shook himself like a dog, but didn't leave the window. There were other leather goods on display, like handbags, briefcases, and portfolios (perhaps plastic?), and there enthroned among them was an eagle with outspread wings. No doubt the idea was to suggest flight, travel. Perhaps the eagle is a migratory bird. The crow certainly isn't—but, come to think of it, nor is the eagle. We're becoming too caught up in symbols. Ion shrugged his shoulders and abruptly moved away. He bumped into an elderly woman, who stopped and swore at him in Hungarian. Ion asked her to forgive him: *Bocsánat!* He repeated the word several times, alternating it with another that meant more or less the same thing: *Sajnálom!* These were two of the few Hungarian words he had learned during the nearly three weeks he had been in Budapest. His humble, though heavily accented, expression of regret didn't calm the woman one little bit: she was so angry her face was entirely distorted. Her chin slid around, her arms clawed the air, and her fists were balled abnormally tight (unless, of course, some fingers were missing). There was something animal-like about her, and Ion felt afraid without quite knowing why. He panicked and ran for the other side of the street, and almost got hit by a truck. The driver screeched to a halt, stuck his head out of the door (or maybe even opened it), and fired off a volley of abuse. Ion made out the Hungarian word for "Gypsy"; he didn't try to stand up to the irate trucker but crept away instead, keeping close to the walls, hunched over, his eyes on the toecaps of his scratched shoes. He felt people staring at him with hostility, but he didn't dare to raise his eyes and be sure. He stumbled over a mutt that was out for a walk with its master, a well-dressed man sporting a mustache and a black felt hat. The dog yelped more than barked. Ion said *Sajnálom!* again and broke into a run; it wasn't much further to Farkas's aunt's place, where he was staying. He went into the inner yard, which was oval shaped like the long second-floor balcony that hung over it. He was out of breath as he climbed the staircase, which creaked beneath his steps. He fumbled in his pockets and sighed with relief: he still had the key. Farkas's aunt wasn't at home, nor was anyone else. He went into the room he slept in, collapsed into a broken-springed armchair, and closed his eyes. Why had he been afraid? How stupid! It's true, though, that the old woman he bumped into outside the leather store was pretty scary. Now it came to him: she looked like a goat, just like in one of his nightmares. He'd often had nightmares, especially in adolescence, when he would wake up bathed in sweat, his heart racing so fast he thought it might burst. But when he'd told Marioara about his dreams, she just roared with laughter. It didn't take much to get her started. You laugh like the village idiot getting screwed, Ion's father, Dinu Valea, had told her more than once. What was that supposed to mean? Maybe just that she was a sensual woman, Ion thought—now, here, in Budapest.

He got up from the chair and walked round the room a few times. He wasn't sure how to spend the evening, except that he didn't intend on going to bed so early. Feeling hungry, he took a sausage out of the fridge and broke off a chunk of bread. Farkas's aunt had been very hospitable to him.

"Just for a few days," Ion said.

"Stay as long as you like," she replied with a smile.

Ion watched himself chew the salami and bread in the large mirror in the living room. Farkas's aunt was far from being an old woman. She still looked good and could even be called attractive: blonde, always made up, hair nicely done. She liked to play bridge. Any day of the week, she'd be at a friend's house with other devotees. Sometimes, if too many showed up, they'd organize two games or take turns at the table.

"Take me along and I'll be the dummy," Ion joked one day—though Farkas's aunt would have been only too glad to let Ion play if he'd known just a little of the language.

"You have to learn Hungarian!" she said, waggling her glove at him. Then she held out her hand, and Ion bent over and kissed it, like an officer in the Austro-Hungarian Empire.

Farkas's aunt was named Zsuzsa, in fact, and like many Hungarians she'd been born in Transylvania, in Romania. She moved to Budapest in the 1970s, after marrying a college professor much older than herself whom she'd known as a student in Cluj. He divorced his previous wife to be with Zsuzsa, who was barely twenty at the time, young and beautiful. There was a huge scandal. People say that the professor's first wife—who, to top it all, was the daughter of some big shot—cracked up after the divorce and had to be committed. From then on, she refused to have men in her presence: she felt threatened by them, persecuted. She complained that she was being followed, or claimed that there was a conspiracy afoot to kidnap her and lock her away in a sultan's harem. She freaked out if a man so much as brushed against her, so that it was very difficult for her to ride the metro, streetcar, or bus—and even in the street there were all kinds of incidents. After many years in a psychiatric clinic, she emerged old and not entirely cured. Unhappiness and psychosis had made her ugly. She looked like an animal—a goat.

The old professor died just a few years after the wedding, from lung cancer, having smoked like a chimney all his life. Zsuzsa remained in the professor's house, and did translations from French to supplement her meager widow's pension. Occasionally she also translated from Romanian, but there was too much competition: so many people in Hungary knew the language—more and more every day, you might say.

As a student, she had come across a short story in the magazine *Luceafărul*; it seemed more like a fragment from a novel, but she liked it and set about translating it into Hungarian. It was called *Fugue* or something like that. She could no longer remember the author's name: all she knew was that he'd gone away to the West, so no one ever wanted to publish the translation—not even later, in Budapest. But what was his name . . . ?

In the 1980s Zsuzsa developed a taste for traveling. She went almost every year to visit relatives in Transylvania, where her brother, Dr. Farkas, had set up shop. She also managed to see a little of the West: Vienna, Trieste . . . One year she went to Paris and had a fling with a Romanian writer there, but his wife—an authoritarian Frenchwoman he described as pathologically jealous—soon put a stop to it.

"Of course, he may have been exaggerating," Zsuzsa told Ion, with a touch of humor. "I had no contact with this wife of his, until the day a tall woman burst in on us with a gun in her hand. Who knows who she really was."

"What do you mean?"

"Well, you know, maybe she was just any old woman, a seventh-rate actress the hack had hired to put on a little show for me. The cretin was afraid I'd stay in Paris and keep bugging him. That's what you Romanians are like: horny and yellow-bellied."

Ion cowered in the big living-room armchair, and for the first time in his life he felt an urge to speak up for Romanians . . . but he quickly thought better of it. It was hardly in his best interests to do so just then.

"You exaggerate," he said softly.

"Oh, you're very good at handling people," Zsuzsa continued. And, whether because of her accent, or simply because, after so many days of continence, Ion couldn't keep his mind off it, the way she said "handling" had very strong sexual connotations for him. She probably realized this herself: she repeated the word with a strange look in her eyes and broke into laughter, raising her plump white arms in a sort of invocation that soon relaxed into a languorous stretching, as though she were alone in the room, hands reaching out toward Ion so that he didn't know quite how to behave and remained motionless but smiling in the armchair, until Zsuzsa got up, went to the sideboard, and took out a bottle of whisky and two glasses.

Their copulatory tussle did not last long. Ion disentangled himself with the speed of a rooster, and while waiting for a repeat Zsuzsa overwhelmed him with so many questions that he was unable to avoid speaking of Maria. The miners' descent on Bucharest interested Zsuzsa less than what had happened to Maria. Ion admitted, almost *sotto voce*, that on the night of the miners he and Maria had quarreled like two old fishwives . . .

"Why?" Zsuzsa probed, stroking the student's abdomen. "What about?"

Ion didn't reply. Zsuzsa's questions were becoming more and more precise, and he was finding it more and more difficult to answer them. She knew how to be specific, to focus on details, and then, all at once, to extrapolate these into something quite significant. And, if she now stroked his sex most tenderly, bending her mouth over as if to speak to it, this didn't mean that she wasn't still waiting to hear about the night when Ion and Maria, having been followed and threatened, took refuge in his room. Ion hoped that the reawakening of desire would bring relief and endeavored to bring this moment on as soon as possible. Zsuzsa wanted to know, simply out of curiosity, whether Ion had hit Maria at the height of their argument, when she had been holding a sickle-shaped knife in her hand. Or perhaps it actually had been a sickle, why not? Ion had previously taken a hammer from the toolbox. No, the Hungarian woman's interrogation served no purpose—she kept inciting him, but at the same time prevented him either from answering her or from acting on his arousal. Enough, the student sighed despairingly. He turned and buried his head between Zsuzsa's ample breasts. She leaned back invitingly, adroitly, helping the young man to cover her with his new surge of enthusiasm. "Tell me!" she murmured mechanically. "What did you do then? Did you hit her?"

Instead of replying, Ion went on to the attack. What followed was a sort of hand-to-hand combat between two equally matched opponents, a brawl that only escalated in violence as each in turn seemed to emerge, temporarily, as victor or vanquished. The battle ended a long time later in their mutual exhaustion. They lay silent, without touching each other. Zsuzsa no longer pestered Ion with questions. In any case, he would no longer have bothered with them.

He unstuck his knee from her thigh and held his breath as he turned over, although this was probably not necessary, since the woman beside him was fast asleep. Only a few strands of light passed into the room through the shutters. He continued to move slowly and cautiously, resting his right arm on the bedside table and allowing the left to slacken like a spring; one leg swung over the side of the bed, immediately followed by the other. There he was, seated on the edge, hands on knees and still groggy with sleep. He turned his head: the woman seemed to be barely breathing. He got up, went to the bathroom, and switched on the light. He saw his timeworn face in the mirror. He looked at his hands, as if he expected them to be dirty or, worse, bloodstained. He turned the hot tap and soaped his hands; the water scalded him. Next came his teeth. He turned the other tap and squeezed some paste onto his brush. Then he realized he'd taken her brush by mistake. He shrugged, looked back into the mirror and smiled. We rather overdid it last night. After a few glasses of whisky, the game of love got a bit too rough. She probably didn't have any complaints . . . but now she was lying there, motionless.

He began to scrub his teeth vigorously. The paste filled his mouth, trickled down his throat, and spilled out over his lips, chin, and nose. Again he'd used too much. He cupped his hands and bent over to rinse his mouth.

Then on to shaving. His beard was thin, not at all rough, spread like grass around his huge-looking Adam's apple. Whenever he shaved, he was afraid that he might cut himself, slash his throat. He wouldn't go to a barber for anything in the world. He'd tried one once, but when the razor got near his apple he stuck out his hand, stood up, and began to squeal like a pig before slaughter. He ran into the street clutching the towel, with foam still on his chin and one cheek, trailed by the barber who probably thought his hand had slipped . . . Whenever Ion thought of that scene, his hand shook and he really did cut himself. The blood turned the shaving foam red. He bent over to rinse his face. It wasn't a deep cut; he didn't need to look for a band-aid. But neither did he feel like finishing his shave.

Zsuzsa woke up and rapped on the bathroom door.

"Why have you locked it?" she asked indignantly.

Ion said nothing. He would have liked to take a bath, but now he felt it would be better to do without. He was both shy and brusque around her. He was aware of this, and would have liked his attitude to be more even, more harmonious. But no doubt she forgave him for his moodiness, putting it down to a lack of experience. Or maybe she liked the combination just as it was; maybe his lack of skill, of *savoir faire*, actually turned her on.

"Open up. What are you doing in there?" Zsuzsa demanded.

Ion wiped his face with a towel and drew back the bolt. Zsuzsa entered, stark naked and white as snow, her large heavy breasts bobbing gently. She began to brush her teeth without giving Ion a glance—but she noticed that he had used her brush, and this annoyed her. Turning around, she rebuked him by waving her damp toothbrush threateningly, level with her ear. He smiled apologetically and quickly pulled on his briefs. Then he looked for his other clothes, which weren't in the bathroom but lay scattered around Zsuzsa's bedroom; his pullover and jacket were still back in his own room. He didn't wait around to be called to breakfast, which they had been eating together for some time. Zsuzsa was taking longer than usual in the bathroom, washing and blow-drying her hair, so Ion put on his pullover and jacket and left without saying good-bye. Too bad if she thought he was angry with her.

He walked along the balcony, then down the massive wooden staircase to the yard. There he stopped in front of the frame that people had once used to beat the dust out of their carpets: who beats carpets in their yard nowadays when everyone has a vacuum cleaner? For a moment he had a crazy impulse to jump and hang from the top bar of the frame, executing the old gymnastic routine he knew he could still manage. But he controlled himself: he didn't dare. Maybe it was time to leave Budapest. It may be a beautiful city, but there are others to see . . . further on. The beautiful things are just beginning.

"Stay as long as you like," Zsuzsa had said, even before she slept with him.

He wandered the streets without any goal in mind. It was quite a cool morning: autumn was setting in. Rusty yellow leaves lay dead on the paving. The telephone is ringing. At first the sound doesn't register, and I sit for a few seconds with my pen suspended above my sheets of paper (rather as a reader might remain open-mouthed in surprise at what he's just read). Of course, it's the telephone—probably Marianne's bored and has found some pretext to call me.

I get up from the table, go down into the living room and pick up the receiver. It's a woman's voice, but it isn't Marianne. She speaks French with an accent so thick you could slice it with a knife. She wants to speak to me, to Mr. So-and-So. "Speaking," I say in French. Then in Romanian:

"Who is this?"

"Ana Pânzaru. Do you remember me?"

I'm speechless. It means that Marianne must have given her my number after all. Now I can't just say, Sorry, Mr. So-and-So is not at home, he's gone for a walk in the forest. Nor do I have the heart to hang up. The woman's never done me any harm, has she? Again I hear Ana's slightly panicky voice:

"Don't you remember?"

I look out the window: a few little white clouds are racing across the sky. There's something strange about their speed. It lightens my mood.

"I do. What was it you wanted?"

"What a pity you're not in Paris!" she says with a little sigh.

"Who gave you the number here?"

No answer. I hear whispering at the other end of the line.

"What a pity!" she says again.

"I don't understand why you're calling. I've come out here to the Forest of Brocéliande . . ."

"Where?"

". . . to the forest, so I can write my novel in peace."

"Forgive me!" Ana says. "Mihai's here too, right next to me. We're both in Paris."

"How nice."

It occurs to me that she may want Roger's address, but doesn't have the nerve to ask for it. In fact, I don't know it either. I would have to phone Gachet, who presumably knows where the valiant driver can be reached.

"Don't you want to speak to Mihai? He only flew in yesterday and would like to say a couple of words."

"All right, give him to me," I say a little irritably.

I hear Mihai's voice. He apologizes for disturbing me.

"Never mind," I say, not too convincingly.

"I also wrote you a letter. Didn't you receive it?"

"It's on my desk in Paris. It hasn't reached me yet."

"So you haven't read it?"

"No, I haven't. Don't you understand that I'm not in Paris?"

"Where are you?"

"I'm in Brittany," I reply after a moment's hesitation. What's it to him where I am?

"What's the weather like there?" he asks, and I get the feeling that he's making fun of me. My voice hardens.

"What do you want from me?"

"Well, er, I'm not sure how to put it . . ." Mihai stutters. "Don't get me wrong, but we, or rather I, think very highly of you. I admire you. And Ana's fond of you too."

"That's great. But I still don't understand . . ."

Again I hear whispering. It gets on my nerves and I hang up. I dial my apartment in Paris, determined to give Marianne a piece of my mind. Why did she give them my number? I specifically asked her not to! But Marianne isn't home: she's out wandering somewhere. She feels bored and so points her car straight ahead and drives off. She's not the only one. That's why the traffic in Paris is so wild.

I sit at the table and try to pick up momentum again. I reread what I've written. Ion wandered the streets gawking at the shop windows. He stopped in front of a leather goods store. It had all kinds of fancy suitcases, but they were terribly expensive—terribly expensive to him, anyway, because he had only managed to put aside a few dozen dollars and a few hundred francs. That was all he had, and he wasn't going to change it into forints. Really, what did he need another suitcase for? His own was still okay, although Maria had made a hole in one corner with a knife—no, with a sickle. I should cross that out: it doesn't work at all. Why not with a scythe? He shook himself like a dog, but didn't leave the window. Et cetera. I stop. I think I can hear the telephone again. I should unplug the thing, call Marianne when she's back home again and really let her have it, then announce that from now on I'm going to leave the phone unplugged.

"And what if something happens?"

"Like what?"

"I don't know. Something serious."

"Who cares. You'll manage. Send me a telegram, what the hell!"

I leaf through the manuscript again. Ion might accuse me of speaking more about myself in this novel than about him.

Well, I suppose I do. But I don't think there's time to change that now, to make this novel a proper *Bildungsroman*: that is, initiation of a young man from the East into the decline of Western Europe; progression of an individual's consciousness to self-knowledge and unhappiness; then a sketched reverse movement of objectification with the aid of the external world—as external as possible—up to the point of self-alienation. A little further and Mr. Fukuyama would be upon us . . .

No, no, the telephone is ringing again. This time it isn't a hallucination. I don't move at first: I stay put—on my haunches, as they say. Then it occurs to me that Marianne might have come back, that it might be her calling me. Now's the time to let her have it, to get it all off my chest. Later, when I'm not quite so angry, I won't sound so convincing. She could even end up turning the tables on me. I hurry down the stairs, so fast that it's a miracle I don't fall and break a leg or rib. And, as I rush, the telephone rings once more. I pick up the receiver and hear a kind of metallic roar, like a bulldozer rummaging in a mound of cans—the voice of a tin god with nothing to say, whose mechanical belching foretells the shape of things to come. A few seconds of pure anguish: the line must be out of order. I put the receiver down and pick it up again, then dial Marianne's number. It rings in empty space. No answer.

Ion's *flânerie* through the streets of Budapest wasn't completely aimless: not that morning, at least, when he'd left without waiting for breakfast, and while Zsuzsa, having finished in the bathroom, was searching the apartment for him. Where the hell has he got to? she wondered in Hungarian as she entered his room without knocking. In fact, he had an appointment at the Hotel Europa, where an old school friend, Toma, who'd left Romania in the age of the Midget, was currently employed. He'd been pestering Ion to get a job there too, if only on a temporary basis.

"I'll find you one, you'll see. A little *job* that you'll like."

He had pronounced the word with the Romanian *J* sound, of course. The point is, however, that Ion forgot the appointment. When he remembered, he panicked and turned straight off in a different direction. Now he was closing in on the hotel, in a great hurry, yet unable to refrain from turning his head left or right to eye whatever girls he passed. You wouldn't have thought he'd just spent the whole night making love to Zsuzsa.

"You Romanians . . ." she began, then broke off; you couldn't quite guess how she meant to continue. Her tone was slightly contemptuous, but then you couldn't be sure she hadn't wanted to dish out some heavy-handed praise, without making it obvious that her intention was to flatter you. Anyway, the compliment or insult remained at the level of innuendo, because she never did manage to finish her sentence.

"I know, we're full of defects," Ion encouraged her.

"If only that was all you had!" she said. "But there are also your so-called good qualities . . ."

This disturbed Ion so much that he didn't even try to analyze it. When he arrived at the hotel, he looked at his watch and hesitated: not because he was five minutes early, but probably because he had lost all appetite for the meeting.

"What kind of job?" Ion had asked, imagining Toma's sarcastic smile at the other end of the line.

"You'll see when you get here."

"Okay, but at least give me some idea."

"It's an honest job. You'll like it."

He went into the hotel and found that Toma wasn't there. He hadn't shown up to work that morning and hadn't phoned in to say why. Maybe he was sick. A girl at reception spoke a little French, but not enough.

"Doesn't he live here?"

"Who? Tamás?"

"Yes, Tamás. Where does he live?"

The girl had no idea. She was blonde and plumpish, always smiling. Then an elevator boy appeared, a Hungarian from Transylvania who could speak Romanian.

"Toma? No, he doesn't live in the hotel. He lives with someone, an Albanian girl."

But he didn't know where and he didn't have a telephone number for him. Maybe there wasn't a telephone where they lived. Ion was confused. He looked at his watch, then at the toes of his scratched shoes. He shifted his weight from one foot to the other, like a basketball player before taking a free throw. The elevator boy asked him whether his name was Ion.

"Yes, it is."

"Someone was asking about you," Ferenc, the elevator boy, reported. "He's waiting for you in Room 621—a Mr. Gagarin."

"What does he want from me?"

"I don't know."

"I've never even heard of him."

"Well, he's certainly heard of you," Ferenc said with a laugh. It wasn't a mean laugh, but still rather inappropriate. Ion looked at Ferenc inquisitively, not afraid but unsure what to make of it all.

"Don't be afraid," Ferenc added. "He seems nice enough, and he doesn't get drunk on vodka like the others do. A decent type."

"And how will we understand each other? Russian's a complete blank for me."

"For me too. But it doesn't matter: Mr. Gagarin is with a young guy, our age—and he speaks Romanian."

"From Moldova?"

"Probably—although I don't think Romanian's his mother tongue. He speaks it worse than I do."

"You speak it very well," Ion said.

"Well, thanks."

Ion didn't know what to think, and certainly not what to do. But, in the end, what did he have to lose? He looked again at Ferenc, then at his toes.

"Let's go, then," he concluded.

They took the elevator to the sixth floor. The hallway was rather dark and smelled of something—probably insecticide or some kind of moth-killer. The carpet was so thick that your feet sank up to your ankles in it. The two young men stopped in front of Room 621. Ferenc knocked. A good minute passed. Then Ion, apparently impatient to meet Mr. Gagarin, knocked a second time. He looked at Ferenc skeptically, who shrugged and seemed puzzled.

"He must have gone out."

"What time did you say you'd bring me to see him?"

"Now, at ten o'clock." Ferenc looked at his watch, and so did Ion. It was five past ten. Ion pressed his ear to the wooden door. Not a sound from inside. Dead silence.

"Okay, no point hanging around," Ion said, with a hint of disappointment in his voice. They walked back toward the elevator, and as they passed Room 612 the door opened on a swarthy, thickset man bathed in sweat, wearing only an undershirt and pajama bottoms. His feet were bare.

"Comrade! Sir!"—and he held out his arm to take Ion by the sleeve.

"Are you talking to me?" Ion stopped in surprise.

"Yes, yes, please come in! After you!"

"Is this him?" Ion asked Ferenc.

The elevator boy shrugged and seemed at a loss.

"No. I don't think so."

"Please, come in!" the fat man insisted. He smelled of perspiration mixed with cheap perfume or deodorant.

"Why should I? What do you want with me?"

There was a wine stain as large as a hand on the stranger's undershirt. But he didn't give the impression of being drunk—frightened, rather, as he looked right and left down the corridor.

"Are you looking for Gagarin?"

"Yes, Gagarin," Ion replied. "That is, he said he wants to talk to me."

The fat man leaned towards Ion and took him by the arm. As he stepped back, his big toe pressed down on Ion's toecap. The student didn't flinch, despite the reek of cheap wine and tobacco that hit him full on.

"They've taken Gagarin away, grabbed him. Kaput, Gagarin!"—and he mimed his throat being slit, fingers extended and tightly bunched. "Kaput! But you can make contact with *us*."

The telephone again! I throw my pen onto the table, beside the sheet of paper blackened with tiny letters swarming like insects in a frenzy. I get up from my chair. What should I do? Ignore it? But it could be Marianne. I'll set a time with her when she's allowed to call me: let's say between ten and ten-thirty in the morning, and between nine—no, later, also ten—in the evening. I'm coming! But I don't much like the idea of racing down the stairs like before.

I get to the living room, and the telephone seems to be ringing louder than ever. Maybe I'm developing an allergy to it. I lift the receiver. It's Mihai again.

"Don't get upset this time. Just listen to me for a couple of minutes."

"I'm listening."

"Our country, as you surely know, has been discredited . . . it's been criticized, slandered . . ."

"Yes, I know."

". . . trashed, pulverized . . ."

"Dragged through the mud."

". . . especially in France, after the business with the miners."

"So? Who's to blame for that?"

"It's true. You're right. But something has to be done."

"Yeah? You think we can glue all the broken china back together again? How shall we do it, and with what?" I ask, suddenly brightening at the prospect of a cartful of crockery on the Champs Elysées . . . or better still the Place de la Concorde . . . all the crockery smashed to smithereens by the miners and now exhibited in the heart of Paris.

"But we have to do something. For example, you could write an article in *Libération* explaining that the Romanian devil isn't as black as he's been painted."

"And how black is he, in fact?"

"Gray," Mihai replied, though perhaps less than serious. Again I could hear whispering and even laughter at the other end of the line—at the embassy, no doubt. "You could write a little article," Mihai repeated, raising his voice. "It won't make your hand fall off . . ."

So now he's getting impudent. I'm losing my temper, but I make an effort and refrain from banging the receiver down on him.

"Why don't you try asking Năstase?" I ask, making myself sound perfectly calm.

"Năstase? The tennis player?"

"No, Năstase the writer. He'll write anything for anyone, so long as there's money in it."

"Still, we'd have liked it if you—" Mihai's voice has reverted to its earlier, honeyed tone. I don't allow him to finish the sentence. Enough!

"I'm busy right now, Mihai. I have to finish a novel. Get it?"

"Yes, of course I do," Mihai says—and, believe it or not, I can detect a hint of admiration, even pride, in his voice. "Please forgive me for disturbing you. Your novel is more important than . . ."

"It's okay. It doesn't matter," I say in a conciliatory tone.

"I told them you weren't like the others," Mihai adds, continuing to flatter me. And I don't know why, but I believe him, I don't contradict him, don't snub him, don't hang up on him. I tell myself that the "kid" is right—that all the so-called "kids," as the Securitate guys were known, are right. What does it matter if . . . With all their files, they know better than anyone what kind of a person I am. Maybe they don't even want me to write an article defending the new regime. Maybe they just need to be sure I'm not preparing to attack it—to write an article about University Square, the miners, and all that.

Ion stayed a good while longer in Budapest. Winter was approaching. The forest is showing all the colors of autumn, but there seem to be more leaves on the ground than in the trees. It's warm, though, unnaturally warm for this time of year, with Christmas around the corner. I've taken off my pullover and scarf and settled down at the table.

He walked fast, sometimes breaking into a run. He bumped into a passerby or two, stopped and apologized: *Sajnálom*, then started up again. He was gasping and sweating profusely. He felt like he was tripping over the tails of his own coat. He was on his way to meet Gyuri, behind Hotel Europa, across from the Romanian tourist office. He was late. All morning he had tried to reach Tiberius in Timișoara, but the lines had been too crowded. There had been a busy signal the entire day.

Ion liked to be punctual. He looked at his watch again. There was no longer any need to run: he could already see Hotel Europa;

it was drawing closer like a huge blue and white ship. There were more people than usual on the sidewalk, even in the street itself. Traffic was at a standstill. No buses were getting through. Three police cars had blocked the entrance to the hotel. Something had obviously happened. The crowd was looking up. At the sky? They must have seen a flying saucer, Ion said to himself, without so much as a smile. But no, they were looking at something lower down, at the roof of the hotel. Pointing to a spot between the satellite dish and the air duct shaped like a ship's funnel, where a stout, almost obese man was standing in his undershirt and pajama bottoms. Ion took up position on the opposite sidewalk, where he could get a better view. The fat man had a rifle, which looked as if it had been fitted with telescopic sights. But he neither was nor had been shooting. Maybe it's not the same guy, Ion thought, losing patience. With all its layers, the story is starting to seem like something out of the *Thousand and One Nights*. Instead of keeping his appointment with Gyuri, he was staring openmouthed at a routine police operation: the arrest of a drug trafficker or some other petty criminal.

He crossed the road and took a little street that led behind the hotel. He was speed-walking, but now and then he turned his head to look back—so it should come as no surprise to hear that he bumped right into another pedestrian in a hurry: yes, exactly, it was Gyuri Farkas, with his red beard and school-boyish zeal.

"What the hell's wrong with you?" Farkas exclaimed when it became clear to him that the clumsy passerby was the same Ion he had arranged to meet God knows how many minutes ago. Their collision turned into an embrace. Farkas didn't seem at all upset that he'd been made to wait so long.

"I'm really sorry," Ion said, and he told him what had happened on the roof of the Europa.

"Maybe it's a terrorist," Farkas said excitedly. "Actually I was on my way there myself."

"Why's that?"

"Well, I waited and waited, and all the time I kept hearing someone or other talking about what had happened in Europa—I mean *at* Europa."

"*On* Europa . . ."

"And then curiosity got the better of me."

"So, what really happened?"

"No idea. You're the one who's just been there."

"I was only there for a few minutes, and I didn't talk to anyone around me. As you know, my Hungarian isn't exactly advanced . . ."

"Well, okay, let's go and see what it's all about."

Ion was of two minds whether to tell Farkas the whole story about Gagarin. It had happened more than a month earlier. He was afraid of looking ridiculous. And what proof did he have that the guy on the roof was the same as the one who . . . ?

They heard a gunshot, then another. Farkas broke into a run, followed by Ion, and they were soon at the hotel. The numerous rubberneckers, having been moved along once by the police, were back for more; curiosity had proved stronger than fear. The man on the roof fired twice into the air, without hitting anyone. Unless it wasn't him who was firing?

No, he was no terrorist. Anyhow, he could see he didn't have a chance: the police were already on the roof. A couple of them were crawling toward him, guns in hand. The fat man took off his undershirt and waved it on the end of his rifle, then collapsed under two policemen.

"I guess we ran here for nothing," Farkas said, and then suggested going for a coffee somewhere.

They went into a cramped little café where they were the only customers. Behind a velvet drape at the back, a female voice was saying:

"For God's sake, how long are you going to be in the bathroom?"

Ion had made a little progress in Hungarian, even though he didn't have the courage to speak it. So he laughed, proud to show Farkas that he had understood the sentence. Farkas was pleased about it himself. The woman shouted something again—less of a question this time, not at all sarcastic, actually somewhat threatening:

"How many times have I told you not to wash your hair in the tub!"

The two friends were in a good mood as they sat at a low table surrounded by red velvet stools. An attractive young woman appeared from behind the drape (it was green), dressed in a way that highlighted her figure—without being too revealing. The curve of her ass was extraordinarily beautiful. She brought them two cups of coffee.

"I met a guy called Georges, a Lebanese," Gyuri said. "He said you and he knew each other."

"No kidding. Here in Budapest?"

"Yes, he was with a group of people I know vaguely. Since he can't speak Hungarian, he was chattering away in French—and hardly anyone understood a thing he said. Then someone told him, 'Speak Romanian and Farkas will translate.' "

"What did he have to say that was so important? Business? Something to do with drugs?"

"No. More like women."

"Women?"

"Yes, yes—a prostitution ring, with lots of Romanian women."

"So, do you think the guy on the roof could also have been . . . ?"

"No clue. I didn't even see what he looked like."

"I did. Fat, darkish, with a face like an accordionist's."

"How could you have seen that much, with him up there on the roof?"

"I took a good look, that's all. But I also think I saw him face to face once, like we are now."

"Really? When was that?"

"More than a month ago. Tell me—" and Ion put his hand on Gyuri's wrist "—I don't suppose you've heard of someone called Gagarin?"

"The cosmonaut?"

"No, not the cosmonaut. Another Gagarin—probably the head of some gang, except that he's behind bars now." Ion swallowed hard and told Farkas the whole story. When the accordionist in the undershirt had said: "You can make contact with us," Ion hadn't protested. He had kept his mouth shut, hadn't asked: "But who are you guys? Musicians?" or something like that, whatever, just to say something. No, he'd gotten scared and hurried on to the elevator. "But that's just the beginning. I mean, Toma was already missing, and then Ferenc disappeared the very next day. No one at the hotel even remembered Ferenc—as if he'd never existed. 'What was his last name?' I asked myself. But I'd known him only as Ferenc—a puny, blondish kid, a little younger than me."

"There are a lot of Ferences in Budapest," Gyuri said.

"Sure, but my Ferenc worked at the hotel, as an elevator boy."

"And you left him in front of the elevator you'd come up on?"

"Yes, he stayed behind on the sixth floor. He said the fat guy had asked him to do something for him. I was a bit afraid. I was out of there like a shot."

"Pretty weird," Gyuri said, scratching his fiery red beard. The waitress returned with two more coffees. She leaned over to put the cups on the table and to take the old ones away. Her hip grazed Gyuri's shoulder, and he stroked her leg gently below the knee.

"And Tamás never reported for work again. He cut and ran."

"Who's Tamás?" Gyuri asked absentmindedly—maybe he was distracted by the young woman's curves.

"I told you: Toma. He's Romanian, an old schoolmate of mine."

"Ah, the one with the Albanian girlfriend." So something had sunk in after all! "There are also Albanian women in the prostitution ring I was telling you about," he added, and he took his hand off the girl's leg as she walked away with a smile. She went behind the drape again, then stuck her head back out to peek.

Gyuri's wandering mind was getting on Ion's nerves. But his friend was oblivious. He kept up the small talk, shifting from one topic to another. He didn't notice the girl looking at him, and so she withdrew behind the scenes again, disappointed. Gyuri lit a cigarette. I do the same. If Marianne saw it, she'd really chew my ear off. But she can't see what I'm doing. She can't even hear it. I've unplugged the telephone.

"Georges mentioned someone named Silvia, a Romanian woman. It's an extraordinary story."

"A campfire story," Ion added, gratuitously spiteful. Pretending not to notice the irritation in Ion's voice, Gyuri calmly began the tale. A few rather noisy people came into the café, so he was forced to raise his voice. Ion didn't have the heart to interrupt him again.

Silvia, see, was a student in geology, geography—something like that. She spent all day at University Square, shouting slogans, singing songs with the others, sometimes dancing. She had a friend, Ana, who was a nurse. She skipped class more and more often. Her boyfriend, who was studying French or Italian, wasn't too impressed by all the revolutionary agitation. In fact, he was jealous. Silvia made friends with other students who hung around the Square. She went out with them some evenings.

I've forgotten the name of the guy who was studying French or whatever. You did French too, didn't you? Well, he was pretty pissed off because of all the trouble Silvia was getting herself into. I wouldn't say he actually missed old Ceașa, but he did make some strange comments. That's what people are like—subjective.

One day—or one night, rather—he began to ask her some pretty direct questions . . . to interrogate her, you know, like the Securitate. And she told him so, right to his face . . . and, well, she ended up with a nice pair of black eyes. They only made up just before the elections.

But then the miners showed up. She was outside the school of architecture, surrounded by other students or young people, some with darker skins than others, if you follow me. They all knew the revolution was over, so they didn't do anything to antagonize the warriors from the coal face. . . It never even occurred to them to fight back, but the miners immediately understood that they were dealing with students—even if they weren't, what did it matter?—and so moved in for the kill. Silvia made a dash for cover a little way off, but she didn't have time to reach safety. A club smashed into her head, then another: she fell flat on her face. A couple of hours later, when the ambulances arrived, she showed no signs of life. They packed her straight off to the morgue, along with a few other corpses. Why waste time taking her to the hospital?

Silvia pieced all of this together only after the fact, based on what people told her and what she was able to reconstruct on her own. She certainly got nothing out of Ionel, the guard at the morgue, because after what happened the poor guy went out of his mind and had to be kept under lock and key. He was known to have some gruesome habits . . . he'd actually been caught once before, but how he'd wept and wailed! "Don't throw me out into the street, I swear I won't do it again!" Everyone had felt sorry for him—even the Party secretary.

Lying there on the slab, Silvia was as beautiful as an icon. Ionel was supposed to put her in cold storage, but he looked long and hard at her, eyes filled with longing. He kissed her face, her cheeks, her lips. He put his thumb in her half-open mouth to feel her teeth. Then he pressed the palm of his hand against her firm but welcoming abdomen. Her thighs were parted slightly . . . it was like an invitation. Ionel's eyes clouded over. He couldn't resist much longer. Hot blood rose to his head—and elsewhere. He pulled the slab into a corner and lowered his pants and shorts. For a moment he thought of undressing completely, so that he could feel the girl's whole body close to his . . . but he didn't have the nerve. He'd never gone that far before. If someone came in and found him naked as a worm on the corpse, it would be pretty hard to find a plausible excuse.

He entered her with a sigh, more of excitement than pleasure. After a few minutes, he felt the body stir beneath him and, looking into the girl's eyes, saw something that suggested life—perhaps more. Bewilderment, terror, pleasure: a strange mix of sensations, in each of their bodies. In Ionel's head, however, it was terror that finally got the upper hand. He froze for a while, then tried to withdraw from the body. He saw its lips move, saw one arm rise to encircle his neck. The legs and thighs too were trying to hold him inside. Ionel pulled away screaming and, his pants around his legs, made a dash for the door.

Silvia didn't revive immediately. After Ionel broke loose and ran, she fell back into a coma. In fact, she remembered nothing of the rape scene later—not even a distant echo, like the next morning after a dream. No, she had to piece it all together herself, adding a few details of her own invention . . . and embroidering still more as she told the story again and again. What's certain is that, when the other guard, Vasile, heard Ionel's screaming, he ran into the room and went to take a closer look at Silvia. She seemed a stiff like any other—or rather a young female corpse, superb but lifeless. He put his hand on her belly, touched her sex, toyed with it a little, and only then noticed a glimmer of life in her eyes: yes, her lashes definitely fluttered a few times.

Vasile kept his wits about him. He'd seen some peculiar things in his time, and he'd certainly heard the expression "apparent death" before. He was also a nice old man, Vasile. After covering her body with some scrubs, he went to call a doctor, or at least a nurse. The girl tried to raise her head but lost consciousness again. When she came round, a nurse had just given her an injection. A doctor arrived too. Vasile waved his hands around as he explained all the details. Only Ionel was missing: the man to whom Silvia owed her life, in a manner of speaking, was locked up in the Central Hospital.

Silvia would have liked to visit him, but she couldn't find out where he was being held. It's true that she didn't insist too much. She was a little ashamed to tell people that she owed her resurrection to him, that instead of sticking her in the freezer he had . . .

Eventually Silvia left for Cluj with Dr. Iroşeanu, where he had some relatives. It was there that she met Georges.

Gyuri seemed delighted with his story. Ion looked out the window, wrapped up in thoughts of his own.

The telephone is ringing.

I end the previous chapter with the ringing telephone and prepare to start a new one. I press my jet-black ballpoint into the white sheet of paper. Ringing telephone? How's that possible? Didn't I write earlier (black on white!) that I'd unplugged the thing? That's really careless. I get up from the chair, then sit down again and leaf through the pages I've already written. I find the place where I explicitly mentioned the plug, where I was lighting a cigarette and worrying about how Marianne would have reacted. After all, it's not long since I gave up smoking. Should I erase the sentence, which creates an intolerable contradiction for the reader, and resolve to pay more attention to such details in future? They may not seem so important at first sight, but they can weigh heavily in the scales of verisimilitude ... I hesitate. Yes, the public is all too used to lugging those scales around wherever they go. I mean, most adult readers carry a pair over their shoulders or have one hanging from their waists at all times ... So I need to be precise.

How can a telephone ring if is has been unplugged? Marianne is undoubtedly right to accuse me of being unserious, of shying away from sustained effort and self-discipline.

It rings again. This time it sounds clearer than usual: not yet the music of the spheres, as in Spielberg's movie about aliens, but pleasant nevertheless. Besides, let's not exaggerate. That was hardly music of the spheres. Sounded more like a few notes from Béla Bartók. Or Zoltán Kodály.

What to do? Shall I go and pick it up? Shall I allow myself to speak into a phone that's been unplugged, that's lifeless, deprived of electrical current, therefore in blatant conflict not only with the science behind Bell's century-old invention but with the elementary logical principle that every effect must be preceded by a cause? The telephone is ringing—that's the effect. What happened before it started ringing? It was removed from its plug. Could that be the cause? Could it be ringing because I unplugged it? If that's the case, there's no point in deleting that earlier sentence of mine. What's written is written!

I feel my head spinning like a telephone dial. The ringing's stopped. All's quiet now. All I can hear is the whistling of the wind as it stubbornly strips the last leaves from the trees.

Ion was scouring the streets of Budapest for Maria. After Gyuri Farkas's story, he got it into his head that Silvia was really Maria. But was Georges the Lebanese really the Lebanese George he'd gone to college with? Ion tried to remember his surname, but none of the Arabic syllables that came to mind sounded quite right: Habib, Habache, Saddam, Aziz, Arafat . . . Nonsense!

Zsuzsa had left him and gone to stay with some friends or relatives, he wasn't quite sure which, in Cluj or Tîrgu Mureş or somewhere else in Romania; she was planning to go from there to Timişoara. She liked to travel: to move around, as she put it. Her student love hadn't exactly tied her to the bed, but Ion had been quite upset nonetheless, and had reproached her, not too harshly, for substituting her *Reisefieber* so soon for the fever of love. Zsuzsa had smiled inappropriately and remained silent. She might at least have waited a little for him to leave first, he said, without appreciating that the one thing she couldn't do was wait patiently for him to pack his bags and abandon her. So she went away and left him to make himself at home in her apartment.

"When you decide to leave, lock the door and put the key in the mailbox."

Ion tried to make their farewells as emotional as possible, but Zsuzsa laughed in his face. She kissed him maternally on the forehead and closed the door behind her. Ion sat motionless in the armchair with his eyes on the door. After a while he began to feel hungry, so he hopped up and did a few jumping jacks to get his circulation going. The fridge was full: Zsuzsa had stocked it with all kinds of things, enough to last him a week, even two if he was careful—or perhaps longer, until she returned. He realized then that he'd forgotten to ask her about that little detail: roughly when, that is, she expected to be back. Most likely he wouldn't have gotten a clear answer. But he still could have tried . . . directly or indirectly.

"Call me before you come back, so that I can give you a proper welcome."

But no, nothing like that. He had just stared at her sadly, with his calf's eyes, as she haughtily picked up her suitcase and paused for a moment at the door, just long enough to flash him a little sign, at once amiable and ironic, a farewell gesture of consolation and encouragement, before she stepped out and gave a sharp pull on the doorknob. The telephone is ringing.

This time I jump up, rush down the stairs, and pick up the receiver. I hear a metallic grating sound, then some piercing, shrieking, eardrum-bursting whines, and at last a faraway voice formulating a question. I know this from the interrogatory tone, but I have no idea what language I'm hearing, or what the words might mean . . .

"Who do you want to speak to?" I ask, first in Romanian, then in French.

I also know how to say it in German, English, and Italian—even in Russian. No answer. I hear a click, then nothing. Not even a tone.

Ion poured himself a glass of buttermilk and drank it quickly. When he took the glass from his mouth, it left a white mustache behind. He didn't wipe it away—either with the back of his hand or with a paper towel. He went to look in the mirror, suddenly happy. He forgot Zsuzsa, thought of Maria—or, to be more precise, of the girl taken to the morgue as a corpse and saved by the perversion of one of the guards.

It would almost make a sort of sense that she's become a prostitute, since it was sex that brought her back to life. Why shouldn't she feel grateful to her savior? Besides, can you really talk of rape when no compulsion was used, when the girl's will or consciousness didn't even enter the picture? Medical science might even draw a valuable lesson from the experience, by concluding that sex should be used in future as one means of verifying the "appearance of death." Don't lifeguards try to resuscitate people through mouth-to-mouth contact—as intimate as the most passionate, erotic kiss? And no one is scandalized by that.

And yet. A prostitute offers her body not out of gratitude but as part of a commercial transaction. So maybe Maria's career change needed a different explanation—though not, Ion was convinced, a venal one. No, she was prostituting herself because of a near-mystical fascination with the opposite sex. In the past, although certainly aroused by a man's touch, she had always needed the emotional pretext of love. During the events in the Square, however, she became a little more available—hence Ion's jealousy, and hence too the consequences of his jealousy.

He took a small fat Debrecen sausage from the fridge and bit into it with gusto. Gyuri had promised to put him in touch with Georges. Ion hoped that something would come of this—otherwise, he'd be on his way sooner rather than later. He'd already bought his train ticket: Budapest—Vienna—Munich. Still chewing eagerly on the sausage, he looked around for some bread. All he could find were a few stale slices. It doesn't matter. Ion is capable of buying bread himself.

The idea of Vienna suddenly excited him. Then a bit of sausage went down the wrong way and got stuck. He coughed as hard as he could, turning red, then poured himself a glass of water and drank it. And after Vienna, Munich! But that's as far as he got. He put the rest of the sausage back in the icebox and went to brush his teeth.

The frame for beating carpets was still there, out in the yard, standing up to the days and the years with dignity. It was rarely used, except by a couple of pensioners, although on public holidays, or during spring-cleaning, other families might also come down and hang their carpets, furs, or skins on it—or so Ion imagined. In any event, during the two months he'd been living there, Ion had only once, on a Sunday morning, seen that old couple drag a proper carpet out and drape it over the lowest rung, looking around, frightened or embarrassed, as if performing a shameful ritual they were unable to give up. But usually they only had enough strength to bring out small rugs, or sometimes an overcoat or a torn fur.

Ion went into the street, shivering beneath a coat that didn't give him adequate protection. He should have thought to put on a thick sweater as well—or maybe two. Plus his jacket. He was crossing the boulevard when he thought he spotted Georges from behind, in the human tide flowing toward the opposite sidewalk. He recognized him from his thick red neck, and from the thicket of wavy black hair that lay over it like a crown. Ion quickened his pace. He bumped into an old woman, who began to scream as if he'd cut her throat—she went on and on. He glanced over his shoulder as he sped along and saw that she was the same lady as on that previous occasion: the madwoman with the goat's face. He accelerated: *Sajnálom!* He was gasping by the time he caught up with Georges and grabbed him by the arm.

Georges didn't have time to chat: he was going to an important meeting. They arranged to meet the next day, at Hotel Europa.

"Is that where you're living?" Ion asked uneasily.

"I'll tell you all about it," Georges answered in his excellent, if accented, Romanian.

Punctual as always, Ion entered through the hotel's revolving door as a heavy man in a great hurry pushed him from behind. Georges was lolling about on a sofa in the lobby, sitting between two gorgeous creatures: one fair-haired, the other a redhead; or at least they looked gorgeous from a distance. Georges asked him to take a seat; Ion found himself next to the grinning redhead.

"Let me introduce you to Bojena. She was born in Sarajevo, but she's mostly lived in Trieste and Paris. You can speak to her in French," Georges said in French. "And over here is Hanka, from Krakow."

Ion nodded awkwardly to the left and right. He felt Bojena's not-inconsiderable thigh pushing up against his own—a position that didn't seem to bother her one little bit.

"You're off to a good start," Georges said, this time in Romanian. Ion didn't know what to say. He tried to take up as little room as possible, his knees close together and his elbows pressed against his sides, but he soon realized this was absurd and did his best to relax. He even extended one arm around Bojena's shoulder, resting it nonchalantly against the back of the sofa. He cleared his throat, as if about to make a speech.

"I'm going to Vienna," he said offhandedly in French. "And from there to Munich."

He tapped his jacket pocket to suggest that the ticket was inside, but Georges wasn't looking at him, perhaps not even listening. He got up suddenly and scurried over to the elevator, where another blonde, probably of the peroxide variety, was emerging. She didn't seem too pleased to see him.

"Where are you from?" Bojena asked Ion, her voice somewhat gruff. She put her hand on his knee; it was a little too large, with bright pink, scalded-looking flesh and long, brick-red, varnished nails. The Polish woman, for her part, took a mirror and some lipstick out of her handbag.

"Bucharest," Ion replied.

Bojena gave an understanding nod, and her hand pressed down more firmly.

"I like you," the Bosnian woman declared, apropos of nothing. She didn't even smile. "Come with me!"

Spending his foreign currency on a woman didn't much appeal to Ion. He shook his head and made as if to stand up. The Bosnian understood at once and began to laugh. Her strong hand dug into Ion's thigh and prevented him from getting to his feet.

"Georges told us about you—he said you were his friend. For you it's free."

Ion let out a laugh, relieved. But he still didn't feel like it. All he could really think of was finding Maria, so he swallowed hard and asked Bojena if she'd ever heard of her . . . a Romanian girl.

"A Romanian, yes, but she isn't called Maria."

"What is she called?"

"Silvia. And she's the boss's right arm."

The Polish woman, who was following the basic drift of the conversation, nodded to confirm what Bojena had said.

"Silvia. Silvia."

Ion was disappointed, but he wouldn't give up.

"I guess that's what she's called now. It's her *nom de guerre*."

"*Guerre*?" The Pole wasn't too hot at French.

Bojena didn't know the expression either and suddenly seemed upset.

"War? What are you talking about? We make love, not war."

And she was proud of this retort.

Georges reappeared then, towing the blonde from the lift. He had a satisfied look, like someone who has fulfilled his duty to the letter. Ceremoniously, he introduced Natasha from Kiev, who didn't offer the slightest attempt at a smile. Her face was creased with anger.

"Ask him. He knows more than we do," Bojena said.

"What's up?" the Lebanese enquired, and he suggested that they all go to the hotel bar.

With a glass of whisky in front of him, Ion repeated his question to Georges. Had he perhaps known Maria while he was in Bucharest?

"There are so many Marias," Georges replied sardonically.

"Maybe so. But I was with one of them, not all," Ion said, annoyed.

The girls were talking among themselves, in a kind of pidgin Russian sprinkled with words from each of their own languages.

"What do you want to know, exactly? Come on, out with it. Don't strut around like a painted crow." This peculiar expression—peculiarly Romanian—suggested that Georges was almost as comfortable with Ion's language as with French or Arabic.

Ion wasn't thrown by the Lebanese's linguistic talents and looked him straight in the eyes: "The girl who's working for you, the Romanian . . ."

"Well, what about her?"

"What's her name?"

"Silvia."

"Not Maria?"

"She said it was Silvia."

"Maybe she was lying."

"How should I know?" Georges laughed, finishing his whisky. "And it doesn't interest me one bit. Shall we have another round? It's on me."

Ion didn't answer. He raised the glass to his lips but didn't drink. He reached out and took Georges by the wrist with his free hand.

"Could I see her with my own eyes? To make sure she's not Maria."

"No, you can't."

"Why not?"

"She's left for Vienna."

"You mean you let her go?"

"It was me who sent her, together with Karim. To get the lay of the land."

Ion went on holding his glass of whisky. Georges wasn't joking. His voice was sharp: it brooked no contradiction. There was no point persisting, then. Ion lowered his eyes. Under the table he glimpsed Bojena's huge thigh; she had taken off her shoes and pulled her skirt up high. She looked happy, relaxed.

Ion left Budapest just in time.

Here's an article printed beneath the banner headline: AUS-TRIA CLOSES ITS EASTERN FRONTIERS.

Imitating its neighbors to the west, Austria is gradually shutting the door on the "poor" of Europe. Beginning this morning at 0:00 hours, Vienna reintroduced visa requirements for Polish citizens for a period of at least six months and sent 1,500 soldiers to the Hungarian border to stem the flow of foreigners—especially Romanian nationals—who are crossing illegally into the eastern part of the country at the rate of two hundred a day . . .

The stated justification for these measures is that the Austrian authorities have been unable to solve the problems raised by illegal immigration and the resulting black market by any other means.

The number of asylum-seekers has increased in recent weeks, and the refugee camp at Traiskirchen, where more than three thousand Romanians are currently housed, is full to overflowing.

VIENNA'S DECISION EMBARRASSES BUDAPEST

Hungary too is afraid of finding itself with many thousands of Romanian refugees on its hands, but at the same time wants to avoid a further worsening of its relationship with Bucharest . . .

After the fall of Ceausescu, Romanians are coming to be seen as Europe's plague-carriers. One by one, the formerly "fraternal" countries have introduced new restrictions to prevent a massive influx of "economic refugees" from Romania. The only exception has been Budapest, which fears the reprisals that might be taken against the Hungarian minority in Romania. Rejected everywhere else, Romanian refugees will inevitably find themselves heading for Hungary.

The situation is critical, said the Hungarian interior minister. We are hemmed in. It is inconceivable for us to close our borders with Romania. Nor is it possible to turn away all refugees indiscriminately, as there are certainly many ethnic Hungarians among them.

One far-right Austrian paper described the Romanians as "the yids of today's Europe."

A hunt for "moles" is under way in Germany. Former spies for the GDR are now coming to light. Tiedge, the best known of them, has taken refuge in the Soviet Union. Before he left, he was apparently offered sanctuary by the Syrian, Libyan, and Iranian secret services (according to *Bild-Zeitung*).

The monument to the Warsaw ghetto has been desecrated. A few months ago, anti-Semitic graffiti appeared all over the Polish capital. They included: "The only good Jew is a dead Jew."

Who are eating the swans in Vienna's Prater? Romanians? Or are they Bosnian gypsies, as the Romanian embassy in Vienna claims?

The families of Soviet "technicians" serving in Baghdad were already repatriated in late August—a sign that the Soviet Union still enjoys special treatment in Iraq.

In a small town in Bavaria, a man punctured his lover's abdomen with a kitchen knife to abort her six-month pregnancy. According to police, the perpetrator was blind drunk at the time. He has only been charged with attempting to perform an illegal abortion, as the woman gave her consent and was in no way forced into it.

Also in Germany, two black American soldiers were stabbed on Wednesday night. According to witnesses, the attackers were eight Turks, who managed to escape by car.

Yugoslavia is sinking into a nationalist fever. Torn apart by the hatred of its own peoples, it has virtually ceased to exist. It is playing no role in the formation of new alliances in Europe. Yugoslavia is now no more than a name . . . Ten years after Tito's death, it is already on the brink of civil war.

On Tuesday, with more than two thousand people in attendance, the Patriarch of Moscow conducted a funeral service for the Orthodox priest Aleksandr Mena, who was killed last Sunday with an ax . . . Father Mena was well known abroad and had published several books there. Jewish on his mother's side, he was baptized as a child in the rites of Orthodox Christianity.

Bosnia-Herzegovina is falling to pieces . . .

A report on the clashes in Tîrgu-Mureş: An inquiry into the interethnic clashes in March 1990 placed the blame upon local leaders of Hungarian and Romanian ethnic organizations.

Between 1983 and 1989, four women on the payroll of Linz Hospital killed several dozen elderly people. Their trial will begin in April 1991.

Television war: The competition between U.S. television channels continues to escalate. Accused of giving too much airtime to images from Iraq, one network had no scruples about launching a patriotic tirade against its detractors.

A little religious history: The schism of 1054 divided Christendom between Catholics loyal to Rome and Orthodox churches rallying to the Patriarch of Constantinople. The fight broke out over questions of doctrine and Papal power. The Orthodox number more than one hundred million believers in Eastern Europe (Russia, Romania, Georgia, etc.) and around the Mediterranean, especially the Balkans (Greece, Serbia, Bulgaria, Macedonia, etc.). They are organized into autocephalous churches, to which four historical patriarchates must be added: Constantinople (Istanbul), Antioch (with its headquarters in Damascus), Alexandria, and Jerusalem. The role of these is now symbolic.

It would have been quite easy for him to stay on the train, cross-legged in his compartment with a book on his knees, and continue reading peacefully until he reached Munich. It would have been a sign of character, especially since he was by no means certain that Maria was hidden behind this Silvia. Maybe Georges had been telling the truth when he said he'd never actually met Ion's Maria—or had met her but no longer remembered.

So, maybe he should go straight to Munich after all, without stopping in Vienna? But what was the hurry? No one was expecting him in the Bavarian capital. Sandu's last letter had been mailed from Jena. Sure, Mr. Fuhrmann lived in Munich, and Ion's father, Dinu, proudly claimed to have been this Fuhrmann's friend . . . they used to play backgammon together . . . But could it really be said that Mr. Fuhrmann was expecting Ion? Dinu Valea had written to him a few months ago, and Mr. Fuhrmann had been kind enough to reply that, yes, Ion could stay with him for a while. But he had also been curious to know whether the young man played backgammon at least as well as his father.

"Write and thank him," Dinu Valea urged Ion.

"And tell him you play backgammon," Marioara chipped in.

"But I'm hopeless at it," Ion said.

"What does that matter?"

Ion wrote to thank Fuhrmann, but without saying when he would arrive. Now, in Vienna, he would be able to write another letter telling him the exact date—and saying that, although he wasn't very good, he did at least know how to play the game in question. He didn't need any lessons. He even knew how to play Gul Bara, the Rosespring variant of the game. But how come Mr. Fuhrmann couldn't find a partner himself—there were plenty of Turks in Germany, after all. Ion found this Oriental mania—on the part of a Romanian German!—a little exasperating.

"Instead of going to the Square to bawl all kinds of nonsense, you'd do better to stay home and play some backgammon with me," Dinu Valea said to Ion, without really believing his son would pay attention. "At least that way you'd get some practice in ahead of time, so you don't make a fool of yourself in front of the Germans . . ."

"You're all playing with fire," Marioara warned. "Mark my words, you'll get your goose cooked one of these days."

Ion didn't waste time arguing; he just cleared out. He wasn't too convinced himself about the nonstop rally on the Square, but he didn't dare miss the daily roll call. All his friends and classmates were there—including Maria.

Before he left for Timişoara, he wrote to Sandu and asked him to reply to Tiberius's address. There was no answer. He wrote him again from Budapest. Again nothing. Hard to believe that both letters had gone astray.

So, he was in no great hurry to reach Germany. What could have happened to Sandu? The more Ion thought about it, the more worried he became. The only other address he had was for Sandu's parents, in Heidelberg. Probably Sandu was there too. He'd actually hinted at it in his letter from Jena, before the "events" in Romania: he hadn't made up his mind, but he was toying with the idea of going back to school and getting a serious degree. A student in Heidelberg!—it sounded good. But that would mean that he'd given up his dream of becoming a star athlete. What a waste of talent! as Fane Ghişoiu used to say. Ion had advised Sandu to head for Berlin: he'd written this in an aside, mainly so that he could then segue into some mention of the Wall, which had just come down. He'd felt a little nervous about doing this—Ceaşcă hadn't yet been toppled and riddled with bullets—but all the greater had been his pride at taking the risk. The revolution wasn't far off: only a few days away. It had already broken out in Timişoara.

Some people don't want to call the events of those December days a revolution anymore . . . they say the word is too pompous, given the results. Some prefer to say "plot," while others . . . well, they do their best to make the entire affair sound as ridiculous as possible. Ion didn't care for that. Even if a handful of people eventually took power, and even if they'd been planning this all along, their "plot" would never have succeeded without a mass movement behind it. It was a revolution, Ion said to himself: stolen, hijacked, but a revolution nonetheless.

Turning these ideas over in his mind, Ion left the station and headed off down the first street he happened to see. Everything was clearly in a different league from Budapest. He followed the flow of people through the streets, slightly dizzy at everything he saw. He had an address in his pocket . . . where he could go to find Karim, and, with any luck, maybe even see Maria again! The thought excited him, but he didn't necessarily find it pleasant. There was a lump in his throat. Maybe it would be best to forget her. He began to regret having gotten off the train. He looked back in the direction of the station. The train had probably left already for Germany. He'd have shown greater strength of character if he had overcome this unhealthy curiosity and continued on his journey. What did he actually *want*, in the end? To see Maria again? After he'd abandoned her in a pool of blood with her head split open? After running like a rat into some alley or other? After crossing the road and shouting some words that didn't even add up to anything?

A car came within an inch of running him over. The man at the wheel swerved at the last minute, preferring to hit the side of another car. Luckily he hadn't been going too fast.

"Gypsy boy!" the driver shouted at Ion.

He stopped in front of a shop window and put down his suitcase. Here was the slip of paper with Karim's address: Pfeilstrasse 5, and a telephone number. In his other pocket he had a letter from Georges for Karim, in Arabic script. He took it from its unsealed envelope, found it impenetrable, stuffed it back in, and pocketed it again. It was clear what he had to do: telephone Karim. But to do that he needed a few coins. Georges had generously provided him with a few five hundred schilling notes. He went to a street kiosk and bought *Die Presse*.

Karim wasn't at all surprised: Georges had already phoned him, so he was very friendly when Ion—having finally found a booth that still took coins—called him and began to speak in German. In fact, Karim spoke French very well—even better than German.

Friendly though he was, Karim told Ion not to hurry. Silvia was still sleeping.

"Ah, okay. It doesn't matter."

Ion enjoyed walking closer and closer to the center of Vienna; he didn't take a subway or bus. Now and again he put the suitcase on the ground and inspected his sore hands and swollen fingers. He went as far as the cathedral, but he couldn't go inside because of the suitcase and had nowhere he could leave it. He stared admiringly at the window displays on Kärntnerstrasse, promising himself that one day he'd stop being so afraid of everything, that one day he'd drop this penniless tourist act and at least take a look inside the legendary Demel's.

Pfeilstrasse wasn't far from the city center. He walked up to the second floor and hesitated on the landing for a long time between two absolutely identical doors: neither had so much as a tiny nameplate or label by its bell. He went up to the left door and, still holding his case, pressed on the button. The door sounded as if it was being torn from its hinges, and the accordionist from Hotel Europa stood in the open frame in his undershirt and pajama bottoms. The terrorist on the roof, the drug trafficker, whatever—I have no idea what to call him. I take my pack of cigarettes and throw it as far as I can away from me.

"*Entschuldigung!*" Ion said, pretending not to know the man from Adam. Nor did the other man show any sign of recognition. So why was he smiling beneath his mustache?

"*Entschuldigung!*" Ion repeated, and turned on his heel.

The trafficker didn't shut his door. He squinted and watched contemptuously as Ion went to his neighbor's. Or perhaps he was sizing him up. Ion had a worn overcoat that was too long for him, and his shoes were scratched. The man in the undershirt waited for him to press Karim's bell. He didn't move: perhaps he was wondering what a bum like this could be doing there. Too much of a sap to be for real? Suspicious? Could the other guys have sent him?

Ion didn't have the courage to turn round, although he felt the man's stare like a claw on his neck. He rang the other bell with all the force he could muster. The door opened at once, as if the young man who now stood before Ion had been watching all the time through his peephole. This was Karim: tall, handsome, with Oriental, Semitic features, but not too pronounced, just enough so that you wouldn't think he was Italian, Croatian, or Greek. Ion introduced himself and Karim flashed a row of gleaming white teeth. He opened the door wide, in an exaggerated gesture of welcome, and bowed with a vaguely feminine elegance. Maybe it was meant ironically. Ion felt uncomfortable: he was thinking of the accordionist, or the trafficker. He still couldn't work up the nerve to turn and look back; he was sure the man was still there, watching. Ion kept his eyes fixed on Karim, who not only looked pleased to see him, but was showing him special consideration: bows, smiles, soothing glances. Hard to imagine him exchanging winks with the guy across the way. Although it's true that looks are here and gone in a flash, like thoughts—the eye is the nimblest of all organs. And Ion had no real reason to trust this romantic lead from Beirut or wherever it was he came from. He could be something other than Lebanese, after all, and Ion wouldn't be able to tell the difference.

"Come in! Welcome!" Karim said once again, in perfect French. Ion glanced rapidly over his shoulder and saw that the accordionist had finally shut his door.

"I got the wrong door," Ion began.

"That can happen."

"There's no way to know . . . no cards, no names."

"We try to be discreet." Karim smiled, and his teeth were whiter than you'd see in a toothpaste commercial. Maybe they're false, Ion thought, leaving his suitcase in a corner of the hall.

"Come, I'll show you your room."

At that moment a young woman appeared, wearing a fairly transparent white silk nightdress.

"Silvia," Karim said, with the same sweeping, formal, slightly over the top gesture.

Ion recognized Sonia and gave a smile of relief. It was Sonia, not Maria. She put her arms round his neck, in the most natural way imaginable. Karim smiled without moving, like a master of ceremonies—no, like a photographer, or rather a cameraman waiting for the director's command, action! before starting to shoot.

Ion kissed her on both cheeks. She took the opportunity to press her lips to his mouth, though not too insistently: a kiss as in the American films of old.

Sonia had joined their group late, introduced by Valeriu, I think. She said she was studying fine arts—maybe she was. One day she had shown up with a folder full of revolutionary posters, not very good ones. She wanted to send them to France, where she'd heard that a poster exhibition about the Romanian revolution was being organized. "What revolution?" Valeriu had sneered. The others had been more indulgent, or simply more polite. "Come on, let's focus on the important issues . . ."

Once she went to an impromptu party at Ion's place, and two days later she came back again on her own. It was a month after Maria's disappearance. She wanted him to help her draft a letter in French, to be sent ahead of, or together with, her drawings: why shouldn't she submit a few posters to the exhibition in Paris, after all? It was also rumored that the big FNAC bookshop there was going to publish an album of the best images. So, Sonia had gone to see him *after* the day of the miners.

Ion pulled away from her embrace, still a little suspicious. The girl watched his expression.

"What are you doing here?" he asked, as if he didn't know.

Sonia didn't answer. Nor did Karim allow them to have a proper conversation. He picked up Ion's suitcase and banged it into the door facing them, pushing it open.

"Come on, I'll show you your room." He was still speaking French, but Ion wasn't sure that he didn't understand Romanian too.

Sonia didn't answer Ion's question, nor did she seem overeager to talk about her life.

I go downstairs and look for Sonia's counter on my map. I can't find it . . . there's no sign of it; it isn't with all the others in my less and less crowded Bucharest, and isn't anywhere else that I can see either. Maybe I never made one for her—never thought she'd end up being so important. I go upstairs again, get a pair of scissors, and cut a piece out of a visiting card, large enough for me to write SONIA in capitals and a tiny Silvia in brackets next to it. After a brief fling with Roger (less than a week, since the trucker had to leave for Turkey and couldn't stick around in Bucharest), Sonia met Dr. Iroșeanu. One evening, after drinking more than screwing, the doctor said to her, with well-meaning cynicism: "Why don't you go to Budapest, like all the other girls with a bit of class? You're not cut out for Istanbul!" It almost sounded like a compliment. She was in the doctor's bed in Cluj when he said it. The next day he called Georges.

I go down to the hall with the freshly made counter and stick it on a pin straight into Vienna, next to Ion's. I forgot to make one for Karim as well. And what about his neighbor, the accordionist? Aren't there getting to be too many characters?

By the way, the whole story about the miners and the morgue was invented by Dr. Iroșeanu, who had more imagination than he knew what to do with, and maybe even some literary talent. He'd written a number of short stories, even published a few in various journals. Unfortunately, he didn't have the time to spend on literature. When he wasn't at the hospital, he was at a bar drinking. And, when he wasn't at either, he was in bed with a member of the opposite sex, regardless of age, creed, or culture. To tell the truth, however, Dr. Iroșeanu didn't fabricate absolutely *everything* in his wild stories. He took inspiration from reality, which, as everyone knows, is richer than any writer's imagination. Having read a short news item in the paper, he retold it—slightly exaggerated—to Sonia and then to Georges, on whom it made a very strong impression. With the consummate skill of the postmodern narrator, the doctor refrained from revealing his source to the Lebanese, who, when Sonia was introduced to him, asked: "Is this Silvia?" The doctor didn't reply, just blinked his eyes—once, twice, three times—lingering so long over each blink that it was hard to imagine they would ever open again. To give even more weight to this affirmative movement of his lashes, he leaned toward Georges and inclined his high forehead, which baldness had extended to the back of his head.

Sonia didn't dislike the name "Silvia": it sounded more Western. And she liked being in Georges's arms even more. When she left for Budapest with him, she hugged Dr. Iroșeanu quite effusively and whispered in his ear: Thank you.

He dreamed of Maria all night long, and then once more toward morning. She was laid out on a slab in a glass-domed lecture hall that resembled a huge greenhouse. Her eyes were shut . . . but, if Ion looked more carefully and ignored all the birds at the top of the giant cage, where light flooded in and gave them hope of flying into the deep blue that weighed on the trapdoor in the dome without ever breaking or melting it down, that is, if he didn't allow himself to be distracted by the winged creatures that often flew down and circled over Maria and himself, giving out little cries of frustration and sometimes forcing Ion to drive them off with his arm, if he succeeded in concentrating on the girl's naked body and pallid face, it seemed to him now and again that she opened one eye or the other, as if to check that he was still there, on watch, amid the eagles, ravens, parrots, cranes, and other much smaller and noisier avifauna.

He went up to the white slab and moved his hand over her thigh; the skin was warm to his touch. Not the skin of a corpse, Ion said to himself, and then he felt the claws of a bird as it landed fearlessly on his hunched shoulders. He struggled to shake it off while the creature tried to peck at his skull; it was a raven, as big as an eagle and as stubborn as a mule. He picked up the sickle lying at the foot of the slab and struck out at the raven. It unstuck itself from his shoulder blades and beat its wings in a vain, desperate attempt to fly away, but the sickle had already cut too much away. The bird fell down cawing. In response to this dying appeal, another ten ravens swooped down onto Ion, who wielded his sickle like a scimitar, defending himself heroically. Black feathers drifted like dead leaves onto Maria's body and little by little covered it over entirely.

Now Ion heard Maria breathing regularly behind him. He grabbed a crowbar, which, being thicker at one end and a little bent, looked like a cross between a grapnel and a hammer. Whirling it around in both hands, he lunged into the birds again: there were even more of them than before, but they were still unable to get the better of him. Maria climbed down from the slab and crouched by his feet for protection, but her arms round his waist proved somewhat of an encumbrance. Our brave fighter no longer had the same mobility. Probably out of fear—why else?—Maria clung to Ion with all her might, and eventually forced him to his knees. He was still swinging his weapon against the winged flood when he felt the girl's hands, and then her lips, exploring every corner of his body. He turned away from the battle for a moment to save his eyes from an eagle's intrepid beak, and suddenly saw that it was Sonia pressing her lips to his mouth and holding him fast with her arms and legs.

Sonia had become a real expert in the art of love, thanks to the school of the Middle East. Her erotic technique was simply masterful. Her body now had something snakelike about it, while her mouth had become a cupping glass, her sex a flesh-eating flower. I feel an immense pleasure coursing through me from head to toe. I open my eyes amid the clicking of the typewriter. The telephone is ringing. This time it has every right to—I plugged it back in a little while ago. I lift the receiver. I don't know how I got down the stairs. I'm shaking and swaying. Dazed.

"What were you doing? Sleeping in broad daylight?" It's Marianne. Reprimanding me.

My mouth feels furry, my lips sticky. Only my ears are working—more or less. I bell like a rutting stag.

"What's the matter with you? Are you sick?"

"Ooo, hoooo . . ."

"Do you want me to call Dr. Gachet? If you can't even fucking . . ."

With great difficulty I manage to unstick my lips and breathe through my nose.

"No, noooo . . ."

"What's going on over there? Are you . . . with someone?"

Marianne is getting suspicious. I can hear the little viper coiled inside her purest French voice.

"No. Yes."

"What's with the forked tongue? What on earth's the matter?"

Her voice has become downright anxious. I make a supreme effort to pull myself together.

"I'm alone. Who do you think I'm with? My characters?"

"A little party for the author and his characters," Marianne says sardonically. "So, are you getting anywhere?"

"Who with?"

"What do you mean who with? The novel . . . Or whatever it is you're writing."

"Yes, yes."

Now her voice gets a little more tender—even frisky, if that's not overstating matters . . . I recognize the tone. It's a good sign.

"And aren't you missing us?"

"Of course I am."

"I'll mail you a cassette. I recorded the Siamese. I couldn't shut him up: he was meowing all day. He's obviously missing you."

"Put him on."

"You mean now? You know he can't bear the telephone."

"That's true."

"Oh, yes, I nearly forgot. Smaranda dropped in to see me."

"No kidding. How did it go? I hope you didn't fight."

I seem to have regained the power of speech. I'm wondering how to light a cigarette without giving the game away.

"We got along very well, thank you."

Marianne's voice suddenly hardens:

"She told me you've been getting calls from the embassy."

"It's true. In fact, I was just about to tell you off for giving them my number here."

"Me?"

"Who else?"

"No idea."

"And how did Smaranda know about it?"

"She must have heard it from someone else. So, what did they want?"

"They wanted me to write an article about Romania."

"An article or a novel?"

"An article . . ."

"Why should you write an article if you're writing a novel? I don't get it."

"Never mind. Anyway I told them no."

"Good. You don't have time for articles too. When are you coming back?"

"Well, I still have to finish the novel."

"You can do that here. I thought you just couldn't *start* it in Paris—can't you finish it at home?"

"Just wait a little longer."

"I've arranged everything for you. Created the ideal conditions. You have a room to yourself, I tiptoe round you, treat you like a prince. What more do you want?"

"Please, just a little longer. So I can get deeper into the subject . . ."

"Or maybe I should come out there? Just for a few days. Is it still raining?"

"Cats and dogs."

"Every day?"

"Yes."

"You're lying. You think I don't watch the weather reports? Yesterday it was beautifully sunny, with just a few clouds."

"Exactly . . . and the clouds are right above the house."

"Yeah, that's really plausible!"

"Please, be patient a little longer. Ion's already in Vienna."

"Alone?"

"Yes. I mean, well . . . there's a girl there too."

"Maria?"

"No, not Maria. Sonia."

"Never heard of her. Where did you dig her up? Is she Russian?"

"You were the one who sent her to me. Don't you remember? The girl in the morgue—the one who came back to life thanks to a guard's cock."

"Nice way of talking you have. I think you do it on purpose, just to provoke me."

"Look, you were the one who cut the article out of the paper. It was news to me."

"So what? Did you have to stick it straight into the novel?"

"No, but . . ."

"What are you writing anyway? Is it porn? Send me some to read, so I can get an idea . . ."

"Out of the question."

"Why?"

"Because I'm writing it in Romanian."

"You're crazy."

Marianne is really seething. After I tortured myself for so long to learn French, and she tortured herself for so long putting up with me (I've never met anyone with so little aptitude for languages!), even after I managed for better or worse to write a couple of novels in her language (God have mercy on those misbegotten books, but they're certainly in French, no one could deny it!), now I'm dropping it all, eh? and reverting to that Danubian dialect, that ragtag and bobtail language, that low slang of bandits and homicidal shepherds . . .

"Calm down!" I say, summoning up my last reserves of dignity. "You're talking about my mother tongue after all."

"You call that a mother tongue! Any kid can learn that screwball language! It has no rules worth speaking of! It should be banned!"

I'm at a loss. It's harder to pacify her at a distance. I promise to speed up, to work night and day and then hurry back to Paris. I promise her the moon and the stars.

"There's another letter for you," she says, as if to change the subject.

"Also from Mihai?"

"No, that's the old one."

"So what are you waiting for? Are you going to send it to me?"

"There's also one from somebody called Gagarin."

"Gagarin?"

"That's right. Do you know him?"

"No. It doesn't matter. Mail it to me anyway."

"I'll send everything off today. Well, guess it's good-bye. And don't be angry about all the things I said."

"Don't worry, I'm not angry. I've forgotten them already."

"Really?"

"A kiss and a hug!"

I hang up and go back upstairs thinking of Gagarin. Obviously he's not in jail like the accordionist claimed. But why's he writing to me? To threaten me? How? What can he do? He has no power over me. Does he want to buy me? Propose a deal? And why doesn't he just call here? Maybe that was him calling a little while ago. Or someone on his behalf—a secretary . . .

I sit at the table, intending to finish the chapter about the morning when Sonia came and started running her hands over Ion while he lay asleep in his room. She did everything necessary and ended up on top of him. Ion sighed with pleasure, shouted out loud. Then Karim woke up, ran into the room, and saw them together.

"Excuse me!"

No, I can't write. I can't get Gagarin out of my mind. Maybe he has plans to harm Sonia in some way, or, worse still, Ion. Then he'll really have me under his thumb. I go downstairs again to call Marianne. I'm lucky: she's still at home.

"Me again! Please, would you mind opening that letter."

"Mihai's?"

"No, you can throw that one out if you want. The other one."

"From Gagarin?"

"Yes, Gagarin. Open it and read it to me."

"Wait, I'll just get a knife. It's taped shut."

I hear her cut open the envelope. Rustling paper, almost metallic, then her voice, dismayed.

"I don't understand a thing. It's in Russian."

"*Merde!*"

"See? You'd be better off back in Paris."

"Can I ask you a real favor, then? Please go and mail it right now. Kiss, kiss."

Ion lay down again, exhausted. The birdcage was also a fish tank: fish, eagles, and ravens all cohabiting. Maria had come back to life, only now she was a mermaid. Ion tried to catch her, to grab her by the tail, but he couldn't manage it. She slipped from his grasp and swam off laughing. Ion pumped his legs as hard as he could to catch up with her, but how can you keep up with a mermaid? At one point he thought that he didn't have enough air, that he was in danger of suffocating, of drowning—but this was clearly nonsense. He clung to an eagle, which bore him up to the area directly beneath the dome. The sky had clouded over. In fact it was raining. The fine drops fell softly onto the thick glass pane covering everything. He didn't hear it. Night was descending, ever so slowly.

Sonia, propped up on an elbow, watched him breathe in and out. He was snoring gently—perhaps dreaming, she said to herself.

He wrote to Mr. Fuhrmann telling him that he would arrive in a few days. He didn't want to be more precise—which in my view was asking for trouble, a good way to alienate his German bene-factor. Still, at least he wrote something—in German no less! He thought this would come as a big surprise, but it was possible that Mr. Fuhrmann considered it natural for anyone who wanted to travel around Germany to have learned German first. Besides, Fuhrmann had no idea what Ion had been studying at univer-sity: he might think he'd been a German major, in which case the occasional grammatical error in Ion's letter—especially the wrong noun cases after a preposition—might really get on the old man's nerves: so this is the kind of German they taught you under Ceausescu, eh? . . . after you'd sold off the Saxon Germans and the Jews! So, in actual fact, it wasn't impossible that Ion's Ger-man would have exactly the opposite effect. Maybe he'd have done better to write in Romanian—or best of all to send a telegram with his date of arrival stated clearly. You don't need to know which case goes with which preposition in order to write a telegram. Just your date of arrival. Conciseness and punctuality.

Ion had been in Vienna for more than a month, doing nothing special: killing time, playing the tourist, strolling around town. Georges had probably told Sonia and Karim to take care of him. The Lebanese didn't seem jealous at all of the nights that Ion was spending with Sonia: noisy nights too, filled with moaning and shouting. He didn't give a damn, apparently. Only once, when they'd woken him up from a deep sleep, did he burst into Ion's room. He said he thought he'd heard screams and thumps and cries for help. But he left immediately, apologizing and looking confused.

One day another girl appeared, a Croatian blonde. She sat at the table, drank a schnapps that Karim offered her, and took an exaggeratedly long cigarette holder from her bag. She blew out the smoke in carefully practiced rings. Her name was Nemira and she was a Muslim: not Catholic like the majority of Croats, nor Orthodox like the Serbs. She only stayed two days. Georges phoned and ordered her to be sent to Budapest posthaste. Sonia went with her.

That day Karim and Ion decided to check out the casino. It was Karim's idea, and he had to insist quite a bit before Ion agreed. Ion didn't really have anything in particular against it . . . and, after all, Karim had been more than friendly to him (even brotherly, perhaps?). So why spoil his fun? Ion allowed Karim to pick his wardrobe from head to toe. He even agreed to wear a tie, though he couldn't stand having anything around his neck, because of his highly developed Adam's apple.

"Don't tighten it too much, leave it loose!" Karim advised, still speaking in French. Does he really not know Romanian? Ion wondered.

They got to the casino early and had no trouble finding places next to each other at a roulette table. Ion seemed a little overawed, perhaps even frightened. He was afraid of losing the pitiful sum that he'd been holding onto for dear life since arriving. He changed a five hundred schilling note into chips, and would have made do with even less if he hadn't been ashamed to face Karim. He placed his thick veiny hands over the tokens: he was in no hurry to play and preferred to watch for a while. Now and then, however, he did put a ten-schilling chip on red, before changing his mind and switching to black. It wasn't a high-risk system, and what's more he won almost every time.

"That's just tickling the cloth," Karim said rather disdainfully.

Ion didn't reply. A strange guy appeared across the table, with a big Mexican-style mustache that attracted his attention. He looked like Țiriac. Then Karim pushed forward all his remaining chips—you might say viciously. A straight up bet. The *moustachu* smiled sardonically. Ion kept right out of it this time. He was already scared enough for Karim.

"What are you doing?" he whispered to him, his voice trembling.

Karim didn't hear a word. He lit a cigarette. The croupier threw the little ball, which span round and round. Ion looked in fascination at the pile of chips covering Karim's chosen number: 13. It'll land on the 12: the thought flashed through Ion's head, while across the table the *moustachu* smiled and nodded, as if he could read his mind. When the croupier's voice announced 12, Ion bit his lips and watched Karim's dignified yet unsteady walk to the bar. He sat still, not daring to follow his friend, aware that it would be a mistake to try to console him. He glanced over at the *moustachu*, who gave him a nod of encouragement.

"Place your bets!" The croupier's voice was an agreeable baritone.

It'll land on 17, Ion thought. The man with the mustache and red tie nodded and quickly took a little piece of board from his breast pocket; a huge number 17 sprawled across it. Ion's arm was shaking as he pushed a humble chip toward the square with the number 17.

"Seventeen *plein*?" the croupier asked, and Ion, stretching his arm interminably, nodded yes.

It landed on 17. Ion's chip multiplied at a vertiginous rate beneath the croupier's nimble fingers. And he left them where they were, on the same number. Ion was numb with emotion, unable even to feel pleased about what had just occurred. He avoided the croupier's eyes, though the man was—quite naturally—trying to determine what Ion's intentions were for the next bet . . . What should he do with all these chips? The *moustachu* again held up the little piece of board with the number 17. It'll land on 17 again, Ion thought. The croupier sounded more irritable than usual when he asked if Ion was playing 17 straight up.

"*Ja, siebzehn!*" Ion rapped out the syllables as though they were a military command.

The croupier bowed his head and shoulders in a submissive gesture. The *moustachu* smiled contentedly. Ion, surprised by the force of his own voice, suddenly felt at ease, fearless, without any anxiety at all, as though he was in his natural element. If he lost, it was no tragedy: he'd only be giving back what he'd just won. To be sure, four hundred schillings or so was hardly an insignificant amount given the state of his finances, but at least he wouldn't blame himself later for passing up a big win. He looked over at Karim. He certainly would have to respect Ion now . . . if he'd seen any of it. Two elderly Englishwomen hurried to place their bets on 17 too. The ball had already begun to spin, but the croupier looked away and said nothing. The man opposite kept moving his eyes between Ion and the ball.

"Seventeen," the croupier announced, struggling to maintain the required composure. He counted out the win, then placed a few large chips—probably five hundred schillings each, if not a thousand—at the base of the pile. It was certainly what they call a tidy sum. Ion tried to calculate the total, but soon lost count. The man with the mustache took out another piece of cardboard and held it in front of his forehead. Ion didn't think twice. The number 14 was already echoing in his head, louder and louder, until it was a deafening noise.

"Everything on fourteen," Ion ordered. The croupier stared at him for a few seconds, but didn't say a word. Using his rake, he transferred the pile of chips from 17 to 14. The house limit still hadn't been reached, so there was nothing he could do—there must have been 15,000 schillings on number 14, but the casino allowed bets up to 25,000.

Meanwhile, Karim had returned to the table—he'd been standing behind Ion for a little while now. He found it hard to work out what was happening, since Ion still had the same chips in front of him as when he had gone to the bar: the kid must be completely spineless. Ion hadn't seen Karim yet and was looking with some pride at his heap of chips. He glanced up and saw the *moustachu* smiling at him. Why the hell doesn't *he* place any bets? Ion wondered, feeling a tightness in his chest. And why don't the others say anything? Don't they see what he's doing? No one protests, no one asks to occupy his place instead of him—they all just keep quiet, preferring to stand on tiptoe and stretch out their arms, or else to throw their chips down from afar and beg the croupier to put them on their chosen number. Ion noticed too that a lot of other players were following his luck and gambling on number 14. Finally Karim's face lit up and he touched Ion on the shoulder.

"Are all those chips yours?" he whispered in his ear.

Ion didn't deign to answer. The Țiriac lookalike smiled mysteriously and tore the card with the number 14 into smaller and smaller pieces. Did he perhaps have other cards in reserve? Ion asked himself. He wondered why he suddenly felt more cheerful. It was a good sign!

The ball was already spinning. Ion still felt entirely impassive. Again he counted the chips remaining beneath his calm, bony fingers. More than five hundred schillings.

"Fourteen," the croupier announced, barely controlling the tremor in his voice. The *moustachu* with the red tie got up from the table and left without another glance at Ion. He was tall and sturdy. Karim, hovering to and fro, put his hand on Ion's shoulder and arm, then wrung his hands as he took a few steps back and a few more forward again. He could see that Ion had hit the jackpot. He opened his mouth to tell him something, leaning over toward his neck and ear, then changed his mind.

Ion demanded his winnings. The croupier, who had recovered his composure, skillfully formed a few piles of the largest, most valuable chips.

"You have won half a million schillings," he said, whereupon the other players, both seated and standing, sighed and groaned and began to whisper to one another. The hum of glory! "It would be best for us and yourself if you agreed to take it in the form of a check," he added stiffly.

Ion turned to Karim, puzzled, and asked him to explain what the croupier had said. After all, how could he have understood it, let alone accepted it, when he'd never in his life had such a thing as a bank account? Did Karim have one? And even if he did—well, Ion's trust only went so far.

"I want the money in cash," he said, and he took a few large chips from the pile and handed them to the croupier. The gesture had an immediate and beneficial effect. The croupier asked to be replaced and got a nice blue box from somewhere, probably one of the plastic ones where he kept the chips he collected during the game. Then he told Ion that he would accompany him to the manager's office and explain the situation. Karim and several other players went with them: a veritable procession. News of the win spread like wildfire to the other tables, and gaming activity ceased entirely for a few minutes. Covetous—or simply curious—stares followed the troop as they wound their way to the manager's office near the pay windows.

"I haven't got a bank account," Ion said, in a German that was improving all the time. "I'm just passing through on my way from Romania to Germany."

It might have been better if he'd kept that last point to himself. The casino manager experienced a powerful twitch in his lower jaw, which moved from left to right and returned to its initial position only after a few seconds of extreme effort.

"Do you have a passport?"

Ion showed his passport, which had been issued before the Austrian government decided to reintroduce visas for citizens of certain East European countries. I don't know whether the manager was up to date about that kind of administrative detail. In any case, such things didn't concern him: they were for the police and the immigration people to worry about. The manager eyed Ion up and down, comparing him with the passport photo. Yes, there was certainly some resemblance. Nevertheless, Herr Direktor picked up the telephone and called the police. Ion and Karim protested, but it was to no avail. They were asked to take a seat and wait. The manager whispered something to the croupier, who nodded vigorously and gesticulated in reply. Ion didn't take his eyes off the blue box. This time around he would have found it much more difficult to apply the well-known fatalistic, mioritic dictum: *He who has nothing, loses nothing!* Karim was cradling his head in his hands.

After nearly an hour, two plainclothes policemen showed up from the vice squad, which was also responsible for casinos. They examined Ion's passport, asked to see Karim's as well, then discussed between themselves how to proceed. They also asked the croupier a few questions in a low voice, but Ion's ear still caught several piously intoned references to the numbers 17 and 14.

Just as Ion was kissing goodbye to his half-million, the policemen gave him a sour smile and returned his passport. That meant the manager had to pay up. The blue box disappeared, and the cashier brought in a pouch stuffed with brand-new banknotes. It never crossed Ion's mind to count them—in any case, there were certainly a lot. But he asked for a plastic bag, filled it in the twinkling of an eye, then asked for another one. He sent Karim off to find a taxi.

When they got to the apartment, the accordionist appeared in the doorway opposite. After some fumbling, Karim eventually found his key and inserted it in the lock, while taking out a sheath knife that glistened like a snake's tongue with his free hand. Ion went in first. Karim followed him backwards, keeping the knife pointed at the massive shape of the neighbor, who stood there watching, calm and motionless.

Now they counted the money. It had been Karim's suggestion, his eyes gleaming with excitement.

"What's the point?" Ion had said, reluctant to open and disturb the wads of notes. "We should have done it there. It's too late now."

They were seated opposite each other on two armchairs. Karim had a look of sincere admiration. After saying a few words in Arabic—perhaps praise?—he switched to Romanian:

"And to think I took you for a sucker!"

Ion, who had suspected for a long time that Karim knew Romanian, showed no surprise. He had the inspired idea of dividing the winnings.

"If it hadn't been for you, I'd never have dreamed of going to the casino," he said, in a voice perhaps too unctuous to sound entirely convincing.

Although pleasantly impressed, Karim proudly refused the offer. Only then did Ion become afraid. The knife had disappeared into the Arab's pocket . . . but it might reappear at any moment.

"It's your dough," Karim said. "You won it fair and square!"

"I got lucky—that's all."

Ion had forgotten to mention the Țiriac lookalike, or had been afraid to. Nor had he breathed a word about those little cards. He took a bag, the one that was only half full, and held it out to Karim.

"Take it. It's your share."

"You're insulting me . . ."

The telephone rang.

"That must be Georges," Ion said.

Karim jumped up and hurried to the phone at the other end of the apartment. Ion didn't hesitate for a second. He grabbed the two bags and raced down the stairs three at a time. A taxi happened to be passing outside.

"*Zum Bahnhof!*" Ion shouted in the driver's ear.

When the mailman rings, I go down and open the door, take the envelope from his hand, and thank him. He's even more cheerful than usual. I ask myself, Why are some people so happy? as I wait for him to get back on his blue bicycle. True, it's a magnificent spring morning. He starts pedaling, upright on the seat. Only now do I notice that he's grown wings: two little ones coming out of his shoulder blades. They flutter awkwardly behind him, irregularly, without any strength. It's obvious that the poor mailman isn't in the habit of using them. You can't even say that his bike moves any faster now than when he pedaled it without wings—and when he probably found it easier to lean over the handlebars, and had less wind resistance to worry about. In fact, the wings prevent him from picking up speed. You wouldn't have thought they'd be such a handicap.

Soon I turn and go back inside. With my mind on the mailman, I'd forgotten the yellow envelope I'm still holding, the one

Marianne sent with such laudable alacrity. I should call her. But first I'll see what's in the envelope. I think I can feel the edges of a cassette. Of course, the Siamese! I get a knife from the kitchen and cut the envelope open. Apart from the tape, there's a smaller pink envelope with my name and Paris address written in Latin characters. On the back, also in Latin characters, is the sender's name: GAGARIN. The envelope has been opened already: most recently by Marianne, who, after finding to her horror that the letter was written in Russian, stuffed it back in and for some reason sealed the envelope with Scotch tape.

I go upstairs, where I know there's a Russian-French dictionary in a corner of the bookcase. No doubt the friend who lent me this place once had ambitions to learn the language of Solzhenitsyn— but soon gave up.

On the stairs I think about the mailman again. Did he always have wings, and I just never noticed it before? I can't believe that. Anyway, they must have started growing some time ago, like wisdom teeth, which need years and years to break through the surface of the gums. And the process is often painful—slow and painful. He probably suffered for a long time, without even realizing the cause of the pain. Maybe he thought he had arthritis or some disease of the spine. Did he see a doctor or just hope it would pass on its own? Was he too ashamed to get help once he saw his wing tips in the mirror? But why should he have felt ashamed? Since when has it been shameful to grow wings? Or maybe it was his co-workers who first noticed the bony excrescences coming out of his shoulder blades? When he was undressing to put on his uniform, another mailman may well have pointed to them, even reached out to touch them:

"Jesus, what have you got here?"

"It feels soft like a bunch of feathers," another added—let's call him Paul.

"Let me touch it too," Marie shouted merrily.

"Be my guest. Whatever you touch just grows and grows . . ."

"Here, let me have a feel!"

"You should see a doctor, you know," Paul said, getting on his bicycle.

They rode off in the same direction, but then one went around the forest to the right, the other to the left. But it was long before Pierre's wings became really noticeable, and certainly long before they became too big to be confused with anything else, that the two mailmen spotted the round, still object hanging in the sky. At first they tried not to mention it to each other, still less give it a name. They were pedaling slowly. Pierre was feeling the usual pain in his shoulder blades: it was dull, like a toothache. He was almost used to it by now. Again Paul urged him to see a doctor, because it wasn't normal to have a thing like that growing on you for no reason.

"I don't even know what to call it," Paul added, braking. Pierre braked too. He was a little irritated. Then he looked up into the sky and said:

"And, you know, that metal bowl up there can't possibly be a plane . . ."

"So what?"

"So, do you know what to call that wingless contraption?"

"No, I don't."

"Well then. You don't know what to call anything, do you?"

I still remember a few things from my seven years of Russian at school, back in Romania. Especially the grammar. You can look up words in a dictionary, but you've got real problems if you don't know how the sentences are constructed.

With much toil and trouble, using the dictionary for every sentence, I finally manage to decipher most of Gagarin's missive.

Gagarin was furious, above all with me. How dare I get him mixed up in such a shady business instead of letting him rest in peace—especially now, in an age he detests and is happy not to have known, since he luckily disappeared in time thanks to what was called a plane crash . . . And how dare I paint him as a gang leader, a little Mafia godfather? Don't I know he was a colonel in the Red Army and about to be promoted to general? Don't I know that, if he needs money now, it's only to help the communist party, which is falling apart, and unless something is done will soon . . . yes, soon lose all its influence? And we know who's to blame for it all, who sold our country to the American imperialists! What happened that evening at the roulette table has to be understood in that light—because under present conditions . . . Objectively speaking, what other solution is there? Can I see one? So, I shouldn't kid myself that Ion will keep the money he won—not all of it anyway. They chose him: he was a mere instrument, someone to make the whole thing possible. They chose him because he looked nicer and more naïve than some of their other options. He hardly had the nerve to start betting at the roulette table in the first place! He put one chip on red, another on black . . . People don't come much dumber than that! And, really, he was so easily influenced . . .

It would be madness to let Ion keep the money and turn him into a target for rival gangs. The accordionist is already after him, and that's *my* fault—because I wanted to make the plot more complicated, more like a thriller. But I needn't worry: he'll leave Ion with a few schillings, at least—maybe even enough to get to Paris. Isn't that what I want? In any case, he and his men aren't to blame if the Romanian student suddenly panicked and ran off like a thief and a dolt, abandoning his suitcase with all his belongings just like he'd abandoned his homeland. When he scurried out of Karim's block, the moron thought that taxi was passing by accident. Ha! An accident, my foot! Everything's planned in advance—from the top down, the very top, where the *вождъ* or is it *дождъ* . . . ? (I don't understand the word and I'm too lazy to look it up.)

When the taxi reaches the station, Ion will finally realize that the driver is none other than the *moustachu* from the casino, the man with the little cards, the one who read his mind so well (or put things into it). But, even then, he still won't know whether to be uneasy or, on the contrary . . . He'll dip into one of the moneybags, take out a wad of notes and hold some out to the driver, pretending that he doesn't know him from Adam. But, after switching off the engine, the *moustachu* will step out of the car and, showing his obliging smile and fire-red tie, ask his passenger to alight. He'll speak Romanian, though with a strong Bessarabian accent. Ion will get out, taking the plastic bags with him.

"Follow me!" the *moustachu* will say.

Ion won't have the courage to refuse. He'll feel weak all of a sudden. He'll walk robotically through the station hall, jostled by passengers hurrying in every direction. They'll be oblivious to the young man with his two plastic bags and his sturdy mustachioed companion, who walks ahead with large sure strides, not even glancing round to see if the other is following. At a certain point they'll go down some steps to the underground level.

I drop Gagarin's letter and tap my hand on a word in the dictionary lying open on the table: *уборная* (toilet). I'm getting a little worked up, losing my cool. If the letter wasn't in Russian, I'd think it was a trick Marianne was playing to get back at me for not letting her visit. Or maybe the embassy up to some monkey business? But why? What's in it for them? Are they trying to scare me off? Make me ditch poor Ion in the middle of his travels, so that he doesn't make it to the West? So that he doesn't serve as a bad example for Western readers, especially young ones? No, that's too ridiculous!

I take out the tape and slot it into the cassette player. From the first notes I recognize Schubert's Opus 100, the Piano Trio no. 2 in E flat major—my favorite trio. A nice little surprise from the Siamese? He knows how much I like the piece, which, though not completely without hope, is shot through with a dignified sadness . . . waiting-room music. However, at the very moment when the violin and cello almost cover the piano and take over with their heartrending chords, I hear the inimitable meowing of the Siamese. Schubert fades into the distance, and the cat's voice takes his place. It's a poignant, sorrowful wail, like a declaration of love mingled with bitter reproaches.

"Finish the novel and come home for God's sake!" The cat has to choke back his tears. "Stop beating around the bush, or no one will want to read you anyway . . ." Then a pause, followed by Marianne's voice likewise urging me to get a move on. It's sad and dignified. They're obviously in cahoots, I say to myself, but just when I'm about to press stop and silence them for good, I hear Schubert's wonderful andante in the second part. The funereal tones of the piano—which now outstrips the other two instruments and leads them to a point that, though inevitable, is not the absolute end—inspires me to persevere, inspires me to see things through to the finish, whatever that may be—and not with undue haste, either. In fact, when I think about it, even Gagarin wants me to go on. That's why he has no intention of harming Ion—of that I'm sure. What Gagarin can't tolerate is that my character has become a millionaire overnight. Maybe he's right . . . What will Ion do with all that dough? It would get too complicated even for me—even for this novel.

All of them are right. I must continue, though I shouldn't waste any more time on these kinds of digressions . . . nor let any more parasitical subplots and intrigues attach themselves to the story. I should get Ion onto the train to Munich, where Mr. Fuhrmann is expecting him, as quickly as possible. First, though, the *moustachu* will relieve him of most of his roulette winnings. That's no great misfortune, and anyway Ion will still be left with a heap of money. The day before, he had only one hundredth of what he'll keep if he's sensible and lets go of that plastic bag he's clinging to so tightly. It would a pity to rip it . . . And that, more or less, is how the *moustachu* will try to persuade him—without brutality, even with a certain gentleness. He'll patiently explain that it's the only natural solution: to give up part of the money that fell from the skies. Besides, did he really win it alone, without anyone's help? And, if he was willing to give some to Karim, who did nothing to deserve it except take him to the casino, why shouldn't he share it with *him*, Haiducu, who sat opposite him all the time at the table and indicated the winning numbers?

Ion will first shake, then nod his head, having seen Haiducu turn crimson, take a pistol from one pocket and lazily slip it into the other. He'll begin to move his head up and down, down and up, clearly suggesting that he's not far from acquiescence. And Haiducu will continue speaking slowly and calmly. Ion will hold out the three-quarters full plastic bag, from which he has transferred a handful of notes to the other bag, as nonchalantly as Haiducu moved his gun from pocket to pocket.

Haiducu laughed, holding his belly with both hands. Ion had loosened his grip on both plastic bags, as if to avoid losing his balance. He too was smiling, but it was a wan kind of smile. They were in a space too narrow for much cheerfulness. Ion sat exhausted in the bathroom stall. The other continued to laugh, his mouth stretching from one ear to the other. Ion held out one of the bags, from which he had meanwhile removed another handful of notes and stashed them in a pants pocket.

"Here, take it. Good riddance!" Ion said.

Haiducu stopped laughing. At exactly the same moment, his arm shot out and delivered a perfectly exquisite slap with the flat of his hand.

"So, you like playing little games, eh?" the Bessarabian asked, his voice almost as calm as before, though he was breathing a little more heavily. Ion's cheek was burning: on fire. He was so taken aback that he didn't respond in any way. Wasting no more time, Haiducu grabbed the other bag, the one now overstuffed with bills, from the student's hand.

"I've left you a lot more than you deserve," Haiducu said, a bit more edge in his voice.

Then he left the bathroom.

Ion sat there dazed for a little longer, head in hands, elbows on knees. The other moneybag lay on the floor. When Ion stood up to leave, he saw it and bent over to pick it up. Then he sat down again and started to count the money Haiducu had deigned to leave him. As he did so, he put the bills in his jacket pockets as extra padding. As Mihai would have said, every cloud has a silver lining.

He was too tired to take the train that night, so he got a room in a little hotel near the station. Unable to fall asleep, he got dressed and went for a walk around the neighborhood. He returned with a girl he'd picked up in a dark back street—a blonde with inexpressive blue eyes. She stripped in double-quick time, then took a transparent knee-length apron out of her bag, made from nylon or some other plastic material, and tied it around her waist. In front of her sex there was an opening just big enough to, well . . . She asked for her "little present" and slipped it into her bag. Ion stared at her, immobile; he'd never seen a thing like that before. The girl lay down, her legs stretched full out but pressed tightly together. She was waiting. Ion felt rooted to the spot, not knowing what to do. The creature on the bed began to wiggle one of her brightly varnished toes. She was losing patience.

"*Was wartest du noch?*" she asked. "Take your pants off."

Ion responded like a robot. He took his briefs off too, but nothing else. He even kept his jacket on. He approached the girl with his penis dangling. She asked for an extra two hundred schillings to get to work on it with her mouth. Ion shook his head vigorously. He'd rather get himself worked up.

The girl said nothing. She waited, gently moving her hips in time with Ion's hand. That helped him to get excited, and soon his friend was standing to attention. The girl opened her legs as wide as she could and raised her pelvis. She had a smile on her face.

The next morning, as he was climbing onto the express, Ion turned his head and thought he saw Haiducu at the end of the platform. He quickly jumped aboard, found an empty compartment, and sat down by the window. After a few minutes, the train gently moved away from the station.

Times does not flow uniformly: a banal truth Ion had figured out long ago. He'd even discovered another phenomenon linked to those uneven leaps in our perception of the temporal flow—a veritable hemorrhaging of being! He had discovered—and now, in the train, he had the opportunity to verify—that there are holes in time into which the thinking subject sometimes falls, as into a dreamless sleep (and inside of which he wakes up in nonbeing?), though it's not in the least a question of sleep (nor of dreams?). Well, such holes can appear anywhere, anytime. And you become aware of them only after you've left them. They are little deaths lying in wait for us, in expectation of the big one—or perhaps as the negation of it (Ion didn't know how to explain this). The most conclusive experience of time, the most spectacular, are those moments of narcosis in which time is completely annulled. These falls outside of time (if it's possible to put it like that) hit you unexpectedly, like an epileptic fit, in the street, on a streetcar, or at the office. It can even happen as you're walking up a flight of stairs: you're on the third floor and you lift your head and you see a sign saying sixth floor. So what happened between the third and the sixth?

Ion was on the train hurtling toward Munich. He was quite sure he hadn't nodded off—on the contrary, he'd been watching the landscape all the time. He was alone in the compartment . . . But then, who knows how, he woke up facing two girls in snow-white jumpers. They were laughing and laughing and passing each other a bottle of disgustingly sweet cherry brandy, unless it was some cheap red wine: there was no label. How hadn't he noticed them when he came in? Clearly he'd fallen into another hole, leaving time and reality behind. What else? He looked at his watch.

A man wearing a Tyrolese (or Bavarian?) hat, short leather pants, and a green cloth jacket opened the compartment door. He was dragging a kind of hunter's game bag, from which a bunch of feathers (probably the tip of a wing) protruded. Breathing heavily, he sat down on the same seat as the girls, with the bag next to him. *Grüss Gott!* The girls stopped laughing and returned his formal greeting. One of them, whose turn it was to have the bottle, hesitated for a moment, then took a swig and said something that Ion failed to understand. The Tyrolean decided to put his bag up in the luggage net and said something himself. The girls giggled. He smilingly accepted the bottle that the lighter-haired of the girls offered him; her hair was an implausible yellow, almost the color of rapeseed, while the other was a blonde with blue eyes, though not really all that blue. The man, who was wearing long pale-green woolen socks and thickly laced boots, first rested the bottle on his pink knee, which was crisscrossed by fine scratches. He then took a big gulp and made a face. So the bottle didn't contain red wine—as he may have thought—but a strong spirit, probably mixed with cherry liqueur or some mountain fruit extract. He handed the bottle back to the first girl, who, still laughing, tossed her golden hair and passed it on to her friend. But, instead of drinking in turn, she turned her eyes to Ion.

"Would you like some?"

Ion understood the question, but he didn't know what to do or what to say. He shook his head. The girl insisted, holding out the bottle as if it were a weapon.

"No, thanks," Ion said, and although he had kept his answer as short as possible his accent probably gave him away. He was obsessed with his accent—as if he could have done something to hide it.

The girls looked at each other, upset. They exchanged a few words in a dialect that Ion found completely incomprehensible. The Tyrolese man joined in, and a conversation developed between them that Ion made no attempt to follow. He looked out the window. The train was now quite close to the Danube: the river snaked its way along a sun-drenched valley, and on the horizon he could make out the massive bulk of a mountain range.

When he looked back, Ion saw the Tyrolean get up and pull his game bag from the net, then sit with it on his knees. The girls seemed very interested. The one by the window went and sat on the hunter's right. But if he's a hunter, why doesn't he have a gun? Ion wondered. The hunter without a gun opened his bag slowly and carefully and took out a bird that was still alive, though wounded. It was a kind of hawk or falcon with gray plumage, the feathers on its back darker than those on its rhythmically pulsating underside. Its yellow beak was desperately clicking left and right. The girl who was then holding the bottle took the stopper out, but, instead of drinking from it, tilted it towards the bird's beak, managing with remarkable deftness to bring the two into contact with each other, so that the hawk drank some of the red liquid beneath everyone's admiring eyes. The Tyrolese gave a loud hearty slap on his fleshy thigh. Without warning, the other girl put her hand into the bag and fumbled around under the falcon's belly; you could see from her look that she had found something completely unexpected and even unidentifiable. When her hand reappeared, it was holding a fish. The rape-haired girl cried out in surprise. The Tyrolese laughed and laughed, and so eventually did the others, Ion included.

Then the conductor appeared on the scene. The girl put the fish back into the bag and sniffed her fingers with disgust. The Tyrolean was still laughing, though more quietly, in hiccups. After its swig of brandy, the hawk had calmed down and its head had stopped jerking; its breathing was also more regular now, no doubt because it was in less pain. The blonde put the stopper back on the bottle, then changed her mind and took it off again. But she didn't drink any more. The conductor, who had a beard and mustache, seemed a little uneasy as he looked around the compartment. The Tyrolese fumbled in his jacket, dug out his ticket, and handed it to the inspector, who took it without paying any attention. Evidently the bird in the bag interested him more than the ticketholder did. He asked some questions about the eagle, as he called it, in an ordinary German that Ion could follow without too much difficulty. He also understood, or thought he could understand, the Tyrolese man's explanations: that the falcon had fallen into a trap, and he was taking it home to nurse it back to health and train it as a hunting bird. The conductor nodded, his beard swinging up and down; he punched the hunter's ticket, took Ion's, then punched that too. Who set the trap? There was no answer. The Danube was no longer visible. The train was skirting the side of a mountain, the sun was setting somewhere behind its wooded slopes, there was less light in the compartment, even though night had not yet fallen. The inspector asked to see the girls' tickets, but they didn't have any. Why didn't they have tickets? They didn't have time to buy them before the train left. But where did they get on? In Linz. And did they have any money? the railwayman asked in a friendly, if not jokey sort of way. No, no money either. The girls laughed, and so did the conductor. One of the girls offered him the bottle of schnapps, but he refused it with dignity. Suddenly he was serious again. The other girl stood up, tall and strong, and began to stroke the back of his uniform. He took offence: he was fifty-something, and, although his short, stocky stature somehow jarred with his carefully groomed and perfumed beard, he couldn't allow such liberties while he was on duty, especially not from passengers caught without a ticket. Didn't either of them have one? Really? The question triggered more peals of laughter. The small man now got really angry, took a step back, right onto Ion's toe. The student reacted automatically with a hefty shove, and the official fell on top of the girl who was holding the unstoppered bottle on her lap. The reddish liquid poured over her white jumper. Furious, she too gave the conductor a push that threw him off balance, and he landed first in the hunter's arms, then in the other blonde girl's im-mobilizing bear hug. The bottle hadn't overturned completely, so the girl in the cherry-stained jumper rose to her feet and opened the railwayman's mouth with one hand (her fingers planted like claws on his beard and throat), while with the other she forced the mouth of the bottle under his mustache and through his teeth. Ion heard sounds of impotent gurgling and groaning. The Tyrolean went down on his knees and gripped the conductor's legs between his arms, leaving him no choice but to drain the bottle dry. Ion closed his eyes to avoid seeing the finale.

When he opened them again, he looked around and saw no one. An empty bottle was lying on the floor, and a few grayish feathers were scattered beside it. The whole compartment smelled of alcohol. The train was in a large, brightly lit station that was swarming with people. He'd arrived in Munich. Ion went bleary-eyed into the corridor. It was deserted. All the other passengers had left. He was the last one onboard.

He hailed a cab and pronounced the street name and house number where Mr. Fuhrmann lived as correctly as he could: Fritz Kortner Bogen, 16. Why not "Strasse" as well, or at least "Gasse"? And what was this "Bogen"? It was in some godforsaken district full of new apartment blocks: not quite Balta Albă in Bucharest, but not much better. The fare on the meter rose at an alarming rate. Ion breathed a sigh of relief when the driver finally stopped in front of number 16, where some kids were playing noisily at hawks and doves. They ran excitedly along the sidewalk and into the road, clambering from time to time onto the steps that led up to the building: that was base, where the hawks couldn't get you. When he got out of the taxi, Ion saw that some pigeons were hopping on the sidewalk, their crops stuffed with all kinds of filth they had diligently collected from the asphalt or around the occasional trees that formed an ersatz green space in the concrete suburb. The pigeons didn't look too impressed by the mock battle between mock birds, nor by Ion's hesitant advance through the ranks of children and pigeons to reach the front door. He went into the lobby and examined the rows of mailboxes, then made his way up to the third floor. He found the door marked "Fuhrmann," rang the bell, and waited. In vain: Mr. Fuhrmann wasn't at home. Glad now that he'd left his suitcase in Vienna, Ion went back down into the street, among the pigeons, where the children had disappeared. He sat on the steps and thought over what he should do next. Worst-case scenario, he would check into a hotel: he had enough money now. His padded pockets told him that he hadn't been robbed while asleep on the train.

A middle-aged woman appeared and asked what he was doing there. He explained in his broken German who he was looking for, but the woman had never heard of the name that he pronounced.

"There's no Urmann around here," she said, and Ion got up to leave without further ado. Placated by his docile attitude, she suggested that he ask at the Gasthaus on the corner, and perhaps wait *there*—as people normally do, with a glass of beer at a table. The woman bore a likeness to the conductor on the train: she even had some down on her cheeks. Seeing this, Ion bit his lips to avoid laughing, then thanked the woman and headed for the bar. It wasn't far. The street curved off to the right, so it wasn't really a proper corner, but the Gasthaus was there at the bend—a bending Gasthaus. On the opposite sidewalk, a little procession of mainly women and children was walking behind two stretcher-bearers. Thinking that he saw the Tyrolean hunter on the stretcher, with a sheet tucked up to his neck, Ion crossed the street, wide-eyed with curiosity. A strapping blonde drew alongside the prostrate figure and pulled the sheet over its face. Ion noticed that the shroud was spotted with reddish stains that probably wouldn't come out in the wash. The middle-aged woman from a few minutes ago was also part of the procession. When she saw Ion coming toward them, she shouted for him not to get any closer: he should buzz off and mind his own business. One of the stretcher-bearers turned his head, and Ion recognized Haiducu. He stopped. Some men appeared in the Gasthaus doorway, shyly gesticulating to Ion. A flock of doves made a low-level pass over the stretcher. Ion turned on his heel and went toward the Gasthaus. The men thronging the doorway made room for him to enter. Ion went to the counter and asked for a beer. Then he asked about Mr. Urmann—*Entschuldigung,* Mr. Furmann. The man who served the beer was darker than Ion: probably Turkish, the Romanian student thought, proud of his perspicacity. The Turk smiled and pointed to the far end of the room. Ion turned his head and saw a group of men clustered around a table.

"There he is, playing Gul Bara," the Turk said, with a strong accent that made Ion feel good.

He took his beer and nervously walked over to where he had spotted Mr. Fuhrmann's silvery head of hair. The man he had come to see was seated at a table with other devotees of the game, moving their pieces energetically and with great skill.

The telephone is ringing. I stand up . . . Sorry! I mean, Ion stood up and went just as he was, barefoot and in his briefs, into the other room. He answered: no, Mr. Fuhrmann wasn't at home. He could just as easily not have answered at all. Mr. Fuhrmann had left no instructions one way or the other. And, in fact, the telephone hadn't rung much since he'd been there, or had rung only when Mr. Fuhrmann had been in—and, of course, able to answer himself.

"*Hallo!*" Ion said, careful to place the emphasis on the first syllable.

"*Entschuldigung*! I'd like to speak to Ion Valea."

The voice at the other end sounded familiar.

"Speaking," Ion said, and at that moment he recognized Haiducu.

"Do you know who this is?"

"Yes," Ion said, too afraid to hang up. It wouldn't have done him any good anyway—if Haiducu knew his telephone number, he also knew his address.

"How are you enjoying life among the lovely Germans?" Haiducu asked. No reply. He was speaking as though Ion were a little boy.

"I see we're not in a talkative mood," Haiducu went on. "Now listen, we've got to see each other . . ."

"See each other?" Ion, terrified now, looked out the window; a flock of pigeons was speeding past.

"Yesterday you almost gave me away," the Bessarabian said reproachfully. Ion shrugged.

"What's that you said?"

"I didn't say anything," Ion said, again shrugging his shoulders.

"Anyway, I don't give a damn what you have to say about it. We're meeting tomorrow at the races."

Haiducu's tone had become peremptory. Ion broke into a sweat. He didn't have a tissue handy to wipe his forehead. Now the flock of pigeons was flying in the other direction.

"Where?"

"At the racetrack."

"But why?"

"You're needed."

Cold sweat dripped down Ion's back. He'd have liked to refuse, although he probably knew he had no choice in the matter. In the end he'd have to bow to the occult forces that had chosen him as their pawn—Ion Valea, a Romanian student eager to see Europe. Maybe they'd picked him at random, or according to criteria he couldn't begin to fathom . . . to achieve a purpose he knew even less about, and had no way of guessing, however much he tried. Best not even to think about it!

But he tried to be clever, at least to gain time—to play for time, as they say.

"I've no idea where the racetrack is."

"Ask Fuhrmann."

"Mr. Fuhrmann doesn't bet on horses. He only plays backgammon."

"He knows all right. And if he doesn't you'll still manage. Ask at the bar, at the Turkish place."

"You haven't said when. What time, exactly?"

"Be there at three. Got it?" And Haiducu ended the conversation.

Ion went back to the room where he slept. He fumbled around under the bed looking for his shoes, but he couldn't find them. He went down on his knees, then on all fours, then on his belly, poking his arm further and further under the bed, until at last he felt something soft, almost fluffy, with his fingers. I guess Mr. Fuhrmann keeps a goose under the bed, Ion joked to himself, smiling, and got back on his feet. He'd left his shoes under the chair where he'd also draped his pants and shirt. He dressed hurriedly, although it was still too early for his appointment, even if the racetrack was in the back of beyond. He looked at his watch, before kneeling in front of the suitcase he'd bought the day after his arrival in Munich, along with some shirts, socks, and underwear, a pair of shoes, and a new pair of pants (German, though made from English material)—oh, and a French belt. *Erster Klasse!* He kept his winnings at the bottom of the case, the bills a little creased since he first got them. He took out a wad, waved it like a fan in front of his nose, and put it in the inside pocket of his jacket.

He went out into the street. Spring was in the air. A few solitary pigeons were pecking at crumbs on the paved sidewalk. That's the consumer society for you: there are always some crumbs to peck at. Ion was pleased with this formulation, which he'd come up with there and then, on the sidewalk, as he trod gingerly past the pigeons. But he didn't look down to verify its truth-value. If he had, he would have seen that the crumbs were few and far between, practically nonexistent. His eyes never strayed down to the level of his feet but remained fixed on the clear blue sky. He'd even managed to push that unpleasant telephone call out of his mind. Or perhaps the idea of some betting at the races excited him, for all the unease he—rightly—felt at the prospect of meeting Haiducu again. He remembered his wins at the Ploieşti races, in his final year at school, when he'd gone there with his and Sandu's coach . . .

He crossed the street and went to the Turkish bar. Mr. Fuhrmann wasn't there. Ahmed smiled nonstop at Ion and offered him a coffee. Ion accepted. A few minutes later he also knew the whereabouts of the racetrack.

It was the day of the trotter races. Ion arrived early, too early, when the place was mostly empty. A space had been cleared between the two stands, a kind of enclosure where the horses would be brought from the stables already attached to their sulkies. They'd walk around this paddock once or twice, then move to the track to warm up. No horses had been brought out yet, however. Ion stood resting against the barrier, which was painted white and green. No bets were being taken, but the currency exchange was open and Ion went to convert his Austrian money into marks. It was rather a frustrating experience, because all he received for his wad of brand-new notes was a couple of sheets of paper—a few hundred marks at best. He should have brought along more schillings.

He returned to the paddock. A chestnut horse had appeared there, with a driver sporting a silk jersey as red as the flag of the former Soviet Union—only the hammer and sickle were missing.

In their place, a single yellow star occupied half of the driver's back. The chestnut wasn't wearing its number yet: it was just being taken for a spin. It would be hard to identify later, as the red jersey and yellow star were the colors of a stable that was fielding a number of horses that afternoon, although only two or three of them were chestnuts. Ion bought a racing form and looked through it several times. No mention.

Someone tapped him on the shoulder. He turned his head and saw Fane Ghişoiu with a broad grin on his face.

"How are you, my boy!" Mister Fane said, hugging Ion to his bosom, as they say, although in fact it was more like hoisting him onto his belly. He'd put on rather a lot of weight, old Fane. But his passion for the horses was undiminished. He could sniff out a racetrack miles away. In that context, it made perfect sense that he was there, and Ion didn't bother asking what he was doing at the races in the Bavarian capital. Maybe Sandu . . .

"Have you seen him?"

"Who?"

"Sandu Economu."

Fane Ghişoiu nervously shifted his racing form from hand to hand, obviously discomfited by the question.

"Why? Is he in Munich?"

"I don't know," Ion said. "The last time he wrote me was nearly two years ago, before . . ."

But Mister Fane didn't seem too interested in the fate of his former pupil. He opened his form and pointed to something in the third or fourth race.

"Nothing much in the first few races. Not worth risking your deutschmarks."

Ion knew by now that his former coach's knowledge of the turf was far from infallible, so he didn't even bother looking at the indicated horse, or even the race in which it was running.

"It's a dead cert," Mister Fane added. "It would be a pity not to bet on it . . ."

Ion didn't want to offend him and would have said nothing at all if the older man hadn't kept on insisting.

"But how do you know, Mister Fane? We're in Munich here, not Ploieşti."

Fane Ghişoiu took a look over his shoulder, then to the left and right, suspiciously. The racegoers were beginning to arrive, taking their time. Fane moved his lips closer to Ion's ear and whispered so softly that all he could hear was the name *Haiducu*.

"Haiducu?" Ion blurted loudly, shocked. "How do you know Haiducu?"

Ghişoiu covered Ion's mouth with his hand, while his eyes implored him to shut up. He put his arm around Ion's shoulder and steered him toward the fence on the edge of the track. There he whispered more words in his ear, the gist of which was that Haiducu couldn't keep their appointment because of some urgent business in the city: that is, he couldn't come at the agreed hour, but he would make it a little later, so until then, if Ion felt like a few bets—but not any old bets, wasting the rest of the money he'd obtained with such difficulty in Vienna—then he should carefully follow Mister Fane's instructions . . .

"Look," Ghişoiu said, calming down, and he again pointed to the middle of the open page of his racing form. But Ion's eyes were elsewhere: the horses were coming onto the track, spruce and sprightly, and their drivers, whips under their arms, were all staring straight ahead, all bent on finishing first. How the hell could you choose just one?

"Did you get the name?" Mister Fane asked with an anxious look. "Don't say later that I didn't give you the right tip. It's number five. But wait, not in this race. Where are you running off to? What are you doing?"

Without saying a word, Ion marched straight over to the betting windows. Mister Fane went after him shouting the name of the horse:

"*Roulette russe!*"

But Ion probably didn't hear. He stopped and lined up at the first window. There were still five minutes until the start of the race.

Ion lost in the first two races. Meanwhile Ghişoiu had vanished—as if the earth had swallowed him up. After scouring the larger and larger crowd, Ion began to wonder whether he'd really seen him after all, really had that conversation. Maybe I dreamed it! Maybe it was all just a dream!—and he chuckled to himself at the romantic cliché that had stuck in his mind, along with plenty more of the same ilk, ideas you don't even think about and—once you become more or less sophisticated—no longer speak or write, since they seem embarrassingly trite. But does that mean they're necessarily false?

Ion was so wrapped up in his thoughts that the third race passed him by. He looked to see the number of the winner. It was 5! He had bet on 14, *Ökologie*, which came in last. Hadn't Mister Fane told him to go for 5? The odds on it had risen to 12/1. Idiot! Why hadn't he taken Mister Fane's tip—especially since it was clear that it wasn't just one of the coach's whims, that Haiducu had fixed the race?

Ion looked at his racing form and tried to pick a horse for the next race. Again 14? Or 17? He lined up at a window and decided to bet all he had on 17. Go for broke! The horse's name was *Jonas*, and its driver wore a red jersey with a large yellow star. Must be the one he'd seen when he first arrived . . . or one of its stable-mates. The horse had been warming up since long before the race, as if someone had wanted to keep the punters from seeing it. Now, on the track, it looked pretty pathetic, barely dragging itself along.

Ion went into the stands to get a better view of the race. *Jonas* was in the second pack, together with ten other horses that all looked far sprightlier. Twenty yards in front, seven others were restively awaiting their starter's orders. Ion's gaze was naturally fixed on *Jonas*. When the albatross wings of the starting gate slowly lifted, *Jonas* reared on its hind legs like a rutting stallion. Calmly and skillfully, the driver managed to avoid an accident and even got the horse back on four legs; *Jonas* then sped off at the trot, already in last place. Right up in front, five yards ahead of the rest of the pack, was number 5, *Rote Fahne*. Haiducu was right, Ion muttered to himself. After the first lap *Jonas* was still last, but it had made up some ground. *Rote Fahne* was keeping the lead, with number 14, *Schwarzer Schwann*, hard on its heels. Now *Jonas* was racing up at breakneck speed, overtaking one opponent after another. At the bend it was up to the two leaders, fearlessly contending on the outside for first place. On the home stretch, all three looked to be neck and neck. *Jonas* was slowing a little after its fabulous catch-up, and Ion was afraid it would finish just behind the others. The little red man with the yellow star on his back looked positively demonic as he whirled his whip over the horse's backside, without actually making contact. The chestnut made a supreme effort in the last few yards, and the photograph left no doubt: it had won, by a whisker.

Ion was counting his winnings—the second time he'd ever had the chance—when Haiducu appeared in front of him, hands on hips.

"Give it here!" Haiducu ordered, pointing to the money that Ion had automatically stuffed into the shelter of his breast pocket.

This time Ion wasn't going to be fleeced so easily. There were plenty of people around.

"It's my money—I won it," he said categorically, and he started heading for the exit.

"You won it, but on my directions. Like in the casino . . ."

"That's not true."

"What do you mean? Didn't Fane Ghişoiu tell you which horse to back? Didn't he tell you number 5?"

"Yes, but 5 didn't win. *Jonas* was first, number 17."

"I'm talking about the third race, dumbo! Didn't *Roulette russe* win that?"

"Yes, but I didn't bet on it."

"You were supposed to—like I told you."

"Anyway, the fact is that what I won, I won on my own."

"Are you sure you aren't lying to me?"

"All you had to do was show up on time, to keep an eye on me. Either you or Mister Fane. Where did he run off to?"

Haiducu didn't reply. He was furious. He could see that Ion wasn't lying, and that it was Ghişoiu's fault for not making him back the right horse. Maybe he bet on it himself. Yes, that's probably what he did, and then disappeared with the money . . .

"Let's go get a beer," Haiducu said, after they had left the racetrack.

"I don't have the time," Ion lied, and he took advantage of a taxi that had just pulled up. The driver half-opened the rear driver-side door, Ion jumped in, and the car sped off—like the wind. Ion looked through the rear window and saw Haiducu left in the lurch on the sidewalk.

"Where are we going?" the driver asked in Romanian, and only then did Ion realize that it was the accordionist. Maybe he hadn't recognized Ion yet, though . . . Maybe he'd just heard him speaking Romanian and felt glad that his fare was a fellow countryman. Why assume the worst? Ion gave him Fuhrmann's address, then thought better of it and said:

"No, first of all downtown, to the Pinakothek."

The accordionist said nothing, didn't even turn his head. Maybe it's not the accordionist after all—that is, the terrorist from Hotel Europa. Maybe he just looks like him, in the same way that Karim's neighbor looked like him, without that necessarily meaning he was the same guy . . . There are so many coincidences in this world . . .

Ten minutes later the taxi was prowling around a huge park: this must be the *Englische Garten*, Ion said to himself. The streets were much greener than elsewhere. At some point he thought he could see Ana and Roger. They were walking with their arms around each other, stopping from time to time to kiss and cuddle.

"Stop. Do you hear me? Stop!"

But the swarthy driver had no intention of stopping. On the contrary, he put his foot down hard. Ion opened his window, but it was too late. The car turned onto another side street, then another: not a living creature to be seen. *Then* the terrorist slammed on the brakes. He turned toward Ion, gun in hand.

"Okay, cough it up!"

"But . . ."

"Get a move on. I'm in a hurry."

Ion gave him a wad of bills, no more than two thousand marks—nearly all he'd won at the races.

"Is that it?" The accordionist looked dissatisfied. "What have you done with the rest?"

"Haiducu took it from me," Ion sighed.

"He took it 'coz you're a sucker. Now buzz off!"

Ion didn't wait to be told again, and he was given a helpful shove. He fell on all fours onto the sidewalk. The accordionist drove away. Ion watched him go, but it was too late to make out the license number.

He scrambled to his feet, wiped the dust off his pants, and felt inside his pockets. Well, he still had a few hundred marks—more or less what he'd gone to the racetrack with. He walked along slowly until he spotted a real taxi.

Mr. Fuhrmann was still out. Ion took off his jacket and shoes and lay on the bed, but he was too exhausted to fall asleep at once. He noticed a stain shaped like a duckbill on the ceiling. He closed his eyes for a few minutes, maybe more. He felt a hand on his brow. A fair-haired, ruddy-faced man was smiling at him from beside the bed: he had dimples too, and blue eyes.

"*Was wollen Sie?*" Ion asked, as good as any Goethe. The stranger answered in Romanian. His name was Lebedev. But why was he so happy, so cheerful?

"My dear Mr. Valeev," Lebedev said formally—with a Russian accent, of course. "My dear Mr. Valeev," he repeated with a smile. "I don't want to disturb you, but I absolutely must look for something under your bed."

Ion didn't know what to say. Should he get angry at being woken by a stranger who mispronounced his name and spoke so pretentiously that you couldn't even give him the benefit of the doubt and assume he was just making fun of you? Lebedev didn't wait for permission: he kneeled down and poked his left arm under the bed, but he hadn't positioned himself right, so he could only reach halfway. Then he stretched out flat on his belly. His arm now extended into the darkness all the way up to his shoulder. Ion stayed put; if he got up he might squash the man, lying like a frog on the carpet. He waited for him to retrieve whatever he was looking for.

"Does Furmanov know about this?" Ion asked. Then he started laughing, a little hysterically, lying on his back and clutching the waistband of his pants. Lebedev twisted his head round as far as he could, but said nothing. Ion finally sat up Turkish-style, legs gathered beneath him—no longer laughing. He looked down, as if from a riverbank or the edge of a swimming pool. The other man persisted in his extractive labor, until finally Ion could see the feathers come into view, not very white anymore, perhaps because of all the dust they had collected for God knows how long under the bed . . .

The next time he woke up, Ion saw Mr. Fuhrmann tiptoeing through the room, on his way to the hall and then to the front door and then to the street.

"I didn't want to wake you," Fuhrmann apologized.

"Where's . . . ?" Ion mumbled.

"Who?"

"The Russian who came to take . . ."

Ion stopped. He realized that his mind was wandering. Fuhrmann had a smile on his face.

"There were a couple of calls for you. Someone named Haiducu. Then a classmate from college—Petrişor."

"Petrişor?"

"That's what he said. Weren't you classmates?"

"Sure we were!"

"So I did right to give him this address? I asked him where he got the phone number from, and he said Dinu told him . . . so I assumed it would be okay. As for the other one, he laughed when I asked him. He knew the address and everything. Who is he?"

"Haiducu?"

"Yes. That's the name he gave."

"I don't know much about him."

"What do you mean? He knows all about you—and about me too. He said I play backgammon at Ahmed's. Did you tell him that?"

"Me?"

"Well, who else? Was he another classmate of yours?"

"No way!"

So, in the end, Ion was forced to tell Mr. Fuhrmann about the business with Haiducu, though he played it down enough so that the older man wouldn't be too shocked. He reduced the size of his winnings at roulette, for instance, and likewise the degree to which the incident in the bathroom had terrified him . . . He also filled Fuhrmann in about Karim and Silvia—which is to say, Sonia.

Fuhrmann didn't understand exactly what Silvia's line of business was, and why she'd changed her name.

"Is she Russian?"

"I don't know," Ion said. And he really didn't know. "One evening she showed up at Petrişor's. Valeriu brought her there."

"Petrişor seems like a serious type," Fuhrmann said. "He wants to study German culture. Not like you: he's not in a hurry to get to Paris. There are other places in Europe besides Paris, you know."

"What makes you think I'm in a hurry?" Ion said. "I've been here bothering you for nearly two months now."

"Yes, but you should see some other German cities. I see you've got a bit of money."

Ion said no more. He was sitting barefoot on the edge of his bed, and, although the talk with Mr. Fuhrmann and the news that Petrişor was in Munich had got him started, it still couldn't be said that he was wide awake. He went into the bathroom to take a shower. Mr. Fuhrmann had business to deal with and left the apartment.

Petrişor showed up before Ion had even managed to get dressed. They hugged each other—Ion not too fervently, Petrişor rather more exuberant. He was thinner than Ion remembered—downright skinny, in fact. Actually, he looked pretty terrible all around: his jacket was torn at the shoulder and had grease and grass and earth stains, probably from sleeping outdoors; he also must have been walking a lot, since his boots were falling to pieces; only his jeans were still holding up.

"How did you get in this state, man?" Ion asked as he took off his pajama jacket and put on a shirt.

Petrişor drew up a chair and sat down. He was completely exhausted—and hungry, of course, though not starving. Thanks to Gică he wasn't too badly off.

"Thanks to who?"

He'd met Gică on his way out of Sopron, a small Hungarian town near the Austrian border. They met on an exit ramp by the highway, while Petrişor was making his way along the meridian, tired of all the walking and worried about how to get across the border without being spotted by the guards—especially the Austrians.

"Didn't you have a passport?" Ion asked, beginning to put on his shoes and socks.

He did have a passport, but not a long-stay or even a transit visa. The Austrians had recently reintroduced visa requirements and were keeping a very close watch. So, with a lot on his mind, Petrişor suddenly noticed a wheelchair beneath a tree. Gică was taking a rest. He'd been disabled since an accident when he was a kid, but after the regime change he struck it lucky when a team of German doctors visited Timişoara, where he was living at the time in terrible circumstances, supported by an old and needy mother. The Germans took a liking to him, and when they heard he hadn't gone out for years they promised to help. The young man was certainly eager to leave Timişoara and Romania and see a bit of the world. "I'm not afraid of anything," he told them. "Anything's better than staying cooped up in that apartment." A German firm that manufactured wheelchairs offered him one of their extraordinary machines so he could travel anywhere he liked. The catch was that in order to earn his chair free and clear, Gică first had to make a record-breaking trans-Europe wheelchair trip, from Timişoara to Paris via Munich. The German company gave him some pocket money, but they covered the bulk of his expenses with a little blue plastic card; they explained how Gică could use it for almost anything—whether he was spending the night in a town, or stopping in a village to eat lunch.

I call Gachet to ask how many miles a young disabled man in a wheelchair might be able to cover in a day. I'm out of luck: the doctor isn't in Paris. Then I call Marianne, who immediately answers: no more than seven to ten miles. I think she underestimates the energy and strength of a young Romanian determined to get out of his country. And I tell her so.

"So why did you ask?" she snaps. "The story doesn't sound very plausible to me. In fact, it makes me feel a little sorry for you."

"Couldn't you find out for sure somewhere?"

"Why don't you try calling Gachet?"

Of course there was always a danger that Gică would become a target for someone up to no good. At first he was rarely on his own: it often happened that someone would accompany him from one village to another. And between Timișoara and Budapest he was escorted by a cyclist the German firm had hired specially for the occasion.

"And what happened to the cyclist after that?" Ion asked, on his way to the kitchen to make something to eat for Petrișor. "Hey, would you like some coffee too?"

Petrișor gobbled down his food and went on with his story between mouthfuls. The cyclist had become involved with a girl in Budapest and left Gică to continue the journey alone. The different stages of his historic journey were strictly defined, and even obligatory: he wasn't allowed to spend more than two days in the same place. Still, he did spend three in Budapest—at Hotel Europa.

"Yes, I know the place," Ion muttered.

Petrișor looked at him with a mixture of admiration and incredulity. He himself had seen the hotel only from outside: he hadn't ventured as far as the lobby. And when he'd been passing through, Gică wasn't yet there. When he did arrive, he was still with Manfred, the cyclist, who defected during their very first day at the hotel. It began when Manfred refused to accompany Gică around Budapest. This was no great setback in itself, since people knew all about the young Romanian's adventure—there had been articles about him in the paper, German and maybe even English journalists had been hanging around and following him in the street, and that morning the TV guys, not only Hungarian but Austrian, had been around to film him. What did he need Manfred for?

He gave him the day off. But then Manfred didn't come back the next day. Gică stayed an extra night and complained both to the hotel management and to the journalists that Manfred had pulled a vanishing act. Two journalists offered to accompany Gică the rest of the way in their car, but on reflection realized it wouldn't be much fun for them driving along behind a wheelchair . . . So then they suggested taking him in their car and swore they'd never tell a soul—but Gică didn't feel he could trust them completely. It might be a trap. And even if it wasn't, the precise timing of the different stages meant that it was too complicated to cheat. How could he show up in Vienna a week early? So, in the end, the journalists stopped insisting and left him to go on alone. It wasn't such a long way from Budapest to the Austrian border . . .

In a village before Sopron he found himself in the middle of a wedding celebration. When he went to bed that night, some time after twelve, a girl who was blind drunk climbed in with him, wanting to know how far down he was paralyzed. She found out—and was only too happy to stay the rest of the night. The next day, when Petrişor came across him by the roadside, Gică was—naturally enough—sleeping under a tree; he wasn't used to such vigorous exercise. You might say that everything worked out pretty well for Petrişor after that. It was about time that it did too—he'd been living from hand to mouth all his time in Hungary. He was broke, he didn't have a visa for Austria, and he had to pass through the damn place to reach Munich.

"Why Munich?" Ion asked, hoping that Petrişor knew someone there who could help him, at least for a while.

No, there wasn't anyone expecting him in Munich, but he'd heard that the Germans granted political asylum much more easily than other countries, and anyway he'd get board and lodging during all the formalities. He'd cite the systematic persecution of intellectuals in Romania, the bloodbath in University Square, and the fraudulent elections too. Ion wasn't about to contradict him; he might end up asking for political asylum himself. But he did point out:

"Isn't it a bit late? That all happened more than a year ago."

Mr. Fuhrmann returned just then. He looked rather shocked at how low a Romanian student could fall. Did he know German at least? But Petrişor dodged the question and went on with the story of Gică.

"A disabled guy who's being sponsored to ride a wheelchair all the way from Timişoara to Paris," Ion summarized for his host in a single breath.

Mr. Fuhrmann seemed very interested. He sat on Ion's bed to listen, hands on knees.

So, Gică was asleep under the tree. Petrişor approached him with nothing special in mind. No, he didn't intend to rob him, although it's true that he was dead broke and barely had enough for his daily bread. Sure, he still had some dollars in his boots, but he'd sworn not to touch them until he arrived in Germany. He didn't want to ask the Austrians for political asylum: they let you starve to death in their camp at Traiskirchen.

So he went up to Gică, but no sooner had he touched an arm of the wheelchair than its occupant woke up and grabbed Petrişor's hand: his strength was quite extraordinary. Speaking Romanian—as if he already knew who he was dealing with—Gică accused Petrişor of trailing him since before Budapest. It was Manfred who had pointed this out, then; he'd spotted him at least two days earlier, he said. "It's probably a refugee from Romania," Gică had muttered.

"Was it true you'd been following him?" Ion asked.

No, it was a simple mix-up. All cats are gray in the dark. There were so many Romanians wandering around Hungary, after all—and neither Gică nor Manfred had eyes in the back of his head head to see them all. In the end Gică believed Petrișor's story, and he accepted when Petrișor offered to push him for a while. "But not for long . . ." Gică said, closing his eyes . . . that girl had really wiped him out. He told Petrișor about the wedding only later, on the other side of the border, when he also filled him in about his other adventures. They split up a couple of miles before the border. As agreed, Petrișor went across the fields and entered a little forest, while Gică followed the highway singing at the top of his lungs to create a diversion.

Mr. Fuhrmann could no longer refrain from asking Petrișor why he didn't have a passport. The students gave him the usual explanations, but Mr. Fuhrmann wasn't feeling quite as hospitable now as when he'd spoken to Petrișor on the telephone.

"If you don't have a visa, you stay where you are."

"That's easy to say in Munich!" Ion burst out, and Petrișor smiled at him gratefully. "Go on with your story," Ion encouraged. Mr. Fuhrmann held his peace.

The two travelers met up again after the border, in an Austrian village where Gică invited Petrișor to dinner and even allowed him to sleep in his room, on a mattress on the floor. The innkeeper turned a blind eye and didn't ask for their papers. Anyway, Petrișor wasn't completely without documents: he had a valid passport, only the Austrian visa was missing.

"And what about a German visa?" Mr. Fuhrmann asked anxiously.

"I've got one here. Look," and Petrişor proudly took out his passport and showed it to Fuhrmann. "When I left Romania, it wasn't necessary for us to have an Austrian visa, you know."

"That's right," Ion confirmed. "I came here without one."

"They changed their policy afterward, when I was already in Hungary."

Mr. Fuhrmann breathed a sigh of relief.

I don't know if that visa story was quite true, but I'm sick of looking at the old man pouting there on the bed. I hear the telephone and go down to answer it. Marianne's a little irritated as she tells me that someone just asked about Ion, over the phone. The voice didn't want to say who it belonged to. He doesn't live here, Marianne explained. The voice insisted. It was a male voice, foreign, with an accent that was hard to identify. "He hasn't reached Paris. He's in Vienna or Munich, I'm not sure which. But who are you?" Marianne asked. "Someone who only wishes him well," the voice replied.

"Do you think it was the embassy?" Marianne asked me.

"I don't know. Maybe it was Mihai."

"He didn't have a Romanian accent. I'm sure about that."

"So what made you think it was the embassy?"

"Who else do you want me to think of?"

"I don't know."

"Yesterday there was a female voice. Asking after you."

"As is my due," I say haughtily.

"Maybe it's your due, but I'm not your damn switchboard operator."

"Didn't you ask who it was?"

"Yes, I did. It was a Miss Ozana . . ."

"What?"

"You heard what I said. And she had the same accent as the guy today."

Petrişor and Gică started to have arguments about what constituted a fair exchange of material benefits. Gică wanted more than just to be pushed along the road, and one sleepless night he finally got around to expressing his wish: he was tired of jerking himself off. Petrişor pretended not to have heard. When Gică then threatened to ditch him or report him to the police, the student countered with some threats of his own, pointing out that he was there secretly sharing the room only because he'd helped Gică to cheat during the day, since Gică was supposed to make it to his destination entirely under his own power. There was a tacit understanding between them that had to be respected. Otherwise . . .

The two of them continued their wheelchair journey to Vienna along back roads; it was better to take a longer route than to expose Petrişor's helping hands to public scrutiny. They went onto the highway only when they had to pass through a town. In Vienna they split up again. The newspaper and television people awaited Gică with great ceremony, while Petrişor blended into the crowd. Only late at night did he creep into Gică's hotel room.

They were approaching the German border. Night was falling, and they still hadn't reached the village that was the next scheduled stop; there were still a couple of miles to go. They had wasted some time chatting in a forest and drinking a few bottles of beer. Then they had taken a nap—Petrişor in his sleeping bag, Gică in his wheelchair. Since they were now running late, they decided to take the main road—but before they could get into the open they found themselves facing a lusty young man in military uniform, though without his cap and boots, pointing a gun straight at them. Petrişor froze and took refuge behind the wheelchair. Gică, not having anything to hide behind, raised his hands and closed his eyes. The soldier burst out laughing. He wasn't going to shoot them: he was drunk, that's all, and just wanted some *Bier! Bier!* Ah, but there was none left. *Geld* then! He was a Russian deserter; he'd sold his boots and was trying to survive from hold-ups. When he couldn't find anything to steal, he went hunting in the forest—but now he'd run out of bullets too. He only had one left, he explained, realizing that his new acquaintances weren't German and could speak some Russian. *Румынский, хорошо!* Petrişor tried to convince the soldier that they were just as broke as he, and couldn't help him: *Деньги нет!* But the Russian was suspicious and wanted to look in their pockets. Their conversation—if this sequence of Russian and German words accompanied with assorted gestures could be called that—threatened to go on and on. It was dark now, and, since they didn't want to tell the Russian they had a room waiting for them in the next village, there was a strong possibility that all three of them would end up spending the night under the stars. The Russian even suggested going back into the forest to light a fire. He was so plastered that nothing seemed to trouble him. Crafty Petrişor suggested that the soldier look after Gică while he sniffed around the village and tried to get some food for them. Gică protested vehemently. If any of them had a chance of cadging some food, it had to be he, the poor cripple—and, of course, Petrişor would have to come along to push the wheelchair. The Russian saw through this, however, and wouldn't hear of being left there alone. So he took his pistol out again, and Gică's hands were back up in no time. The soldier looked at them, then at his gun, and finally sat on a mound of earth with his head in his hands. Was he weeping? The gun, which he still held in one hand, was close to his temple. The other two didn't move. The Russian pressed the barrel of the gun to his head and pulled the trigger. Nothing. He held out the gun to Petrişor, but the young Romanian had no burning desire to play Russian roulette. Then the Russian gave it to Gică, who looked at it and calmly pointed it at the soldier, whose head was back in his hands. "Go on, shoot, what are you waiting for?" Petrişor whispered. Gică pulled the trigger, and there was an absurd little click. Again it hadn't fired. "This gun doesn't have a single bullet in it!" Gică said angrily, and he pointed it at Petrişor. The student threw himself flat and crawled beneath the wheelchair. Gică spitefully tossed the weapon down beside the soldier. *Keine Kugel!* The Russian was no longer crying. He took the pistol from the grass and again lifted it to his temple. The shot rang out loud, far into the distance. The soldier fell onto his side. Petrişor jumped up, overturning the wheelchair. Gică found himself on the ground, next to the soldier, and began to scream. The student ran off in the direction of the highway. Anyway, it was too late that day to avail himself of disabled Gică's hospitality. In darkest night he puffed his way toward the border.

I copy out some of the press cuttings from the scrapbook where I stuck them in with Scotch tape.

Four hundred racially motivated crimes this May in Germany:

German extremists have caused the death of five people: a Turkish woman and her children were killed in Solingen in one of thirty-three arson attacks recorded by the German government. Another fifty-nine assaults were reported, as well as 308 "lesser incidents" such as threats and insults. In West Germany, in 1990, 270 racially motivated attacks were committed. After unification, the number rose to 2,280.

Again in Germany, a neo-Nazi was sentenced yesterday to seven years' imprisonment for wounding a Nigerian asylum-seeker with a knife.

The number of violent xenophobic attacks doubled in the first six months, by comparison with the same period last year.

In a hostel for refugees in southern Germany, five Chinese asylum-seekers were wounded by a dozen Albanians who had left a week earlier following an argument with them. The Albanians returned with sticks and iron bars, looking for revenge. Police are holding three of them for questioning.

Romania:

The Association of Independent Journalists has accused Romanian President Ion Iliescu of molesting and insulting a journalist at an election rally on Saturday in Constanţa. Following his example, bodyguards attacked another ten reporters who were on the scene.

The main suspect in the "Bulgarian umbrella" scandal has disappeared:

Francesco Giullino, a Dane of Italian origin accused of assassinating the Bulgarian writer Georgi Markov in London in 1978 with a mysterious weapon known as the "Bulgarian umbrella," has managed to flee from Denmark as the evidence continues to pile up against him.

Germany:

Four Russian soldiers died in a shoot-out on Thursday evening at Taucha, a town near Leipzig in East Germany. For reasons unknown, the men—who were escorting a food convoy armed with pistols and a machine gun—opened fire on one another.

Romania:

Mein Kampf will be banned following a demand by President Ion Iliescu, who described Hitler's book as "an act of fascist propaganda forbidden by the Constitution." The President also denounced the fact that parties with a fascist orientation now exist in Romania.

Former Yugoslavia:

A new wave of violence erupted this Monday in Sarajevo and the rest of Bosnia. The commander of the Serbian forces in Bosnia, General Ratko Mladić, threatened to shoot down planes carrying humanitarian aid, on the grounds that—in his opinion—they were parachuting in weapons for the Muslim Bosniacs. The leader of the Bosnian Serbs, Radovan Karadzić, proposed the closure of "a number of detention centers." In Bonn, the interior minister announced that Germany would not accept any more refugees, as "it is time for other countries to make similar commitments."

Britain:

Three people were wounded on Friday by booby-trapped parcels delivered in several towns. Police blame the attacks on an extremist organization devoted to the protection of animals.

An American woman has lost five hundred pounds in six months:

Carol Yager, who now weighs 680 pounds, hadn't been able to walk for nine months when she was admitted to the hospital in mid-January. Some fifteen firemen were needed to move her. They wrapped her in canvas netting and rolled her down a slope to the ambulance.

Ethnic cleansing:

The co-chairmen of the Geneva conference on the former Yugoslavia, Cyrus Vance and Lord Owen, traveled on Friday to Banja Luka (in western Bosnia) to investigate claims of a new program of "ethnic cleansing," while fierce fighting was reported in the north of the republic. They were due to hold talks with representatives of all sides in the conflict, and with local officials of the International Committee of the Red Cross (ICRC) and the UN High Commissioner for Refugees (HCR). The Serb leader in Bosnia-Herzegovina, Radovan Karadzić, who was in Banja Luka for the occasion, maintained that "the situation is not so grave." The day before, one of his advisers, Nikola Koljević, denied that a new ethnic cleansing campaign was being initiated in the region, and claimed that Merhamet, the local humanitarian organization, was involved in arms trafficking.

Romania:

A general strike has paralyzed the country for twenty-four hours. Strikers are demanding a raise, as current wages are now only worth about forty percent of their value before prices were deregulated in October 1990. The strike is being organized by two of the three union federations: Frăția and Cartel-Alfa.

United Arab Emirates:

A one-year-old child, left alone at home, caught a snake, bit it to death, cut it in two, and used it as a toy, all without getting so much as a scratch.

Germany:

The German Justice Department is investigating links between local right-wing extremists and the American Ku Klux Klan, according to a communiqué issued yesterday by the prosecutor's office in Karlsruhe. Early in the year, activists from Berlin had a meeting with "Grand Imperial Dragon" Dennis Mahon.

Russia:

The Russian Justice Department opened an investigation on Tuesday evening following the death of a Zimbabwean student, who was killed by a policeman in front of Lumumba University.

Japan:

Mainichi reports that a forty-year-old fisherman arrested on Wednesday in the west of Japan has been charged with using his wife as shark bait. Motoichi Nishimura and his cousin decided to "punish" the young woman by wrapping her in a net and dipping it repeatedly into shark-infested waters.

Croatia and Bosnia—Joint Defense:

The Croatian and Bosnian presidents, Franjo Tudjman and Alija Izetbegović, announced that they signed an agreement yesterday to coordinate the "defense efforts" of the two republics of former Yugoslavia. The agreement was made public at a press conference held at UN headquarters in New York.

Romania:

A total of fifty-four skeletons dating from the 1950s have been discovered on the grounds of a former Securitate headquarters near Bucharest. Many of them bore marks of a violent death.

Risks of the Trade:

At least seven journalists appear to have been wounded during clashes between Muslims and Orthodox Christians in Sarajevo: five reporters from the Bosnian daily *Oslobodenie*, BBC correspondent Martin Bell, and Curovici, a reporter for Radio France Internationale.

Ion went into Ahmed's bar, where Mr. Fuhrmann was already playing backgammon with a Greek. At least that's how the bald corpulent man introduced himself, although if he hadn't spoken he might just as easily have been thought to come from Armenia, Israel, or another country in the Middle East. In fact, the Greek claimed to live in Istanbul; he was just passing through Munich on business. This was of little interest to Mr. Fuhrmann. Concentrating on the pieces and the dice, he barely listened to what his opponent told him in an approximation of German that made Ion—seated discreetly a little way off—feel delighted with his own linguistic abilities, leafing through a newspaper attached to a rod.

Ion made a sign for Ahmed to bring him another coffee. At that moment a breathless girl entered the bar and looked all around with the air of someone being chased. Was she looking for someone? Was she in danger? Her eyes settled on Ion, and she walked to his table with quick little steps. She was holding a plastic bag; she dropped it into his arms.

"Hide it!" she said between her teeth, before hurrying to the bathrooms in the back.

The street door opened again, revealing a man who, though dressed in ordinary gray trousers and a beige sweatshirt, couldn't possibly have been anything other than a cop. Without thinking twice, he headed for the back of the café and reappeared a few moments later marching the girl out by the arm. Ahmed pretended not to have seen any of this. The backgammon players certainly weren't interested. Ion was the only one worried by it: he had been hiding the bag behind his back, holding it there with his arm conspicuously bent, but fortunately the policeman had found Ahmed more worthy of his suspicion. The Turk was busy behind the counter, rewashing the glasses he had just washed. The street door was still open, and a gray BMW could be seen parked outside. One of its doors opened and swallowed up the girl. The cop in the sweatshirt returned and again went to the back of the bar. He passed alongside Ion, who was now holding his newspaper with one hand and concealing the plastic bag under the table with the other. So the policeman saw nothing. He was convinced that whatever he was looking for had been hidden in the bathroom, but he came back empty-handed. He planted himself at the counter and began to question Ahmed. Fuhrmann gave a short but powerful shout: the cry of victory. The policeman turned to look at him. It was a peculiar sight: a serious gentleman, white-haired and properly dressed, holding both arms up, shaking them like a madman. The Greek put on a weak smile and suggested another game. Fuhrmann immediately accepted. The policeman left the bar. Ion stood up too, stuffed the plastic bag into his jacket pocket, and headed toward the door. Ahmed followed him all the way with his eyes, clicking his lips in something like admiration.

"What about your coffee?" Ahmed asked, but Ion didn't hear him. The Turk shrugged.

Ion went up to his room. Petrişor was gone. He said he'd be off looking for work. He'd already applied for political asylum, and while awaiting a decision he wanted to make as good an impression as possible. "What, do you really think someone's following you around? That the German state pays good money to keep an eye on you?" (Ion was teasing him at the time, but he didn't know yet where Petrişor would disappear to. If he'd had any idea . . .)

He opened his suitcase and put the plastic bag inside . . . he assumed it contained several packets full of white powder. He'd never taken drugs, and wasn't especially curious to find out what it was like. Maybe that's why he was so calm. He wasn't afraid because he didn't feel the least bit guilty. Under the circumstances, however, his innocence wouldn't necessarily be clear to anyone else. He was acting like an accomplice, like a link in the supply chain. Fuhrmann wouldn't have been pleased: he'd have hit the roof.

So, why not just dump the packs of cocaine? Flush them down the toilet?

He sat on his bed, head in hands. He'd liked the girl and become her accomplice: it was as simple as that. Instead of handing the plastic bag to the cop, he'd hidden it from view—from the cop's view. That was already breaking the law, and he could be put away for it. Now—only now—he was getting scared. He stood up and reopened his suitcase. Flush it all down the toilet? But what if the girl comes back and asks for it? It's true the police hauled her in, but they had no evidence against her. So she'll be back, that's for sure.

Two or three days later he saw her at Ahmed's. She was calm, beautiful. She smiled at him. She paid for the fruit juice she'd ordered, stood up, and made for the door. There she turned and made a sign to Ion with her head: she wanted him to follow. He glanced at Ahmed, but he didn't seem to have recognized her. Fuhrmann was playing backgammon with the owner of the pizzeria across the street. There was also a group of young people drinking beer. Ion went outside and looked around, but there was no trace of the girl. He started walking, just like that. At the entrance to an apartment block, he felt someone grab him by the arm and pull him inside.

"Where's the bag?" the girl asked in a low voice.

"At my place."

"Go on then."

It was like an order. Ion never thought of disobeying. He crossed the street: Fuhrmann's building was only a few dozen yards away. He turned to check that the girl was following. Not a soul. She doesn't take any chances, he said to himself. Afraid of being tailed, no doubt. And she's right to be afraid! Ion went up the three steps at the entrance and then into the small lobby. As he waited by the elevator, the girl ran in, breathless.

"Which floor?"

"Third."

She was already climbing the staircase. Ion hesitated before following her. He soon caught up, but they didn't stop before reaching the third floor. He opened the apartment door and the girl slipped in under his arm.

"Come in here," Ion said, opening the door to his room.

"I'd like a glass of water."

When Ion returned with the glass of water on a plate—as Marioara had taught him!—he found the girl seated on the bed, her legs pulled up to her chin. She'd taken off her shoes and jeans.

"What's your name?" she asked, before taking the glass and emptying it.

"Ion."

"Are you Greek?"

"No."

"Turkish?"

"No. Romanian."

"Ah, *Zigeuner!*" she exclaimed, with a kind of pleasure or excitement in her voice. She wasn't blonde and she had brown eyes. "Sit here next to me. My name is Hilde."

They made love. Hilde had a very lavish way of expressing her enjoyment. Against a background of moans and groans, she sometimes let out a long sharp squall. A dolphin's cry. Or a siren's . . . At first it rather frightened Ion, but he got used to it and began to grunt himself, until by the end he was squealing like a pig whose throat was being cut. As a finale, they both joined in screaming blue murder.

"Do you live alone?" the girl asked, once she had more or less regained her composure.

"No, but there's no one else here right now."

They didn't have a lot to say to each other. Hilde asked for another glass of water. She drank it down while Ion waited, holding the plate. Finally she pronounced the key question:

"Where's the bag?"

Ion looked surprised, as if he'd forgotten all about it. He took a moment to respond, so Hilde panicked and demanded in a harsher tone:

"The plastic bag! Give it back! Do you hear me?"

"Sure, sure. Right away."

Ion put her glass back on the plate, and the plate on a table. Then he turned and took his suitcase by the handle. He pulled it out quickly. He didn't feel like opening it in front of Hilde, so he took it with him into the kitchen. He returned with the plastic bag and handed it over to the girl. She opened it feverishly, counted the little sachets, then opened one of them and smelled the contents.

"It's okay," Hilde said finally, with a smile on her face. "Come. Do you want to again . . ."

Ion guessed what she meant, but he looked at his watch and shook his head.

"It's getting late. The others will be here soon."

The girl didn't press him. She started to get dressed, looking out the window as she did so. A strange airplane, with a single curved wing, hovered motionless in the sky. She saw it, but didn't say anything—just continued to dress.

"This is how we'll do it," Hilde said, and she gave him back the bag. They arranged to meet at the subway station.

"Take down my phone number. Or give me yours," Ion said.

She took out a notebook and jotted it down.

Once in the street, Ion grasped the plastic bag he had stowed under his jacket and looked all around him. Nobody there. He walked to the subway station, without turning to look behind him. He went down the stairs. Hilde arrived at a run. "The bag!"

And she vanished down a corridor with the bag and everything. Ion returned to street level.

He almost forgot Hilde after that. He got to know an Italian girl, a waitress in the pizzeria. One evening the telephone rang, and Fuhrmann answered and called for him.

"It's a German girl," Fuhrmann said, mildly impressed.

It was Hilde. They met the next day, at the same subway station. He hardly recognized her: she'd lost weight and looked sick. They went to a bar. Ion didn't dare to ask any precise questions, and Hilde didn't exactly volunteer information. Just to say something, Ion talked a little about Mr. Fuhrmann, but Hilde didn't find this an exciting subject, and called poor Fuhrmann an old fart. Then Ion told her about a "friend" who had crossed Hungary and Austria on foot, where he met a disabled guy who was making the same journey in a wheelchair. Hilde was only half listening.

"What's his name?"

"The one in the wheelchair? Gică."

"No, the other one."

"Oh! Petrişor Horhoianu."

"What a funny name!" Hilde said. "I ask because some time ago there was a Roma squatting at our place . . ."

"A Romanian!"

"Whatever! We were afraid of him at first. We thought he was a stool pigeon. Some of us still do. But what can we do? He's got Franz behind him."

"Who?"

"Franz. He's kind of our squat leader, and he likes boys . . ."

Hilde was living with a whole bunch of dropouts, apparently, in a big, rundown, abandoned house. They weren't paying any kind of rent. When Ion went to see her there for the first time, Hilde was alone, in a magnificent dress, waiting in a drawing room furnished with only a few scratched armchairs and a long mahogany table—or maybe it was some other rare wood.

"No need to ring, no need to knock . . ."

The house looked impressive from outside: virtually a palace. The lattice gate at the street entrance was unlocked. At the back lay a huge park, which had also gone to pot, naturally enough. Ion went up the flight of stairs, pushed on a massive door of sculpted oak, and found himself in a hall from which two staircases rose in wings to form a kind of oval, supporting the gallery on the first floor. The doors leading out from the hall were wide open. Hilde was standing up straight, in a long blue taffeta dress, beside a parrot cage that was taller than herself. The bird's feathers had all the colors of the countries belonging to the European Community.

"You go up an internal staircase and at the top you'll see the open doors of the drawing room."

He didn't meet anyone, but to the right of the staircase, or, to be more precise, beneath it, he thought he saw two shadowy forms trying to hide from him. The whole house was dimly lit—except for the part of the drawing room where Hilde was standing, thanks to a window behind the parrot's cage that cast a little more light.

"Come!"

She opened a door into another room, which, though much smaller, was furnished with a bed.

Unable to persuade Ion to join in, she sprinkled some of the white powder onto the back of her hand and snorted it alone. Then she gave a little pull on the belt of her dress, which opened at once. Hilde stood naked before Ion.

"Correct me if I'm wrong, but did you do it last time without a condom?"

"A condom?"

"Yes, a condom—don't you know what they are?" she said, lying on the bed.

"Sure I do."

"Well?"

"I don't really carry them around . . ."

"Buy yourself some! But today I'll let you use one of mine," Hilde said, reaching under the pillow.

The next day, while chatting with Petrişor to find out whether he too ever frequented the house on Venedigstrasse, Ion told him about the condom question.

"Do you think that means she's . . . ?"

"HIV? Not necessarily . . ."

"What do you mean?"

"I mean she doesn't entirely trust *you*. That's only normal."

"Yes, I guess so."

Anyway, it was good with the condom too, and Hilde was as wild as before—though Ion wasn't quite as impressed this time, especially since the condom, by reducing the direct stimulation, not only prolonged the act but also brought a certain detachment from it. That's why he noticed when a biker came into the room dressed as a deep-sea diver: he was carrying a girl's body, dripping water. They'd probably come from a swimming pool or God knows where. The biker-diver muttered something into his helmet and quickly retreated.

One morning Mr. Fuhrmann handed Ion a letter that had arrived from Romania. It was from Dinu Valea. He was glad to have an address where he could write to Ion at last, and this allowed him to hope that he might perhaps receive a few lines in return from his tramp of a son. He'd written before, to Ludoşan in Timişoara, who had replied, politely enough, that he didn't know Ion's whereabouts—probably in Budapest, although he didn't have an address for him. It was also possible that he'd already moved on to Vienna, or farther still. Dinu also said the police had come around twice now, asking about Ion. Once they made the old man go with them to headquarters, where they asked him a bunch of questions in connection with Maria. But he didn't know anything: after pestering him for more than an hour, they let him go home. It's not quite like under Ceausescu, after all! This new guy, Iliescu, hasn't been on television so often since he won the elections. Otherwise, life goes on. You can find everything at the market now, only everything's more and more expensive. And he, with his wretched little pension, well, it's hard to make ends meet.

Not a word about Marioara. She's probably run off again, Ion said to himself.

Mr. Fuhrmann liked to talk with young people. He was also a real, old-fashioned ecologist—not just one of those "defender of nature" types, who are so easy to make fun of (like practically every German you run into, especially the very young and very old), but someone eager to establish an ontological foundation for what he called an anticipatory projective morality.

"I don't get it," Petrişor said. He too claimed to be an ecologist, and maybe he was—but he knew Ion would greet with skepticism, if not outright mockery, any hint that he was simply signing up to Mr. Fuhrmann's views on the matter. "I don't understand how you can be moral in advance. Morality depends on individual circumstances—that is, on the present moment."

Ion nodded, more or less in agreement. Mr. Fuhrmann smiled with delight, settling into his armchair and taking his time to reply. The seconds passed. He was probably searching for the right words in Romanian; he didn't seem to have any problems with the language—it had been his too, after all—but he hadn't spoken it for a long time. Strange to think that he'd used it more than his mother tongue during all the years he'd worked as a Romanian railways conductor, just like Ion's father, before applying to emigrate to Germany. But he liked to read, and in recent years he'd been buying all kinds of books in German—so his recent enthusiasms had never found a footing in Romanian. He was an autodidact, Mr. Fuhrmann, and that is why there were some unexpected gaps in his knowledge. Ecology was his pet subject, but his curiosity didn't stop there: He'd read through shelves of history books, especially about the Second World War, which held a personal interest for him because his father had been deported to Siberia; German was very useful when it came to this kind of research. More recently, he'd been making efforts to read philosophy—a late passion that he couldn't explain even to himself. At his age! Many times he'd even neglected backgammon for philosophy's sake—but, precisely at his age, maybe he needed philosophy more than at any other.

Petrişor was impatient to get another word in. That's young people for you, Mr. Fuhrmann thought: the less they know the more they talk. He took a banana from the fruit bowl on the table.

"If I understand correctly," the young man said, "projective morality means taking responsibility for the future effects of your actions. I mean the harmful effects, a long time into the future . . . And this applies even if the person responsible is well-intentioned or is unaware of the consequences of what he does. But . . . the effects are distant and uncertain. So, how can you punish someone before you know the effects? That would be criminal!"

"I admit it would be difficult to pass legislation along those lines. The first task is to change the existing morals, because that always comes prior to the writing of laws. That's where we have to start. Otherwise, the nihilism that's taking a firmer and firmer hold will cause the void that's already surrounding us to deepen and grow . . . We have to fight it with secular instruments," Mr. Fuhrmann added, struggling a little for breath. "The Enlightenment and everything that's happened since then have eliminated the sacred dimension."

"What instruments do you mean?" Ion asked in a low voice.

"Fear. The heuristics of fear."

"I still don't understand," Petrişor sighed.

Mr. Fuhrmann smiled, feeling pleased with how their conversation was going. He half rose from his armchair, then sat back down. Petrişor read his mind, hurried to the kitchen, and returned with three bottles of beer from the fridge. It just took a few seconds. Fuhrmann didn't even have time to decide whether he should talk to them about Hobbes and the *summum malum*, which is more persuasive—because it produces more fear—than the *summum bonum*. In fact, things are more complicated, he thought, pouring himself a beer. In Hobbes the fear is pathological—as Kant would say—not spiritual.

"You mean fear keeps the garden better than the gardener," Ion joked. He was drinking straight from the bottle—which irritated Fuhrmann more than his recourse to paremiology. It was a sign of haste and loose thinking.

"You talk like someone from the suburbs, and a *golan* at that," the German complained, unaware that Romanian government circles had recently been reviving this Ceausescu-era word for "tramp" or "good-for-nothing" and using it to smear youthful opponents.

Petrişor didn't follow Ion's lead and take his own turn at bat—ridicule is Romania's national sport—but instead added a grave admonishment of his own. Ion responded by calling him a sanctimonious hypocrite, but he soon calmed down. Silence then. When Mr. Fuhrmann set down his empty glass, it was clear that the students were waiting for him to speak. He now had a little frothy mustache under his nose. He was looking for the best way to phrase what he had just been thinking.

"Evil dissuades more than Good persuades," Fuhrmann said, and again he paused to allow the boys time to digest his words. "And that's even true of the greatest evil of all."

"You mean death?" Ion whispered, in a return to gravitas.

"But, from an ecological point of view," Petrişor broke in, "evil most often manifests itself after the fact—perhaps even after the death of those who perpetrated it."

"You're right," Fuhrmann said, again with a smile.

This one thinks he's some kind of Socrates, Ion said to himself, slowly refilling his glass. He didn't like his beer to have too much of a head.

"Some solution has to be found," Mr. Fuhrmann said, after a few more minutes of silence. "Humanity doesn't have the right to commit suicide."

"Why not?" Ion asked dryly.

Petrişor was just then raising his glass to his lips. He shuddered. Drops of beer fell blithely onto his chin, neck, and shirtfront. This Ion is crazy, he said to himself. He's trying to pick a fight, and in the end Mr. Fuhrmann will explode and kick us both out . . . into the streets we'll go.

But Petrişor was wrong, poor guy. Mr. Fuhrmann's lips were spread wide, in a smile of delight.

"A very good question," he said. Petrişor wondered if he wasn't being ironic. Precise and ironic! Yes, rather than get angry, maybe he was mocking Ion in response to his impudence. But Ion looked mighty relaxed—he knew the old man better, knew who he was dealing with. Petrişor wasn't going to stick himself between these two.

"Why should an individual be allowed to commit suicide, but not the species? That's an excellent point."

"*That is the question,*" said someone in English.

Who?

Fuhrmann looked at Ion, but he hadn't said a word. Neither had Petrişor. The old man's lips twitched and his eyes bulged. How strange!

"Did you hear that too?" Ion asked, looking more afraid than insolent now.

"Maybe there's an Englishman in the house . . ." Petrişor suggested.

I put my ballpoint down and allow myself a little smile. I wonder how Marianne will react when she reads this bit. Whatever I do, I can't pull the wool over her eyes. She knows my voice too well.

Petrişor went to the fridge and opened the door.

"You don't think he's hidden in there, do you?" Ion asked, ready to start joking again, whether out of fear or spite. Putting on a brave face!

But Mr. Fuhrmann scowled: he was in no mood for jokes, and the complexities of the Romanian soul left him cold. For a moment he'd thought that Ion was genuinely interested in discussing the problem of ecology, but all either of them was interested in was getting more food and drink from the fridge. The youth of today! The Germans are no better, but at least they've got more flesh on them—they're not just skin and bones. Sure, they vote Green, some go on demonstrations or to rallies, but they don't have any coherent ecological ideas . . . Of course it's better that they defend nature instead of making racial purity their big thing—although some of those skinheads are still obsessed with that; it's enough to give you the shudders. Most of them are in the old GDR, it's true. In Rostock, for example, one Saturday night, they attacked a refugee hostel: mostly full of Romanians, which is to say Gypsies, but so what? You either accept them or send them away: you don't start killing them. Hundreds of Molotov cocktails rained down on the hostel, and people from the neighborhood came to gawk and even applauded the arsonists. When the police showed up, the crowd actually tried to stop them from arresting the skinheads.

"All from the same earth and the same water!" Mr. Fuhrmann sighed, pleased at having remembered this classical Romanian quotation.

As he came back with three more bottles of beer, Petrișor saw immediately that old Fuhrmann was getting angry, even watching his server a little suspiciously. Surely he doesn't think I'm a ventriloquist, Petrișor thought, giving the old man a little smile, trying to humor him. But Fuhrmann didn't return the smile. In Yugoslavia too young people are the most vicious—because they're also the most ignorant. And they don't have any memory of the old regime, which was on its last legs when they first began to get a political idea or two . . . A load of morons, that's all they are!

The German's brow was becoming more and more furrowed. Fortunately the telephone rang, its diabolical tinkle sounding much louder than usual. Fuhrmann got up and shuffled over to answer it. He still looked deadly serious, standing there with the receiver to his ear, though he began to get a strange look in his eyes. There seemed to be a tremor in his voice. Fear or respect . . .

"Herr Haiducu . . ." Fuhrmann said. "Yes, I'll put him on right away. *Sofort! Sofort!* Ion, come and speak to Mr. Haiducu."

"The writing's on the wall, I guess," Ion brooded, again resorting to cliché. He dragged himself up, stiff as an old man.

"Yes, hello?"

"So, your little buddy's back with you," Haiducu said contemptuously.

"Yes."

"Maybe all three of us should get together."

"What for?"

"*That is the question!*" And Haiducu laughed: a bleating sound like a goat—or an old woman bent over her cane, and when she turns her head you notice she looks like a goat . . .

Ion stood firm. He wouldn't agree to meet Haiducu, even when the gangster threatened to show up at Ahmed's bar. Ion didn't really care, now that Fuhrmann was more or less filled in about the difficulties he'd faced during his travels . . .

"If you want to stop by, that's up to you."

"You'll regret this, just you wait and see," Haiducu said, before hanging up with an angry clatter.

Ion stood thinking for a few more seconds, with the receiver still in his hand. Then he replaced it on the cradle, slowly and deliberately.

"Who was it?" Petrișor asked.

"You weren't very polite," Fuhrmann said reproachfully. Ion just shrugged. "You get nowhere by being impolite," the old man went on. "You make enemies."

Although Fuhrmann knew about Haiducu's role in Ion's adventures, the penny didn't really seem to have dropped. Admittedly, the student had withheld one or two essential details—for example, that Haiducu was the man who'd held up the little cards at the casino—but, after all, Ion had also predicted the numbers himself, and other people at the roulette table would have seen the cards too . . . As for the racetrack, Ion had shown that he could win all by himself. He didn't need Haiducu. Long ago, at Ploiești, there had only been Fane Ghișoiu and himself, and Ion had done pretty well for himself, no? There was nothing strange in his not revealing every little thing to Fuhrmann . . . It was no big deal that Ion had more money than the old man thought; Fuhrmann was only interested in loftier matters, in being able to converse with someone at a certain level of abstraction. (It was Petrișor that Ion had to be careful with as far as money was concerned.) Besides, there were some things he *couldn't* tell Fuhrmann, who was too rational and might misunderstand, or anyway refuse to believe, certain details in Ion's story. That had already happened once! And look at the asinine advice the old man gave him—as if politeness was the main thing to worry about right now . . .

"You should have invited him over, so we could talk things out properly."

"But who was it?" Petrișor asked again, with no more success than before. Since there was nothing left in his bottle, he made another trip to the fridge.

In Fuhrmann's eyes, Haiducu was probably nothing more than a casino conman, or at worst a petty blackmailer. But what could he have on Ion? Had the kid done something stupid during the student demonstrations? Maybe he'd been forced to leave the country? But Fuhrmann didn't have the nerve to interrogate his guest. In fact, even if he'd bitten the bullet, Ion wouldn't necessarily have told the whole truth and nothing but the truth.

By the time Petrișor returned with three more bottles, Fuhrmann was no longer upset. They're just kids, after all, running away from a benighted land. Mr. Fuhrmann had always regretted not having children; they would have been Ion's age by now, and probably similar to him: frivolous and self-centered. Still, it's stupid for a parent to blame his children for being selfish. There's no reciprocity in the parent-child relationship, except perhaps at the emotional level. As far as duties and responsibilities are concerned, we're talking about a one-sided phenomenon. Parents protect their offspring without asking anything in return, without counting on any reward. They do it by instinct. This should, therefore, also be the basis of ecological morality, Mr. Fuhrmann said to himself—and he slapped his forehead with the palm of his hand, rather as Archimedes did before leaving his bath, causing no small amount of confusion in the two Romanian students, who had been sipping their beer and thinking of something completely different.

"Do you need anything? Don't you feel well?" Petrișor asked politely.

Fuhrmann looked like someone who's just heard he's won the lottery. His eyes were swimming in tears of joy, his power of speech temporarily lost. Great happiness is beyond words. The only time Ion had seen him look so radiant—his forehead red and glistening with perspiration—was when he beat Tariq, the unofficial backgammon champion at Ahmed's bar.

Not knowing how to share his joy with the young men, nor how to pick up the thread of their conversation about ecological philosophy, Fuhrmann raised his glass for a toast—the only problem being that his guests had again finished their bottles.

"What's wrong with you kids? Sitting with empty glasses in the homeland of beer?"

Petrişor didn't wait to be asked twice.

"There are only two bottles left," he shouted from the kitchen.

"We'll buy some more," the German called back proudly, and he took out his wallet. Then he had a better idea. He flicked through his address book and—under the eyes of the new generation—dialed a number with his ring finger. Although he spoke very quickly in his native German, the invaders from the Orient understood that he was making an urgent order. Two dozen bottles! The old boy's lost his mind, Ion thought.

The local store took less than fifteen minutes to deliver. A few bottles were straight from their own refrigerator, so that the customer could start drinking at once. Mr Fuhrmann took three glazed mugs with lids from his sideboard.

He began to speak: slowly and hesitantly at first, pausing between sentences to find the right words and to get his ideas in order, then more and more quickly, with ever greater fluency and fervor . . . He didn't start with Adam and Eve but with the Flood. Until then people had lived in real harmony with nature, even though they'd already been banished from the Garden (did they feel like exiles?). In other words, they were no longer simply animals: they'd learned to work and to think. The watery assault, caused by incessant torrential rain, was considered a betrayal, an abandonment by the Mother Nature in whose bosom men and women had, till then, developed more or less as little children. They adopted three kinds of attitude in the face of this axiological apocalypse: Noah's response, which under Abraham led to the emergence of monotheism; Nimrod's response, which paved the way for the scientific mentality by way of the construction of the Tower of Babel; and then the Greek reconciliation with nature, to which Hegel, for one, adhered for a time. In reality, the last of these approaches was never fully accepted, even among the Greeks; it may therefore be considered utopian, albeit sound. The other two ideals, particularly the first, involved submission to a higher, divine power that could mediate our relationship with nature and protect us from its caprices; it was even believed that, by worshipping that higher power, humans would more and more get nature to obey them. We are the "chosen species," after all! Among the Greeks, however, the relationship between man and nature was managed by a host of gods, and man's ambition to wrest more and more privileges was often rejected or condemned. Prometheus's betrayal drew a terrible punishment, remember. Man didn't try to make peace with nature, just maintain a certain equilibrium with it . . .

The hiatus between man and nature, symbolized by the Flood, may also be seen as the separation of Subject from Object, a split carried to the point of estrangement and even open hostility. To heal this wound, Abraham imposed monotheism and, in a related move, a twofold tyranny over nature: man was the slave of Jehovah, and nature was the slave of man. Go forth and multiply! Master the whole world! Such was God's command to the human species.

The Judeo-Christian God is violent and cruel. He accepts evil in the world and, through human agency, even commits it Himself. The correlation between God and man is evident, here. Who, in the end, created whom, "in his own image and likeness"? It doesn't much matter. Either way, the result was disastrous. If we can no longer be believers, this is due to our recognizing how low the human individual has sunk . . . To believe in Him, we must also believe in ourselves, and how is that possible these days? God has His faults, of course, but at least He has the excuse of being a projection of our own . . .

"Okay, but He was also a way for man to justify his own crimes," Ion interrupted, taking the argument in a different direction.

Fuhrmann remained unruffled.

"That was clearly an unconscious projection, and it only made things worse. Morality . . ." (Here I feel like adding: the impulse behind morality must be duty to others, hence to the species . . .)

"It can't be based on a deal with the divinity," Ion continued, in a slightly declamatory tone.

Fuhrmann nodded. He was proud that the boys were no longer just listening to him but also understanding. They needed to be patient a little longer, however, since he hadn't finished what he wanted to say.

"So, paradoxical though it may seem, the religious attitude fueled Nimrod's attitude, which sought to confront nature without divine aid. The Tower of Babel was human pride in its pure state. And, if God prevented its completion—the confusion of tongues made it impossible for the workers to communicate with one another—He did it out of fear that the gigantic edifice would reach heaven itself: that is, that men would dispense with Him, no longer need a protective master . . ."

Ion blinked, unsure of what Fuhrmann was getting at. Did he mean that both science and religion are anti-ecological? In that case, well, man himself . . . But he didn't want to interrupt the oratorical flow again.

"Let me go back to Abraham for a moment," the German said, looking quite pleased. "As you know, Abraham was willing to sacrifice his only son, just to prove his blind obedience to God. In nature, the perpetuation of the species is an instinct, an end in itself, the red thread running through life on earth. Only man has been able to disturb this vital instinct, to sacrifice the future of his species for the sake of an ideological construct. The angel stayed Abraham's hand, but he *would* have killed . . ."

"Maybe he'd already seen him, so knew he wasn't risking anything," Ion suggested.

"Seen who?"

"The angel."

"Again with the jokes!"

Well, anyway, he would have killed Isaac, that's what we're told, and Isaac would have accepted it without flinching: in essence, he would have committed suicide. An ecological murder, so to speak—the perfect genocide. The Hebrews pioneered this idea, and then the Christians took it up and made it the cornerstone of their thought: God Himself had agreed to kill his only begotten son. Was this a way of atoning for His own original sin: the subject-object dichotomy? A reprieve for a humanity that was now entirely at sea, and whose morality was on the rocks? However we rationalize this sacrifice, it's clear that Christian compassion isn't applicable outside the human realm. Man continues to think of himself as the lord of nature, when in fact he's a petty tyrant . . . a Ceausescu.

The Judeo-Christian mentality is fundamentally anti-ecological, and that fact is the source of all the difficulties in the way of a shift in humanity's priorities. Ecological morality must be based on a new sanctification of our survival instinct: for instance, the idea that the coming generations will be our own flesh and blood . . . which, of course, is perfectly true! We have a responsibility for what will happen to our grandchildren and great grandchildren, and it depends mainly on us whether and under what conditions they will exist. Sanctification of the species, not of the individual!

What can stop Mr. Fuhrmann when he's philosophizing?

Only one thing: the Absolute; pure transcendence.

The two students, heads buzzing from the beer and the hot summer of 1991, hoped that Mr. Fuhrmann would soon tire himself out and rest content with his prolegomenon for a new morality . . . Perhaps then he would take a little break, at least long enough for them to hazard a modest proposal:

"How about stopping by Ahmed's? Maybe Tariq's back from Baghdad."

Ion and Petrişor slipped out of the bar, leaving Fuhrmann in single combat with the Iraqi champion.

It was a pleasant evening in early autumn. It had been raining for an hour or two, and the asphalt was still wet and shiny. They had nowhere special to be. Suddenly Petrişor stopped, sighed, and said:

"What are we doing here, Ion?"

Ion had no answer to the question, which until then he'd managed to avoid raising himself. He'd posed other, vaguely related questions, and one thing might easily have led to another, but he'd never come right out with the big one. For example, he'd asked why he hadn't ever taken a chance and gone to look for Sandu in Heidelberg. True, Sandu hadn't answered the letter Ion sent him a few days after first arriving in Munich—and that was several months ago now. And, also true, Sandu's parents hadn't answered either, hadn't sent back a simple note, just a few lines with Sandu's current address . . . Surely they would have seen the sender's name and realized that he, Sandu's best friend, was in Germany—just a stone's throw away? He'd waited patiently, but nothing had come. He then began to speculate that Sandu had left Europe entirely, shipped off to the United States, for example, and that his parents had forwarded Ion's letter to him there. But Sandu would have had time to reply by now, to tell him what had happened in his life, why he had decided to emigrate a second time; to argue that there's no point staying in the Old World if you're really serious about sports, that only American universities turn out world-class athletes nowadays . . . Sure, it's not easy to succeed over there: the competition is fierce. Just think of all those blacks: if they don't go in for music, what else will the Americans let them do except play sports—mainly baseball and basketball, but also track . . .

Sandu *could* have written all that, but he didn't. In the end he couldn't be bothered.

So, Ion didn't answer Petrişor's question. They were walking slowly, in silence. And Petrişor didn't repeat the question.

After a little while Ion said, "Why don't we go to a nightclub? It's on me."

"What, you struck it rich all of a sudden?" Petrişor asked, with a stupid grin.

Ion quickened his step.

When they got to the nightclub, a girl with bare breasts popped laughing out of a barrel and invited them in. Then she crouched back down inside the barrel. Petrişor wanted to take a peek.

"You're not supposed to do that," Ion warned.

A bouncer well over six feet tall grabbed Petrişor by the belt and pulled him away. The girl again came out again smiling from ear to ear, her breasts bouncing around.

"He's with me," Ion said in German. And he put his hand into his inside pocket, as if looking for his wallet.

They went in and sat at a table near the stage, which was separated from the hall by a red velvet curtain. Ion ordered a bottle of champagne.

"You're crazy," Petrişor said admiringly.

A black cat appeared and sneaked along the curtain, standing out sharply against the red material. It went to the other end of the platform, then turned and came back. A blonde grabbed the cat from behind the curtain. She held it to her breast like a newborn babe. She was wearing a white jumper, and Ion thought she looked like Maria. He nudged Petrişor with his elbow and said:

"Don't you think she looks like . . . ?"

"Who?"

"Maria."

"Are you kidding? Can't you see she's blonde—and German?"

"Maria was blonde."

The curtain lifted very slowly. Again they saw the black cat, which seemed to have grown in the meantime. Two men in white smocks walked on carrying the recumbent blonde on a mortuary slab.

"Maria was blonde too," Ion repeated softly. He didn't want to disturb the rest of the audience, who were taking a keen interest in the goings-on, craning their necks and sitting up in their seats. Trembling with excitement.

"Was she?" Petrişor asked. He sounded doubtful. He raised a champagne glass to his mouth, but didn't go beyond moistening his lips. He was in a good mood.

"Yes, she was a pretty blonde . . ." Ion confirmed, and it dawned on him that one of the two male nurses was none other than Fane Ghişoiu. Not really so implausible, since he'd already seen him in Munich once . . . at the races. Ion didn't bother telling Petrişor—he might never have met the coach back home.

The orderlies laid the slab on a kind of hospital bed. The girl wasn't moving, didn't even seem to be breathing. She was wearing a white jumper and a short skirt that didn't reach anywhere near her knees. Mister Fane made a comical gesture of complicity with the audience and raised the girl's upper torso in such a way that, although her eyes were shut and her head was still resting on the coach's belly, she seemed to be lying flat on the bed, her legs straight in front of her. The other man removed her shoes and socks. Her soles, like Maria's, were quite large and quite reddish.

"You see, you've even forgotten what she looks like," Petrişor scolded. Instead of focusing on the stage, he glanced from time to time at a corner of the hall where he thought he had seen Ana. But, of course, he said nothing to Ion about this, so as not to encourage his delusions about Maria. The two girls were inseparable . . .

Mister Fane tried to pull the girl's jumper over her head, but he found it too difficult and she apparently began to feel stifled beneath the wool. The other nurse roared with laughter, turned his head, and winked at the audience. Then Ion caught sight of Ana too, who was following the scene onstage as though her life depended on it. Beside her, Roger was pouring whisky into a glass. He was placid. Or blasé. Ion almost whispered a few words to Petrişor about what he'd seen, but thought better of it.

With a triumphant shout, Mister Fane (or the man resembling Mister Fane) finally tore off the white jumper. The girl's head reappeared, her blond hair tousled and her face flushed. No, she wasn't dead. Nor was she Maria. Applause.

The skirt proved easier, and it wasn't long before she stood in her black panties and bra. One of the men sat beside her on the bed and stroked her thighs, while the other undid her bra and released her breasts. Then they pulled off her panties. The audience applauded again. The man still on his feet opened his fly and displayed his organ. The girl's eyes were wide as windows, her mouth a gaping cavern.

Petrișor had never seen an act of fellatio performed in public before. He poured himself another glass of champagne. Unfortunately, the curtain came down just as things were getting going.

"Are you convinced now that it wasn't Maria?"

Ion pointed to the table where he thought he had seen Ana and Roger. They were gone. He looked back at Petrișor, but his friend's eyes had already wandered off again.

"It's like each of us has a double."

"Excuse me?" Petrișor looked back at Ion. Was he serious?

"We each have someone who's like an identical twin. A brother . . ."

". . . or sister."

Petrișor shrugged, then snatched the champagne bottle out of their ice bucket and poured himself another glass. The curtain was motionless, as was Ion with his head in his hands. He hadn't even touched his champagne. Soon, a tall stocky man—he looked like a band member (not a Party member!)—came up to their table. He stared for a few seconds at Petrișor, who was calmly sipping his champagne, then at Ion, who still had his face hidden. The man reached out and tapped Ion on the shoulder, winking at Petrişor and prompting him to break out in an anxious smile.

"Is he sleeping or crying?" the man asked. Ion was ignoring him.

Petrişor wasn't surprised to hear the guy speak Romanian. He drank another mouthful, that stupid smile still on his face.

"May I sit down?" the swarthy musician asked, with an excessive politeness that Petrişor probably interpreted as sarcasm. But, not knowing what else to say, the student opened his hands and gestured to an empty chair. Then he leaned over to Ion and whispered in his ear:

"Who is this guy, Ion?"

Only then did Ion raise his head and look at the dark-skinned stranger, who had sat down and was pulling Ion's full glass over to himself.

"The accordionist!" Ion whispered, his despair almost comical.

The curtain rose on a naked man with large swan's wings; he was moving them with difficulty: they were heavy, and not exactly white. The accordionist, having emptied Ion's glass in one gulp, was looking greedily at the rest of the bottle—but then he swung around on his chair and began to watch the performance like everyone else. The swan-man waddled awkwardly to the other end of the stage, where a girl draped in a thin, transparent shroud was lying on a sofa and waiting. It might have been the same girl from the earlier act.

Ion reburied his head in his hands. Petrişor poured some champagne for himself and for the accordionist, the latter still using Ion's glass. The bottle was empty now, and Ion was already regretting his generosity.

"Let's order another bottle!" the accordionist shouted. Petrişor wasn't sure who was supposed to pick up the next round. In any case, he was broke . . .

But Ion looked up and, to Petrişor's surprise, said in a calm voice:

"Okay. I'm thirsty too."

He sat up in his chair to attract the waiter's attention, but there was no sign of the man. Ion really *was* thirsty too: he hadn't gotten so much as a drop from the first bottle. He stood. Meanwhile, two girls on stage were holding a large red flag, one corner sewn with a golden hammer and sickle.

"What are you doing?" Petrişor asked, his voice sounding thicker than before.

The accordionist arranged his chair in such a way that he could sit back comfortably without taking his eyes off the girls. They proved to be very talented strippers—removing their clothes while passing the flag between themselves as necessary. Ion cast them a last look before he went off zigzagging between the tables. He passed to the right of the stage and began to descend an endless staircase—an unusual rumbling could be heard from far below. The stairs didn't lead to the bathrooms or to the kitchen—Ion went down and down into the dark. At last he heard happy, excited voices nearby—snatches of songs, jukebox music, a tango . . . Arriving in front of a half-open double door, he peered through the gap and saw a dimly lit room where two pairs of dancers were gliding between a few long rectangular tables. Maria and Ana were seated at one table next to Roger; both wore very light dresses—one might even say slips. Maria had an exaggeratedly long cigarette holder and was blowing smoke rings. Ana was sipping from a brandy glass. Haiducu sat enthroned at the head of the table, dressed in a tuxedo with a chrysanthemum in the buttonhole. Ion knew some of the remaining characters, but others were strangers: two girls in claret-colored jumpers who looked like twins; the bouncer he'd run into on the way in; the girl in the barrel, who, as Ion only now realized, was actually Bojena, the Bosnian from Budapest, although, wait, he wasn't absolutely sure . . . And yes, of course, Fane Ghişoiu of all people, well, he couldn't have been left out: he had a glass in one hand and was calling for silence; he wanted to make a speech, but no one took him seriously—Ana was trying to fit one of her breasts into her brandy glass, so everyone had their eyes on her instead, while the former coach's teaspoon taps on table and wineglass merely irritated the others. Haiducu finally reached out, and—making a violent yet precise sweeping motion—brought Ghişoiu's glass crashing to the floor.

"I'm the one who's giving the speech," Haiducu declared in his baritone.

Ghişoiu didn't make a sound. Not even Roger had the courage to stand up to Haiducu, or even to point out that he couldn't understand a word of his Romanian blather, and, really, if he was going to make an election speech now, that would be that, as far as he—Roger—was concerned: he'd go back upstairs and watch the girls take their clothes off . . . that would be much more fun. No, he didn't say any of that; he just muttered something in Ana's ear, but she put a finger to her lips to shut him up. One of her breasts was still resting in her brandy glass, but everyone had forgotten about it now—watching, fascinated, as Haiducu got up on a chair and looked down over the assembled crowd. Not even the dancers were dancing any longer. Nor was any music to be heard.

"*Дорогие товарищи,*" Haiducu began in Russian. With the exception of Roger, who was drinking cognac straight from the bottle, everyone was hanging on his every word. Ion didn't understand everything, but he got the gist of it: namely, that this infra-terrestial world was only one stage, one fleeting moment, on the way to the luminous Beyond where the great Gagarin was watching over us. This was why one and all had to fulfill their missions heroically, without any consideration for themselves.

At the back of the hall Lebedev began to beat his wings . . .

It was a pleasant, sunny blue morning. Ion opened one eye and looked at the clock on his bedside table. Then he opened the other, to make sure, and jumped up like a jack-in-the-box. He was going to be late.

After just five minutes he walked out the front door munching a pretzel. Once in the street he broke into a run, accelerating when he saw a bus heading for the station. He leapt onto it at the last moment.

I come back from shopping and pass in front of Europe hanging there immobile and indifferent on the wall. I stop. The little counters are all in their places, like the pennants representing troop positions on an army headquarters map. In their places? Actually, I'm pretty sure the things are out of date: my map no longer reflects the real situation on the ground. For example, according to the latest information, Ana and Mihai have left the embassy and are working at Radio Free Europe, in Munich. Ion has seen them a number of times; the circumstances didn't allow him to stop and chat, but that doesn't mean they were hallucinations. As for Roger, given his job as a truck driver, he could be almost anywhere in Europe—even in Turkey. Sonia also moves around a lot, between Budapest, Vienna, and Prague—sometimes with Karim, sometimes with the boss himself, Georges. Speaking of which, Georges has been away in Lebanon: he took Hanka, the Polish girl, along with him. Sonia didn't exactly appreciate that, but she kept her mouth shut. Business hasn't been too good lately: there's a lot of competition . . . When Georges gets back, he won't be pleased to hear that another two of his protégées, Bojena and Nemira, have run off into the great wide world. Bojena is probably in Munich; nothing is known about the other one. There's a rumor going round that she's mixed up with some terrorist organization.

After a few months wandering around Transylvania and the Banat, where she spent some time with her cousin, Dr. Farkas, Zsuzsa returned to Budapest and has been spending most of her time playing bridge. In Timişoara she met Tiberius and discussed Ion with him several nights running. Neither Tiberius nor Gyuri Farkas knew the current whereabouts of our adventurous student. Zsuzsa did her best to sound offhand, even sardonically humorous, when she spoke about Ion, but Gyuri wasn't fooled by this front. By the way, I should move his counter too, since he's now moved to Budapest for good; he has a very interesting job there and is engaged to a woman who owns a café.

Other characters are significantly less mobile. It's a question of age. Mr. Fuhrmann, for instance, only ever goes to Ahmed's, at the corner of his street, or very occasionally takes a bus to the downtown bookstores. The same goes for his former workmate, Dinu Valea, who's retired now and spends whole days without so much as stepping outdoors. It should be said that Marioara has left him again, and this time probably for good. She's found someone younger and more solvent.

Other characters still have vanished without a trace. In particular, nothing is really known about Maria, whose story is so complicated that it's best, perhaps, to close the file on it for good. Neither do we know much about Dr. Gachet, for instance, who left on an expedition to Afghanistan and hasn't been heard of for months. Smaranda gets along without him as well as she can. She's been seeing more and more of Marianne, who likewise considers herself to have been abandoned. They go together to the theater or the movies.

As for Sandu Economu, let's assume that he's crossed the ocean and settled into life on a university campus in California. There's been some ugly talk that he made friends with Valentin there, who happened to be on assignment in the U.S., but that their friendship didn't last long, because Valentin ended up getting himself shot dead in a bathroom. We can't be sure about this, however. When Ion finally went to Heidelberg, he couldn't find Sandu's parents at the address he'd been given. The neighbors were completely bemused. When Ion asked if they remembered a family of Romanians with a Mercedes in the yard, they laughed in his face: What yard would that be?

Ion went back to the train station, not even curious to see a little of old Heidelberg. He looked at the castle from below without climbing up to it—the castle that French troops set alight in the age of Louis XIV. Then he rested his elbows on a bridge overlooking the Neckar; the water was dirty and sluggish. Ion didn't really know what to do with himself: unfortunately he'd left Sandu's letters behind in Romania, and, although he'd jotted the address down in his notebook (along with Fuhrmann's and many others he'd needed on his travels), he wasn't absolutely certain that he hadn't just made a mistake. Could he have got the name of the street wrong? What else sounds like "Hölderlinweg"?

He ran into the hunter on the train, but didn't recognize him at first, since the man was wearing ordinary clothes. The hunter without a rifle . . . And this time he didn't have his game bag either. He was lying stretched out on the seat, alone in the compartment. The other compartments were almost full, so Ion asked politely if he could sit on the seat opposite. The hunter answered as if they'd known each other for ages. He had a weak voice, in contrast to his rather stout frame and chubby face. Ion sat by the window and tried not to look at the hunter, especially since he was reminded of the scene on the Vienna-Munich express whenever the other man spoke. No, he wasn't dressed in the Bavarian (or Tyrolean?) style this time, but there could be no doubt that it was the same man. Ion was itching to go look for a seat in another compartment, or even stand in the corridor—as long as he could get out of there. But he didn't have the nerve. What was he really afraid of? In fact, what he felt was a more complex emotion, with perplexity as the dominant component. Not fear—or, rather, not a normal, every-day fear but a rarer state of mind, a general apprehension in which his reason was paralyzed. Perhaps he was afraid of understanding—though at the same time it was precisely fear that fueled his urge to understand . . . To understand what? He didn't know.

His head was turned toward the window, but he was watching the hunter out of the corner of his eye. The hunter, for his part, kept staring straight at him—smiling. You could even say that he was appealing to Ion, asking him to turn around, asking for his attention before he started to speak.

"Are you wondering where you know me from? Where you saw me before?" the hunter asked.

"Er, no . . . no," Ion stammered, without turning his head. He pretended to be absorbed in the landscape.

"Are you afraid to look at me? Do I disgust you? Or maybe you pity me, is that it?"

Now Ion saw a girl in the compartment he hadn't noticed before. Had she come in through the door? I mean, had she slid open the compartment door without his noticing? Had she come in from outside?

She sat smiling by the feet of the hunter, who quickly, happily, cleared a space for her next to him.

"All the other compartments are full," she said, with a Slav accent.

The hunter pointed to Ion, who was still staring out the window, and said, spitefully:

"He's pretending to be interested in what he sees out there."

"So?"

The girl beamed a smile at Ion, and he couldn't resist smiling back. He turned around and, looking straight into her eyes, smiled again.

"Where are you coming from?"

"Heidelberg."

"No, I mean which country?"

Ion hesitated. He couldn't say he was Austrian, nor did he want to say he came from Hungary. It would have been simpler, but it just struck him as craven. What—was he ashamed of being Romanian? The girl waited patiently. The hunter made a sudden movement and hit his head against the metal bar on the window.

"Transylvania."

The hunter let out a groan, then a growl. Finally, the sounds coming out of his mouth were sufficiently articulate to be intelligible:

"Exile is a slow death," the recumbent figure murmured. "A death agony. Look at the state I'm in . . ."

Ion looked at the hunter, then at the girl, who made a wry little face, as if to say: Don't take the gentleman seriously, can't you see he's only talking to keep himself awake?

"When I was back home, in my forest over the mountains . . ." the hunter declaimed. The girl started laughing, and so did Ion.

Then all three of them laughed.

"Tell us about Maria," the girl said wistfully, pulling her dress far up her thighs. She had quite thin legs, with bony knees.

"Yes, come on, tell us," the hunter said stridently, grimacing.

Ion started weeping. Soon all three of them were in tears.

As the train was pulling into Munich, the hunter spoke one last memorable phrase under the girl's mocking eyes. She had just taken off her dress; she had neither breasts nor pubic hair.

"Go to France," the hunter said. "Don't waste any more time here. Go to France. You're expected there."

Ion got off the train at the last minute. His state of acute bewilderment was now accompanied with a sense of malaise, of discontent. He was weary inside, I don't quite know how to put it. He'd lost the plot, and this produced a kind of exhaustion, even nausea. He felt like throwing up. He wanted to go to the station bathroom, but he suddenly felt afraid. He thought he could see . . . But no, it wasn't him. That was just Ion trying to justify his fear. What if the hunter lying on the train seat had been right?

Ion dragged himself toward the bus stop.

Mr. Fuhrmann was home: he had a headache and wasn't in the mood for anything. Ion noticed this and would have been happy to leave him alone—all he meant to say was good evening. But then he suddenly felt obliged to explain why he was back so soon.

"I couldn't find anyone at the address I had," Ion said. He stood in front of Fuhrmann, who was sunk into an armchair.

"No one, really?" Fuhrmann asked, mildly surprised, opening one eye but otherwise sitting perfectly still.

It was almost dark outside. Mr. Fuhrmann had closed his eye and was groaning gently.

"Don't you feel well?" Ion asked, ready to go to his room. It's hard to say which is more civilized in such situations: to show concern and risk disturbing the other person, or to tiptoe by and risk seeming indifferent.

Fuhrmann didn't reply, and Ion hurried away to his room. Maybe he's had a fight with Petrişor, Ion speculated, while checking that the suitcase was still under his bed. Maybe he's simply thrown him out. I'll have to ask. Ion went to the door and gripped the handle, but then he thought better of it. That just isn't done! It would be like asking Fuhrmann to give an account of himself. Whatever might have happened, he'd been pretty generous, really—not only to Ion, but to Petrişor too ... putting them both up, and putting up with them! Ion sat on the sofa. Yes, Fuhrmann must have kicked Petrişor out, told him to get going. And now he feels bad about it. That's why he's sulky and doesn't feel like talking. His conscience is bothering him. But why didn't he say anything? He could have just said, deadpan, in as few words as possible: That Petrişor is unbearable, I showed him the door. But no, Fuhrmann had hardly even looked at Ion, just opened one eye. Mr. Fuhrmann, usually so polite, didn't bother to respect convention this time—What do you gain by being impolite?, as he was fond of saying. Maybe he's really angry, even with me! Ion thought. He stood up. It's not out of the question that he'll give me my marching orders too.

He crossed the few steps to the sofa-bed and took another, closer look at his suitcase: it wasn't shut! He put one of his hands on it. He always closed it after taking something out. How could he have forgotten? A dark suspicion began to form inside him. Someone had opened the case while he was away. Petrişor!

Ion felt the ground give way beneath him. He sat back on the sofa and ran his hand across his forehead. He was sweating. He got to his feet again, bent down, and pulled the suitcase up. Opening it wide, he removed the two shirts, the briefs, the socks, the tie, and the handkerchiefs he had laid on top of his money. It was still there! But no—there were only a few wads left. Ion sat down next to the suitcase, breathing hard. He tried to compose himself, then began counting. Soon he got confused and stopped. But it was clear enough: Petrişor had made off with more than half the money, like a thief. He'd fallen out with Fuhrmann over something or other and his solution had been to poke around in his friend's suitcase. Ion's head went back into his hands; he sat and pondered what to do. To start off, should he tell Fuhrmann or not? It would probably be best from every point of view to tell him, to complain. At least it would ease Fuhrmann's conscience, if it was really his conscience that was troubling him. And it would cast Ion himself in a better light: the innocent victim. But, then: should he tell Fuhrmann that Petrişor had stolen practically *all* his money? And that he wanted to leave for France, as he'd planned from the beginning, but was afraid that he no longer had enough money to make it? Maybe Fuhrmann would feel sorry for him and take out . . . how much? A few hundred deutschmarks? But that's next to nothing, Ion thought, knowing that he still had enough schillings left to buy himself a few *thousand* marks, not a few hundred.

"I'd like to head out for France," Ion announced that evening, after he had told Fuhrmann about Petrişor's vanishing act with the money. The German had been horrified, eyes bulging and a hand raised babylike to his mouth.

"As you wish," he replied, once the wave of emotion had passed.

And they spoke no more of Petrişor. With the help of a few beers, Fuhrmann recovered his appetite for life and conversation, and began explaining the myth of Prometheus and Epimetheus to Ion.

"Both of them?" Ion asked in surprise. "I only learned about Prometheus."

"You were taught a truncated version, which is usually what happens in Romania. Prometheus stole fire from the heavens . . . But Prometheus stole fire and brought it to man because his brother, Epimetheus, whether from carelessness or stupidity, had forgotten to create human beings—or, to be more precise, had done it too late, once the show was over, as they say." Fuhrmann chuckled, then continued: "He created them after the flora and fauna, after he had more or less successfully established an ecobalance both within and between those two realms. Do you understand? Man, the latecomer species, was doomed to disappear, and that's what would have happened if it hadn't been for Prometheus's courageous intervention."

"Why's that?"

"What do you mean, 'why's that?' Don't you see that man was surplus to requirements, a troublesome afterthought who'd have been eliminated if Prometheus hadn't decided to help out—partly, it's true, because his brother's stupidity had put him in a tight spot. Prometheus gave man something that wasn't part of his nature: technology."

"Fire stolen from the gods."

"Exactly. So, man survived thanks to technology. You could say that, right from the beginning, man was against nature. He was an artificial species—that is, forced to resort to artifice, to break the harmony with nature, and, worse still, to gradually disrupt the initial equilibrium from which he had, by definition, been excluded. That's what the Greeks teach us. Read Plato's dialogue about that Sophist, what's his name?"

"Gorgias?"

"No, the other one. Protagoras! He was an extraordinary figure, far ahead of his time. Among other things, he coined the famous maxim 'Man is the measure of all things.' Yes, yes. Do you know what one of his works is called?"

"No."

"*Truth, or The Discourse to make you fall flat on your back . . . !*"

". . . In astonishment?"

"I don't know. Could well be. Astonishment is the mother of philosophy."

"So who's the father?"

Fuhrmann gave Ion a dirty look. He wasn't used to this kind of Romanian banter anymore. He couldn't bear it, especially when his brain was really humming and producing such important ideas. He could see that Ion understood very well what he meant. Sometimes the young man seemed actually interested, asking questions and really participating in their conversation . . . But then he'd suddenly lose interest and come up with this kind of nonsense. Ion had to know it irritated him. Fuhrmann had told him as much more than once. But it didn't seem to make a difference.

"Is it really so hard for you to be serious for more than a few minutes at a time? It doesn't matter how we start out, you always end up making a big joke out of it all. What a waste of a good mind! I'm sorry to say that . . . because I like you, you know? You're not a stupid kid—just a rough diamond, I suppose!"

Ion said no more and hung his head.

Fuhrmann continued his philosophical discourse until late into the night, weaving together banalities and flashes of legitimate insight that he didn't know how to express well in words. Whenever he tried to fit one of these into the flow of his speech, it sounded a little odd and unconvincing. Sometimes too he got his facts wrong . . . for instance about that dialogue, in which Plato—far from being an ecologist—is simply trying to demonstrate that man is a social/political animal imbued with a sense of honor and justice.

So, now I am forced to move my *Ion* counter to Strasbourg.

He was whistling as he climbed down from the train. His suitcase was light; the overcoat he'd bought the day before his departure was slung over his other arm. He seemed in a good mood. He might be seeing Hilde in a few days. She had an aunt in Strasbourg, and she'd given him the number where she could be reached.

"Do you have anyone in France?" Fuhrmann asked him before he left.

"I do, in Paris."

"Who?"

"A writer."

"A writer? A Romanian?"

"Yes, from Romania."

"In exile?"

"Yes."

"What's his name? Is he well known?"

"I'm not sure."

"You're not sure of his name?"

"No. He only gave me his phone number."

"Where did you get to know him?"

"In Bucharest."

"After the . . . events?"

"Just after. He came in a truck, with a truckload of medicine."

"No kidding!"

"He was with a doctor from Médecins Sans Frontières. Mihai met the guy first and then introduced him to the rest of us. He invited him around to his apartment, where a number of us were getting together that night."

"But you said you don't really trust Mihai?"

"So?"

"Who knows what your writer's mixed up in? You can't trust anyone these days," Fuhrmann said. "You saw that with Petrişor. Who would have thought it!"

Ion was glad he hadn't said anything about Hilde. When Fuhrmann asked him why he was stopping in Strasbourg, he just muttered something about the cathedral, and the German was suitably impressed.

"You should also stop in Cologne. The cathedral there is the biggest and most impressive. I'll even treat you to a hotel."

So Ion came out of it with a little extra. Poor Fuhrmann! Was he just naive, or did he just want to help in as tactful a way as possible? In fact, it's very likely that he was sorry to see Ion leave; he'd no longer have an audience for his philosophizing. He'll have to go back to backgammon all day in Ahmed's bar—when he's at the table there, he doesn't say a word; some people even prefer not to play with him because he's so taciturn. It's not only that he's silent himself: he won't let his partner talk either. He refuses to respond to any questions, so the other man eventually loses interest and goes quiet—or else, if he does keep up a noisy monologue, Fuhrmann hisses, puts a finger to his mouth, or even calls aloud for silence: *Ruhe!*—"Well, well, he's not mute after all," the Turk or Serb or Greek opposite him exclaims.

Ion checked into a hotel near the station. Even the cheapest room seemed horribly expensive to him, but he had no alternative and he wasn't down to his last cent. He'd have to think about the future, though. Perhaps Miodrag hadn't been bragging and would be able to find him a job. Ion had met him in Munich, at Ahmed's, where the whole Balkan Peninsula seemed to gather. He was a Serb, from Bosnia.

"What are you fighting about there?" Ion asked him once.

"Fighting? Do you see me fighting?"

Miodrag did indeed look peace-loving—until the day when, feeling insulted by a Turk, he flashed his knife in the air. This too happened at Ahmed's bar. The Turk had no interest in fighting, probably didn't even have a weapon. He ran behind the bar and, with Ahmed's help, managed to get into the kitchen. Miodrag soon calmed down and didn't try to follow the man: He had defended his honor! (Is that the same kind of honor that Plato was talking about? Ion laughed and shook his head, his mop of black hair.)

When Ion left the hotel to go for a walk, he took all his money with him. There was less weight now, substantially less—not only because of Petrişor, but also because Ion had changed some of his schillings into large deutschmark notes. Not far from the station, he changed one of these again: into francs. He felt relieved: he got a good rate of exchange. Now he could understand why, as Miodrag had said, people from Strasbourg went looking for work in Germany. The border is just down the road, and being more or less German themselves they don't have any problems with the language. If they find work across the border, they take it and give up their job in France. They can still be home for dinner and sleep in their own bed. That was roughly how Miodrag had put it. What's more, the French hate moving, so the jobs they leave vacant aren't filled at once, and it suits the bosses fine to hire unregistered workers—that is, immigrants or unemployed people who are willing to work for less in order to be kept off the books and continue receiving benefits. That way, everyone's a winner.

"And the state foots the bill!" the Serb had concluded triumphantly.

"But who's the state? Where do you think it gets its money from?" Ion might have pointed out. "And, anyway, what's the state still good for nowadays?"

Miodrag gave him a telephone number in Strasbourg: a certain Slobodan, who had married a Portuguese or Spanish woman and started a small business there.

"Tell him I sent you—and that you're Romanian . . . But Romanian, not Romany!"

In keeping with his favorite proverb ("Never do today what you can put off until tomorrow"), Ion didn't call the number right away. He felt like seeing the cathedral first. Having broken his promise to Fuhrmann by giving Cologne and its cathedral a wide berth, he thought he should make up for it as soon as possible by seeing its sister in Strasbourg.

It was huge. If you looked at it without moving away from the walls, you became dizzy and frightened, as though the mass of stone was threatening to collapse. Ion felt small and pitiful, no more than a worm. His neck and eyes hurt. He looked away, in other directions. Stalls and booths with souvenirs lined the sidewalk opposite the cathedral. All those glaring, parrotlike colors—curiously matching the flags of the European Community states that fluttered overhead with all their petty, ephemeral energy—brought Ion back down to earth . . . to the mundane. The humility of the moment before was replaced, at least in part, by feelings of disgust and contempt. It was the first time he had dared give a name to this feeling: Yes, contempt, that was it precisely, there was no other word for it, not even "disillusionment" would do. Here in Strasbourg, in the capital of Greater Europe, Ion was surprised to feel contempt for the consumer society, its ostentatious wealth, its new, superficial, provisional opulence expressed in little knickknacks at once insignificant and aggressive, all like a cloud of mosquitoes next to the calm massive wealth of the cathedral—the only true wealth in that part of the city.

That was more or less what he would write to Fuhrmann in a few days. The sincerity of Ion's tone and the occasional stylistic flourish would bring a kindly smile to the old German's face. And if a few elements of ecological critique happened to be mixed in, he would even feel like replying—but where to?—to congratulate and encourage the young man. It's also our fault (everyone's fault) if Europe has come to this pass, Fuhrmann would say. It's all we have, though, and things are even worse elsewhere . . .

However, instead of deploying a few choice phrases to show that he understood the eco-crux of the problem, Ion opted for a narrative register and wrote to Fuhrmann about his encounter with Gică. Yes, the disabled Gică had been begging for alms beneath the cathedral walls, one hand outstretched, eyes shut as if he were blind. Maybe he was ashamed, Ion thought, and like a child was closing his eyes so as not to be seen. He sat there in his wheelchair, which looked about to fall apart—or, anyway, it was no longer the pristine wonder (was it actually the same chair, in fact?) that the Germans had brought to his home, removed from its packaging, and presented to Gică in bed, causing him to sit bolt upright, cry out, and clap his hands like a madman. He'd wanted to fondle it, and when the Germans held it up for him to get a closer look, he'd tried to kiss it all over—especially the wheels.

What an invention the wheel was! Fuhrmann would exclaim as he read Ion's letter. But this would only be a brief philosophical aside: he'd have his work cut out to read all the results of Ion's night-long scribbling. That hadn't happened to him for ages!

The encounter with Gică left a deep impression on Ion. In the first place, he was amazed at his own perspicacity: how could he have known that the guy in the wheelchair was none other than Gică? Petrișor had never described him, never tried to sketch out his features; he hadn't even told Ion that Gică was fair-haired—an important advantage for a Romanian, since otherwise the locals might think he was a Gypsy. For a disabled person—for a cripple in a wheelchair, forced to beg—it's naturally much better to be blond. People usually take it for granted that your hair color is real. Tanned as he was, Gică could have had his hair dyed, and it wasn't impossible that this might have occurred to someone, but it was never likely to become a coherent thought, or to be spoken aloud in earshot of other passersby.

Ion didn't notice Gică at once. At first you have eyes only for the cathedral. Then you turn away dizzy and see the stalls and booths with all kinds of garbage for tourists. Only then do you look back toward the church and take in the people stationed in front of its walls—the rejects of the consumer society. Among them, a young blond man sitting with his eyes shut—just like the Surrealists used to photograph people when they wanted to suggest a gaze directed inward. Gică had an advantage over the other beggars: begging from a wheelchair is much less tiring than begging on your feet; he could even perch his hand on one of his armrests as he stretched it out in supplication. The others were forced to stand, switching their bowls from hand to hand every hour or so, or else—for the few with neither legs nor wheelchair—to sit on the ground at the foot of the walls, moving around on their hands in a way that developed impressive muscles. Probably someone came along in the evening to help them get back home, or wherever it was they spent the night. They must have been quite well organized. They looked askance at Gică, no doubt feeling envious of him.

Ion went up to Gică and whispered a few words of Romanian in his ear. The cripple opened his eyes and smiled. But then his face clouded over and you could see the suspicion in his eyes.

"Who are you? What do you want from me?"

"Nothing," Ion replied, in as gentle a tone as possible.

Of course, he didn't think it a good idea to mention Petrişor. In fact, it would have been a real mistake; he was absolutely certain that Gică would be nursing a grudge against him. He'd spent the whole night and much of the next day beside the dead body of the Russian, where that bastard Petrişor had landed him. He tried in vain to climb back into the wheelchair, and in the end he just went to sleep, cheek to cheek with the soldier's corpse. It stank of anything you might care to name: blood, sweat, above all vodka. Toward morning, before he woke up, he saw an old goat-headed woman (or was she leading a goat on a leash?), who had knelt down and was licking his face. She had a rough tongue, like a cat's. Gică shouted and sat up, looking all around him. The Russian was still there, smiling. With a great effort, Gică managed to somersault alongside the wheelchair, then he gripped its seat and one of its wheels and again tried unsuccessfully to hoist himself aboard. He could get halfway there but no higher. He fell back impotent onto the grass, one hand stuck in the spokes of the wheel. He felt like weeping, from rancor and from helplessness. The road was some distance away. There wasn't much traffic passing, and he couldn't even see it from where he was, down among the blades of grass yellowed by the exhaust fumes that had wafted over . . .

He began to yell: *Hilfe! Hilfe!* But who could hear? The cars sped by, and the hiss of their wheels on the asphalt smothered his shouts. As evening approached, he spotted a hunter: a man wearing short leather pants, a green cloth jacket, and a feathered hat. Or maybe it was featherless—anyway, typical of the region . . . or of his occupation. His game bag was knocking against his side as he came walking out of the forest. There was no sign of a gun.

"He didn't have a gun?" Surprised, Ion shifted on his seat in the café where he had offered to buy Gică a coke.

"No."

"So how do you know he was a hunter?"

Gică fell to thinking, and Ion didn't press him. He finished his coke and ordered another. He was thirsty.

He accompanied Gică to the hostel where he was spending the night with two other disabled persons, one of whom was actually perfectly healthy. Only then did he hear the end of the story.

Mr. Fuhrmann neatly stacked the pages of the letter on his table and went to the fridge to get another beer. I put down my ballpoint, next to my writing pad, and look out the window. Pierre is winging his way up to the house on his bicycle. I think happily of the answering machine I've installed, which will save me a lot of time and a lot of effort going up and down the stairs. I'll no longer be at the mercy of mystery callers and metallic voices from a computer or God knows where. I ask Pierre if he'd like a glass of something (coke? orange juice? no alcohol while on duty), but he declines with a slight dip of his wings. He's probably still not used to them. They seem to have grown a bit since he was last here.

Mr. Fuhrmann poured his beer, holding the glass at an angle so that it wouldn't foam up. Then he resumed Ion's letter.

So the hunter came up to Gică and asked the usual questions in such a situation. The soldier was sleeping the big sleep, no doubt about that. But why was his hand gripping the pistol? Had he shot himself in the head? Gică moved his lips. His German was largely a matter of guesswork, and sometimes he understood exactly the opposite of what was being said. *Kaput! Kaput!* he kept repeating. The hunter got irritated and gave up. "Stay here until I get back," he said, and he went to the highway, waved down a car, and came back with a driver who was holding a mobile phone to his ear. After a quarter of an hour, three policemen arrived and began to question Gică—but he wasn't capable of saying any more than *Kaput! Kaput!* He didn't even have any ID. The cops searched his pockets and found nothing: neither papers nor money. Petrişor had taken everything. Mr. Fuhrmann bit his lip in indignation. What a filthy little bastard! And he poured himself another few drops of beer. He liked to drink slowly, taking his time. But maybe Gică was lying about that part. Or maybe Ion was exaggerating—trying to make his ex-friend (who had, it's true, behaved like a sneaky thief) look worse and worse. You never know where you stand with these Romanians: they lie like nobody's business. And Fuhrmann swallowed the rest of the beer in his glass. He thought for a few moments, then decided to finish the letter in bed, after he'd had a bite to eat and gone through another bottle.

Three swans, two white and one black, were gliding down the canal. Night was falling. Ion pushed the wheelchair, while Gică, happy to chat in Romanian, went on with his story. Of course the highway patrol took him to the border police, where he was given something to eat and drink. They also found someone to act as an interpreter, so that Gică was able to explain who he was and what had happened the previous night. Unfortunately, no matter how hard he tried, he couldn't remember the name of the company that was sponsoring him; maybe he'd never known it. "Are they in Munich?"—"Yes, most likely, anything's possible . . ." Poor Gică! The policemen felt sorry for him. They put his wheelchair on an examination table and, demonstrating the famous Germanic thoroughness, searched every inch of it for the manufacturer's name or, failing that, some other clue to the company's whereabouts. But, apart from *Made in Germany*, they found nothing. At least that was something to go on. They obtained a list of companies likely to make wheelchairs in Germany, and Gică concentrated on the names in the hope that something would jog his memory. His finger hovered over *Bach und Sohn*, which sounded a little familiar. The policemen phoned at once. Herr Bach didn't recall having sponsored a Romanian disabled person, but he did think it was an interesting idea and asked the policeman what the young man looked like. When he heard that, though Gică didn't speak German, he was blond and came from Timişoara, Herr Bach said: "I'll get right in my car: it's not far from Munich to the border." He was there in less than two hours.

He drove Gică into Germany in his car. The Austrian police had no problem with this: they just got Bach to sign some papers, and gave Gică a permit to cross the border. The old wheelchair remained behind, in case the other company wanted to reclaim it as their rightful property. Gică looked at it wistfully for quite a while, but he had no choice in the matter: He would have to trust Herr Bach, who shook hands with the policemen before they went on their way.

They crossed no-man's-land and reached the German border post, where the guards simply waved them through. Either they trusted their Austrian counterparts or they just didn't want to waste time. Probably both.

Bach and Gică went straight to the wheelchair factory and tried out a number of models. The Romanian had his eyes on a little electric number, but Bach explained that these were difficult to maintain and much more fragile than ordinary chairs. It would also be more attractive to thieves, of course. "Simple, but state-of-the-art—that's what you need," Bach said, helping Gică to get into the chair in question. It was indeed easier to maneuver than his old one, and it even seemed to go faster.

Gică stayed in Munich for a few more days. He rested up in a small hotel and then went sightseeing. Ion could easily have bumped into him there, as could Petrişor, who had arrived by this time and was already staying with Mr. Fuhrmann. Here Ion almost let the cat out of the bag to Gică.

"Well, I don't mean to say that he *was* there, but, you know, he could have ended up in Munich too . . ."

No, Gică hadn't seen Petrişor, and, frankly, he never wanted to lay eyes on him again. Herr Bach gave him some money and a new credit card, and they arranged to meet in Frankfurt in two months. He also presented him to some journalists, so that Gică's picture appeared in the papers—though without his name, which might have caused problems with the other sponsor. Herr Bach had thought of everything! He also advised him to say that he was from Bucharest rather than Timișoara. "Why's that?" Gică asked—"It's for the best," Bach replied, before heading off. He was in a hurry: he had other things to do. Gică had a hard time facing the press alone, given the poor state of his German. Fortunately, one of the reporters spoke Romanian: a large, dark-skinned guy who looked like an accordionist. Claimed he worked for Radio Free Europe.

"And did you make it to Frankfurt okay?" Ion asked, pausing on the bridge over the swan canal.

The swans had disappeared. It was darker still.

Gică sighed. In a village near Stuttgart he'd begun to feel someone was following him. He looked around and saw a cyclist pedaling along, more or less at the same pace as his wheelchair: neither faster nor slower. Instead of resting for a moment and allowing his pursuer to overtake, Gică speeded up. He should have stopped at a Gasthaus—it wasn't long before he passed one—but it was still too early, and he told himself that it was only another three or four miles to Stuttgart. He looked over his shoulder again. The cyclist had stopped and was digging through his pockets. Maybe he wanted a smoke. The village seemed to be deserted. Heading out into the country again, the sense of being followed came back stronger than ever. Gică heard the whirring of wheels other than his own and turned his head. The other man was only ten yards away. Gică started to go faster, then suddenly hit the brakes. The stranger stopped beside him and said in Romanian, with a Russian accent: "Why are you in such a hurry?"—"What do you want from me?" Gică shot back—"Nothing. I want to help you." Gică considered returning to the village, but he decided to press on. "Are you heading for Stuttgart?" the tall man on the bicycle asked. Gică didn't answer. The two advanced like that, alongside each other, for a mile and a half. Some cars passed and, each time, Gică raised his arm for them to stop. No luck. The drivers probably didn't even notice. "What's the matter? Why are you thrashing around like that?" the cyclist asked, planting himself right in front of the wheelchair, with one foot on the ground. Gică didn't have time to brake; the stranger leapt aside like a toreador and gave him a hard shove that landed him in a ditch.

When he came to, Gică felt around his head and mouth, then reached into his breast pocket for the money and the little blue card he used to pay his hotel and restaurant bills. Gone—plus he couldn't even find the permit to stay in Germany, which Herr Bach had obtained on his behalf from the Bavarian police. His head ached terribly.

Mr. Fuhrmann fell asleep indignant.

I hear the telephone and get up to answer it. Then I remember I now have a robot to do it for me. The telephone rings three times and stops. Out of curiosity I go downstairs and move my head, my ear, close to the device. I hear the grating metallic voice that's been tormenting me for over a month. Another cryptic communication. But how can I figure out what they're trying to tell me?

Ion didn't manage to find Slobodan. He called several days running but never got an answer. Then a voice claimed there was no Slobodan at that number. It was a woman's voice, groggy, as if she'd just woken up. Thinking that he might have misdialed, Ion tried again—but got the same voice as before, only more irritated. He hung up and called Hilde's aunt. He'd been putting off contacting her—Hilde had told him to hold off as long as possible, if he could, when she'd given him the number.

"I'd like to speak to Hilde."

The woman at the other end, who had started with a "Hello, yes," went quiet. Ion repeated his request, very politely.

"Where did you get this number from?" It sounded like an old woman—quite possibly the aunt herself.

"Hilde gave it to me when we met this summer in Munich."

The woman again fell silent. After a few moments she said gruffly:

"This summer in Munich?"

"Yes."

"This is some kind of joke—a very sick joke."

Her voice was more weary than irritated: the voice of an old and exhausted woman.

"I'm not joking at all, believe me," Ion said, brushing the keypad with his index finger. He was in a booth near the cathedral. A wedding procession was just emerging from the great church.

He heard the characteristic sound that modern telephones make when the other party hangs up. It was all very mysterious. The woman seemed to know Hilde: she didn't say he had the wrong number, and, whether it had been the aunt or someone else, the name Hilde was clearly known to her . . . Otherwise she'd have said so. She definitely had a German accent—though that didn't prove anything one way or the other. The bride was taller than the groom, making him look like a dwarf beside her. His head barely came up to her shoulder.

Ion wondered if he should call back.

The bride, in fact, was taller than any of the men in the procession. She was wearing high heels, practically spindles, even stilts. Ion didn't want to jump to the conclusion, however, that she was wearing them just to tower over everyone else—to make herself feel big. He looked at the keypad, inserted another prepaid card, and redialed the number of Hilde's aunt.

"Please forgive me," Ion said, frowning. "Hilde herself gave me this number. She wrote it down for me on a piece of paper. That's the truth."

"Hilde's dead," the aunt whispered.

"Dead? Dead?" Ion repeated robotically. "How did she die?"

"She died, a long time ago."

The aunt's voice was husky, grave, washed out. Ion put the receiver down and forgot to take back his card. It was an honest telephone, and it pointed out his mistake, but Ion was still feeling so shocked that its warning fell on deaf ears. Looking up, he saw the wedding procession had disappeared from his field of vision. He left the telephone booth and spotted Gică by the cathedral walls, one outstretched hand supporting itself on his wheelchair's armrest, the other waving for Ion to join him. The student dragged himself over.

"What's wrong?" Gică asked, worried to see Ion white as a sheet. "You feeling sick?"

Ion shrugged.

"I'm going to the café," he muttered.

"I'll come with you," Gică said, releasing his handbrake. Ion walked ahead. Seated at an outside table, he ordered a calvados. Gică was a little surprised.

"You're starting early . . ."

Ion didn't feel like talking. Gică could only wait patiently for him to down his glass of calvados, order another, and feel the need to say a few words instead of sitting there gulping like a fish. Perhaps he'd even explain why he had that funereal look . . .

"Did you see the wedding?" Ion asked.

"What wedding?"

"What do you mean 'what wedding'? The one that just left the church . . ."

"You mean the cathedral?"

Ion's head found his hands. Afraid that he'd offended him, Gică tapped him lightly on the arm. Ion ignored him. A waiter brought another calvados, and the invalid took the opportunity to order a tomato juice. Two Japanese tourists who were machine-gunning the cathedral with ultrafast cameras stumbled over a chair; one of them fell on his knees and then on his stomach. By keeping his arms over his head, as though the ground had flooded, he managed to avoid any damage to the camera. Ion didn't find this at all funny. He raised his head, flushed with heat and emotion, and watched the scene unfold—without laughing. No, even a Japanese man swimming on his belly in front of a Gothic cathedral couldn't produce a chuckle. Gică, in stitches, made a much better audience. Finally the other Japanese tourist bent down and helped his traveling companion to his feet.

"He didn't keel over in awe or astonishment," Ion said softly.

"No . . ."

"He fell during a technical exercise meant to justify his trip to Europe. He fell on his belly."

"Maybe he's on vacation."

"Or on a mission," Ion snickered.

"A mission?"

The fallen tourist struggled up and bowed to his friend in need, probably to apologize for the shame he had brought on them—in front of foreigners! Only, look, he's not going to commit hara-kiri for a little thing like that, Gică thought, with one eye on his pensive and melancholy companion. Ion was staring into space. Had that really been Hilde's aunt on the phone? For a moment he was tempted to tell Gică everything—even about Maria. But he held back. The hick wouldn't understand a thing. Although, actually, that might make him the perfect . . .

I straighten my back. Goddamn sciatica is playing up again.

The telephone woke Zsuzsa very early in the morning. A male voice suggested they meet to talk about Ion, the student from Romania.

"Do you know him?"

The voice was in a hurry, eager to end the conversation. After lunch Zsuzsa went, as agreed, to the lobby of Hotel Europa, where a tall middle-aged man was already waiting for her. He rose quickly from the armchair and came toward her smiling. So he knows me, Zsuzsa thought, a little naively. The man invited her to the bar, and she accepted a small whisky.

"Tamás, give us two whiskies," the man said to the bartender.

At approximately the same time, Dinu Valea was talking with a police inspector in Bucharest, and Tiberius Ludoşan with another one in Timişoara. All of these characters were interested in Ion. They wanted to know where he was now, when and where he was last seen and under what circumstances, etc. etc.

Well, if you ask me—but no one's asking me, no one comes around here to ply me for information, to loosen my tongue, to worm anything out of me, although they ought to know . . . anyway, if someone were to put the right questions to me, I would definitely be able to tell them that right now, without a doubt, Ion is leaving the café near Strasbourg Cathedral—and no, I don't know its name, I never pay attention to those things. So, at this very moment, Ion has paid the waiter (who gave him a long hard look) and left the café, and is now pushing Gică's wheelchair. He stops in front of a telephone booth.

"Would you do me a favor and call someone for me?"

"Who?"

"A girl's aunt. But you have to ask to speak to the girl."

"What's her name?"

"Hilde."

Gică agreed, delighted. Ion looked in his pocket for his calling card but couldn't find it.

"Wait here a second. I'll go buy another one."

He soon returned with another card, inserted it into the slot, dialed the number, handed the receiver to Gică. The wheelchair only half-fit inside the cabin.

"It's ringing but there's no answer."

"Be patient. She's an old woman."

Wait as they might, the aunt didn't answer.

"Who's this Hilde?" Gică asked, wheeling his chair back out.

"A girl I met in Munich. It seems she's dead."

"What?"

"She died."

"When did that happen?"

"A long time ago, before I met her, apparently. I don't know . . ."

Gică shook his head, covering his mouth with one hand. Guy's lost his mind. Gică didn't bother asking to hear more.

"I don't feel like begging anymore today," he said.

Ion didn't hear: his mind was elsewhere. He'd been in Strasbourg nearly two weeks and hadn't done anything he'd planned to do, and Slobodan wasn't answering at the number Miodrag gave him: either he'd gotten the wrong number from Miodrag or he wrote it down wrong. He even thought of writing to Mr. Fuhrmann and asking him to ask Miodrag for the right number, since they both hung out in Ahmed's bar. Of course, more than anything, Ion was furious with himself. How could he be so absentminded? And now he realized he didn't even have Mr. Fuhrmann's telephone number. It wasn't that he forgot to bring it—he'd never had it in the first place. He'd jotted it down once on a piece of paper and promptly lost it. He hadn't even made any attempt to memorize it. Intolerable!

"I just don't feel like going on today," Gică repeated. Ion said nothing as he pushed the wheelchair toward the cathedral wall.

He still had some money, but he didn't know how much. His hotel cost a lot. It might be a good idea to accept Gică's proposal.

"Stop!" the cripple shouted.

"What's up? Why are you yelling like that?"

"Because you're stone deaf. I told you I don't feel like begging anymore today. Let's go see a movie. It's on me."

There was a multiplex not far from the cathedral. One of the films, *The Two Marias*, had started a quarter of an hour before. At least that's what the woman at the box office claimed. Gică didn't have the patience to wait around for the next show. He took out some money and Ion bought two tickets with it. The usherette helped Ion to carry the wheelchair down the steps to one of the auditoria. It would be harder going back up . . .

Two half-naked women were trying on dresses in a hotel room.

"Wow, what a beauty!"

"Yeah, not bad. But the other one's more your style—give it a try!"

One of the women looked like Zsuzsa, the other like Maria. Now Ion realized how much they'd always resembled each other: both in the film and in . . . Sure, Zsuzsa's plumper, also more mature—much more mature.

Maria undresses.

"You've got beautiful breasts," the other says—what's her name? Of course, it's also Maria; they're the two Marias.

"A little big, no?"

"No, no . . ."

Maria lets herself be fondled. She glances over to a cage by the window. An eaglet is jumping around behind the bars. It obviously doesn't have enough room.

". . . like a couple of sacks."

And she laughs.

"I like them."

Maria cups one of Maria's breasts with both hands, then leans over and takes the nipple in her mouth. Gică is fidgeting in his chair. He knocks into Ion with his elbow.

"How greedy you are!"

The woman on the screen gently tips the other's head back and kisses her on the eyes and forehead.

"Now it's your turn."

She searches through a cupboard and takes out a white silk dress, longer than the others. A wedding dress? She holds it out with touching pride, but also a touch of embarrassment . . .

"Look!"

Ion loves the swishing sound of the dresses.

Then she's dressed, perched on a chair in a bar beside a man holding a glass of whisky.

"But when did he leave?" the man presses her.

The woman seems confused, or rather put out. It's clear that she doesn't at all enjoy being interrogated like this . . . not at all. Who knows what details might come up next . . .

"I don't know. I told you I was away traveling."

"And you left him alone in your apartment?"

The woman shrugs without replying.

"And when you got back?"

"He was gone. He'd left."

She suddenly looks sad. But the man doesn't let go easily.

"Yeah, yeah, but when? How long were you away?"

"Oh, a long time. Two or three months."

Then a railway station appears on the screen, looking tiny at the edge of a forest.

It's raining. A tall peasant with a scythe over his shoulder enters a room, probably a storeroom. People are shooting dice in a bar, at a table. The cubes roll on the worn green cloth. On a chair lies a stationmaster's peaked cap, the color of a rotten sour cherry. A gendarme comes in. He asks about Maria. No one seems willing to answer. A small bearded man comes out of the frame and slips off through a rear door. He has a hammer in his hand.

An eagle in flight, gliding over the forest. The moon like a pale sickle.

A flock of sheep crosses the square in front of the hotel, followed by a light truck full of suitcases, bags, and all kinds of paraphernalia. A man at the steering wheel with a cigarette in his mouth. His family following him, pushing a wheeled platform loaded with old rags and crockery. An oldish woman, maybe the peasant's mother, frantically pulling a cart that has a cylinder of bottled gas on it.

"Are you leaving?"

"Yes, we're off."

"But what's happening? Have you all gone crazy?" the gendarme asks aggressively.

"If you're not capable of protecting us . . ."

"What kind of movie is this?" Gică groans desperately, fiddling around in his chair.

Ion doesn't answer.

Maria gets angry and sweeps the two glasses off the table with the back of her hand. They fall to the ground and shatter. The man pushes her onto her back; she rolls over on the bed and, with the wall for support, rises again with arms outstretched and threatening, beautiful as a houri.

The stationmaster crosses the square: a dead sheep is lying right in the center. He stops and examines the carcass, then raises his head to look at the sign:

HOTEL EUROPA

She seems asleep. As the shot widens, you can see the clotted blood on her hair and the red from the top of her skull trickling down to her neck. She was hit right in the softer part of the skull.

The stationmaster's peaked cap moves forward through the tree branches. An eagle hovers above the forest—no, it's not an eagle, probably not an airplane either . . .

"Say, what's with that metal dish in the sky?" Gică asks, perking up at the sound of an engine. "It doesn't look much like a plane."

"What do you want it to look like?"

"Son of a bitch, it looks like a saucer!"

Ion thinks: Of course we're lost, we came in halfway through. He says this to Gică. Will they have to watch the whole film over again?

Gică's had enough: he wants to get out of there.

"But aren't you curious to see how it ends?"

"How it begins, you mean."

"It's the same thing."

A serpent at the foot of a tree weighed down with apples. Maria beside it, buried in the grass. It's easier with a book. You turn the pages, skip boring passages, then throw it away. Someone to Ion's right heads for the way out, stumbles over Gică's wheelchair, falls on his knees. He gets up again, furious. Gică laughs into his beard: it's funny, funnier than the film. He's still laughing as the station-master with the cherry-colored cap wanders along the platform, flag in hand. The sound of the plane or God knows what flying machine. It gets louder and louder. The sky is blue, empty, clean. The lights go on in the hall. Ion looks for Gică but can't see him. The few people in the audience have all left. No sign of Gică. Ion goes toward the bathrooms. He finds Gică chatting to the usherette, who has a cheerful smile and is fiddling with her flashlight; it's switched off, of course. Gică sees Ion and waves him over, toward the exit.

In the café-cum-kiosk by the station, Gică tried to persuade Ion to leave the hotel where he'd been paying through the nose since he arrived in Strasbourg. It's true that the manager, who had no reason to complain of Ion, had hinted that same morning that, if he was thinking of staying in the city for another month or two, and of course if he paid cash in advance, then a considerable reduction might be forthcoming . . .

"How much?" Gică asked.

"I don't know. I didn't ask."

"Well, you should find out."

Ion's terse replies came out in a lazy drawl. He seemed tired, although he may only have been bored. Little by little he came back to life. He stared Gică down.

"Don't think I enjoy spending so much on a hotel, especially since I'm beginning to run low."

"I didn't ask how much money you've got," Gică said, arrogant and a little offended. "I asked how much it would cost you a month, after your reduction."

"I don't know," Ion said, shrugging.

"How much did you pay last month?"

"Nearly three thousand francs."

"That's a fortune!" Gică was shaken.

"Other places in town cost even more."

"You don't have to stay in a hotel."

"Where else is there?"

"You can come stay with me. Listen . . ."

As if afraid that the other customers would hear, Gică pushed his wheelchair closer and whispered in Ion's ear:

"We have a mighty fine hotel all to ourselves. You'll see . . ."

"A hotel?" Ion asked, raising his eyebrows. He'd seen how Gică usually lived: a tangled mass of people in a basement smelling of piss, which they shared with rats and slugs.

"That's what I said. A disused hotel. In fact, it used to be a hotel for dogs, although people put other pets up there too when they went on holiday and didn't want to *encumber* themselves."

"Didn't want to what?"

"Encumber themselves," Gică repeated, not realizing how odd this French-sounding turn of phrase—plus many others, since the Revolution—sounded in Romanian, and how he was contributing to the formation of a dialect that might become, in fact had every chance of becoming, the Romanian of the twenty-first century.

To whom does the Romanian language belong?

After I write this pretentiously rhetorical question, I cross it out, delete it, or, if you prefer, strike it through. I don't say rub it out, because an eraser wouldn't really get rid of the question—in fact, it doesn't disappear whatever you do. Anyway, all kinds of improprieties are perpetrated through considering a language as one's property. Or, to put it another way, property justifies all kinds of improprieties. Gică, sitting there in his wheelchair, seems to have power of life and death over the Romanian language, especially since all the realist novelists will hasten to reproduce his manner of speech and thereby encourage him, reflexively, to continue exercising that right, which cannot be described as arbitrary, because it is actually collective—that is to say, Gică shares it with other speakers living in the same territory who are more or less in contact with one another. Is the language being degraded? We hear that question from old émigrés who, having lost touch with Gică and his pen-wielding supports, feel challenged, if not excluded—that is, feel what they are: exiled. For the true exile is the linguistic exile—any other kind of exile can just be thought of as a long European (or world) trip. Émigrés can say as proudly and grandiloquently as they like: "My fatherland is the Romanian language!" But the Romanian language remains just where it is—with everything else: far away.

How can one know for sure, especially here in Strasbourg, whether Gică is mangling or enriching the Romanian language?

After Gică moved into the pet hotel, one of his fellow-occupants used some black or red paint to spray HOTEL EUROPA on all the walls. Gică told Ion about this, not necessarily in a mocking tone.

"Europe belongs to us all!" he exclaimed, and then another character, who had just entered the café, came up to their table and said in Romanian:

"How well you speak!"

Colonel Burtică, as he introduced himself, sat down opposite the two young men and took out a pile of *tiercé* betting slips, which, giving a quick smile, he began to fill in. He didn't have to think too much: either because he was selecting the horses at random, or because he'd studied up on all the possibilities and already made up his mind. Maybe he's one of Haiducu's gang, Ion thought, feeling a sudden tightness in his chest. The colonel was still marking his crosses when yet another character came up to their table, probably an acquaintance of the *tiercé* gambler, because he had that air of exaggerated jollity that southern peoples—especially Romanians—affect when they meet again after a separation. He addressed the colonel in Romanian, with a slight Transylvanian accent:

"You'll blow all your pension like that!"

"Don't you worry about me," Burtică replied calmly, looking up from the slips for no more than a second.

"Are you two also Romanian?" the newcomer asked.

Ion and Gică mumbled something and nodded their heads up and down, impressed by his powerful physique and baritone voice.

"It's full of Romanians in here," the punter growled. He counted his slips, stacked them atop one another, and stuffed them into his pocket. "You run into them all the time."

"Have you just arrived from Romania?" the baritone asked. Let's call him Spirea and agree that he was once a good rugby player, who went to France with the national team for a friendly match in the 1960s and never found his way back to the Fatherland.

"Yes, as a matter of fact," Ion said quietly. He'd been about to say no, from Germany, which was also true in a way. But this would only have drawn the subject out, since the others wouldn't have been fooled.

"So what's it like there nowadays?"

"What do you mean?"

"Since the overthrow."

"It's pretty sad," Ion replied.

"Pretty sad," Colonel Burtică repeated, with evident satisfaction. "Life is hard . . ."

"Sure, because the communists have stayed in power," Spirea chipped in.

"The communists?" the colonel protested. "And who might they be?"

"Iliescu and his crowd."

"You call them communists?"

"What are they, then?"

"Whatever. Free-traders, that's what they are! Full of hot air."

"What do you mean?"

"They'll say anything to stay in power. Promise the moon and the stars. A bunch of demagogues!"

"Communists!"

"They've got no principles."

"It's better like that. That's all we need—for them to have principles!"

The two young men remained spectators, taking no part in a discussion that seemed more and more like an argument and threatened to degenerate into a shouting match. Gică was quiet as a mouse, while Ion uttered no more than monosyllables confirming or reinforcing the views of the two old émigrés from the 1960s. Come to think of it, though—I mean, if we try to follow

Spirea's nebulous ideas—I'm not so sure the two of them should really be placed in the same category. With Burtică, for instance, things are a little more complicated. He settled in Strasbourg only a few years ago, and his background was rather unclear even then. Some gossips said he'd worked for the Securitate. But so what? Wasn't the other guy—the general who fled to the United States—a former head of the Securitate? And look how he turned things around. He spilled the beans in print, then had plastic surgery to get rid of his girlish features, so that no one would recognize him. Yes, he churned out a book exposing the regime, exposing Ceausescu. Burtică, on the other hand, has remained the same, wearing exactly the same face as ever: square-jawed, flap-eared, nose like a potato.

The argument between the two men suddenly died down.

"So, why did you leave?" Burtică turned to ask Ion. "I mean, why now, after the new regime took over? You can't complain that you don't have the right to say whatever you like."

Ion shrugged. Clearly he was in no mood to discuss his reasons for emigrating.

"Leave the kid alone," Spirea broke in. "Can't he travel if he wants to? See a bit of Europe?"

"You're right," Burtică relented. "See that life is hard everywhere."

"It's not quite as bad as that," Spirea said softly.

Burtică called the waiter over and ordered drinks all round. Maybe he thought a beer or two would loosen the two youthful tongues. Not so that they'd tell him anything in particular: he didn't really give a damn. But he liked to sit and chat, and Spirea did too. That's why they met at a bar or a café from time to time. Their relationship never got beyond the same sort of chatter over a glass of beer. Usually they'd discuss international politics, or other subjects about which they could more or less agree. The Yalta Conference or the Malta Conference—a rhyme they'd always found a little suspicious.

"They've sold us down the river again," Burtică sighed.

"Yes, that's clear."

The beer had its little effect. But the tongue that loosened was Gică's, not Ion's. He told them how he went to stay with his mother, a doctor in Timişoara, a year or more ago—and how he met a rich Frenchwoman, a countess, who took pity on him and offered to get him a state-of-the-art wheelchair. He chose one from a catalogue that she happened to have in her bag, and it arrived two or three months later. As he was about to leave, the beautiful and generous countess—her name was Madame de Ségur—invited him to stay with her in the south of France, somewhere near Avignon. She had a castle there, yes, a real *château*. Absolutely, she was a countess and she had a *château* on a hill overlooking the village of Lacoste. After a few weeks of intensive training in the streets of Timişoara, and then on the Arad Road, Gică—heart in mouth—set off in earnest.

Ion listened in silence, allowing Gică to go on saying whatever came into his head. Nothing he told them matched either Petrişor's account or what the cripple himself had said earlier. What's more, at one point in the story, Petrişor had a cameo part as a shady type claiming to be a student called Valentin, who had probably been sent by the Securitate to put a spoke in Gică's wheels. As for the name of the countess . . .

"But why would the Securitate have been interested?" the colonel asked, a little tetchily.

"The Securitate has been disbanded," Spirea said, playing along.

"Don't ask me!" Gică said. "Maybe they wanted to stop me getting to France. You'd know more about these things than I do!" and here he looked Burtică right in the eyes, making him feel distinctly uncomfortable. Spirea gave out peals of triumphant laughter. Ion laughed as well. Colonel Burtică rose angrily to his feet and went to hand in his betting slips. Cool as a cucumber, Gică went on with his story, so that by the time the colonel returned he had already come across a Russian tank unit that was stranded, out of gas. The soldiers left their vehicles by the roadside and went into the forest, where they soon found a clearing and got a fire going. They drank vodka and sang in chorus. Night was nearly upon them when they spotted the cripple's heroic advance along that Austrian highway through their field glasses. Never before had they seen a wheelchair move at such high speed. The soldiers stopped singing, went out to the highway, and split their sides laughing as they set up a little roadblock. There they picked up Gică, wheelchair and all, and took him to their camp in the forest. A couple of girls were there too now, dancing wildly and taking off more and more of their clothes. The soldiers sang and clapped their hands. The girls were tall and very blonde. Real beauties! They whirled around the flames like fairy bewitchers on a midsummer's night.

"Why are we listening to this bullshit?" Burtică grumbled, still on his feet. He didn't want to sit down with them again.

"Let the kid express himself," Spirea said. "Come on, tell us some more."

But Gică had his dignity too. He ordered another beer and drank it in high dudgeon. Not for anything in the world would he agree to continue the story. A sullen silence ensued. Spirea and Burtică started bickering again and soon stormed out, slamming the door behind them. Only when the waiter arrived with the bill did Ion realize that they had left without paying. The situation became tense when the young men refused to pay for the old émigrés—it wasn't fair . . .

"*Qui a passé la première commande?*" Ion asked the waiter.

"*Je m'en fous moi, ça ne me regarde pas,*" he replied.

The manager appeared.

"*Vous n'étiez pas ensemble? Je vous ai entendu baragouiner en romanichel,*" he said, keeping calm. "*Allez, vous payez maintenant! Ou alors j'appelle la police.*" The threat was delivered in the same unruffled voice.

Gică tried to exploit his disability and pointed to the wheels on his chair, but the manager didn't give a shit. Ion paid up.

The next day he moved into "Hotel Europa," having bought himself a sleeping bag. He took a tiny room, more reminiscent of a kennel, naturally enough, which had a strong smell of dogs—but even that was better than in the basement, where Gică was sleeping. Everyone had their own room. At the end of the yard there were Turkish-style toilets, and closer to the rooms a cold-water tap for washing. I don't know whose idea it had been to buy a hose, but this also functioned as a makeshift shower when it was attached to a rope running from the toilet roof to the nearest tree. Ion managed to wash Gică using this method, and even the legless Bulgarian who moved around on a kind of widened skateboard (he'd stepped on a mine dating back to the Second World War somewhere near Karl Marx Stadt—but what was a Bulgarian doing there?). In fact, it was easier to dress and undress the Bulgarian, since he had no pants and didn't present the same problems that Gică did with his soft limp legs. Now and then his sister (or was it cousin?) showed up at the hotel: a well-built, unfussy sort of girl who went with anyone who wanted to sleep with her. She was called Draga and she'd found work on a building site on the outskirts of town. She had a crush on Ion, but he didn't really find her attractive: or, to be more precise, he was afraid. He'd gotten it into his head that he might catch that terrible disease that Draga and all the others didn't seem to care about.

"AIDS is for rich guys," she used to say.

But Ion wasn't convinced, so he avoided plumpish Draga and she found comfort with everyone else who came along. He could always try his luck elsewhere, even with honest-to-goodness French girls . . . Why not? People said they smelled like flowers and wriggled like snakes.

Ion still had a little money left: he was richer than all the other poor souls who'd ended up at the Hotel. That was why he lived in a state of constant anxiety. He kept his money in a little plastic bag, on a piece of string tied around his waist. One day he asked Gică:

"Where do you keep your money?"

"What money? You're nuts!"

At that time only ten or so people were living in the Hotel, plus the Gypsy to whom they had to pay a small room fee. Yes, he was the manager! He'd set himself up in the largest room, once used by the man who'd run the place in the old days. He had his own private bathroom, complete with a tub that he didn't use because the hot water had been cut off. Gică had needed to ask the manager's permission for Ion to come and stay with them, even though the student wasn't a beggar and therefore had no income. Originally from Hungary, the Gypsy could also get by fairly well in Romanian; he was what you might call a polyglot, since he also had more than a smattering of Serbian, German, and French.

"He's a parasite," he said, when he heard that Ion didn't want to beg.

"He's my assistant," Gică retorted. "And there's not enough space for both of us in one room."

"Okay, but he'll have to pay twenty francs a night."

"He can't pay twenty: he's got to eat as well. Make it five."

"*Ça va pas?*" the Gypsy snarled.

The haggling went on all day, with occasional breaks. From time to time Gică would say to Ion, in earshot of the Gypsy:

"Why don't you sleep in the park or at the station? It's free. This guy's trying to screw you. He's a greedy bastard."

And he winked.

In the end they reached an agreement: it would be ten francs.

Apart from Ion and the Gypsy boss, the only person in the hotel who was sound of body was an old man they called Milord. But he wasn't sound of mind. He claimed to be related to the queen of England, and said that in his childhood he'd known King Michael of Romania and had visited him before the war. Then he was disgraced and ended up in the street, supposedly because he'd fallen in love with a German officer, an angelically beautiful Gestapo man.

"What was his name?" Medina, for example, the one-armed Portuguese, might ask.

"What was he called?"

"Yeah, what was his name?"

"Rudolf."

"Rudolph Valentino?"

"No, Rudolf von Himmel," Milord replied dreamily.

There were a number of versions of his story, but the common element, which should be mentioned first—the invariable that formed the narrative backbone—was Milord's time as a prisoner of war. One night, he said, back when he was a fighter pilot, Milord had been escorting some British bombers on a mission over Germany. He was hit by anti-aircraft fire and was forced to bail out. He was captured, and, after various adventures that changed with each telling of the tale, he found himself being interrogated by none other than Rudolf.

"Aren't you perhaps the king's nephew?" the German asked.

"Indeed I am," the Englishman replied, thunderstruck by the beauty of the Nazi officer.

It's said that Von Himmel was equally sensitive to the young lord's charms. Perhaps trying to deny this attraction, he walked up to the pilot and hit him with his crop, right across his eyes.

"You're lying, you swine!"

The symphonic chords of Beethoven's Fifth wafted in from the next room. Milord didn't flinch at the blow: his blue eyes were mirrored in von Himmel's blue eyes, and in his mouth he felt the taste of his own blood—likewise blue! This dominance of blue was another structural invariable in Milord's otherwise rather luxuriant and irregular diegesis. Nor should we fail to mention the erotic scenes and, in particular, the detailed descriptions of the German's genitals. When he got to this part, Milord remembered Romania,

King Michael, and the king's father. With rare exceptions, he didn't take the narrative any further. The death of von Himmel (who was captured by the British shortly before the end of the war), and above all the likely circumstances of his execution, were a shock from which Milord's mind never recovered.

Constitutional Storm in the Bundestag:

The opposition has called for a special session of the Bundestag to reexamine the decision to send German troops to the Adriatic to oversee the embargo on the former Yugoslavia. According to a recent poll, sixty-five percent of Germans would support a constitutional amendment to allow the German armed forces to take part in UN peacekeeping operations—a proposal that is supported by the Social Democrats. But sixty-five percent also firmly oppose any extension of this proposal to include collective armed intervention, the pet project of Chancellor Kohl and the two architects of Germany's new foreign policy: Defense Minister Volker Rühe and Foreign Minister Klaus Kinkel.

In Citadel Park in Strasbourg, which is well known as a rendezvous point, Entr'aides and Info-Gay activists move around in pairs at night handing out condoms to any couples they come across.

Whether during in-person conversations or via their Minitel on-line information service, the most frequent question is whether protection is necessary for oral sex. Martine and her team recommend the use of a condom. Two blonde girls admitted they would be ashamed to buy condoms in a pharmacy. [. . .]

Occasional prostitution is spreading even among young people from relatively well-to-do families, since it seems to promise an easy life. They come up from Metz or Mulhouse for a single night of work and catch the morning train back, having made enough to buy whatever they like for months on end. Even so, there are not enough to meet the demand. Meanwhile, Martine and Alain continue their "hunt." Since January, Entr'aides activists have distributed nearly 30,000 condoms in the area.

"Ethnic cleansing" has begun in Alisić:

Surrounded by Serb towns, the 280-family Muslim village of Alisić surrendered without a fight. The inhabitants live in a state of terror and have only one wish: to emigrate.

A new charge against Erich Honecker:

On the anniversary of the construction of the Berlin Wall, the prosecutor's office in Berlin has placed Erich Honecker and former East German Prime Minister Willi Stoph under suspicion of "complicity in homicide." It is alleged that in 1960 the two leaders ordered the execution of a border-guard colonel, Manfred Smolka, who, after crossing to the West, was recaptured by the communist regime and sentenced to death by a court in Erfurt. [. . .] Erich Honecker, now aged seventy-nine, has been in prison since July 29. He has been officially charged with forty-nine murders and twenty-five attempted murders of East German citizens trying to cross the Wall.

In Mantes-la-Jolie, a policeman suffering from depression aimed his weapon in a state of oneiric confusion:

It was night. Dominique Songeon was strolling around in civilian clothes, on Avenue de la République. André Peste was standing in front of an ATM. The policeman, who was wearing a balaclava and waving his arms like wings, ordered: "Get a move on. Withdraw everything you've got or I'll blow your brains out!" He then fired in the air several times. The other man did not panic, but simply returned to his car and drove to the nearest police station to report the incident. Two days earlier the policeman, who was on sick leave, and the woman he was living with had ingested ten times the prescribed dose of a powerful anxiolytic [. . .] Taking the view that Dominique Songeon had been sufficiently punished by fifteen months of preventive detention, the prosecutor only demanded a sentence of eighteen months and a ban on Songeon's being allowed to carry firearms in future. In this connection, the prosecutor took the liberty of making a historical point for the benefit of anyone surprised by the fact that the police might be in the habit of carrying their weapons while off duty: namely, that this practice dates back to the time of the Algerian War—or, more precisely, to a ministerial order issued by the then minister of the interior, François Mitterrand.

In Paris, two young people from Czechoslovakia were found dead yesterday with their throats cut, in a sleeping bag in a square on rue de la Marseillaise. Their bodies were discovered by a municipal gardener responsible for the square's upkeep. The victims, a man aged twenty-one and a woman aged twenty, had been traveling together through France for approximately a month. They were probably spending the night in the square, which is a few hundred yards from the Pré-Saint-Gervais youth hostel, where no one recalls having seen them.

The girl was naked, and her sleeping bag had been ripped open. The hypothesis that the attack was sexual in nature has not yet been confirmed. The victims' clothes and personal effects were found not far from their bodies; it is difficult to say whether money was a factor in the crime. The victims' identity papers have also been recovered.

An appalling crime in a village in the south of France, not far from the Château de Lacoste:

A man killed his wife by battering her head in with a sledgehammer. The woman tried to defend herself with an old rusty scythe and succeeded in cutting her husband's foot to the bone. This explains why he was unable to flee the scene of the crime.

Death of John Cage:

The century's only philosopher of music? The greatest practical joker in the history of composition? Whatever the truth may be, the pioneer of the prepared piano, electroacoustics, happenings, musical collage, and the "open work" . . .

[. . .] Avant-garde by nature, like the Dadaists, like his role model and friend Marcel Duchamp, who, like himself, was a passionate chess player [. . .] "Many people," Cage once wrote, "see Marcel Duchamp's work as an enigma, a problem to be solved [. . .] for me it was enough to be beside him and to play chess with him."

In *4'30"*, Cage asked a musician to sit in front of his instrument and listen to his own silence for the time indicated by the title. He discovered that music is born out of any event, so long as it is limited to a fixed interval of time. Music is first of all the cross-listening of a performer and an audience. You wait for the sound before it exists. You have the void. A profoundly metaphysical theory. [...]

Cage, like so many others, visited Schoenberg in his American den. And Schoenberg gave him a clear diagnosis: "In order to write music, you must have a feeling for harmony." Cage explained he had no such feeling, and Schoenberg replied that Cage would soon find himself coming to a wall through which he could not pass. Cage replied: "In that case I shall devote my life to beating my head against that wall."

Mr. Fuhrmann kept turning the envelope that had arrived from the USA over in his hands. Poor Ion, how long he had waited for it! Every day he had asked, Hasn't a letter come from the States? And, well, now it's come at last, but several months late. That's how these things are. So, what next? The old man didn't even know where to forward it.

Ion had written him from Strasbourg, but without an address on the back of the envelope. No hotel, no nothing—as though he was sleeping in the street, a park, or the train station. So what to do? Send the letter on to Paris? But, again, to what address? All Ion had left him was the telephone number of that writer he'd met in Bucharest, who'd traveled there with a consignment of food and medicine immediately after . . . the events. But he hadn't even told him the writer's name: most likely he'd forgotten it himself. That meant it couldn't be Paul Goma: no, he's too important, *everyone's* heard of him; Ion would never have forgotten Goma's name. Radio Free Europe has been harping about him for years now. There's also a place in Africa called Goma, somewhere in Rwanda or the Congo. Fuhrmann had discovered that a few days ago, but only now did he make the connection. Bizarre! Maybe he had some African ancestors. Like Pushkin!

No, the writer with the medicine wasn't Goma. Goma's too busy to chat with some snot-nosed students—not to speak of giving them his phone number! Why should he? So they can come and disturb him, stop him from writing? He's not that dumb. When you're a great novelist, a national figure like Goma or Breban, you don't have time to worry about others, except maybe when you're being interviewed or writing some polemical piece. But that's not Goma's style: he's a sober, responsible type. A kind of Havel! Or anyway a Havel who's been kicked out of his country: Ceausescu stripped him of his Romanian citizenship by a presidential decree (as Larousse will confirm). Why? To get rid of him! But wouldn't Goma have left Romania anyway? No, not even a tank could have dragged him away. He was the only person keeping the opposition alive! He was stripped of his citizenship while on a trip to Paris, where he launched a journal that published all the dissidents from the Eastern bloc, Havel included. The Midget of Bucharest couldn't tolerate that, if only because he had to save face in front of the leaders of Romania's "fraternal" countries. After Ceausescu's death, Goma gathered in more and more admirers: the less they'd done to oppose the old regime, the more they revered the old dissident. The same conformism, but turned inside out like a glove.

Fuhrmann went to the telephone.

He dialed the country code for France, then Paris and then the number: 45-84-84-29. A woman's voice answered and informed him in French that no one was at home and that she herself was in Moscow at the moment. Fuhrmann told her in something like French that he'd like to get in touch with Ion Valea, who'd given him this number but not an address where he could forward a letter that had just arrived from the United States. *Et je vous demande pardon pour le dérange*, he added. After he hung up, he realized that he hadn't left his own number, so he called again and waited for the Frenchwoman to recite exactly the same sentence as before. Then he said who he was—*je suis un vieux ami de son père*—and dictated his digits one by one: *sept, zéro, zéro, deux, cinq, huit, six*. He realized he'd left out the codes for Germany and Munich. Should he call back again?

The only address he had to which he could have immediately forwarded Ion's letter was Dinu Valea's—not such a bad idea, in fact. After thinking it over for a couple of days, during which there was no word from Paris, he decided to send it off to Bucharest after all. He began to draft a letter for Dinu, whom he hadn't written to since Ion's departure for France. There had been no reply then, but he knew that Dinu didn't like to write; he was a verbal sort of person, like most Romanians. The simplest course would have been to call and ask him if he maybe knew the writer's address in Paris; that's what he'd have done if he'd known Dinu's new phone number (he'd asked him for it many times but never got an answer). It even occurred to Fuhrmann that Dinu Valea no longer had a telephone at all; he couldn't see any other explanation. He'd sent Dinu his own number, so his friend could have called him, told Fuhrmann his number, and then waited for a call back. But, in one of his rare letters, in which he always forgot to mention his number, Dinu said that the whole process would have taken too long. It's perfectly true that there was still no automatic dialing between Romania and the rest of Europe. But how long, really, would he have had to wait for a connection? All he had to do was call the operator and put in a request, then pick up a book and kill some time. He didn't have much else to do now that he was a pensioner. Obviously, Dinu no longer had a telephone. No doubt the poverty in Romania is getting worse and worse, and although Dinu hasn't complained directly that doesn't mean he's not living from hand to mouth. I realize life isn't a bed of roses for you, Fuhrmann wrote. And, although I'm certainly no nabob, I could try to help you out a bit if you needed it. I won't buy any books for a few months and I'll send him the money instead, Fuhrmann thought, touched by his own intentions. It wouldn't be easy: a nice sacrificial gesture. How would he occupy himself if he didn't buy any books? After he finished reading the few books he hadn't yet started, he would go to Ahmed's more often to play backgammon or Gul Bara. If he was unlucky, he might lose more money than he would have spent on the books he'd given up to help Dinu. So he could offer him some help, but not much . . . He tore up the sheet of paper and began another letter, plainer and more informative. But, however he turned it, he always ended up mentioning books. The day before, at a second-hand bookshop, he'd bought a volume about Hegel by a certain Kroner. The author quite shamelessly praised the "miraculous unity" of the real and the ideal in German thinkers. The book was written in the 1930s. And indeed, Fuhrmann mocked, when Hitler dreamed up his racist idealism, the realism of the German spirit soon found a (final) solution: the gas chambers. Why am I writing all this? Fuhrman asked himself. Now that he was alone again, he felt a growing need to write something, anything. Before Ion had arrived, the old man had begun to fill a notebook with ideas for a future ecological morality. But then he came across Jonas's *The Imperative of Responsibility* in a bookshop and threw his own notes away. It's all been written already, he sighed. But maybe that doesn't matter; maybe it should be written again, with other words, from a different angle, perhaps even drawing different conclusions. You never know. Instead of playing backgammon like there's no tomorrow with all these shady Orientals—as greasy as they are irrational—maybe he'd do better to pick up a pen and write . . . even if he tore it up afterwards, as he's been doing with his repeated attempts at a letter to his friend and former co-worker in Romania, in which he wants to explain that someone has sent an envelope from across the ocean in the hope that he would know where to forward it so that it might reach Ion Valea.

Dinu Valea was puzzled for a few minutes. Hadn't Fuhrmann been the last to see Ion? Wouldn't you think he'd more or less be up-to-date about the boy's movements through the West? Dinu himself certainly had no idea, nor did he know the writer's address. He'd heard of someone named Paul Toma, the richest and brainiest of them all—but how would Dinu know where the guy lived? Even assuming Ion knew himself, he'd never said a thing to Dinu about it, just as he'd said nothing about far more important matters than that. Now Dinu found himself alone: everyone had abandoned him. Marioara had skipped out, tired of living with a poor old wreck—and this time he was pretty sure it was for good: she wouldn't be coming back. He threw the American envelope on the table, from which it slipped onto the floor. Only the next day, when he reread Fuhrmann's point that Ion had been eagerly awaiting a letter from his friend in America, did Dinu think that it might be a good idea, perhaps, to send it on to Tiberius Ludoşan, in Timişoara. He found Tiberius's address in a drawer and scribbled a few lines explaining the situation. Then he went to the post office, glad to be rid of the envelope and whatever might be inside it . . .

That same day Tiberius had a date with Livia, who had just taken her final exams and was in a cheerful mood. She told him that she was thinking of leaving for Germany. What's got into everyone? Who'll be left in this godforsaken country? Only graybeards and Securitate types—and even then only the second-rate ones, the down at heel and poor in spirit, the least guilty . . . The rest have already cleared off, or will be doing so at the first opportunity. Of course the exodus can't continue. The West has already begun to close its doors: you have to line up for weeks to get a German or French visa, and then only after you've already given them supporting documents such as an invitation from relatives living abroad and proof that they can maintain you for the duration of your visit. No one was able to leave like Ion had anymore—on the pretext of tourism.

"Get to know your own country first: it's more beautiful than many others," a German embassy official told Livia, when she applied for a visa without asking her relatives in Bochum for support. She had an uncle or something there—maybe he didn't even remember her.

And, once you have a visa, you still have to worry about scraping some money together: for the train or plane ticket, at prices that have been jumping every three months. Some leave without a visa and try to cross the border from Hungary or the former Yugoslavia, risking their savings or their health or even their life. Few get away with it. Most find themselves in a camp in Germany waiting for their asylum application to be processed, having done their best to paint a picture of the terror brought on by their government with the help of miners and Securitate agents dressed as miners or Gypsies. That used to cut some ice, especially at the beginning, after the events in University Square . . . a few unfortunates were given political asylum. But recently most have been forcibly deported.

Tiberius asked Dr. Farkas for the address of his son Gyuri in Budapest, who had travelled there with Ion and arranged for him to stay with his aunt, Zsuzsa. He could have sent the envelope directly to Zsuzsa, but she and he had had a falling out after her visit to Timişoara. Zsuzsa had made advances to him one night, and he—though willing enough—had been unable to do very much.

"You're not good for anything," she said over her shoulder, before leaving the room and slamming the door.

This made Tiberius angry, and he shouted some pretty nasty things after her. But later, when he thought of her, he felt a kind of disgust mixed with pity. It can't be easy for her, chasing after young students at her age!

Gyuri Farkas had been giving beautiful Eva a hand in the café. He took the envelope from the mailman, read Tiberius's name on the back, opened it, and found an airmail envelope addressed to Ion. Stuck to it, or rather stapled to it, was a page from a notepad folded in two. He told Eva what it was about and reminded her that he'd been with Ion on the day they first met. It was Ion who'd insisted on going into her café. Nearly two years had passed since then . . .

"Time flies." Eva shrugged impassively and went to take another order.

"I didn't think that guy would turn out to be so adventurous," Gyuri muttered when Eva returned.

"Three small coffees."

"Look, he's in France now, and he might be off to America, where a friend is expecting him," Gyuri said, waving the envelope.

"Sounds like you envy him."

That evening Gyuri Farkas called his aunt, Zsuzsa. Maybe Ion had left her an address, maybe she had some idea of how to get hold of him.

"He said he was first going to stay with a friend of his father—a Romanian German living in Munich."

"He's not there any more. He left for France."

"France? Wait a minute. Yes, he did say something about France . . ."

"What did he say?"

"He knew an exiled writer there, someone who hinted that he might help him."

"Didn't you meet a Romanian writer when you were in Paris? That's what Father said."

"Your father's always saying something. Anyway, do you think there's only one writer in Paris? That's where they all go. All the Romanians, I mean."

"And don't you know the address?"

Zsuzsa didn't much like the idea of getting mixed up further with a boy the police were after. She hadn't told anyone about her interrogation at the Hotel Europa bar. Should she tell Gyuri? Of course, she wasn't absolutely sure the guy had been from the police. He never showed her any ID, although he did act as if . . .

"Hello?" Gyuri said impatiently. "Are you still there?"

"If you want to talk about it, come to my place tomorrow evening. Right now I'm off to a bridge match," Zsuzsa said in Romanian. She hung up, and a little afterclick could be heard.

The next evening she asked Gyuri into her kitchen, as far as possible from the telephone, and poured two glasses of whisky. She told him that an extremely polite but persuasive voice had called one fine morning inviting her to Hotel Europa. She'd gone there and met a tall well-built man who offered her a whisky. Gyuri couldn't believe his ears.

"And you agreed to be questioned like that, without being sure he was a policeman!"

"I did feel sure at first. He even looked like one. But—what do you think he was really?"

"I don't know. There are all kinds of crooks in the world. So what did he want from you?"

"To tell him where Ion had gone."

"And did you?"

"I said I didn't know."

"So you lied."

"No. Listen to me: I wasn't here when he left. I was in Romania, in Kolozsvár."

Zsuzsa poured herself another whisky. Gyuri hadn't been drinking his: he'd just moistened his lips and put the glass on the table, enthralled by the conversation. Now he picked it up and took a gulp.

"He was a bit loony, that kid," Zsuzsa said.

"He made a good impression on me. But you probably got to know him better," Gyuri said, grinning.

Zsuzsa didn't get upset. She shrugged and sipped her whisky.

"But didn't you ask why the police, or whoever, were looking for him?"

"No."

"Are you really such a sucker, or what?"

Zsuzsa stood up and said:

"I'll go look for the writer's address."

I know that Marianne would hold it against me if I said nothing about the Moscow putsch. ("He's capable of anything," she once said, gossiping to Smaranda about me. Though I could just as easily say the same about her.) So I hasten to inform the reader that, if I haven't written a word about Marianne for many pages now, the reason is simply that she left Paris and Europe to visit a friend of Smaranda's in Moscow. That's right, Moscow! And, two days after she arrived, the putsch took place. I'll go into a little detail, so she won't have any more reason for complaint.

Shortly before she left, she called to let me know about her trip.

"Okay," I said, "but what will you do with the Siamese?"

"I'll send him to you."

"How will you do that? By mail?"

"I'm in a hurry—let's skip the jokes. I'll send him with someone who'll anyway be in those parts and was kind enough to offer."

And, indeed, the Siamese arrived the very next day, on Pierre's bike.

When I heard the rustle of wings, I was hard at work on a new chapter. I didn't feel like going downstairs to chat with the mailman, as I usually do—but he did feel like it. The bell rang, long and shrill.

"*J'arrive! J'arrive!*"

Pierre was smiling in the doorway, with a little basket in his hands. The tomcat stuck his whiskered head out and, as soon as he saw me, uttered the most stunningly beautiful meow. After this emotional reunion, the mailman explained how it had come about: On the road that skirts the forest to the southwest, a car suddenly braked alongside him and a gentleman with glasses asked where such-and-such a writer lived. Pierre said he was just on his way there. The gentleman, being in a hurry, asked whether Pierre would be so kind as to deliver a nice little animal, to put it directly into the hands of the writer, who was eagerly awaiting it. That's the report Pierre gave, probably thinking it would make the Siamese feel important. He was still in the basket, which I was now holding in my arms. I put the basket on the ground and opened it wide. The Siamese emerged slowly and took a cautious look around. I gave Pierre a handsome tip, and he shook his wings in appreciation. The Siamese took up position in front of a tree, undecided whether to climb up it or come back to me. I put an end to this dilemma by calling his name. Perhaps he was hungry. Now I had to take care of him. I had no choice. My chapter went on the back burner.

Pierre was already cycling off vigorously. He had a new way of using his wings, which allowed him to stop pedaling after the initial momentum was gained. He flew along at not much more than a foot above the ground: a goose or a swan taking off, Hermes disguised as Jupiter, half bird, half mailman; the metamorphosis had not been carried through to the end.

I called Marianne and told her the cat had arrived safely. Her recorded voice informed me that she'd already left for Moscow. From now on I could only follow her in my imagination—not easy, because I'd never been to the capital of the Soviet Union. On the other hand, I've seen many photos: the Kremlin, Red Square, Lomonossov University (which resembles its little sister in Bucharest, Casa Scânteii, named after the Communist daily paper, although I think it has since been changed to House of Truth or Freedom or something like that).

I guess there must also be a Hotel Europa in Moscow, in the lobby of which I can see a happy pair of friends advancing, eyes straight ahead, behind the boy loaded with their luggage. Both are Westerners, both proud of their much-coveted knickknacks and the perfume they give off around them. Yes, that may well be what's going through their heads. I wonder if it corresponds to reality. After all, they're not the only foreigners passing through Moscow. And, God knows, Russian women working in this international hotel also earn enough to make themselves look and smell flashy—to attract attention, men's in particular. Are they tasteless? Of course: that is, they dress according to Moscow tastes. And it is also in accordance with Moscow tastes that these Muscovites judge other women: French, German, American, whatever. So-called Parisian elegance doesn't cut it with them. The two foreign friends will soon come to the same conclusion.

They'd reserved two rooms through the same travel agency that had booked their flights. When they reported to reception, they handed over their passports and a whole arsenal of other papers, and in return they received two keys attached to veritable cannonballs, almost as big as the ones that used to be dragged around on chains by deportees to Siberia. *Поход на Сибирь!* That had been back in the Tsarist era, the one to which many Soviet citizens dreamed of returning. They hadn't enjoyed life much under Stalin—and they also turned their noses up at what followed, under Khrushchev, Brezhnev, etc. It's said that there was greater freedom in Siberia in the time of the Tsars than in Moscow under the communists. Marianne was sure of that. They went upstairs in an elevator that smelled of cabbage or borshch. They looked for their rooms on the third floor, as they'd been told at reception. Empty halls with worn, blood-red carpeting, stained here and there with something black: maybe tar, maybe oil. They found the room allocated to Smaranda, but the key didn't fit. Much as they wriggled it in the lock, trying to turn it with their right hand while holding the cannonball in their left, much as they pushed and pulled and maneuvered and banged, growing more irritated all the while, the door refused to give way. Marianne started to rap on the door with the key and its massive attachment. No one came out, of course. They returned to the elevator, waited, fulminated; no doubt the thing had broken down. They took the stairs, and on the floor below they came across a chambermaid leaving a room with several rolls of toilet paper cradled to her chest. They rushed up to her and didn't understand why she took fright and ran off round the corner, probably to hide in another room. Then Marianne remembered their luggage. They returned to the monumental marble staircase (genuine marble?), whose steps were covered with an endlessly long and narrow carpet, a paler red than the one upstairs and emblazoned here and there with the hammer and sickle. (Smaranda stopped to admire it with semi-ironic glee.) When they reached the first floor, they saw a *moustachu* with a huge briefcase. Huh, there's Ion Țiriac, Smaranda said to herself, but even she didn't believe it was really the famous tennis-player. The *moustachu* stopped in front of them and smiled. Then he headed off down a hallway.

"Say, isn't that Țiriac?" Marianne asked excitedly.

Smaranda shrugged, without replying. She looked tired, exhausted. Back at reception, the man who had given them their keys was no longer there: he'd been replaced by a fair-haired young man with dreamy blue eyes. He smiled. The two Parisians told him indignantly what had happened, but the Russian continued to smile placidly. After a good few minutes, during which more anger expressed in the language of Yves Montand ("Russians adore him," Marianne had assured Smaranda on the plane) had not the slightest effect, the Russian told them calmly in English that they were wasting their time: he didn't understand French, and if they really wanted to communicate with him they should do so in the language of Stallone. Yes, not Stalin, Stallone.

Marianne spoke the language of Stallone quite well, so she started *dal capo* and gradually shed the indignation of a few minutes earlier. The young man listened, patient and amused, and roared with laughter at the bit about the chambermaid who fled down the hall clutching rolls of toilet paper. Far from being angry now, Marianne was positively proud of her narrative talents.

"We do need to have our keys, though . . ."

"Okay, okay!" the blond boy repeated, by now in such a good mood that he placed his large white hand on Smaranda's, which barely covered half of the cannonball.

"And the suitcases . . ."

"Как?"

"The suitcases, baggage, trunks—the ones we brought from Paris."

"Ah, luggage . . . Paris."

"Yes."

"Where are they?"

"What do you mean, where are they? I have no idea. That's what I'm asking you." Marianne, again upset, banged the keys on the desk.

The receptionist, who came from Siberia, seemed unflustered. But he was no longer laughing. He rubbed his cheek with the back of his hand.

"Do you have your passport?"

Marianne felt she was choking. So she gave up English and began to shout in French, to the despair of the receptionist, who couldn't understand the reason for her deplorable regression from a rich and widely used language to a pathetic vernacular that was fast becoming extinct. Marianne saw the look in his eyes, at once helpless and contemptuous, and reverted to English. She asked to speak to the manager. The manager?

During lunch?

"Why don't you two ladies go to the restaurant and make yourselves comfortable? Aren't you hungry?"

He was right. They were both hungry. They ordered vodka and caviar and wondered how it could be so cheap. Their good mood returned. After the caviar, they pointed to the Pozharski chicken—that is, escalope, with peas and potatoes. Marianne had eaten it before in Paris. A few tables away, the fake Țiriac was sitting with three equally suspicious-looking individuals, who now and then eyed the two ladies up and down. They were chattering and laughing: the vodka was beginning to take effect. Țiriac caught Smaranda looking at him and his mustachioed mouth rose into a smile. Soon he was standing in front of them.

"May I sit down?" he asked in English.

Taken aback, Marianne and Smaranda said nothing. The man didn't wait but took a seat, lighting a cigarette.

"My name is Haiducu."

Smaranda's heart began racing.

"Are you Romanian?" she asked, in the thinnest of voices.

"Almost. I'm Moldovan."

"Bessarabian, that is," Smaranda tried to correct him, but Haiducu gave her a dirty look. Then, mellowing, he said in French:

"I'd like to introduce some friends to you."

Marianne shrugged. What is this polyglot after? Even when he'd asked to sit down, it was clear that he was more communicating his intentions than giving an opportunity to refuse. And yet, why refuse? Maybe these gentlemen could help them recover their luggage and get their room keys. "*Quelle histoire!*" Marianne exclaimed. She still hadn't made up her mind whether she should be indignant or have some fun.

I stop here because the Siamese is breaking my heart with his mewling. Does he want to go outside again? Or is he just bored? I go downstairs and find him watching the telephone with hostility. He lingers in front of my map and gives me a questioning look.

Of course, the map still isn't up to date. All the characters have scattered like partridges. I can't keep an eye on them all the time. Some of them I've lost sight of altogether. Sandu Economu, for example, wandering all over Germany and Switzerland: from Stuttgart to Tübingen, then to Berne, back to Frankfurt for a short

415

while, and on to Jena, Nuremberg, and his parents' home in Heidelberg. Before flying to the U.S. he also dallied a while in Berlin, where he fell in love with a Dutch girl. She was the reason why he crossed the Atlantic. But fortunately she dumped him there for a black basketball-player. Are you sure it wasn't some other color? Come on, stop kidding around. Okay then, but why "fortunately"? That's a long story, which Sandu wrote about in the letter he sent to Ion before he left Munich. No, I haven't read it. Zsuzsa, or, to be more precise, Gyuri Farkas, forwarded it to our address in Paris, where it's probably still sitting in our mailbox. In Moscow, right now, Marianne is in conversation with Haiducu, who's telling her about it, about the letter.

"There's no point in Ion getting the letter," he says. "That jerk's entirely capable of ditching Europe for the U.S.—leaving all of us high and dry. After everything he's done . . ."

"And what's he done?"

Marianne couldn't really fathom Haiducu's interest in Ion—he seemed to know more than anyone about him—or in the letter that was now haunting Europe like a spectral manifesto. She really had no idea what could be in it. How could she? She hadn't written it, after all. Haiducu must be mixing her up with . . .

The tom is choking with laughter.

This is the kind of reader I like: one gifted with a sense of humor; one who doesn't begin to identify so completely and crassly with any of my characters that he's actually afraid for their safety—and then throws his book away because the author has hinted that the main character, for whom the reader has developed a certain liking, or anyway familiarity, is going to, yes, well, depart this life. That kind of thing is plain ridiculous!

The Siamese assents with his whiskers and rubs his back against the door. Again he wants to go out.

Perhaps Marianne thinks that Haiducu is making advances. If she does, she's making a terrible mistake. Anyway, he didn't show up for the date they made in the hotel lobby, on the evening of the putsch. The earth, as they say, had swallowed him up. She and Smaranda waited half an hour for nothing. On the other hand, a man and woman appeared speaking Romanian. Marianne had heard the language enough to recognize it, but that doesn't mean she understood much of anything. Smaranda, however, turned white as a sheet.

"What's the matter? You feeling all right?"

Smaranda didn't answer. Her eyes were fixed on the newcomers; or, rather, her ears were glued to them, pricked up like a watchdog's.

"They're Romanians, aren't they?"

"Yes."

One of them, let's say the woman, spoke Haiducu's name and kept staring at the two friends, who—especially Smaranda—were waiting apprehensively for the scene to progress.

"Do you know them?"

Smaranda hesitated for a few seconds, then realized that she had no way of concealing their relationship. Ana and Mihai had spotted her and were coming toward her, smiling with that typically Romanian joviality, exaggerated but not necessarily false. They were both working at Radio Free Europe and had come to do a report from Moscow. When she introduced herself, Ana said: "I'm Maria!" Smaranda preferred to overlook this: she had neither the courage nor the interest to make an issue of it. Besides, the fact that they worked for Radio Free Europe was a sign of respectability—even Marianne probably thought that.

"Have you heard the news?"

"What news?"

"There are tanks in the streets. They said so on television. One of the people around Gorbachev also announced it in a speech. I forget his name: I've got it written down here somewhere." Mihai fumbled in his pockets for a while. Ana didn't bother to offer any help—everyone has their own particular memories . . .

"They also sent them into Budapest and Prague, and a fat lot of good that did them!" Marianne joked.

"And Gorbachev?"

"Gorbachev's under arrest in the Crimea," Mihai said with a certain satisfaction.

"But nothing's really clear," Ana broke in. "Some say he's actually behind . . ."

"Behind the tanks?"

"Behind the whole thing. He wants to set up a hard-line regime."

"Nonsense!" Mihai said. "Gorbachev's a wimp, or else he's working for the CIA."

All four went out to see the tanks and headed for Red Square. A column was indeed making its way along the main thoroughfare. People were crowding around, apparently without fear. Some began to erect barricades. They overturned a streetcar. They were all shouting. At one point, a sturdily built man showed up and started yelling. The crowd applauded wildly. It was the mayor of Moscow, someone by the name of Yeltsin.

When they reached the barricades, the tanks stopped demurely and rotated their turrets. No one opened fire. From time to time, the blond, rather frightened head of a young gunner popped up. A few women, mothers and grandmothers it seemed, approached the tanks with pots and cans of borshch. "Give them a bit of vodka too," someone shouted. Everyone laughed, in a friendly sort of way.

The only man who seemed frightened by the putsch was the president of France, François Mitterrand, who appeared on television and read out a cautious, half-approving statement. After three or four days, the organizers of this palace revolution were arrested. One of them committed suicide, in prison. The others will all be let off in the end.

At Hotel Europa life goes on. The two Parisiennes are beginning to get used to the hotel and the characters milling around the lobby. They are longer surprised at the odd things that happen sometimes: for example, the cavernous voice that emerges from one of their showerheads and gives a little speech. "It must be attached to the telephone cable somewhere," Smaranda said pensively. Once, the telephone rang in Marianne's room when she was alone. She picked up the receiver and heard a horrible metallic screech, as if a garbage can was being dragged along a stretch of ground strewn with nails, barbed wire or some other little metal objects. Then the noise became clearer, and she could identify a corkscrew being pulled vigorously across a can of Coke, which may also have contained vodka—why not? you can never be sure of anything these days. A voice tried to out-shout all these sounds and, believe it or not, finally succeeded. Marianne made out the magical word GAGARIN, followed by many more words, probably in Russian, Ukrainian, or Belorussian, one of which she did actually understand. It was *автор*: not aviator, or actor, but author, yes, author . . .

"This is the author's wife," Marianne shouted into the receiver.

"Жена?"

"Да."

But the voice was able to speak other languages too: German, English, even French. It must be the polyglot himself, Marianne thought. And finally she asked what he wanted.

"Nothing special," he replied. "It's about Ion."

"Do you really intend to keep pestering me about this Ion of yours?"

"Really, we just want you to be nice to him," the polyglot said. "Persuade him to go to Brittany instead of wasting any more time in Paris. That city just leads you to perdition."

"Paris?"

"Yes. Please forgive me for saying so, perhaps I'm being a little unkind. But it's not the same if you come from another country. You see, for foreigners, Paris . . ."

Marianne didn't want to hear any more. She hung up.

The Siamese is mewling with boredom, or quite simply displeasure. So I won't go on reading to him. It would be too complicated or tedious to explain Gagarin's role in all this. Everyone will make of it what they like and what they can.

When Ion returned that morning from the latrines, he didn't immediately notice the Gypsy crouching by the door. So, without suspecting anything, he walked toward his sleeping bag, which was spread out against the wall. Only then did he hear and see him. The Gypsy sprang up and blocked the way out, a knife gleaming in his hand.

"All right, hand it over!"

Ion tried to stay calm and shrugged his shoulders.

"Hand what over?"

The Gypsy stepped forward.

"Take your clothes off!"

"What do you want from me?" Ion asked indignantly.

"Hurry up! Drop your pants!"

"You're crazy . . ."

"Come on, speed it up!"

Ion saw the game was up. He considered using the stool by the window to defend himself—the yard was empty, everyone had left to go about their daily business. But the stool was a little too far away for him to grab it and hit the Gyspy in one movement. The mugger guessed his thoughts and grabbed it first, banishing any dangerous temptations from Ion's mind. Now the Gypsy held the knife in one hand, the stool in the other. Ion didn't have a chance. This guy wouldn't think twice about slitting his throat or cracking his skull open—he could take his pick. The Gypsy had made careful preparations, had chosen a moment when Ion was forced to go out without locking his door—he'd asked for a key, but the Gypsy had laughed in his face—and then entered the room and searched his sleeping bag and suitcase. Then he'd lain in wait, sure that Ion had the money on him.

Ion undid his shirt and belt and, turning around, tried to hold his waistband up while also untying the knot that kept the plastic pouch attached to his right hip. The Gypsy gave a grunt of satisfaction and went to help him: that is, to cut the knot with his outstretched blade. A real Alexander of Macedon!

The knife left a fine reddish mark on Ion's skin.

"Leave me a little," he asked, but the Macedonian put the pouch straight into his pocket.

"I'll keep it safe for you," the Gypsy said, with the utmost seriousness. Then he turned on his heel and went out.

Ion sat dazed on the stool. All he had left now were the few bills in his shoes. He hadn't hidden any more, stupidly thinking that he might tear or spoil them as he walked. What an idiot! He hoped he still had enough to buy a train ticket to Paris, maybe also food for a few days or a week—certainly it wouldn't last much longer than that . . . He didn't dare take the money out now to count it, in case the dark fiend returned, that stinking little vulture! He carefully folded his sleeping bag, slung it over his back, and picked up his suitcase.

Gică was already at his post, beneath the cathedral wall. Ion motioned for him to follow. No sign of the Gypsy around there. Avoiding their usual café, Ion turned onto a little street behind the cathedral. Gică puffed along behind and, eventually catching up with him, reached up and tapped him on the shoulder. Ion stopped. Gică braked hard and almost fell on his face, having forgotten to strap himself in.

"That Gypsy scumbag robbed me," Ion announced.

Gică said nothing as Ion gave him a potted account of what had happened.

"So what are you going to do now?" he finally asked.

"I'm off to Paris."

Silence. Then Gică said decisively:

"I'll come with you."

The hardest part was getting out of the city. Although the road was well marked with boards and signposts, it seemed to go on for ever and ever. The traffic was heavy. Ion was almost running as he pushed the wheelchair, sometimes turning his head to look back. When the Gypsy found out they'd gone, he'd come looking for them. He wouldn't give up until he got his hands on Gică. He didn't give a damn about Ion now that he'd robbed him, especially as the student wasn't a contributing member of their society.

Ion was panting.

"Don't go so fast. We're at the highway already," Gică said, clutching Ion's suitcase, which now held his own things as well.

All this time abroad, on the road, had taken away some of Ion's taste for theory. In Romania he amazed or bored everyone with his "philosophical prattle," as Valeriu once called it. He could have let himself go at Fuhrmann's, but he hadn't bothered. The German was the superior blabbermouth, the superior philosopher, and right from the start he had intimidated Ion with his ecological data. In that domain Ion was still a novice, so he kept quiet and listened—a passive, if not subaltern, role. Sometimes he would open his mouth to ask a question or crack a silly joke, at the risk of irritating Fuhrmann. He did it to please Petrişor—at least that's how he justified his schoolboyish humor to himself, as if it was any excuse. When he was alone with Fuhrmann, he generally showed himself to be much more serious and cooperative—which meant it was mainly Fuhrmann who spoke and he who listened. That should really have been Gică's role—the listener—but precisely because he was ignorant in so many areas, he didn't hesitate to voice all sorts of risky speculations. He wasn't afraid of anything. And his physical disability, which condemned him to comparative immobility, encouraged him to think about things that other young people of his age and circumstances preferred to avoid, or to consider only superficially, like their parents and relatives, using the readymade formulas of so-called popular wisdom, whose distant origins are religious in nature and sometimes even predate Christianity.

"In your place I wouldn't have given in," Gică declared, and although Ion understood the allusion he tried to buy himself some time.

"What do you mean?"

"I wouldn't have let the Gypsy have the money."

"So what would you have done?"

"I'd have fought."

"He had a knife."

"So what?"

"He'd have cut my throat."

"Death doesn't scare me," Gică whispered.

"He wouldn't necessarily have killed me—and he'd have got the money one way or the other."

"Yes, but it wouldn't have been you who gave it to him."

"Big deal!"

"Very big. You'd have shown the strength of your will . . ."

"My will to power? He was the one with the power. The knife . . ."

"You'd have shown you weren't afraid of him. You should have met his power and his threats with scorn!"

"You've got to be joking."

"To be unafraid of death is to be free! And it also makes you the stronger one in any confrontation."

"But he was the one with the knife."

"Makes no difference! That doesn't mean he wasn't afraid of you. On the contrary . . ."

"That's all bullshit! Don't imagine he'd have gone away empty-handed."

"I don't know. But at least you wouldn't have knuckled under."

"Okay, but one of us had to. So I knuckled under and stayed alive."

Gică fell silent. Ion took this opportunity to expound on the well-known Hegelian theory of the dialectical relationship between master and slave—the apple pie of philosophy, the all-purpose theory of human society. True master that he was, Gică couldn't grasp why Ion said it was the slave who came out on top in the end.

"His truth is the master," Ion emphasized.

"I don't understand. Which master?"

"We're not talking about one person but about an attitude of mind. The slave's mentality is supple, dynamic, forward moving. The slave is better equipped to understand reality and life. Do you follow? On the other hand, what does the master have left to do after he's triumphed, after he's put his life on the line and proved that he's not afraid of death? Do you think he's really satisfied? Or, if he is, how long will his self-satisfaction last? Soon he'll become aware that the recognition he's won is unstable, since it depends on the mirror held out by a slave. The master then finds that he can't maneuver, that he's become stiff and rigid, like a corpse."

Gică listened. Ion pushed his wheelchair and went on with his speech. From time to time he paused and stepped in front of Gică, hoping that this would make what he had to say more convincing. The cripple listened, then made a sign with his head as if to call Ion to order, to reality, whereupon Ion went back behind him.

"To escape from this stasis, to negate it and move forward, the master has to find a master of his own, stronger than anyone else, whom he can fear and serve. That master can only be God, a fantastical but overwhelming master."

"There's also death," Gică said, apparently understanding more than Ion had assumed. "Death: the master of us all!"

They spent the night in the fields, in a hut that had probably once served as a rain shelter. Ion helped Gică get ready for bed. He'd never have imagined himself capable of such submission, or, to be more precise, such devotion. But, where could he hide his money? The thought flashed into his head and out again, like a fly.

"Are you asleep?" Ion asked.

"No. I'm thinking about what we were talking about earlier."

"In Hegel's theory, the confrontation between master and slave explains the formation of self-consciousness and the certitude that comes with it—in other words, the transition from the animal to the human."

"From ape to man."

"If you like."

"Were the ones confronting each other always two males?"

Either he hadn't understood after all, or he was in a joking mood. But Ion replied:

"Not necessarily."

"Well, if there was also a female . . . She'd have had to give in anyway. So it would have ended with a bit of fucking," Gică said.

"Yes, but that's not what counts."

"What does count?"

"I'm not going to go over the whole theory again. I thought you understood that it wasn't a clash of material interests, the desire to possess an object, for example, that drove these guys to confront each other. So, the mere desire to possess a woman wouldn't have been the motivating force either. The key factor is the desire to be recognized as something other than an object or an animal, the desire or need for recognition as a subject, which is something only you yourself know for certain."

"So, with women then . . . it's much the same."

"Yes, except that in those days—I mean, in a majority of cases—women were forced to knuckle under, to recognize men's dominance. Men had force on their side. Though, in fact, I guess some women could have been sincere in their admiration or recognition . . ."

"Yeah, right!"

"No, really, just think about it a minute. How could they not have admired a male who fought others off and came out on top, or who had the courage to wrestle with wild beasts? Physical strength was the decisive factor at the beginning of patriarchy, and continued to be so until the time when weaker but smarter men invented all kinds of stuff to replace muscle power."

"Anyway, all that patriarchy stuff is over now!" Gică exclaimed. "Women have started to resist, to fight back. Now you've got to beat them senseless if you want to get on top of them."

Gică thought he could hear Ion sigh.

The next day they left at the crack of dawn. By the time the sun was in the sky, they had reached a small road, where a signpost pointed to a village just a mile and a half away.

"A hot coffee wouldn't go amiss," Ion said cheerfully.

"With some croissants or toast."

Their feet and wheels began to move faster.

They came to a village where a film was being shot. Dead sheep and steers were strewn around the square, and an abandoned cart lay on its side in front of the *mairie*. Amid all this were gendarmes, townspeople, and the film crew. An agitated, perhaps slightly tipsy man was waving his arms around and shouting at the top of his voice: it was obviously the director. Four men were carrying a woman on a stretcher from a large hotel pompously baptized Europa, or, to be more precise, from the hotel café. Behind them was a man wearing a uniform with a stationmaster's peaked cap. He shouted "Maria!" and held out his right arm, while the camera moved along some rails for a few yards. "Maria!" he shouted again. The stretcher-bearers crossed the square, avoiding a lamb's carcass, and turned left instead of right.

428

"To the station! To the station!" the agitated figure yelled. Then, a second later: "Stop!" The foursome halted and lay the stretcher on dry ground—I mean, asphalt—not far from a dead cow. The woman sat up, rubbing her eyes as if she had just woken up. No one was filming her anymore, of course. Three of the men had walked away a few yards, and she tugged at the pants of the one still standing beside the stretcher. When he looked down to see what she wanted, the actress pointed up to the sky. Gică looked up, but he saw nothing.

"Okay, let's do the scene again," the director said. "Only closer to the camera this time."

The four picked up the stretcher again. The stationmaster took off his cap. He was sweating, so he wiped his forehead and neck with a handkerchief. Gică raised his arm toward something in the sky: a plane, a bird . . .

Here I'd planned to develop my theory of musical composition as it relates to writing—as if showing off to the tomcat: that is, repetition, development of themes, variations, and other assorted tricks. But I worry he'll say that I've already done all that in such-and-such a book.

"Who read it, though?" I sigh, staring straight into his yellow Siamese eyes.

"Anyway, the references there were contemporary."

"Highly contemporary," I add—this is a joke.

"You mentioned Berlioz."

"Who?"

"Sorry, I meant to say Boulez."

"Ah, that's different."

"Anyway, the fact is that you're regressing."

"You're right. But I'm not to blame."

"Who is, then?"

"The readers."

The Siamese roars with laughter, or maybe with indignation. He sputters and spits and meows like a wildcat as he crosses the full length of the room. He jumps onto the table and sniffs my pile of typewritten sheets. Placing one paw on the typewriter, he doesn't mince words:

"The truth is that what you write gets worse and more convoluted all the time. You grope your way from page to page—which proves that you have no plan, no real purpose. You dart off in one direction, then another . . . you can't manage to put together the simplest plot, or to say anything even remotely important or interesting that readers can really sink their teeth into."

"You're just parroting what you heard from Marianne," I say, standing up in a huff.

There they are, back on the road, tired and hungry. Ion is no longer pushing the wheelchair but marching alongside it, suitcase in hand, sleeping bag on his back. At one point a hill comes into view, and Ion thinks wearily that he'll have to help Gică to roll up it. The countryside is more uneven in France than in Germany. He didn't take that into account when he agreed to have Gică along for the ride. He was only thinking about money at the time—or not even that: more about the blessings and advantages of begging. Naturally, Gică would have more luck than Ion picking up alms; no one would give anything to a strapping young man like him. Why didn't you stay in your own country? they'd ask. Who'd ask? Well, anyone would. Or else they wouldn't ask, but they still wouldn't give him anything—not a cent! Admittedly, he hadn't tried it yet, just to see what would happen if he held out his hand . . . But you can't beg when your pockets are stuffed with deutschmarks. That's true. Now the marks are in his shoes. But how many? Not a lot. He still didn't want to stop and count them, not while someone was watching . . . not that Gică really counted as a witness: one of his best qualities was his lack of curiosity. The cripple was lagging twenty or thirty yards behind.

"Come on, speed it up! We'll never get there at this rate."

The road was already sloping up. The angle was gentler than it had looked from a distance, but Gică could feel it, he was having a really hard time. Ion stopped and waited, feeling sorry for him as he sweated and furiously pushed at the wheels of the chair. Finally Ion dropped the suitcase in Gică's hands and went behind to push him.

"I wasn't doing myself any favors when I took you along!"

The cars passed at great speed. Not one of them stopped. More in jest than in earnest, Ion said he was placing his hopes in the truck drivers.

"I'll stick you in a refrigerated truck," he shouted in Gică's ear.

"Why not a gas tanker?"

A car passed with an empty horse cart in tow. Ion made the classic sign with his thumb, but too late. The road was now going downhill. Gică no longer needed to be pushed, as the wheelchair was gliding along smoothly enough. The suitcase was still in Gică's arms. *Tant pis!* Ion was taking it slowly, deep in thought, when a black car flashed past and nearly ran him over. It stopped alongside Gică, and three men got out, one of them unmistakably the Gypsy. They surrounded Gică, yanking him off his seat. "Help, Ion, help!" he yelled at the top of his lungs. Ignoring Ion entirely, they hustled Gică into the car and tied his wheelchair to the roof, which was equipped with a special set of bars and ropes. After hesitating for a few moments, Ion ran rather half-heartedly toward them, then stopped. He had the impression that one of the trio was Petrişor. He jumped off the road and ran alongside, crouching below eye level. Then he suddenly raised himself to full height and shouted: "Petrişor!" None of the three turned his head. They all disappeared into the car, which raced off and was soon out of sight. The whole thing had lasted no more than a minute.

Ion sat on the grass and removed his shoes. The deutschmarks were still there, creased and dirty from all the sweat and dust. He put them down and wiped them with the palm of his hand. He had enough to catch a train, even to keep the wolf from the door for a few more days. He carefully folded the money and slipped it into his pocket.

I must help him get to Paris as quickly as possible. He shouldn't waste any more time on the road: the simplest thing would be for him to hitchhike. It would be easier now, without Gică. He didn't look too shady: even if he'd lost his luggage, he came across as a young tourist, especially with his sleeping bag slung over his back—perhaps a student who didn't have enough for the train or preferred to travel most of the way on foot: keeping himself fit, admiring nature. Look, he's picked some wild flowers and even put one behind his ear, like a young German Romantic, a sportsman or ecologist. He might even catch the eye of a lady driver bored with the monotony of her life. Or else a gentleman in the same situation. In fact, it was a gentleman who stopped, opened the passenger door, and asked with a smile where Ion was heading. Ion got in. The gentleman continued to smile: bald, middle-aged, well-dressed, polite, gentle, friendly.

433

When Ion answered "Paris," the driver gave an inviting nod and pointed out that it was a long way to Paris. He was going to Metz. He was an accountancy expert. And Ion? The student replied that he was studying French, loved France, admired the French . . . And so it had occurred to him to go to Paris, where he knew a writer.

"What's his name? Is he famous?"

"I don't think so."

"But anyway, what's his name?" the expert insisted, and he put his nicely groomed hand on Ion's thigh. He only left it there for three seconds, then moved it to the stickshift, to the steering wheel, back to Ion's thigh, and finally to the buttons of the car radio.

Ion confessed that he didn't know the writer's name. He told the driver how he had met him, under what circumstances. The elegant expert in accountancy was very interested in the countries of Eastern Europe: he'd heard about the revolution in Budapest, sorry, Bucharest, and even about the student movements, University Square, and so on. He reeled all this off with the evident intention of pleasing Ion, who responded in monosyllables or, more often, remained silent. Ion watched the sun slip behind the hills and reappear at the end of a valley, then disappear and reappear again, hill and dale, dale and hill, a truly mioritic landscape, even more mioritic than the landscape of Transylvania. It's rather odd . . .

"What's odd?" the man at the steering wheel said, with a worried look. "We'll be in Metz soon."

"Could you please drop me at the train station?"

"Sure. But don't you think it's a bit of a drag spending the night on a train? You haven't even booked a couchette. It would be better to leave tomorrow. Look, you can stay at my place tonight. We'll talk about Romania, er, just a moment, what's the name of your president? Not Ceausescu, I know, you cooked his goose. The other one: the one who was freely elected. Wasn't that what happened?"

"Iliescu."

"That's it, Iliescu! He has a nice, happy face."

"You think so?"

"He looks like a friend of mine . . . died poor and alone a while ago. He played with fire once too often. Had that horrible disease that's going around everywhere."

"Do you really think Iliescu looks like a nice guy?" Ion asked, frowning, and the accountant realized he hadn't said quite the right thing.

"Maybe I'm wrong, you'd know better than me," he backtracked, landing a hearty slap on Ion's muscular thigh. "And, look, we'll have a drop of wine. There's a nice restaurant on the corner of my street. You'll see, it's really great!"

They polished off two bottles in no time. Ion was a little far gone. Iliescu's admirer kept refilling his glass. The wine was excellent, as indeed was the whole meal.

Around midnight, back at the accountant's place, Ion shouted desperately:

"*Je ne veux pas, je ne peux pas! Elle est trop grosse, elle est énorme!*"

"*Du calme,*" the accountant said. "*Alors, lêche-la!*"

The train ride from Metz to Paris took no more than four and a half hours, even though it's not a high-speed line. Ion dozed in the corner of a compartment. Two blonde girls were reading opposite him. The garish cover of one of their books had the title: *Maman était une extraterrestre.* The train stopped only once. Another passenger joined them: a man dressed as a hunter. He had a beret pulled over one ear and a baguette under one arm, but his short leather pants and differently colored leather jacket and high-necked pullover left no room for doubt. Only he didn't have a rifle. Ion closed his eyes and even managed to get some sleep. He woke up in Paris, at the Gare de l'Est.

He didn't rush out into the streets to get his fill of the city. First a station news vendor. So here's the City of Light, in picture post-cards: Eiffel Tower, Louvre, Place de la Concorde in the mist, Arc de Triomphe, a sightseeing boat on the Seine, another *bateau-mouche* opposite Île Saint-Louis, a woman with one breast bare and the other covered with a tricolor, François Mitterrand in the guise of a frog. He also looked at the newspapers. One headline attracted his attention: *The Mysteries of Goma*. No, of course it didn't mean *that* Goma . . . But, by a chain of associations, the multiple Gomas and their multiple fames (town, football-player, pen-pusher . . .) triggered the thought that Ion ought to make a telephone call. He looked through his pockets for the little notebook in which he'd jotted down the writer's number. He couldn't find it. Maybe it's in the sleeping bag, although that's so unlikely it's hardly even worth checking; it's almost certainly in the suitcase he left on Gică's lap. Just to be on the safe side, however, he did look in the sleeping bag. Of course it wasn't there. Now what? Fuhrmann would know the writer's number, because Ion had given it to him. But how was he supposed to get hold of Fuhrmann? It would take at least a week by mail (Fuhrmann could reply to general delivery), and how would Ion manage in the meantime? *Dam Project in Brocéliande Forest Under Attack—Dam Would Increase Water Reserves—Ecologists Prefer to Target Pollution.* Ion stood up and saw a little paper goods section in the news kiosk, beside the novels. He bought a note-book and ballpoint pen, then looked for somewhere quiet to sit on his sleeping bag and write to Mr. Fuhrmann.

He only wrote a couple of sentences, clear and to the point. He'd lost his address book (he didn't bother giving details) and needed the telephone number of the writer in Paris. Would Fuhrmann please send it to him at the poste restante at the main post office, rue du Louvre. PS: plus a little cash, because he didn't have a cent.

After he had sent off the letter, Ion finally went walking in the streets of Paris. In fact, he did have a little money now, which the accountant had slipped into his sleeping bag, and which he'd come across only while searching through it at the station. He was especially sorry to have lost the address book, since it contained not only addresses and telephone numbers but also newspaper clippings, short items and major stories alike. He'd begun to collect them in Austria, on a sudden impulse, no doubt partly because he'd been so happy that he was beginning to understand the language. In a way, the news and facts gathered in this way had had a personal dimension: they'd been his travel journal.

At Place Pigalle he bought an ice-cream bar and stood looking at pictures of naked girls. They weren't any more naked than in Vienna, Munich, or Strasbourg. Tired of licking, he bit off a large piece of his treat and immediately felt a pain in his teeth because of the cold. He spat out what he had in his mouth and threw the rest away. A swarthy type kept winking and inviting him into a striptease parlor. But Ion had become thrifty—and anyway, what was there to see? If he could have done more than watch . . .

He started following a girl with enormous breasts. She went into the front hall of an apartment block, and he did too. She pressed a button, and a sinister yellow light came on. There was a staircase at the end of the corridor. Without stopping, the girl muttered something over her shoulder.

"Three hundred francs?" Ion exclaimed indignantly.

She climbed some of the stairs, then stopped and turned with a faint smile. She bared one of her breasts and, as if weighing it, made it dance around in her hand.

"Two hundred and fifty," she whispered, as if afraid that someone might hear her lowering her rate.

Ion joined her on the staircase, but despite the obvious attraction he didn't feel like handing over a sum that could otherwise be invested in a large number of sandwiches. The girl got angry and began to shout abuse at him. She growled at him down the stairs, and, when Ion touched her breast more or less inadvertently with the hand he was holding to his chest—he was still moving upward and it was a narrow staircase—she slapped him on his hand and swore like a sailor. Still he kept going up, no longer having the nerve to look at the foul-mouthed girl standing with her hands on her hips. He turned a doorknob and found himself looking into a room where people were playing chess. He remained in the doorway, shy and awkward. A tall, distinguished woman of quite advanced years smiled at him from an armchair and invited him in. He took a few steps and stopped at a table where two players were moving their pieces around lightning-fast, simultaneously hammering the buttons on a clock. Ion knew how to play, but not as well as Petrişor, for example, not to mention Valeriu, who had won some student tournament and was considered the strongest player in the college of philology. Before the revolution, of course . . .

The action at another table was calmer, slower. The players stopped to think between moves: it was supposed to be an intellectual game, after all. A few other people were watching from their chairs: one of them, a still-youthful man with unruly hair, kept looking at his watch. He probably needed to go, but was reluctant to do so. In the end, though, he stood up and made for the door.

"Monsieur Pastenague," a voice called after him.

With his hand on the doorknob, the man stopped and smiled and gave an embarrassed shrug.

"I've got to run," he said, so softly that it was doubtful whether the person who had called from the other end of the room could have heard him. "I'm already very late," he went on as he opened the door.

"Just one second," the other implored, standing up from a table. He was holding a book up as a kind of trophy.

Pastenague closed the door again and took a couple of steps toward the fairly elderly gentleman, who, partly because of his weight, had some difficulty in moving. Pastenague took the book, thanked him and, once more at the door, called out:

"I'll phone you."

He disappeared from the scene. Ion turned his eyes back to the nearest chess table, where not much had been happening: complicated positional maneuvers with no piece exchanges or obvious threats. Rather boring . . . A cat rubbed against the door frame. The club secretary was on the phone, laughing now and then; she was evidently a cheerful, exuberant sort of person. Ion needed to use the bathroom and looked all around for it. A door was visible behind the secretary, but it probably led to her apartment. The cat had vanished. He was too embarrassed to ask any of the people watching. He felt enough of an intruder already. What was he doing there? If the lady talking endlessly on the phone hadn't encouraged him to enter, he'd have immediately turned around and gone. Now he felt obliged to remain, to pretend he was interested in the boring game going on in front of him. The chair that Pastenague had been using was now empty, but Ion still didn't sit down. He kept his eyes on the chessboard, as if he'd become fascinated with the game. What an idiot! He should have left together with Pastenague. He shuffled from one foot to the other. One of the players at another table got up and went purposefully to the door behind the lady on the phone. Hope dawned. Clearly the guy needed to take a leak. Here he is back already, with the relieved smile of someone able to urinate in peace. Ion walked toward the same door, smiling at the secretary as he passed her. She returned his smile and winked at him. Ion felt a little disconcerted, but he continued advancing toward the place that offered him relief. He turned the handle of the door.

The room he entered was dimly lit by a blue lamp on a table. His feet sank into wool, causing him to stumble and fall onto one knee. He could feel an extremely thick and soft carpet under his hands. Behind him, he heard a key turn in the lock—once, twice. Had he walked into a trap? He took a few steps forward, ears pricked up. He could make out wailing sounds, as of a baby, or perhaps it was the mewling of a cat. It seemed to be coming from another room. After a few more steps, he found himself in a corridor with a pink light that grew brighter and brighter as he advanced. This led into a brightly lit area where something horrible was happening . . . At first he didn't understand what the eagle was doing there, its claws sunk into the leather of an armchair, its little head moving rhythmically up and down, its wings half-open to help it maintain a delicate balance. He kept away, at a distance of a few yards, not brave enough to get any closer. He tried to guess what was happening. The bird was pecking at some prey: that was clear enough. Its characteristic position left no room for doubt. But who or what was the prey? Where was it? Ion could only see the eagle: no Prometheus being tortured, no hero chained or otherwise immobilized. Ion moved to the side to get a better view, and horror of horrors it was . . . the Siamese. It was lying in a pool of blood, and its eyes, though staring vacantly, weren't glassy like those of a corpse, but human, more than human—the eyes of a demigod who has accepted his own sacrifice as a duty, or as a rightful punishment . . .

I shouted out and hurried toward the eagle. My fingers closed over its feathers, which seemed to rustle like paper. I find myself furiously typing away on a sheet of paper. I pull it out, crumple it up into a ball, and throw it into the wastepaper basket. The Siamese is mewling like a cat possessed. He's at the foot of the stairs, too lazy to climb up. He's hungry, or God knows what's the matter with him.

The following article appeared in the daily *Libération*, under the headline: "The ET Beliefs of Raël's Disciples."

An encounter of the third kind occurred in a casino near Clermont Ferrand. On the movie screen, a formation of flying saucers descends on Jerusalem. A UFO lands on a spotless platform. When the extraterrestrials appear, in a clip taken from a film by Spielberg, more than six hundred people cheer wildly in the belief that the virtual images are about to become reality. They all call themselves "Raëlians," disciples of Raël (in Hebrew: the one who has seen), the bearded prophet dressed in white from head to toe and seated in the front row. The Raëlians all make financial contributions for the building of a base that's supposed to receive the "emissaries from heaven" in the Holy City. All that remains is to collect twenty million dollars more and to get the approval of the Israeli government. It has been given a friendly warning: if it refuses, Israel will be wiped off the face of the earth.

Over three days of celebrations, the Raëlians marked their twenty years of preparing for the "golden age" of humanity. The movement currently claims to have 30,000 members in a total of thirty-one countries, including four thousand in France. [. . .]

Raël is really Claude Vorilhon, aged thirty-seven, born in Vichy of a Jewish father and a Catholic mother. Before he set himself up as the messiah, Vorilhon had tried his hand at sports journalism and done some singsong in Left Bank cabarets. His big hit: *Miel et Cannelle* [Honey and Cinnamon]. But, on December 13, 1973, while out getting some fresh air in the Auvergne, he came across an extraterrestrial in the crater of the Lassolas volcano. The creature dictated to him *The Book Which Tells the Truth*, then whisked him off to meet Moses, Jesus, Mohammed, and Buddha on an Edenic planet.

Vorilhon's belief in flying saucers, plus his air of a slightly crazy backpacker, earned him a number of television appearances thanks to Jacques Chancel and Philippe Bouvard. Public speeches completed the transformation of this guitar strummer into the prophet of an "atheist religion open to the infinite," whose roots lay in a highly seductive sci-fi script. In short, Vorilhon explains, we are nothing but biological robots connected to the great central computer of the Elohim. There is no God and no soul, only a human species manufactured in a laboratory using DNA. After death, "nothing exists unless science does something to make it exist." The central computer spits out the balance sheet of each life, and if it is positive the dead person takes up eternal residence among the Elohim, where he can make full use of creatures entirely subject to his desires.

Claude Vorilhon would probably have returned to his hikes in the Auvergne if he hadn't attracted dozens, hundreds, indeed thousands of followers. Then his playful spirit left the UFO domain and entered New Age sociology, with a set of arguments that were a little more complex than the jumble you might expect. With the Elohim as his centerpiece, Vorilhon preaches a "selective democracy" or "geniocracy" and denounces the fact that "society nowadays lavishes more attention on the mentally deficient and physically disabled than on those with exceptional talents." It is a eugenics program with spine-chilling echoes, which Raël plays down by emphasizing his total opposition to racism. He has also changed the emblem that all Raëlians wear on a chain around their neck: a swastika—"signifying that everything is cyclical"—in the middle of a Star of David. The swastika is rounded off in the star, "so as not to shock the many Jews in the movement." The Raëlian breviary makes no distinction between the artificial computers built by humanity and the "biological robots" that make up Homo sapiens. The only difference, Raël says, is that we are "self-programmable and self-reproducible." Love is a purely "chemical reaction that occurs automatically when a human being has been correctly programmed." [. . .]

Vorilhon considers psychoanalysis to be "one of the plagues of humanity." "You are what you want to be," he says. "If you want to be a bell, then you're a bell. If a cathedral, you're a cathedral. If the infinite, you're the infinite."

During those three days of commemoration, the six hundred Raëlians attending at Clermont Ferrand thrilled to the testimony of "the best" among them, whom Raël had promoted on the basis of merit in accordance with a five-level pyramidal system. An Italian girl: "It's like I've been born again. Now I know who I am: a set of particles assembled according to a genetic code that describes my personality." Christelle: "The messages from the Elohim were what I was lacking. Now I bathe all the time in a bath of love."

There are also some former drug addicts: "Raël has confirmed what I felt all along: the world isn't what they keep ramming down your throat—that life means suffering." Nor is there a lack of young scientific and professional workers, often marked by a previous association with "guilt-inducing" Catholicism, such as the technician who joined the movement after flirting with Buddhism and "the paranormal," and who has found a hedonism to his liking in the Raëlian movement. "Pleasure keeps you tied to life. Without pleasure we'd all commit suicide. Everything works when you're sexually content."

Vorilhon continually draws on sexual imagery, presenting himself as a painter who "makes colors [that is, his disciples] ejaculate." "Paradise," in the mountainous region where the Raëlians gather every summer, is something between the branch of a biblical sect—as seen from an ET perspective (Noah's Ark as a flying saucer)—and a nudist colony where "swapping" precludes any jealousy. In Raël's kingdom, AIDS doesn't seem to have done much to cool the ardor of correctly progammed molecular love.

Vorilhon: "For sixteen years they've been advising poor humans to use condoms. The Elohim already knew that an epidemic was about to hit the planet and asked me to raise the awareness of Raëlians."

More prosaically, Raëlians are asked to contribute ten percent of their annual income to the movement, in addition to selling tapes and pamphlets by Varilhon. "But, as nothing is compulsory for us, it must be said that this target is, as yet, far from being achieved." As the "prophet" himself testifies, the Raëlian movement makes a profit of two million francs a year. A hundred and fifty million are collecting interest in Swiss bank accounts, theoretically for the construction of an embassy for the Elohim in Jerusalem. The prophet says that he is as poor as Job, but he is lucid in his way when he declares to the whole world: "I am only a transmitter . . . or emitter of trances." Which is confirmed by a female follower: "Even if Raël told us loud and clear that everything he's said up to now is bullshit, I'd still continue to believe."

The article is signed: François Devinat.

How do I know Marianne's returned to Paris? Very easy: she called me. Naturally she wants her Siamese back.

"You don't care about me, though," I say, half joking, half serious, and she replies sulkily that after all this time she's used to being without me. I shouldn't imagine that I'm irreplaceable.

"I don't."

"Put him on, will you."

"He's in the garden climbing some tree," I say with unrestrained satisfaction. I look out the window and see no sign of him. The sky has turned scarlet above the forest, and high up, at the zenith, I think I can see that round thing like a tin skullcap or the cat's metal bowl: the one he drinks milk from.

"Go find him!" Marianne shouts. Her voice is more and more metallic, more and more grating. It scratches my eardrum.

"Calm down. Why not tell me something about Moscow?"

It's not that I'm really curious, but I want to change the subject and get her to relax. Even so, I don't let her spout more than a few sentences before I break in with a pointed question:

"Did you meet Georges the Lebanese there?"

Silence. It's clear she doesn't know what to do, what to say. She wasn't expecting the question, which came down like a giant meteorite on Mecca. On the one hand, she's tempted to hide the truth—she's in no mood to go into details, to be forced into giving too many explanations—but, on the other, since she intends to send Georges and Smaranda to pick up the Siamese, she sees no point in lying. It's simpler to tell the truth.

"Yes."

But this bald statement isn't enough for me. I want some details. When did she meet him? Under what circumstances? Was he alone (which would surprise me!), or was he with his usual bevy of beauties?

"He was with Sonia, or maybe it was Silvia—not exactly what I'd call a looker."

I don't think Marianne has fallen in love with Georges. Smaranda, who's younger and quicker, probably got there first. But I wonder if she knows the reality of what the Lebanese does for a living.

"The reality?"

"Yes, the reality."

"What do you know about reality? After all that stuff you write, you've got a nerve to talk to me about reality. As if you have a clue what it is . . ."

Ça y est! She's on her high horse and galloping in the Arc de Triomphe stakes. No one can stop her now. These descendants of

Molière have an ease of expression that really takes your breath away. It's the language that carries them away—French, that genuine thoroughbred. They talk as though they're in a book—especially when they come back from Moscow, where they've had to try and get by in English. They have to make up for all the lost time! So I let her get on with it. I don't contradict. I don't interrupt. I wait for her to burn herself out, to get everything off her chest, even to throw in some idle chatter in the hope that it will stop me asking even more in-depth questions about Georges or Moscow. I could, for example, ask her about Haiducu. Yes, that guy with a drooping mustache like Țiriac's, à la gauloise! I could ask her if she wouldn't like to . . . No, not a mustache like Stalin's. It's been all over with Stalin for a long time. This is the age of Țiriac—of Țiriac and Haiducu.

"What are you doing? Why don't you say anything?" Marianne is upset again now that she's almost used up her reserve of words. The battery's dying.

"I'm thinking."

This unwise admission unleashes another stream of words. The Siamese appears at a window. I nod to him in complicity, without saying anything to Marianne. I see she's forgotten about him. She has other things on her mind.

"We'll talk again another time," I say, slightly bored.

"Aren't you unhooking the phone any more?"

"No."

"No more mysterious messages?"

When did I talk to her about messages? I don't remember, but I guess I must have—otherwise, how could she know? After all, she's not the . . . author.

"What messages?"

"Well, in Moscow, even if you're in the bathroom . . . I mean, if you want to take a shower—a bath is more difficult, because there's never enough hot water or the plug is missing . . ."

"What's missing?"

"The plug. And the water overflows, so you can only take a shower, understand? But, anyway, if you listen carefully, put your ear close to—what's it called, that goddamn round thing? . . ."

"Let's drop it . . ."

"Didn't you ask me about Moscow?"

"Yes, yes. But this is not the time . . . I can see the mailman coming."

Pierre rides down the garden path, stops his bicycle by the door, and, although his wings clearly interfere with certain movements, comes up to the window frame. He stretches out his arm to pet the tomcat, which purrs with pleasure.

"Let's talk again tomorrow."

Sulky Marianne hangs up. In the first place, she's annoyed with herself because she didn't handle things the right way. Instead of telling me straight out: yes, I met Georges the Lebanese in Moscow, he's a very nice man, she hesitated and tied herself in knots. Why did she hesitate? She met him—so what? Is that forbidden? This is no longer a patriarchy, after all. She's lying on the bed, her chubby arms beneath her neck, dreaming like an odalisque in a painting by Ingres.

Ion walks down the steps of the main post office, carrying his sleeping bag on his back. He looks dejected. Fuhrmann still hasn't sent him either the telephone number or the money. Eight days have passed already: he could have done it by now. Ion sent the letter on Monday, so let's say it arrived on Wednesday or Thursday; Fuhrmann could have sent him the number that same day. But he probably spent the whole of Thursday playing backgammon at Ahmed's: yes, he'd have hurried off in the morning without even looking inside the mailbox, and in the evening he'd have come back late, tired after a day of really hard work hunched over the board, throwing the cursed dice time after time, moving the pieces here and there, all day long, with only a short lunch break to gobble sausage and chips and down a beer—and in the end not even winning, which means, in a word, losing. Admittedly, he had some tough opponents that day: he put up an honorable resistance to Tariq, but Aristopoulos completely outclassed him. That Greek was so intimidating—maybe because of his name . . .

Furious and bewildered, Ion wanders the streets aimlessly. Hunger pangs hit him all at once as he passes a restaurant called *Au pied du cochon*. The city is one restaurant after another. But he doesn't dare to set foot in any. He comes to a monumental church that is neither Notre Dame nor the Sacré Coeur. Ion has been living on sandwiches ever since he arrived in Paris. Now he stops in front of a stand selling pancakes, the famous Breton *crêpes*.

The telephone wakes Zsuzsa up. She recognizes the voice. Another summons to the Hotel Europa lobby. She tries to resist, says she'll be tied up all day.

"All day?"

"Yes."

The caller then agrees to meet the next day. He seems in no hurry: calm and collected, just doing his duty, but firm and unyielding.

On the edge of the bed, Zsuzsa pulls on her tights and admires her legs in the wardrobe mirror. They're still beautiful! She falls on her back, suddenly languid with desire.

Georges and Sonia (or Silvia, if you prefer) are sipping from two tall, differently colored liqueur glasses at the Café Flore. Let's say one is pink, the other yellow. They aren't talking, as if they're waiting for someone. Not long after, a lean and lanky man with a mustache—thicker than Georges's and droopy—stops in front of their table.

"Dr. Gachet?" Georges asks, and the man tilts his head a little and nods. He is wearing a blue Mao-style tunic.

Afterwards Smaranda appears. Dr. Gachet jumps to his feet, as if propelled by a spring. Georges smiles and winks at Silvia (or Sonia). Smaranda seems totally impassive. She leans over to kiss Georges, then Sonia. Then she turns to Dr. Gachet.

"So you're back," she says in Romanian, and Silvia can't stifle a laugh. Georges also laughs, but he contains himself better. Dr. Gachet says nothing. He is hanging his head.

"So where have you been wandering around?" Smaranda asks, this time in French.

But Dr. Gachet hesitates before answering. It finally emerges that he hasn't been in Asia (that is, Afghanistan), as Smaranda and various friends thought, but much nearer, in the old world—Bosnia, to be precise.

"Bosnia?" But it's not clear why Sonia is so surprised.

Yes, he's been in Bosnia, with a medical team called in by the Équilibres organization. And, if his stay there was longer than planned, it wasn't by choice.

"What do you mean?"

"They put up a road block and forced us to stop. Then they took us to a village hidden between two mountains. They raped Maria the first evening."

"Who's Maria?" Smaranda asked.

"The nurse who was riding in our truck."

"A Bosnian Muslim?"

"I'm not sure."

Dr. Gachet looked uncomfortable. Eventually he admitted that Maria was Romanian. They were held prisoner for a good ten days. Maria got pregnant . . .

"Who by?"

"She gave birth in captivity."

Dr. Gachet didn't know who made Maria pregnant. He nervously twisted his mustache. What's all this questioning? Do you think it was fun? It was really horrible, especially at the beginning. They got drunk on plum brandy and forced him to . . .

"To what?"

It's not easy for Dr. Gachet to talk about life in the camp in front of so many other others. People at the next table are also straining their ears. It's not pleasant at all.

"It's easier to write about it," he says in a low voice.

The mailman has brought me an envelope with a completely blank sheet of paper inside.

"Maybe it's written in invisible ink," the Siamese meows sardonically.

Gică is sitting beneath the cathedral wall, eyes closed, hand outstretched. His face is bruised: yellow and purple. That helps with the begging. His turnover has almost doubled—to the satisfaction of the Gypsy, who keeps an eye on things from his position in the shade. Petrişor and three other individuals, including one with a fine Gallic mustache, are eating and drinking at Chez Yvonne.

Two young people are running away from each other on a Metro platform. Ion thinks he can see a knife in the pursuer's hand. He cowers against the wall, making himself as small as possible, his sleeping bag clutched tightly to his chest. He'd be better off sleeping in the open. Anyway, they clear everyone out of the Metro after midnight. The fleeing pair have disappeared down a corridor to another platform. Ion heads for the exit. The street is empty. Again he feels pangs of hunger. They are really getting to him: the more his money dwindles, the hungrier he becomes. He could spend a whole day eating. At a street corner, a dwarf—or monkey?—is climbing a rope. Or perhaps it's a sailor? But what is the rope attached to? Curiosity now, of course, but also fear. Ion crosses the street. What if the rope isn't attached to anything? A limousine passes at high speed, almost running him over. He just catches sight of a woman in white, like a bride. Next to her is an enormous cage . . .

The telephone rings. It interrupts me in mid-sentence, breaks my flow. I'll need more than an hour to get into it again, maybe even longer, since Marianne has returned to the charge. She wants the tomcat.

"How I long to have him back!" she whimpers.

"Be patient a little longer. I'll bring him with me."

"You? Why, are you finished?"

"Almost. I've still got to write the ending."

"Ha, ha! I know you. You could quite easily get 'blocked' and sit there another month. Or else feel unhappy with what you've written and start all over again."

"It happens."

"You see!"

As usual, she knows exactly what she wants: to get Georges and Smaranda to drive over and pick me and the Siamese up. We haggle for a few more minutes. I try to convince her that the novel is practically complete. But it's not easy, because I'm not entirely convinced of it myself. I'll have to see what I do with Ion, who's lying in his sleeping bag against the fence of a square in rue du Bac and has just been woken by a tramp's hand moving inside the bag and his pockets too. Ion grabs him by the arm, but with his free hand the tramp manages to start punching Ion in the face. Ion shouts out.

"So you agree," Marianne says, taking my silence as consent.

I shrug and mumble something indistinct. In the end, I don't care . . . let them come—I may even go back with them. I'll save on the train fare that way. It's beginning to look as if Marianne has won again.

Fuhrmann stands up and raises his arms: victory! Aristopoulos preserves his Olympian calm; a little smile that might be thought sardonic forms on his lips. He's thinking, okay, the German has to win once in a while, otherwise he'll lose heart and stop playing. That's also the philosophy of Platonov, a new face at Ahmed's and a passionate but silent spectator. He can hardly say two words in German. He rarely plays—and never with Aristopoulos. Only Fuhrmann still has the courage to challenge the Greek.

One day at Catholic Aid, a Romanian student introduced Ion to some older émigrés, who were greatly excited at the prospect of talking to a hero of University Square. That was how Valeriu described him. But Ion didn't feel comfortable speaking about that period.

"Did you know Munteanu?"

His terse, equivocal reply failed to satisfy their curiosity, but it encouraged them to indulge in the pleasures of speculation. Well, it doesn't matter if the student is tongue-tied; they know all about "the events" anyway, they don't need to have been there. You drown in events when you're too close to them, one of them proudly explained. You miss their wider significance because you can't see the general.

"Can't see General who?" Colonel Burtică asked. Ion hadn't recognized him at first.

"The universal," the speaker clarified.

"Ah!" the colonel sighed with relief.

He was visiting a friend in Paris, who had worked for a long time at Radio Free Europe. Someone named Lăptaru.

So then, of course, they widened the perspective. Like a helicopter gradually gaining height, their discussion rose further and further above the contingent events of University Square, the miners' "day of action," the subsequent election of President Iliescu, the particular country called Romania . . .

"Everything is connected to everything else," Lăptaru said.

"It must be seen in a world perspective."

"Romania is just a pawn on the global chessboard."

"Yes, but it occupies a strategic position. It could become . . . a buffer."

"Come off it! That was in the old days."

"When there was proper diplomacy."

"Nowadays they can't even speak properly."

"But you have to admit that the old ambassador . . ."

"What, that guy with a hotline to the *golani*—those 'revolutionary' good-for-nothings who had him dancing to their tune?"

"Well, yes."

"It wasn't serious. He wanted to attract attention to himself, that's all."

"Ah, the good old days of diplomacy!"

"Diplomacy, wheat, petroleum, and pretty girls."

"Don't we even have pretty girls any longer?"

"We do, but they don't have class."

"You're still living in the days of Mata Hari."

"Malta Harry," Valeriu risked, and his wordplay went down well. They began to discuss the meeting on the island of Malta.

Ion had lost weight and grown a beard, yet Colonel Burtică, an excellent physiognomist, having explained to everyone the new division of the world planned by Bush and Gorbachev in Malta . . .

"But now Gorbachev is history," Valeriu objected.

"That's what you think," the colonel said. "He's still there, watching from the shadows."

So, having clarified this important chapter in Russian-American secret relations, he turned to Ion and said:

"I know you from somewhere."

"From Strasbourg," Ion said.

"Yes, of course!" the colonel concurred, almost happily. "You were with a rather sick-looking boy in a wheelchair. Did he stay there?"

"Yes," Ion replied, a little embarrassed.

I get up, go downstairs and move nearly all the map counters to Paris.

In the street Mihai runs into Roger. Trying to go unnoticed, he bends down and pretends to tie his shoelaces, then takes out a handkerchief and blows his nose long and hard. Roger stands and waits in front of him, so that Mihai has no way of escaping. Roger offers to take him somewhere for a drink, but Mihai declines. He has an important meeting with a Czech journalist who, like himself, works in Munich for Radio Free Europe. Roger doesn't give two monkeys about that; he wants to track down Ana, not having seen her for several months.

"I don't suppose you know where she's got to," the truck driver asks.

"No," Mihai says. "I think she went back to Romania."

"That's impossible. A few days ago I met that old coach, what's his name?"

"I don't know."

"Yes you do. A great lover of horseracing."

"And?"

"He told me Ana's in Paris. He's seen her."

Mihai says he's in a rush and scuttles away, leaving Roger alone on the sidewalk. He watches Mihai go, eyes full of mistrust, even suspicion, but never thinks of following after him. Had he done so, he would have seen Mihai sit down at a café table a couple of blocks away, to be joined five minutes later by Ghişoiu and Ana. They order three cognacs, drink them down, and laugh.

Dinu Valea has drunk half a bottle of plum brandy all by himself; now he's lying in bed, determined never to get up again. He thinks he can hear the flip-flop sound of Marioara's slippers. But he can't see her. What he does see is the disfigured girl, whose photos the prosecutor showed him that morning.

"Don't you recognize her?"

Dinu Valea shook his head.

The room is turning and swaying like the gondola of a balloon. He'd like to go to sleep and never wake up.

Livia finally has her visa for Germany. Tiberius says nothing. No comment. He looks down at his toecaps, then again at the girl and the dark brown, rather handsome young man accompanying her.

"Let me introduce Karim."

The two shake hands without saying a word.

"I'll try to make it to Paris as well," Livia adds.

Marianne has gone out to meet Smaranda. She looks in the mailbox and sees an envelope gleaming discreetly at the back. She unlocks the box and takes out the envelope from Budapest, which contains the letter from Sandu telling Ion that he's struck it rich and married a millionairess. He's given up training and runs only for pleasure now, mostly around the swimming pool under Patricia's admiring gaze. He hopes to see his friend from Romania, but as Patricia doesn't want to go to Europe, the simplest thing would be for Ion to go to San Diego. The letter is signed: Alexandru Hurst.

"How do you know what he wrote?" the Siamese mewls, jumping on the table and sticking his nose in things that don't concern him. Can't you see Marianne hasn't even opened it yet? And, even if she had, she wouldn't be able to make head nor tail of it, as it's written in Romanian.

"She can understand . . ."

"Oh yeah, sure!"

Smaranda is already lining up at a little cinema in rue Saint André des Arts. A rather grimy young man with a sleeping bag on his back is standing in the line beside her. He's trying to dig out some one or five franc coins from his pockets: he doesn't seem to have enough. Then he removes his left shoe and takes out a badly crumpled fifty-franc note. Smaranda smiles. This one must come from somewhere in Eastern Europe, she thinks. At that point Marianne joins her, a little late because of the letter. For a moment she was tempted to open the envelope—an idiotic curiosity that she soon overcame. She went back to the apartment and put the envelope on the living-room table. But on her way out she changed her mind and put it in her handbag. Not that there's any point to this: neither she nor Smaranda knows Hungarian. Is she jealous perhaps? In the car she decided to send it on to the addressee the very next day. She almost had an accident worrying about it. She got into the right-hand lane and wrote the address in Brittany.

"It's good you made it!" Smaranda says.

"I'm sorry."

"It's okay. But I don't think I'll be able to see this film."

There are two women on the poster: one young, the other somewhat older. A cage containing a huge parrot stands between them.

"It's supposed to be a great film," Marianne says, annoyed. "All the critics are raving about it."

"I know, but I can't stay for it. I have an appointment with a publisher. Just across the street here."

"A publisher? What's his name?"

"I don't know, I can't remember. It's a Polish name, or Russian. Something ending in *ovsky*."

"Doesn't ring a bell. Can't be well known, I guess. But what's up? Have you written a book? *Journey to Moscow*?"

Marianne laughs, really laughs, as if she's just made some fantastic joke. Ion also laughs—first into his beard, then loud and openmouthed. Only then does Marianne notice him and think he looks rather nice. Dirty, but nice. Or anyway, happy.

"Cut it out. I'm not going for myself."

"Who for, then?"

Smaranda hesitates.

"Gachet."

"Well, well, well, so Dr. Gachet's resurfaced." Marianne was almost shouting. Ion raised his eyebrows. "Where has be been?"

"In Bosnia. Sarajevo."

"How extraordinary!"

Smaranda heads off across the street. Ion goes with Marianne into the film: *The Two Marias*. They sit next to each other. The student has already seen the film, or anyway half of it. He stuffs his sleeping bag under the seat, unintentionally touching his neighbor's generous thigh in the process. Later he does it again with his knee.

A small station on the edge of a forest. It's raining. A man holding a sickle goes into a room, probably a storeroom. A woman on her knees is hitting a pot with a hammer there. The noise of a smithy at work. Then the whirr of an engine. The man and woman go to the doorway and look up at the sky.

The eagle.

A flock of sheep crosses the village square behind the station. A man with a game bag and a Tyrolean hat, but without a gun, is coming from the station. He's fat. His pink chubby cheeks are seen in close-up. Then the camera lingers on a hotel sign.

Ion fidgets in his seat. He looks out of the corner of his eye at Marianne, who is fascinated by the film. He can't say the same for himself. He's seen it all before—and the same goes for the following scene, the one in which a woman propped up against a bar is forced, or agrees willingly (though not gladly!), to answer a man's questions. She bears a certain resemblance to Zsuzsa.

The film tells the story of an exodus. The population of a village, or even a whole region, sets off for the big wide world, young and old alike. A fair-haired young man in a wheelchair is pushed along by another who is much darker and stronger. He could move under his own steam, by pushing the wheels with his arms, but why shouldn't he take advantage of this opportunity? He looks cheerful, perhaps even happy to be embarking on this unexpected adventure.

Ion takes Marianne's hand. She lets him do it, but she's obviously more interested in the film than he is. Having bought his ticket out of the little money he had left, Ion is now thinking of getting up and leaving. But he's held back by the woman's warm silken skin, her large and ample thigh.

In a hotel corridor, four men are carrying a woman on a stretcher. One of them, much shorter and younger than the others, has a black beard and slanting Japanese-style eyes. He's so short that the others have stopped holding the stretcher any higher than waist-level, and he, for the same reason, has to resist the temptation to rest it on his shoulder.

"Careful!"

"Stop! Right, that's better."

"Go ahead."

"Maria," the young one says, but he doesn't dare turn around to look at her. He has to keep looking ahead.

"Yes."

"How are you feeling?"

"I'm okay."

Maria's head is bandaged. Blood has seeped through the gauze in a few places.

"Don't go too fast!" the man dressed as a stationmaster orders, and he goes down the staircase first. The group crosses the hotel lobby. Zsuzsa is smoking at the bar and replying irritably to the man's questions. She looks like the woman on the stretcher. Each of the bearers is wearing a lit miner's helmet, even though it's broad daylight. They probably have a long journey ahead of them, which will last late into the night.

Ion still doesn't understand much, although like everyone else he came in at the beginning. One thing is clear: the eagle is only a symbol; it conceals a much more serious, much more menacing reality.

"What's the book called?" the fair-haired man asks. He seems not to be ageing too gracefully. Smaranda, giving him her best come-hither look, takes her time to reply.

"*Somewhere in Europe*," she says finally, holding out the thick but tightly rubber-banded typescript.

The publisher makes a face.

"That's been used before."

It's no longer raining. The clouds have begun to break up, leaving a clear sky; above the forest it's taken on quite a vivid color—not blue but rosy, then gradually darker and darker shades of red.

The telephone rings. I go downstairs, angry at this new interruption. It's Mihai.

"How are you doing? Have you finished?"

"I'm writing the last few pages."

"Fantastic! Could we do an interview with you for Radio Free Europe? I'm with Ana."

"Where are you?"

"In Paris."

"And what do you want from me, exactly?"

"We'd like to come there, to do an interview with you."

"All right," I say. "But not today and not tomorrow. The day after."

"Perfect. I'm deeply grateful. All the best."

The stationmaster is on the platform, flag in hand. The sound of an aircraft. The camera doesn't point to the sky but remains on the weed-covered tracks, far into the distance. The stationmaster stands quite still. Then he raises the flag and salutes an invisible train—or something else, up there in the sky. That infernal round thing revolves as it floats overhead.

Ion takes his hand away from Marianne's. He closes his eyes. When he reopens them, the lights are on in the theater.

Only in the car does Marianne ask his name.

"Ion."

"Are you Romanian?"

"No, Greek."

Fuhrmann finally discovers Ion's letter, not having opened his mailbox for more than ten days now. Poor Ion! Fuhrmann feels terribly sorry for the boy and promises himself that he'll go to the post office first thing the next morning. He's too tired now.

He played backgammon all afternoon with Platonov—really gave him a beating.

He unsticks his knee from her thigh and holds his breath as he turns over, although this is not strictly necessary, since the woman beside him is fast asleep, inert. No more than a few streaks of light enter the room through the shutters. The sun is just coming up outside. He continues to move with the same caution: almost like someone in a Bob Wilson play. He rests his right arm on the wooden bedside table, while the other relaxes like a spring; one leg swings over the edge of the bed, immediately followed by the other. He finds myself perched on the corner, hands on knees and still dopey from sleep. He turns his head. The woman is still motionless, but snoring softly—asleep: that is, alive.

He soon finds his clothes and hurriedly puts them on in the bathroom, without washing or even brushing his teeth. Shoes in hand, he again passes through the bedroom. He looks toward the bed: the woman is sleeping quietly. He looks in her handbag on a chair near the door, then changes his mind and just takes everything without bothering to search it. He pulls the door closed behind him and tiptoes into the living room. But the parquet floor creaks underfoot. He opens the apartment door and, without waiting for the elevator, walks down the stairs. He comes across a guy wearing a motorcycle helmet and a deep-sea diving suit.

Once in the street, he takes a series of deep breaths. It's daylight. He feels just like a filmgoer does when the movie ends and the lights suddenly go on. The telephone rings. A grating synthetic voice, a precise non-human computer's voice, asks to speak to Ion.

"Ion isn't here."

Apart from the voice, is there also an ear there on the other end? Does it understand what I'm saying?

The same voice, though it seems a little sharper:

"*La fin approche.*"

Maybe it's just a practical joke, I think, but I don't really believe it. The map of Europe flutters before my eyes: from right to left, left to right. A draught? No, the cat is pushing it with his paw. It's his idea of fun. *C'est tout de même plus rassurant lorsque la cause est là, en chair et en os, derrière l'effet.*

I return to my work table and start rereading aloud. It's no longer raining. The clouds have begun to break up, leaving a clear sky; above the forest it's taken on quite a vivid color—not blue but rosy, then gradually darker and darker shades of red. Is the sun rising or setting? Ion goes into a square that suddenly appears in front of him. He sits on a bench next to a statue of Chateaubriand and rummages in the handbag. First he finds the purse and counts the money inside: not a lot, but I won't turn up my nose at it. Then he fishes out a letter from Budapest. It was sent to the writer whose address he lost or never had or left at Fuhrmann's in Germany, and whose telephone number he's still waiting to get from Fuhrmann. But another hand, probably female, has crossed out the address in Paris and replaced it with one in Brittany. Ion is tired: he didn't sleep enough and crept out like a thief at daybreak. But he does understand. He gets to his feet and heads for the Metro station. It's only two stops to Gare Montparnasse, but he's in a hurry. He wants to get it over with once and for all.

I hear the doorbell and look out the window. I obviously didn't notice when Georges's Mercedes pulled up outside. I have no choice: I can't even complain that I wasn't told in advance. I go and open the door. Big smiles all round. Even Gachet seems in a good mood: "Forget Bosnia!" Smaranda runs up to kiss me. Silvia does too, even though we don't know each other, so to speak—we've never actually set eyes on each other before. Georges is more reserved. He bows with Oriental politeness. Gachet squeezes me in his arms, happy to see me again.

"Please, come in."

I offer them something to drink. Sonia takes the Siamese in her arms, but he struggles like a wildcat and breaks free. Nor does Smaranda succeed in taming him, although they know each other and have met many times before. Maybe that's the reason why.

Gachet begins to relate a tragicomic incident in Sarajevo, when a bride was blown into the air by a mortar shell and landed up a tree. We laugh.

I ask Georges when he last saw Ion. The Lebanese looks at Silvia and whispers something, as if he is making an effort to remember. You see, he wants to give me a precise answer and is concentrating. He puts his hands to his forehead, then rests two fingers on his lips: the last thing he wants to do is speak in haste and misinform me. Dr. Gachet begins to describe another scene, this time from his period of captivity.

"*C'était un camp de nettoyage ethnique,*" Georges says with a shudder, relieved that he no longer has to answer me.

"*Il a écrit un livre,*" Smaranda tells me. Dr. Gachet glances down for a few seconds.

"*C'est du Soljenitsyne!*" Georges adds.

"*Du Dostoïevsky!*" Sonia outbids him.

"*Va chercher le champagne*," Smaranda orders.

No, this isn't addressed to me but to Georges. He stands up and goes out the door together with the Siamese, who's fed up listening to our chatter. They both run along the path to the Mercedes. The sky above the forest is a purplish red.

"It'll rain," Dr. Gachet says.

"Don't worry," I reassure him. "In these parts the clouds come and go."

Georges reappears with two bottles of champagne.

"There's some weird machine above the forest," he reports cheerfully. "A kind of satellite."

"An observation satellite," I explain calmly. "It's needed for studying the weather."

"Ah, yes," Georges says, wrestling with the cork.

Ion gets off the train at Rennes. He forgot his sleeping bag in Marianne's bedroom. The handbag he threw into some bushes. But he has the envelope with him—the envelope from Budapest. He'll hand it to the addressee personally.

Fuhrmann sends money and the telephone number: Paris—Louvre—Poste Restante. When he returns home he finds another letter from the United States, also for Ion. It's from Alex Hurst. Who might he be? the German wonders, a little puzzled.

Sandu-Alex Hurst is running round the swimming pool, admired by Patricia from her chaise longue. An unusually large cage sits beside her, a millionaire's cage that could hold a toucan.

"Let's drink a toast," Georges suggests, once he's poured the champagne with the flourish of a waiter in a stylish restaurant.

And again we hug and kiss and wish one another every happiness. Then the telephone rings. I recognize Ana's voice.

"We're on our way to your place. We stopped in a village for a coffee. Petrişor came along too. Do you remember him?"

"I thought I told you to come tomorrow, not today."

I try to sound severe, though I realize it's too late to do anything about it. We'll have everyone on top of us, that's all!

"Please forgive us," Ana says, "but we've heard there are some strange goings-on in your area."

"Really?"

"Yes. A UFO has been reported over Brittany."

"Over Great Britain, maybe . . ."

"No. We got a phone call from Munich. The information comes direct from Washington." Ana's voice is grave: it positively oozes importance, especially when it pronounces the name of the capital of the United States of America. Then Mihai takes the phone.

"It's not a joke," he says.

"Maybe not," I say, "but I'm busy right now. I haven't finished the novel. I can't interrupt it just like that—because you've suddenly got some idea into your head." When I finish speaking, I hear Gachet's voice, the clinking of glasses, and Smaranda's laughter.

"Sounds like you're having a party," Mihai says, in that insinuating way I know all too well. I've never forgotten it.

"Well, if there's got to be a party, let's all let our hair down and enjoy it."

"What did you say?"

"I said, why don't you come too? The more the merrier!" I shout into the telephone. "Let the ball commence! The final ball!"

Silvia has taken off her dress to show Gachet a scar on her back, on one of her shoulder blades.

"They also hit me on the head," she says. "You can't see it because of my hair."

"Let's polish off the second bottle as well!" Smaranda says, coming toward me. She embraces me, gives me a real kiss on the mouth. I only manage to wriggle out of her arms with great difficulty.

After he leaves the station, Ion wonders whether he should go left or right. Which is the way to such-and-such a village? Someone tells him there's a bus, but only twice a day.

"When?"

His informant takes a pipe out of his pocket and begins to pack it with a special instrument called a tamper. Ion thanks him and heads off toward the highway. He stands by the side of the road vigorously waving his thumb—his thumb, not his index finger! Sooner or later someone will stop: man or woman, young or old. So he waits. Nearly an hour passes—nothing. Not one car even slows down. The loss of his sleeping bag has probably put him at a disadvantage: it would have been a tangible sign, a detail conferring his identity as a tourist. Like this he just looks like a tramp, suspicious. What's he doing there on the edge of the city? He might as well start walking. So he sets out down the road, in long measured strides, stopping now and again to repeat the classical hitchhiker's gesture. No result. He shrugs his shoulders and walks some more, looking at the cars as they speed past him. He's selective, in a sense: he only sticks his arm out at certain cars, ignoring the majority. At one point he thinks he sees Georges the Lebanese in a Mercedes, with Sonia (or Silvia, as they called her in Vienna) sitting next to him. But he's not at all certain. The Mercedes flashes by at more than a hundred miles an hour, overtaking everything else on the road. Besides, Ion has been suffering from all kinds of strange thoughts lately, not to say hallucinations.

I leave them all in the living room and go back upstairs to work. But, before I manage to finish a page, I see a car stop in front of the house. I hesitate for a moment, but then I recognize Mihai, who's put on weight and is wearing a checkered cap and baggy trousers. He gets out first, with Ana soon following. I find her much more attractive than in Bucharest. Mihai takes a few steps to stretch his legs. Then, as if suddenly remembering, he leans over and opens the rear door. Another man comes into view—a young man, to judge by his movements and the ease with which he gets out of the car. But he is dressed in an elegant, old-fashioned style: dark suit, black wide-brimmed hat. Meanwhile Mihai opens the trunk and takes out a crateful of bottles, probably also champagne. All three, with Ana in the lead, walk to the front door, which opens as if by magic. I no longer feel obliged to go straight down to welcome them. I have my work to do. And they do all know one another—well, more or less.

Ion is tired. He sits on a milestone, eyes shut, and puts his head in his hands. He remains there for some time, until finally a car pulls up in front of him.

I hear steps on the staircase. Raising my eyes from the pages, I see Ana climbing the stairs; she pauses on the last one, afraid to go any further.

"Am I disturbing you?"

The sound of voices and glasses has come upstairs with her. I wave her closer, and she beams a seductive smile at me that, as always, I find irritating. On a chaise longue by the swimming pool, Sandu is speaking with Fuhrmann on the telephone; he must know the number from one of Ion's letters. His friend is by now comfortably installed next to a man with a large drooping mustache, driving with one hand. Ion didn't look at him before getting into the car, and anyway he was so tired that he'd have accepted a lift in the devil's own Rolls Royce. He isn't afraid. Curious as it may seem, he feels somehow more at ease now that he's run into a man he already knows—a man, one might say, with whom he is already familiar.

Ana is holding a pair of binoculars. Frenzied music can be heard downstairs. The cork of a champagne bottle makes a deafening pop.

"Won't you come and join us?" Ana says. "It won't be much longer now."

And she points out the window, probably toward the forest. I don't look as far as she's pointing but rest my eyes on a pied wagtail boldly advancing through the long thick grass. I don't look up, but I know that the sky above the forest is as bright as the houselights in a theater.

"Not much longer," Ana repeats.

I don't ask who or what we are waiting for. The tomcat sneaks in behind her and, in passing, rubs languorously against her legs. Marianne is watching television—or perhaps a video of the film she saw yesterday. Yes, why not? She sprawls on the sofa like a Walachian princess from the age of the Phanariot rulers. An eagle is gliding up above, in the television sky.

"I'm sorry," Fuhrmann says. "I assure you I've done everything in my power."

"But what about now? Where is . . ."

"I sent it to Bucharest, to his father Dinu."

"I'm not talking about the letter!" Sandu Hurst snaps irritably, and Patricia comes closer, alarmed.

Poor Fuhrmann had no way of knowing . . . Ion gets out of the car, which immediately speeds off and leaves him at the edge of the forest. He takes a few steps, then stops. The earth is soggy underfoot, as if it's been raining for two whole days. The bird cries are strident and provocative; short or long, they pierce the even rustle of the leafy waves. Strange gasps reach Ion from beneath the earth. What can they be doing down there? But I don't stop . . .

"Won't you come down?" Ana insists.

. . . groans mixed with growls and grunts, a steady squeaking, roars, persistent crackling, and, above everything, owl cries and woodpecker salvoes, the hoarse howling of wolves, or rather the barking of foxes, and again the earlier sounds and the fierce beating of little wings.

"Come!" Ana puts the palm of her hand on my shoulder and glues her thigh to mine. She leans over and brings her mouth close to mine.

"But who will do the writing?" I ask, pushing her away with a superhuman effort of will. I get to my feet. We both go downstairs into the infernal sound of reggae, but no one is there. I hadn't noticed it when they all went into the garden, and then onto the road by the cars. They look with fascination toward the forest. Georges has a pair of binoculars, probably army issue. He climbs onto the roof of the Mercedes. The others would like to see too. But what can you see? they ask. They protest, bump into one another, laugh, clink, and drink. Mihai opens another bottle of champagne. The cork pops like a pistol, scaring Georges, who very nearly loses his balance and falls off the Mercedes. Sonia is only wearing her panties now and holding her arms around her breasts. Perhaps she's cold. Smaranda has kept her slip on, but she has nothing on her feet.

"We'll have a better view up there," I say, going back upstairs. Ana and the cat follow.

I open the window, then think better of it. I don't need either the window or binoculars. I see Ion just as well like this, in my mind's freely roving eye. Now he's turning his back to the forest, and I can see Postman Pierre get off his bicycle and stand beside him.

"It won't be much longer," Pierre encourages him, with a slight movement of his wings. Then he looks at his watch.

I sit at the table again and smooth the white sheet of paper with the flat of my hand. It doesn't bother me that Ana is standing at the window and blocking my view. The Siamese has jumped onto the sill beside her. I pick up my pencil and see Pierre and Ion talking as if they've known each other all their lives. They move their eyes between sky and forest, and of course Ion is doing more of the talking: he moves his lips but also his hands, making countless gestures as in an Italian film. Pierre nods, flaps his wings, encourages Ion to continue; he seems interested in everything he has to say, and from time to time opens his mouth reassuringly:

"It won't be much longer."

Feeling bolder and bolder, Ion starts to tell the mailman what he read a long time ago—he was still in Romania—in a book translated from Swiss . . . Pierre laughs.

No, he can't remember the name of the author, or what language the original was in, only that he was Swiss. And that's no laughing matter—on the contrary. Well, according to him, that is, according to the Swiss writer, the origins of humanity—or, to be more precise, of the first humans, who did after all have descendants, no?, who in turn also had descendants . . . Well, to cut a long story short, the first humans in fact lived as a penal colony;

they were slaves being punished by their masters, who were actually from some other planet.

"Really?"

"Yes, really. At least that's what the Swiss writer said. If he lied, then I'm lying now too. The first humans were forcibly deported here, to Earth, in these kinds of pot-shaped, well, saucer-shaped, flying machines."

"Don't you want to look for yourself?" Ana offers me the binoculars.

But I scarcely lift my nose from the paper. I haven't the time. And, since she's being so generous, that probably means there's not a lot to see. I know how her mind works.

She shrugs and turns toward the forest again. Binoculars to her eyes, she stands there stock still.

I don't have time to look out the window. I have to write. My hand forms letters and words in a language that, whatever else may be said of it, is my mother tongue: the one I imbibed with my mother's milk, then from a nursing bottle, and then from assorted bottles of wine, țuică, vodka . . . And no one is to blame—certainly not the language—if I feel that I'm too slow, if the words don't come fast enough or not at all. I stop for a second to check that Ana is still by the window, cat by her side, and then I start to move my right hand again as quickly as I can, shaking my head at the same time, no, I'm not at all sure that's right, I have to find something else, I cross out a word, put another in its place, above it, and I'm still not satisfied and delete both, I'm writing too slowly, much slower than the rhythm of Ion's speech: the words crowd together on his lips, but not beneath my pen . . . Another correction.

Exiles! Exiles on Planet Earth! That's the expression I've been searching for. Pierre flaps his wings in approval. He likes the word. I stop writing. I want to tell Ana, first timidly, in a whisper, then shouting it out, but she still doesn't hear. Her motionless back is turned to me as she looks out avidly, covering the sky and forest with her body; she looks out patiently and hopefully, concentrating hard, deaf to anything else. She is waiting—to see.

DUMITRU TSEPENEAG is one of the most innovative Romanian writers of the second half of the twentieth century. In 1975, while he was in France, his citizenship was revoked by Ceausescu, and he was forced into exile. In the 1980s, he started to write in French. He returned to his native language after the Ceausescu regime ended, but continues to write in his adopted language as well.

A translator from Romanian, Spanish, German, French, and Italian, PATRICK CAMILLER has translated many works, including Dumitru Tsepeneag's own *Vain Art of the Fugue* and *The Necessary Marriage*.

FOR A FULL LIST OF PUBLICATIONS, VISIT:
www.dalkeyarchive.com

MAX FRISCH, *I'm Not Stiller.*
Man in the Holocene.
CARLOS FUENTES, *Christopher Unborn.*
Distant Relations.
Terra Nostra.
Where the Air Is Clear.
JANICE GALLOWAY, *Foreign Parts.*
The Trick Is to Keep Breathing.
WILLIAM H. GASS, *Cartesian Sonata and Other Novellas.*
Finding a Form.
A Temple of Texts.
The Tunnel.
Willie Masters' Lonesome Wife.
GÉRARD GAVARRY, *Hoppla! 1 2 3.*
ETIENNE GILSON,
The Arts of the Beautiful.
Forms and Substances in the Arts.
C. S. GISCOMBE, *Giscome Road.*
Here.
Prairie Style.
DOUGLAS GLOVER, *Bad News of the Heart.*
The Enamoured Knight.
WITOLD GOMBROWICZ,
A Kind of Testament.
KAREN ELIZABETH GORDON,
The Red Shoes.
GEORGI GOSPODINOV, *Natural Novel.*
JUAN GOYTISOLO, *Count Julian.*
Juan the Landless.
Makbara.
Marks of Identity.
PATRICK GRAINVILLE, *The Cave of Heaven.*
HENRY GREEN, *Back.*
Blindness.
Concluding.
Doting.
Nothing.
JIŘÍ GRUŠA, *The Questionnaire.*
GABRIEL GUDDING,
Rhode Island Notebook.
MELA HARTWIG, *Am I a Redundant Human Being?*
JOHN HAWKES, *The Passion Artist.*
Whistlejacket.
ALEKSANDAR HEMON, ED.,
Best European Fiction.
AIDAN HIGGINS, *A Bestiary.*
Balcony of Europe.
Bornholm Night-Ferry.
Darkling Plain: Texts for the Air.
Flotsam and Jetsam.
Langrishe, Go Down.
Scenes from a Receding Past.
Windy Arbours.
KEIZO HINO, *Isle of Dreams.*
ALDOUS HUXLEY, *Antic Hay.*
Crome Yellow.
Point Counter Point.
Those Barren Leaves.
Time Must Have a Stop.
MIKHAIL IOSSEL AND JEFF PARKER, EDS.,
Amerika: Russian Writers View the United States.
GERT JONKE, *The Distant Sound.*
Geometric Regional Novel.

Homage to Czerny.
The System of Vienna.
JACQUES JOUET, *Mountain R.*
Savage.
CHARLES JULIET, *Conversations with Samuel Beckett and Bram van Velde.*
MIEKO KANAI, *The Word Book.*
YORAM KANIUK, *Life on Sandpaper.*
HUGH KENNER, *The Counterfeiters.*
Flaubert, Joyce and Beckett: The Stoic Comedians.
Joyce's Voices.
DANILO KIŠ, *Garden, Ashes.*
A Tomb for Boris Davidovich.
ANITA KONKKA, *A Fool's Paradise.*
GEORGE KONRÁD, *The City Builder.*
TADEUSZ KONWICKI, *A Minor Apocalypse.*
The Polish Complex.
MENIS KOUMANDAREAS, *Koula.*
ELAINE KRAF, *The Princess of 72nd Street.*
JIM KRUSOE, *Iceland.*
EWA KURYLUK, *Century 21.*
EMILIO LASCANO TEGUI, *On Elegance While Sleeping.*
ERIC LAURRENT, *Do Not Touch.*
VIOLETTE LEDUC, *La Bâtarde.*
SUZANNE JILL LEVINE, *The Subversive Scribe: Translating Latin American Fiction.*
DEBORAH LEVY, *Billy and Girl.*
Pillow Talk in Europe and Other Places.
JOSÉ LEZAMA LIMA, *Paradiso.*
ROSA LIKSOM, *Dark Paradise.*
OSMAN LINS, *Avalovara.*
The Queen of the Prisons of Greece.
ALF MAC LOCHLAINN,
The Corpus in the Library.
Out of Focus.
RON LOEWINSOHN, *Magnetic Field(s).*
BRIAN LYNCH, *The Winner of Sorrow.*
D. KEITH MANO, *Take Five.*
MICHELINE AHARONIAN MARCOM,
The Mirror in the Well.
BEN MARCUS,
The Age of Wire and String.
WALLACE MARKFIELD,
Teitlebaum's Window.
To an Early Grave.
DAVID MARKSON, *Reader's Block.*
Springer's Progress.
Wittgenstein's Mistress.
CAROLE MASO, *AVA.*
LADISLAV MATEJKA AND KRYSTYNA POMORSKA, EDS.,
Readings in Russian Poetics: Formalist and Structuralist Views.
HARRY MATHEWS,
The Case of the Persevering Maltese: Collected Essays.
Cigarettes.
The Conversions.
The Human Country: New and Collected Stories.
The Journalist.

FOR A FULL LIST OF PUBLICATIONS, VISIT:
www.dalkeyarchive.com

My Life in CIA.
Singular Pleasures.
The Sinking of the Odradek
Stadium.
Tlooth.
20 Lines a Day.
JOSEPH McELROY,
Night Soul and Other Stories.
ROBERT L. McLAUGHLIN, ED.,
Innovations: An Anthology of
Modern & Contemporary Fiction.
HERMAN MELVILLE, *The Confidence-Man.*
AMANDA MICHALOPOULOU, *I'd Like.*
STEVEN MILLHAUSER,
The Barnum Museum.
In the Penny Arcade.
RALPH J. MILLS, JR.,
Essays on Poetry.
MOMUS, *The Book of Jokes.*
CHRISTINE MONTALBETTI, *Western.*
OLIVE MOORE, *Spleen.*
NICHOLAS MOSLEY, *Accident.*
Assassins.
Catastrophe Practice.
Children of Darkness and Light.
Experience and Religion.
God's Hazard.
The Hesperides Tree.
Hopeful Monsters.
Imago Bird.
Impossible Object.
Inventing God.
Judith.
Look at the Dark.
Natalie Natalia.
Paradoxes of Peace.
Serpent.
Time at War.
The Uses of Slime Mould:
Essays of Four Decades.
WARREN MOTTE,
Fables of the Novel: French Fiction
since 1990.
Fiction Now: The French Novel in
the 21st Century.
Oulipo: A Primer of Potential
Literature.
YVES NAVARRE, *Our Share of Time.*
Sweet Tooth.
DOROTHY NELSON, *In Night's City.*
Tar and Feathers.
ESHKOL NEVO, *Homesick.*
WILFRIDO D. NOLLEDO,
But for the Lovers.
FLANN O'BRIEN,
At Swim-Two-Birds.
At War.
The Best of Myles.
The Dalkey Archive.
Further Cuttings.
The Hard Life.
The Poor Mouth.
The Third Policeman.
CLAUDE OLLIER, *The Mise-en-Scène.*
PATRIK OUŘEDNÍK, *Europeana.*
BORIS PAHOR, *Necropolis.*

FERNANDO DEL PASO,
News from the Empire.
Palinuro of Mexico.
ROBERT PINGET, *The Inquisitory.*
Mahu or The Material.
Trio.
MANUEL PUIG,
Betrayed by Rita Hayworth.
The Buenos Aires Affair.
Heartbreak Tango.
RAYMOND QUENEAU, *The Last Days.*
Odile.
Pierrot Mon Ami.
Saint Glinglin.
ANN QUIN, *Berg.*
Passages.
Three.
Tripticks.
ISHMAEL REED,
The Free-Lance Pallbearers.
The Last Days of Louisiana Red.
Ishmael Reed: The Plays.
Reckless Eyeballing.
The Terrible Threes.
The Terrible Twos.
Yellow Back Radio Broke-Down.
JEAN RICARDOU, *Place Names.*
RAINER MARIA RILKE, *The Notebooks of*
Malte Laurids Brigge.
JULIÁN RÍOS, *The House of Ulysses.*
Larva: A Midsummer Night's Babel.
Poundemonium.
AUGUSTO ROA BASTOS, *I the Supreme.*
DANIËL ROBBERECHTS,
Arriving in Avignon.
OLIVIER ROLIN, *Hotel Crystal.*
ALIX CLEO ROUBAUD, *Alix's Journal.*
JACQUES ROUBAUD, *The Form of a*
City Changes Faster, Alas, Than
the Human Heart.
The Great Fire of London.
Hortense in Exile.
Hortense Is Abducted.
The Loop.
The Plurality of Worlds of Lewis.
The Princess Hoppy.
Some Thing Black.
LEON S. ROUDIEZ,
French Fiction Revisited.
VEDRANA RUDAN, *Night.*
STIG SÆTERBAKKEN, *Siamese.*
LYDIE SALVAYRE, *The Company of Ghosts.*
Everyday Life.
The Lecture.
Portrait of the Writer as a
Domesticated Animal.
The Power of Flies.
LUIS RAFAEL SÁNCHEZ,
Macho Camacho's Beat.
SEVERO SARDUY, *Cobra & Maitreya.*
NATHALIE SARRAUTE,
Do You Hear Them?
Martereau.
The Planetarium.
ARNO SCHMIDT, *Collected Stories.*
Nobodaddy's Children.